Praise for *Once Upo*

"A school psychologist works to accept her own past while also fighting for her students...A heartwarming story of how a young woman confronted dyslexia and went on to help others...Kabrich reveals an engaging story of self-actualization."

~ Kirkus Reviews

"Mary Avery Kabrich has written a book that is like a verbal tapestry. Three stories are woven together here, each with its own gift to the reader: a tale of dyslexia and how it alters a life for good or ill, depending on how it is regarded and treated across the life span; a story of an educational professional whose power to discern what is needed by children with learning challenges is challenged daily, both by her unwitting colleagues and her own history; and finally, the story of story itself, with its power to lift us and transform our lives."

~ Maryanne Wolf, Professor and Director, Center for Reading and Language Research, Tufts University

"Maddie is a bright, imaginative third grader who, in spite of well-meaning adults, is unable to read. With moments both heart-breaking and inspirational, the story follows the child Maddie's tenacious journey while interweaving the adult Dr. Mary's inescapable struggle to accept herself and recapture her dream of becoming a writer. A story that honors the real lives of people touched, and too often damaged, by a lack of understanding of dyslexia."

~ Dorothy Van Soest, author *Just Mercy* and *At the Center*

"This book offers a unique window on 'why some children learn to read as effortlessly as a bird learns to fly, while others flap their wings so hard they almost break, and still end up in a nosedive.' Written in the compelling, lively style of a personal narrative, this book offers deep insight into the perspectives of educational professionals who deal or do not deal effectively with dyslexia in school settings and the emotional consequences of dyslexia across the life span for affected individuals. The book is highly recommended reading for the general public and school professionals as well as individuals with dyslexia or family members with dyslexia."

~ Virginia W. Berninger, Professor and Research Affiliate,
Educational Psychology, Center on Human Development and Disability,
University of Washington

"The book is engaging from page one and throughout. It is very rare to read a novel that addresses dyslexia, let alone portraying it from the eye of the beholder. I loved the magic and wonder around words and the imagery and imagination throughout the story."

~ Dr. Pauline Erera, cultural diversity scholar

"This beautifully crafted story has heart and soul, validating the life of anyone who ever felt 'less than.' Readers will cherish this book."

~ Jennell Martin, Child Welfare Worker of the Year,
Western United States, Child Welfare League of America

ONCE UPON A TIME A SPARROW

MARY AVERY KABRICH

OPEN
WINGS
PRESS

Published by Open Wings Press
140 Lakeside Ave. ste. A-#144
Seattle, WA 98122-6538

This is a work of fiction drawn heavily from the author's experience.
All names, characters, and places are products
of the author's imagination.

ISBN 978-0-9972332-0-9
1. Self-acceptance — Fiction. 2. Psychological fiction.
3. Dyslexia — Fiction. 4. Catholic — Fiction. 5. Minnesota — Fiction

Designed by Partners in Design, Seattle

For my family

2 0 0 5

MY MOTHER crawled into bed, adjusted her flannel nightgown, and fingered the smooth glass beads of her rosary as she began to chant Hail Marys. Somewhere between "full of grace" and "thy will be done," she drifted into a sleep so deep she never woke again. This is precisely how she had hoped to die, an admission she'd shared with me over a steamy bowl of split pea soup in early December.

As her only daughter, I was special; this was made clear by the mantra she'd spontaneously call out as I drove her home from the mall, or while hemming her dress, or when trying out a new recipe together: "A daughter is a daughter for life; a son is a son until he has a wife." When I heard this as a teen, I would roll my eyes; as an adult, I wondered if Mom missed the unique but attentive ways my three brothers showed their affection. She'd sense my uncertainty, fix her gaze upon me, and add, "If you had a daughter, you'd understand."

I was wholly unprepared to find her lying in bed as though asleep but with her face drained of color, lips parted as if in prayer, and her eyes, not open or closed, but sunken. Even as my heart raced, the steady part of me couldn't help but notice that a calm surrounded her body like an ethereal blanket. She had passed the way she had said she wanted to. I wonder if she had had any idea she would die so young? She was only seventy-two, an age I no longer view as old.

Mom left us in the cold of winter. The Minneapolis School District was generous in granting me an entire week of paid bereavement, which I had hoped would be enough to at least patch the hole in my heart. A month later, I still couldn't shake the bitter chill. I walked the halls of Milton Elementary wrapped in a perpetual blanket of frostbite.

Now it's spring, and life goes on with fragile normalcy. Surely, three months and two days should be enough time for a grown woman of forty-seven—a psychologist, for God's sake—to make peace with her mother's death.

As a school psychologist, I have no analyst's couch in my office, just a collection of briefcases filled with tests designed to measure a range of aptitudes—unfortunately, with little precision. My interest in psychology has always been narrowly focused on the nature of intelligence; why some children learn to read as effortlessly as a bird learns to fly, while others flap their wings until they almost break, and still end up in a nosedive.

I'm resting on Mom's beige microfiber couch, relieved to have stayed steady and productive all afternoon. In the course of the past three hours, I've filled five packing boxes and six garbage bags, now amassed in the center of her twenty-by-thirty living room. I've managed not to shed a single tear. Gazing out her picture window, I notice a glimmer of lime-colored foliage unfurling from the buds of small shrubs.

Hanging lopsided on the adjacent wall is a family photo. I've avoided it all day, even after knocking it askew. Now I find myself rising up to straighten it, as if Mom were in the room. I'm suprised that one of my brothers didn't snatch it up when we did our walk-through last month. My oldest brother, Rob, flew in from Los Angeles, where he works as a district attorney, but left his wife and two kids behind. My two younger brothers, Jack and Danny, live within forty minutes of Mom's house, in the suburbs of St. Paul. I live a universe away from them in the Powderhorn neighborhood of Minneapolis. On a good traffic day, I can get to her place in less than an hour.

It was the first time since growing up and leaving home that the four of us had gathered without the buffer of spouses, children, or our mother. I doubt more than thirty minutes elapsed before we had completed a visual inventory of what to keep and what to donate. Unlike in my own home, everything of Mom's is neat and has its place. My brothers and I stepped lightly from room to room, starting in the kitchen with that hideous green linoleum floor and the pansy wallpaper. Still, seen often enough or through the right eyes, the space was filled with warmth. Lined up along the two generous windowsills sat three decades of mismatched vases, porcelain figures, and various trinkets. At age five or seven or nine, we had imagined that she would treasure them. They were purchased with our limited weekly allowance—we gave them for Mother's Days and birthdays—and she saved, displayed, and dusted them on a regular basis.

As my brothers and I gazed upon the collection, mutual eye contact was enough to communicate that not one of us had a place in our own homes for any single orphaned item. We fell into a silence of collective respect for the care she had given to each cheap relic we had gifted upon her.

It's probably not fair to call the photograph her favorite family portrait since it's the only one. It was taken with my parents' Polaroid Automatic before Jack disassembled it in his quest to find out where the pictures came from. It was 1966. The year Grandma O'Leary died. I was in the third grade.

When I was eight, my world consisted of long, drawn-out Monopoly games with my brothers while snow drifted onto our rooftop, springtime expeditions to catch frogs, and school days that made me want to bury myself deep in the lining of my black coat. Rural Minnesota kept us sheltered, wrapped tight in an insulating blanket while much of our nation pulsed with adolescent exuberance, defiance, freedom, and angst. It wasn't until ninth-grade history that I became aware of the war that couldn't be won and the many protests against it. There was so much that bypassed the one thousand white citizens in our town centered in the middle of cornfields. Betty Friedan, Martin Luther King Jr., and the summer of love. The Beatles did reach through the airwaves to our home on the lake. I can still recall dancing in the kitchen and bellowing, "Lucy in the Sky with Diamonds." In my mind, Lucy was a fairy.

The picture, framed in quarter-inch copper, captures the six of us dressed as though we'd just arrived home from church: my three brothers each with their shirts tucked in, Mom and I both wearing dresses. My six-foot-four father towers above us all. The corners of his mouth are turned upward, but his brow is creased as if he is about to give a lecture. His eyes are focused on some point far off in the distance. He always knew right from wrong, and not one of us would ever have dared to challenge his conviction. My mother, an entire foot shorter than my father, peers directly at the camera, and even though she was in the midst of raising three rambunctious boys and a girl who had her own set of convictions, her smile radiates a warmth I would give plenty to bask in one more time.

Jack is grinning big—he's only in second grade—and I remember that face. I used to tease him about having chipmunk cheeks, because he always kept his lips closed when smiling and his cheeks became fat pouches. Jack has our Uncle Joe's fair hair, while the rest of us have shades of brown to black. Six-year-old Danny also grins, his smile revealing two missing front teeth. He's looking not at the camera but sideways at Jack, his hero. That year, Danny and I were the best of friends. Rob was about to finish sixth grade, but to me it seemed more like he was finishing high school. His glasses seemed to offer proof of his intelligence. He ended up skipping seventh grade.

In the photo, my thick brown hair is cut in a blunt bob just below my ears, and my bangs line up above my eyebrows. Mom cut our hair. The boys, including my father, got traditional buzz cuts. My brothers all had cowlicks, which created endless discussion and teasing. It's clear to me my smile is as forced as the folded hands in my lap, as I tried to look ladylike for the camera. I was envious of my brothers. I wanted what they had—fewer rules and more smarts. I even thought I wanted to be a boy but wouldn't have dared to say so. Instead, I put my efforts into becoming a nun.

I leave the picture hanging, certain Jack or Danny will want it, and return to the couch, plopping down to take a mental inventory. All that's left is the bedroom. Last month, with unexpected ease, we divided the contents of Mom's jewelry box. Each of my brothers has children who deserve to own something of their grandmother's. Because I was never one to adorn myself with strings of gold or silver, my sentiments fell upon the Bible and rosary sitting in tranquility upon her bedside table. I knew that these two items, more than anything else, had absorbed something of her spirit. Her Bible had rested daily in her lap as she fingered each and every one of the fifty-nine translucent amber beads of her rosary.

I shake myself out of a daze as I replay my phone conversation with Danny from the previous night.

"Are you sure you don't want a little company and help tomorrow? I have the weekend off, no Little League."

"Thanks, Danny, it's really okay." I yearned to spend time alone in the small house Mom occupied for more than twenty-five years. The funeral had become a blur, leaving me to wonder if I had truly said good-bye. "Believe me, there'll still be plenty more to do—like schlepping the bags to Goodwill and hauling the furniture out."

"If you say so. You have my cell. Give me a call if you need anything or change your mind."

Other than her Bible and rosary, I didn't expect to lay claim to anything. My townhouse is small and well furnished, and I don't need an extra set of dishes or blankets or (God forbid) knickknacks. But when we entered her bedroom and I averted my eyes from where I had found her, they fell squarely upon the Lane hope chest pressed against the foot of her bed, a loosely crocheted rose-colored lap blanket draped across the top.

When she graduated from high school, my grandparents surprised my mother with the modest, simple four-by-two cedar chest that would later house, among other things, her wedding dress. That's the one piece of furniture I wanted and could make space for.

I look at my watch, 3:45 p.m., and make a firm resolution. In five more minutes I will rise up from this couch, go to her bedroom, and finish sorting and packing, starting with her large walk-in closet. I know what has created my roadblock—it's the bed. She looked so peaceful, but truly, her death was a freak of nature. My mother, who walked two miles a day, played golf, bowled, and, as a former nurse, monitored her health, up and died of a heart attack with no warning. Don't most healthy women live to eighty and beyond these days?

Ten more minutes pass. Finally, I leave the couch and grab a couple of empty boxes from the kitchen and peel a plastic garbage bag off the roll, determined to finish before the sun drops. I enter the room wearing make-believe blinders, focusing only on the closet, where I skim an accordion of color organized by length, from blouses to skirts to long flowing dresses. Mom's preference had always been for bright colors, showy and bold. Each Christmas, I'd receive at least one fuchsia-colored garment with a gift receipt tucked in the box. She was such a good sport, never commenting when I failed to wear it.

I avoid lingering on any one familiar outfit, reminding myself that what I'm seeing is simply the way she dressed—not her. I stay focused on the message I had chiseled on my mind when I viewed her foreign, discolored features: my mother's essence has moved on. Painstakingly, I fold each and every outfit, my mood lifting with the knowledge that someone, a kindred spirit of flashy, yet classy, outfits, will be thrilled with my mother's clothing. I'm pleased to have finished what I set out to do while still witnessing the last bursts of radiance from a sun that has not yet set. I'll be home before dark.

The closet is now empty; the things that gave my mother comfort are neatly packaged for someone else to enjoy. I too feel empty.

I look back upon the hope chest. I kneel on the braided rug in front of my inheritance and lift the lid, releasing a fragrance of mothballs and cedar. As expected, folded on top is the white satin wedding dress that she showed me years ago. She had a vision that I might wear it, but at five ten, I took after my father, and there was no way my mother's only daughter would ever be able to squeeze into a dress designed for a petite woman of five four. Since I'm now divorced, it was no great loss. Beneath this, I find her favorite baby outfits, but since her sons have only daughters, the blue, navy-blue, and shades-of-brown getups have all stayed put. These will be fabulous finds for thrift store shoppers.

After a peek at each jumper and doll-sized version of a Sunday best, I refold every one along the same creases. Lifting a baby-blue sleeper to my face, I breathe in a combination of cedar and laundry soap and imagine my mother holding it up, taking in its scent, and anticipating seeing the tiny pajama on a grandchild or great-grandchild. When I remove the last layer of sleepers and elastic-waisted corduroys, I'm puzzled to find the bottom of the chest lined with black quilted material.

As I reach for it, I know it doesn't belong, that it's some forgotten outcast, an interloper inserted among my mother's things. Sitting on my haunches, knees inches from the chest, I lift the bulky black material. Immediately, my stomach lurches in recognition. It's my coat from third grade: its inner lining torn loose, the elbows ripped, the hood hanging like a limp sock.

As I hold the tattered relic, my arms begin to shake, my heart races, and I fall back in time. I'm in third grade, bundled in this coat from the moment I leave our house in the morning until I return in the afternoon. I keep it on despite teasing, my mother's frown, and regardless of weather. I'm always cold.

My head is airy and spinning. I start to rise up, but a heaviness upon my shoulders sends me to the floor. I bury my face in the coat's thickness, and tears saturate this soft armor from my past. My effort to stop the steady outpouring of liquid generates a heaving sound from deep within my chest.

Hours later, I notice the lavender sky has emptied of color, ushering in the night.

2 0 0 5

MY FATHER used to say, "You can't fit a square peg into a round hole," but I'm certain he had in mind a much more literal interpretation than what haunts me these days. So many of the children I encounter are uniquely shaped in ways that make it impossible to pass through the public school system without their spirits being crushed. If you don't fit the learning mold, watch out. The consequences can last a lifetime.

Most days, my job as a school psychologist is deeply satisfying. Twelve years ago, following six years of graduate school, I traded planned lessons and individualized objectives for a caseload filled with exasperated teachers and frustrated parents. I've always been drawn to children who don't fit in round holes. Now, instead of being a teacher, I give IQ tests, look at the numbers, and tell a story about sharp edges, curves, and what's possible when the right fit is made. I strive to raise the expectations of teachers and parents blinded by what's not working. Interpreting IQ scores is not my most useful skill. In fact, it has little relevance compared with my ability to remain calm and patient in the midst of despair, something I've always been good at. That is, until recently.

I had hoped my final good-bye two weeks ago to Mom's tan-and-brown bungalow on East Irving Street, along with the packing away and tossing out, and the huge release of tears, would somehow restore a state of tranquility, that I would return to work with enough steadiness to finally catch up.

But then I found the coat.

When I returned to my office at Milton Elementary—test kits masquerading as briefcases, a shiny four-drawer file cabinet safe-guarding reports filled with quantitative specs of children who process the world in unique ways—I knew nothing had changed. Each week I seemed to regress.

Every day, I start in neutral, something trips me up, I fall off balance, and before I can gain control, I'm behaving in ways I don't even recognize.

I want to blame the coat. I can't shake its startling image and my surge of anger and confusion. I can understand my mother keeping the fifty-cent vase I gave her in first grade, but a tattered coat? The one that she continuously tried to coax me to take off. Why?

I eventually ended up tossing it where it belonged—in the trash. After I had regained my composure at my mom's house and made peace with the fact that I would be traveling home under the night sky, I sat, exhausted, leaning against the chest with the coat resting on my lap as I stared into the empty closet. The corners of the room were dark; a 60-watt bulb in the middle of the ceiling cast a dim light. I had cried more than I could ever remember, and yet, felt no catharsis. If anything, the desperate ache provoked by the coat was amplified.

Before throwing it out, I checked the pockets. Reaching into the coat's right-hand pocket, I felt a smooth, hard circular object. When I pulled the acorn out, it appeared ordinary, aside from its large size. I grew up with acorns—they were as common as dandeli-ons. This one was no different. In a fleeting, dreamlike moment, I saw my father's large hands wiping clean an acorn with a white hand-kerchief. His voice, stern and serious. "Take a close look, Maddie." I gazed more intently and witnessed this most ordinary acorn shift to an object of exquisite perfection—its uniformity of color, the faultless spherical line where the cap once sat—no wonder nine-year-old me had placed it in my pocket. I did the same again, slipping it in the front pocket of my jeans.

The windowless conference room has a stale scent about it. I glance at the clock, relieved to see that I'm three minutes early. Lately, it's been hard to arrive by 8:00 a.m. I turn toward the door and see Matt Henderson, my buddy and the school counselor, coming down the hall. He's a gentle father figure to the children who visit his counseling office. His soft, round features, and the way his stomach slightly spills over his belt, add to his teddy bear appearance.

"Dr. Mary," he says in a playful voice, his eyes twinkling. He's the only one who calls me this. We've been working together for six years now. We meet here three times a week for student intervention team meetings—aka SIT meetings—with teachers to brainstorm about interventions for children. Much of my caseload has its genesis here, but lately my participation has been woefully off-kilter.

Matt settles into a chair diagonally across from me. His eyes search my face. I suspect he's wondering who will show up. I flash him a smile, letting him know it's the old me, the one who stays calm regardless. Instead of smiling back, he too glances up at the clock and then out the door into an empty hallway. He leans forward.

"You know this SIT meeting is with Karla, right?"

"Of course. I popped into her class last week to catch a glimpse of the new kid, Simon."

His brows rise.

"Actually, I didn't observe too long—her monotone voice still bores me to death."

A stiffness forms around his mouth. He eyes me.

"Why?" I ask.

"Just checking in. I know you've had issues with her . . ."

"Matt. I'm fine. I saw Josiah—that's who we're discussing today, right?"

Matt nods.

"Actually, I suspect he was bored out of his mind too."

"That may be. But—"

In walks Penny Stanton, our special education resource-room teacher. Penny settles in with her usual cheery, "Hi."

While she shuffles through her notebook for a clean sheet of paper, I lean forward and whisper to Matt. "No need to worry. I'm going to be real low-key here. I know this kid is not destined for a special ed eval. I'll let you take the lead."

I wink at him, but it's forced as my heart sinks. I shouldn't have to be reassuring him of my own mental stability. I know I've been off lately, but Matt's acting as if the last six years of consistent performance amount to nothing.

"Guess what?" Penny says excitedly. "Grace Adams won the poetry slam contest."

"That's fabulous," I say. "Doesn't surprise me; she's so bright." I first met Grace in kindergarten. She qualified for special education due to her difficulty with acquiring pre-reading and writing skills. Penny's news fills me with warmth. I add, "And creative. I'm so proud of her. She's making really nice progress. I think since being accepted into the gifted program, her confidence has increased." I make a mental note to congratulate her next time I see her.

Karla Clifford, fourth-grade teacher, enters the room. She scheduled this SIT meeting three weeks ago, but I can't imagine why she'd waste our time here with Josiah. I noticed him the day I was observing Simon; Josiah was the kid completely absorbed in a book.

I'd wanted to rush over and see what kind of book had captured his attention. Observing his laser focus on the text, I had also wondered if he attended the gifted program with Grace.

I remind myself that I am here to be present for and patient with Karla. Except I feel put off by her thin lips pressed with conviction, her perfectly applied eyeliner. Not a single auburn strand of hair is out of place. She matches her teaching style. Karla has taken the concept of a structured classroom to the extreme.

"I'm very concerned about Josiah," Karla starts. "He hardly ever participates in discussions."

Because they're too damn boring.

"When I call on him, his answers are way off topic—or it's some idiotic thing to get the class going." She makes a sour face and rolls her eyes.

Good for him.

"But most the time, he's in his own world." Karla bats her thick eyelashes, and I wonder if this last statement is merely a nod toward sympathy.

Matt jumps on it right away. "Is it possible that he's depressed?"

Penny's curly bronze hair bounces as she nods her head up and down in a perpetual yes motion. Her special kids adore her. Most of the kids on my caseload end up receiving her special education help with one skill or another.

"Oh no," Karla says. "It's just that he resists following the rules. He's never on task. He's always doing sneaky things."

"Do you mean like reading from a novel instead of listening to the science lesson?" I ask with as much innocence as I can muster. Karla turns away from me, but I can feel the heat of Matt's gaze.

"That and pretending to be working on keyboarding skills while connecting to the Internet and messing around." She pauses with a fake frown. "Of course, I had to write him up," she proclaims with way too much elation in her voice.

I feel an anger snake up my spine.

"It's the third time since January." She produces a partial frown and then continues. "Kept him in during recess all last week. He never turns his homework in."

I take several deep, calming breaths and then say, "I notice you've recorded his standard scores on the district test all at the ninetieth percentile and above."

Matt's attention is on me; he must have detected the edge in my voice. I won't say any more.

"I don't trust those scores. Wouldn't put it past him to have cheated. He rarely finishes the questions at the end of the science chapter. In math, he refuses to show his work. I suspect he cheats on that as well, otherwise he'd be able to tell me how he got his answers."

I can't help but roll my eyes.

Penny, in her infinitely patient way, suggests using a behavior contract that she will help develop. I love Penny's optimism and wish teachers took her more seriously. Nothing any staff member ever says in this room is offensive to Penny. She makes it her mission to figure out a way to improve things, doing whatever it takes to fashion a fit between unique-but-square-shaped children and round classroom expectations.

Matt offers to see Josiah for a couple of counseling sessions. I study Karla. It amazes me how her expression stays the same, like makeup. It's applied in the morning and nothing seems to alter it. It's because her mind is made up: Josiah's a loser, and there's nothing to be done. *Jesus. She's missing his brilliance.*

I start to draw in a deep breath but switch course and blurt out the obvious. "He's bored! I was in your class last week observing Simon, and I was bored too. How do you expect a bright kid to stay engaged when all you do is read out of a textbook?"

My pounding heart is making it hard to breathe. All at once, I know who Josiah reminds me of: Bobby, a homely dark-haired kid from my childhood. He was in the highest reading group, an Eagle, and no one told him how smart he was.

Karla turns to me. I catch an almost hateful glare flare up in her eyes. I turn away. I have nothing more to say.

"You're missing the point," she says in a voice devoid of inflection. "I wouldn't bring a child to the SIT meeting if the problem was merely boredom. I'm here because I know there's something seriously wrong."

My fist clenches under the table. "Such as?"

"There's something wrong with Josiah's brain, and he needs help."

Wrong with his brain? What in God's name could be wrong with a kid who'd rather read than listen to her monotone?

"Karla," I snap. "I can guarantee you his brain was fine until he entered your class."

The air drains from the conference room, and my heart goes staccato in my chest. I see Matt's jaw open, but I can't stop myself. "In fact, it's still fine," I say. All three of them stare at me. Karla's made-up face looks as though it's about to crack into a million pieces, and I see pain in her eyes. I squeeze my right thigh so hard a welt forms, and I realize it is the silence I can't stand.

"I'm sorry. I need to leave." My chair scrapes the burnished cement floor. I shove the meeting notes into my briefcase and stride out of the stuffy room. *Damn!* I blew it, and Matt will be upset with me. But I'm right. Karla has no business announcing there's something wrong with Josiah's brain. I wish I could move him out of her class.

Poor kid.

CHAPTER 3

2 O O 5

IT'S MONDAY. A new week, a new start, and my morning schedule is packed with three back-to-back meetings starting at eight o'clock. I'm not worried about the first two; it's the nine thirty meeting with the third-grade team that's giving my stomach butterflies. They plan to discuss Kaylee Leman, whom I evaluated last spring. Since Kaylee is already in special education and they have concerns, this must mean it's a meeting to consider "retaining" her. They know my views about keeping a kid back—generally, it's not a good idea. I'm not the only one who has this opinion; the National Association of School Psychologists agrees. So why have they invited me? Regardless, I am determined not to behave the way I did with Karla.

The first two meetings go well, strengthening my fledgling confidence. The initial meeting is with a high-achieving parent concerned that her first-grade son is not reading chapter books as she did at age six. She suspects a disability. Had I dared to share how long it took me to learn to read a chapter book, I'm sure she'd have stared in disbelief. The second appointment is a consultation session with Tina Luca. Tina is a first-year kindergarten teacher gifted with five-year-old Jason, a pudgy redhead who is brilliant and has autism. I love it that she too understands that he will teach her a set of lessons absent from the best of textbooks. Tina embraces my idea of enlisting other kindergartners to be social ambassadors to Jason. I wish I'd had a teacher like her in kindergarten. I had felt equally clueless, not with reading social cues, but with reading letters.

I leave the kindergarten class, making my way to Jan Kramer's third-grade classroom with rising optimism. I flash back to the first day I met Kaylee, a year ago last spring, when she was referred for an evaluation. She reminded me of Ramona Quimby from Beverly Cleary's series of children's novels. Ramona, age eight—short hair cast askew, freckles, and huge blue knowledge-seeking eyes. I had asked Kaylee my usual opening questions, including, "What are your dreams for the future?"

"I'm going to be a scientist and discover ways to save giant panda bears from becoming instinct," she replied.

I had gently corrected her, saying the word was *extinct*.

"No," she said assuredly, "it's *instinct*, because *exit* means to leave, and that's not what we want."

She went on to share everything she had learned about the bears from the Discovery Channel, and I recall thinking, *There is so much more she could learn from books. Please, dear God, help this child learn to read.*

Kaylee met the state's criteria for special education services in the simplest of ways—a significant discrepancy between her IQ and her reading level. Her intelligence was apparent within the first five minutes of conversation. One look at a writing sample, and I knew she'd qualify. However, test scores were required to quantify these simple observations. It's the documentation of a severe discrepancy between a child's so-called potential and his or her academic achievement that qualifies a child such as Kaylee for special education.

But documenting a severe discrepancy has never been enough to satisfy me.

My thirst is to understand why a bright child can't make reasonable progress with reasonable support. This is the quest that has me chasing after a range of additional aptitude and process measures look-ing for answers. At the very least, I want to be helpful to those whose job it is to open the doors and make reading possible. I understand. I started out as a special education teacher and was handed plenty of evaluation reports full of meaningless numbers. I know in the hidden recesses of my heart that my recommendations also fall short: eight to fifteen pages documenting failure and two to three paragraphs of questionable analysis and suggestions aimed at being helpful. If I had better tools and more time, it would be the other way around. In the end, I'm not so sure my reports matter. What does matter is a teacher who cares, believes, and has the skill to put these qualities to use.

Jan Kramer's classroom is set up in a cooperative learning style—two desks wedged together facing two other desks to make a foursome. The chairs sit fixed, empty, and waiting. The classroom walls are sug-ared with displays of color and a plethora of words. I see the life cycle of butterflies and moths and realize an entire wall is dedicated to envi-ronmental science, Kaylee's favorite subject.

"Dr. Meyers, thanks for joining us," Jan says, motioning me to the oblong table in the back of the room.

Her formality irritates me. Jan appears to be about ten years older than I am, but this might be an illusion. She wears her iron-gray hair in a tight bun at the nape of her neck. I've inherited my father's slow-to-gray hair genes, and my tendency toward quick and practical leaves me with a no-fuss short clip.

Shelby, new this year, bats heavily made-up eyes at me with no comment. Her young face looks freshly powdered, and she's wearing a tight dress that accentuates her curves. To her left, sitting prim at the conference table, is Donna, whom a number of us on the staff speculate to be a good ten years past retirement age. Donna can't weigh more than eighty pounds wet. A gold-colored chain loops around her neck, connecting a pair of wire-rimmed glasses. Donna makes it clear that she already knows everything there is to know about teaching, so I rarely have anything to say to her. I smile and nod; the three teachers shuffle grade books and planners.

"Will Penny be coming?" I ask.

"She has students at this time," Jan says.

Of course. A tremor of irritation rises in my throat, and I try my best to respond calmly. "It's too bad this meeting couldn't have been scheduled at a time when *all* of Kaylee's teachers could be present."

"It'd take a month to get on the SIT schedule, and this is the only time all three of us have planning together. Besides, we did share our concern with Penny."

I sigh nice and loud, and then I say, "Good. I'm glad you collaborated with her. She's very good at figuring out how to help children compensate for weak skills. She's a wonderful resource to have." I look each of them directly in the eye because I'm sure Penny would have given me a heads-up if she knew what I suspect is going to happen.

I notice a stack of papers in front of Jan. On the top, I make out Kaylee's name. Below are two or three scrawled sentences; without punctuation, it's hard to tell. Jan follows my gaze and holds up the heartbreaking writing sample.

"This is Kaylee's report on the life cycle of moths." She then displays the next two papers—entire pages filled with correct paragraph structure. "And here are two samples of what most third graders produce."

My body stiffens. Obviously, Jan has chosen the most gifted students as comparisons. "Children who struggle with reading typically have even more difficulty with writing," I say.

"Of course, we understand this," Jan says. Shelby nods, and Donna adds her expert endorsement in the form of a muffled "uh-hum."

No, you don't understand.

"She doesn't have problems with ideas and concepts," I continue. "I bet Kaylee can dictate a fabulous report. Her challenge has to do with recalling how to form each letter and figuring out the spelling. It saps her ability to express her ideas."

"We understand," Jan chirps too quickly. "And Kaylee has been receiving resource-room support with Penny all year. Our concern now"—she pauses, briefly making eye contact with Shelby and Donna—"is fourth grade." Her voice drops on the last two words.

"But of course she'll continue to receive support from Penny next year," I counter a little too loudly. No one responds. My palms are sweaty. *Stay calm.*

Jan shifts her gaze to Donna, who throws her shoulders back. Her frail frame shakes with a mild tic that causes the thin strands of silver springing from her head to shimmer. Her voice is anything but frail.

"Even with special-ed support," Donna says, "it would be a *shame* to send this child on to fourth grade when she's barely reading beyond a first-grade level." She glares at me as though it is the first time I've heard this argument. But I hear this every spring as I sit in meetings with teachers afraid to allow children to move on to the next grade, fearing failure. What they don't understand is that flunking is the ultimate failure.

Even so, I feel the sting of a fresh slap upon my face as they make their claims. My heart speeds up—as if I were the one threatened with being held back a year. I take a deep breath, ready to dispute their position, but when I look into their eyes, I regress to a nine-year-old with a voice that is soundless.

Jan says, "I'd love to have Kaylee another year; it would give her a chance to develop her literacy skills and build confidence." Shelby vigorously nods. Jan pauses, sizing me up.

I struggle to keep a neutral expression. *I'm not going to lose it.*

"Since Kaylee and her family know and trust you, Dr. Meyers," Jan continues, "we thought it would be helpful if you would attend the spring parent conference when we share what we think is best for her."

So that's what they want.

"But . . ." There's so much to say. "I don't agree."

The air thickens. I listen to the clicking of the wall clock. In that moment of hush, I wonder if they can hear my heart pounding.

Donna, the "expert," speaks first. "She can't possibly be successful in fourth grade. She'll get further and further behind. I've seen it happen."

Jan chimes in, "We want what's best for her. She'll feel defeated trying to make it next year."

"It would be an absolute tragedy to move her on."

"While I would love to have her another year, she could have Donna or Shelby."

No screams deafeningly inside my head. I open my mouth, scrambling to find words, but they hide from me. Again, I try to speak, but my voice is lost. I squeeze my eyes shut and remind myself, *I'm Dr. Meyers.* I bring my gaze back to Jan's gray hair, bobbing up and down with assertion. My face reddens. I pull in a deep breath, willing calm. Instead, a mountain of embers ignites from somewhere deep. I'm on my feet.

"Why would you do this to her?"

"Dr. Meyers . . ." Donna, Jan, and Shelby stare at me.

"Do you have any idea how humiliating it'll be?" My legs are shaking. I have to get out. But first, I say, "Just because she can't read doesn't mean she can't think!" And now it is dead quiet. I must leave. But there's more they need to know. "She wants to be a scientist, and you're destroying her dream." I stride out the door and slam it, but not nearly loudly enough.

My office is suffocatingly small, and I welcome the confines of its walls. I close myself in and drop to my desk, holding my throbbing head between my palms. *This isn't me. I'm the one who guides teachers, draws upon research. I don't lose it—it's my job to calm those who do.*

The rhythmic thump in my head fades, and a woozy vacuity slips in. A wave of nausea rolls up from the back of my throat. The slightest scent of food, and my stomach will heave. I breathe deep to stabilize, and the lump in my throat threatens to take over; it's demanding I curl myself into a ball and cry. I place my hands on my desk and make myself sit up.

I shake my head and train my eyes on the stack of student files to the left of my computer, each an overstuffed manila folder, collectively on the verge of toppling over. All I need to do is open one and get started.

The file I begin with, the one on top of the stack, is that of Marcos Del Quintos, ten years old, referred three weeks ago. He comes with a dense outside psychiatric report. Reading the evaluation is the place to start. I focus on the words, but my eyes swim over the letters, over and over them, until I notice a period and realize I haven't read a single word. Not one in the entire sentence. Like Kaylee, I can't read a goddamned thing. My eyes blur and I wipe them dry, but still they're blurry. *I can't read.*

CHAPTER 4

1967

MRS. ZINC STANDS like a statue, with steel-gray hair bundled tight, waiting for the six of us to sit soundlessly with our hands in our laps. Then she smiles her pretend smile—the one that tries to say, "This is fun"—as she holds up a card with a bright red apple on it.

"Okay, Sparrows, let's review. Remember, you need to know the vowel sound to read the words."

Six voices chime together, "*A, apple*," and then make only the beginning sound of apple: long and drawn out as if we're about to sneeze, but only the *a* part of *achoo* comes out.

The day I found out I'd be a Sparrow for the second year in a row, I zipped my black coat up tight. I was cold. Later that evening, I waited until Mom and I were alone to share the disappointing news.

"It's not fair. I was a Sparrow last year. I'm in third grade now, and I know all about what Sparrows do—it's boring."

Mom was busy frying onions and ground beef to make spaghetti sauce. The smell made my stomach growl. I thought she might ask me to stir the pot, but instead she said, "Sweetheart, Mrs. Zinc's a good teacher. Rob had her three years ago. I think she knows what's best for you." I didn't want to stir anymore.

Mrs. Zinc holds up the next picture card, an elephant. It's the same set of cards from second grade. I let my voice get lost with the others. I make myself look in Mrs. Zinc's direction. I see Mrs. Zinc hold up the card with the letter *o* and an octopus, and I chant along, like during dinner prayers, but my imagination takes me flying in a whole different direction. I imagine Mrs. Zinc's smile changing to the one that means a good surprise is about to happen.

Mrs. Zinc flings the cards across the room and announces, "Children, it's a beautiful day, and you've all been working so hard. We'll skip reading and go outside for a game of kickball!"

I reach the playfield first, ready to kick a home run, except bratty Bobby Wallace sneers his chip-toothed face at me and insists on being the first one up, so I let him. He kicks the ball hard. It flies sideways and smack! hits Mrs. Zinc squarely in the head.

Mrs. Zinc's head bobs back and forth as if attached to a spring. I see stars circling above her eyes as she falls to the ground in a big heap, her cream-colored dress all dirty and wrinkled. While everyone is trying to figure out what to do, I take off for the hospital where Mom works. I know exactly how to get there, and since I can run faster than anyone, I reach the emergency room before the others can even get to the office secretary to explain that Mrs. Zinc is knocked out cold.

I'm bursting through the hospital doors when Mrs. Zinc interrupts. "Madelyn."

I jerk my head up, blink, and tell myself, *To be continued.*

"You're not following along. How do you expect to get better at reading if you don't pay attention?"

The pause is long enough to make my face turn red. I imagine shouting out, *This is boring!* Instead, I do my usual and say nothing, but I scoot further down into my chair until my knees bump against the desk bottom.

"Cheryl, will you kindly help Madelyn find her place?"

I zip up my coat. Even though my face burns red, I'm cold. I reach for the hood, ready to pull it up, and then remember: Mrs. Zinc no longer allows it. Cheryl sits up in her chair as tall as her short body can.

She tucks her long blond hair behind her ears and points to where the previous round-robin reader left off.

No one expects me to read this next sentence; besides, it's a stupid story. I place my finger where Cheryl points, even though it makes me feel like a baby.

Whoever invented letters must have made them confusing on purpose—why should it matter what side of the circle the straight line is on? If it were up to me, I'd make *d*'s, *b*'s, *p*'s, and *q*'s all the same letter so no one would have to work hard at trying to remember which is which.

"We're all waiting for you," Mrs. Zinc says, and then, with a sigh adds, "Cheryl, since Madelyn was not paying attention, would you mind repeating the last two sentences?"

"Over the hills," Cheryl reads, "and under a bridge, that dog Spot ran with glee. Then he saw the tall jackrabbit off in the distance."

Oops. I looked up. My finger slipped down the page, and I've lost the place again.

"Start here," Cheryl whispers.

I blink hard and then begin to sound out, one letter at a time, the four letters in the first word. "Ss-*tu-ah-p*."

"Spot," says Cheryl, and again puts her finger to the word.

Ugh. I land my finger under the first letter of the next word and move it like a snail, letter by letter, in the direction Cheryl moves her hand. We're back to reading *Spot the Dog*.

The day Mrs. Zinc introduced this story, I was on a mission trying to rescue Mr. Dreadsly, our principal. He had been captured by Martians who tricked him because they could change their bodies to look like children. I was deep inside a secret tunnel under the school when Mrs. Zinc picked up the flat book sitting on my desk and slapped it back down, startling me, then demanded that I read the title. I think she surprised everyone, because all six of the Sparrows looked first at her and then at me. I wasn't going to use my finger for just a few title words, so I took a quick look and blurted out what I saw: "Stop the God!" Everyone but Mrs. Zinc laughed, so I made myself laugh too so they'd think I made the mistake on purpose.

"Spot tucks of—" I continue reading.

"Spot took off," Cheryl says.

"Spot took off afraid the—"

"—after the," Cheryl says.

"—after the jock—"

"—jack," Cheryl says.

"—rabbit." *Whew. All done for now.*

CHAPTER 5

1 9 6 7

EASTER was last week, and I'm still a Sparrow, me and three others. I liked it better when there were six of us because then I didn't have to follow along so closely, and it was easier to invent my own story. We continue to say letter sounds and read boring flat books, over and over. If you're an Eagle, like my friend Paulette Oakley, or like Bobby Wallace, who is not my friend, you get to read chapter books. The same is true for Bluebirds and Robins.

My favorite part of the day, besides recess and PE, is when Mrs. Zinc reads to us. She reads for an entire forty minutes minus the question time, which I also like because I'm really good at answering questions, as long as I don't have to read them. My hand is always up first, but Mrs. Zinc usually waits to call on me to give the others a turn. My favorite story used to be *Charlotte's Web*, and I couldn't imagine a better story ever, but now I know I was wrong. The very best, or as Grandma O'Leary would say, "most marvelous," is *The Fairy Angel's Gift*.

Story time begins at 2:20, unless someone, and it's usually Bobby Wallace, makes too much noise. Mrs. Zinc is patient. She's willing to do her quiet standing and waiting for as long as it takes until we sit as still as statues. She sometimes reminds us, "Third graders, it's your choice: we can have a long story time or a short one." I can tell from the way she says it that it really doesn't matter to her.

Some days, waiting for 2:20 is as hard as waiting for Christmas.

I'm good at telling time. The other Sparrows can't tell time, which I know because it's telling time that makes it possible for me to be first in line for recess every day. I've given up signaling to them when our reading time is about over. They continue to act surprised when Mrs. Zinc makes that announcement. Not me. And then later, when it's finally two o'clock, keeping my mind on the worksheet in front of me and on writing down answers, instead of drawing tiny pictures that I will later erase, is the hardest part of the school day. Two o'clock means only twenty more minutes before we can finally pack up our things and listen to the most marvelous story ever told.

Paulette is my helper. That's what Mrs. Zinc calls her. Last year, lots of different kids helped me with words; this year, it's Paulette's job. I wouldn't need a helper if the worksheets didn't have words. Lately, I've been thinking about how cavemen used to tell their stories with pictures and how even today, hundreds of years later, we can still read their stories. I doubt that people hundreds of years from now will be able to read *Spot the Dog*. Actually, they wouldn't want to.

Paulette is smart, like my older brother, Rob, and they both wear glasses. Rob wears wire rims, which made my father angry because he thinks they make Rob look like a hippie, even though he has short hair. Paulette's glasses are round brownish plastic, and they always seem to be sliding down, even though she has a big nose. Maybe reading a lot makes you need to wear glasses, because Mrs. Zinc also has glasses that she only puts on when she reads.

Paulette doesn't always take the time to help. Like yesterday, I was checking the clock and waiting for it to be 2:20 when Paulette asked if I wanted to copy her answers to the worksheet. Paulette's desk touches mine, making our two desks look like one big long one. Mine is smack in front of Mrs. Zinc's. To my left are big windows that come in handy when I'm waiting for the time to pass. I looked down at my page of blank lines, which Paulette also saw. She slid her worksheet over to my side.

"Can you read me the questions?" I asked. Paulette glanced up at the clock, which I had just checked, and then at her paper. There were only ten minutes left before story time.

"There's not enough time. You haven't even started. Here, just copy my words." She was right; there were way too many words to read and listen to in ten minutes. No wonder everyone was working so hard.

Paulette's handwriting is the opposite of mine. Hers is neat and easy to read, but I draw better pictures. I don't understand why I can draw marvelous horses and churches but have a horrible time drawing letters. Maybe it's because it took me so long to decide if I was left- or right-handed, and finally Mom just made me be right-handed like most everyone else.

I was halfway through the worksheet, copying one letter after another, when Bobby Wallace came by to use the pencil sharpener next to Mrs. Zinc's desk. I smelled him coming; he smells like rain-soaked leaves mixed in a puddle of dirt.

"You're cheating," he sneered. I looked up; Mrs. Zinc was on the other side of the classroom helping Lisa. I wasn't sure if I was cheating or not, but it sort of felt like cheating, so I added it to the confession list I keep in my head. "Just because you can't read doesn't mean you get to cheat," Bobby said, saying the word *cheat* even louder.

"It's not a test," Paulette said in her teacher voice. "Besides, it's none of your beeswax." I grinned. Paulette can be a good friend.

The first day Mrs. Zinc introduced *The Fairy Angel's Gift,* I knew it would be the best book she had ever read to us. She held the book in outstretched arms and circled them like a second hand on a clock from one side of the room to the other. I scooted to the edge of my seat, craned my neck, leaned over to Paulette's side, and caught the fairy before Mrs. Zinc had even twisted toward the windows. When she turned in my direction, I saw the fairy's lavender tunic, her long yellow-gold hair, and rhinestone boots. By the time Mrs. Zinc lowered the book, I'm sure I spied a smile on the fairy's face.

Mrs. Zinc told us that we'd need to use our imaginations; unlike *Charlotte's Web*, there were no pictures in this book.

Imagination. Mrs. Zinc turned it into a bonus spelling word later that week. Paulette and all the smart kids got an extra point for knowing how to spell it, but I knew the meaning of *imagination.*

"Who can tell me what *imagination* means? Yes, Madelyn?"

"It's when you make something you can't see become real in your mind." All I had to do was think of Saint Rita. I pray to Saint Rita every night. She's as real to me as Mrs. Zinc standing tall in front of us all.

My catechism teacher, Miss Stanley, introduced Saint Rita to me last year when I was in second grade. Miss Stanley became my favorite teacher the first day I met her at the beginning of the year. I expected her classroom to be white walls with a crucifix over a chalkboard in the front, but instead, there were pictures of saints everywhere. I could tell they were old because they were paintings. Saints lived a long time ago, before cameras. I didn't notice Miss Stanley when she first entered the room because the other kids were loud and noisy, running around, and because I was busy studying the pictures trying to figure out the saints' names, but she tapped me on my shoulder and asked my name right away.

She didn't even look like a teacher. Her hair, the color of peanut butter, toppled below her shoulders with a scarf draping down. Her scarf was orange, yellow, and red, the colors mixed together the way I color the sun. She had it wrapped above her forehead, and my first thought was that if it had been all black or all white, it would have looked like a nun's habit, except nuns don't usually show their hair.

I told her my real first name—Mary—so she knew I was named after the Virgin Mary. I then said, "I'm planning on being a nun when I grow up. Can you teach us about all these saints?"

"Madelyn's right, that's a correct definition," Mrs. Zinc said. I sat up tall in my chair and unzipped my coat. "For example, some children pretend to have friends that are not real—they're called imaginary friends."

"How can you have a friend that's not real?" Bobby asked without raising his hand. Mrs. Zinc answered anyway.

"Well, they're not real friends, they're imaginary friends. They're real only in a child's mind. Children pretend to have these friends by using their imaginations."

Bobby gave a short half laugh and muttered, "Weird."

Mrs. Zinc had made it clear that this book was fiction just like *Charlotte's Web*. Fiction means it's not true. But I've seen fairies, and Grandma O'Leary also saw a fairy when she was about my age. I'm not so sure it's true that animals don't have conversations behind our backs, and who knows, maybe spiders are much smarter than we ever realized. These are thoughts I keep private.

If *The Fairy Angel's Gift* was about just any old fairy, I might not pay so much attention. But the fairy in this story is unlike any I've ever heard about. She isn't a dingbat—a word Grandma O'Leary used to mean stupid—like Tinker Bell, who kept losing her shadow. She's as smart as some of the saints that Miss Stanley has taught me about. The fairy has a special name. Her name started out Dottyrambleon, but when she decided to be an angel, she did what nuns do and changed her name. I know all about this since I'm going to be a nun someday.

Dottyrambleon became Yram. She could have turned into Dotty, but that would have been an ordinary name, just like my first name, Mary. There are two other Marys in my class, Mary L and Mary J, but I'm the only Madelyn. Madelyn is my middle name, and Yram is the middle of Dottyrambleon.

It's tricky to figure out. Mrs. Zinc showed us by writing Dottyrambleon on the chalkboard. I counted thirteen letters. Then Mrs. Zinc erased four letters in the front and five letters in back, leaving *y-r-a-m*. *Ee-ram*. Usually, I don't pay attention to letters and sounds, but this time I wanted to understand. I raised my hand.

"Yes, Madelyn." Mrs. Zinc said.

"Yram's name starts with the letter *y*, not an *e*."

I heard a muffled "duh" coming from Bobby, who sits on the other side of the room by the door. Paulette scratched something on a piece of paper and shoved it in my direction.

I ignored her and watched as Mrs. Zinc wrote *Dotty* on the board, underlined the letter *y* and said, "Listen to the sound *y* makes. Just like in the word *happy*, you hear a long *e*."

Paulette was tapping her pencil on the word she had written on the paper. When I looked, I saw my own name, Mary, with a circle around the letter *y*. I felt my face turn red; I should have known this. Except I don't ever remember sounding out my own name, like I try to do to new words.

The first day Mrs. Zinc read from *The Fairy Angel's Gift*, I kept waiting to meet Yram, but instead we learned all about Ethan. At first,

I wasn't sure I liked him. He made me think of a spoiled baby even though he was ten, a year older than me. He had something wrong with his heart that made it hard for him to catch his breath, walk, or run. But he was very smart and could read anything, just like my super-smart brother, Rob, who's in sixth grade. Rob also has something wrong with his breathing—asthma. Ethan got to stay home from school and read books all day, but he was lonely and unhappy. If I could read like Rob and Ethan and had to stay home alone, I would never get lonely—it would be like story time all day except better.

The second day Mrs. Zinc read to us, Yram showed up, and that's when I knew this would be my most favorite story forever.

Ethan had tried to join in a baseball game in the playfield next to his house. He knew he needed fresh air, and he wanted to be like the other kids. He kept missing the ball, and the players made fun of him. When he finally did hit the ball, he could barely run and was tagged out before he got started toward first base. This made me think of Darren Olsen and how he must feel when we play kickball and it's his turn to kick. Darren is another Sparrow, and he flunked third grade last year, so that means he's a year older than everyone. He gets teased a lot, but I never tease anyone because I know how it feels.

Ethan went back to his room and decided that since he could read, he could travel places without stepping a single foot outside his door. That's when Yram decided he needed her help. Later that night, she showed up in his bedroom.

After the third day of listening to Mrs. Zinc read *The Fairy Angel's Gift*, I knew I had to figure out a way to keep the story alive. I said extra prayers to Saint Rita because if I could learn to read, I'd be able to make the story last forever. That Sunday, I brought my weekly allowance to church, and as we left, I told Mom I wanted to light a candle and showed her my dime. I'm sure she thought I was lighting a candle for Grandma, which I did do several other times, but this time I lit it for myself. Monday, nothing had changed—I was still a Sparrow and I read words like a Sparrow.

I told Saint Rita I wasn't angry with her. That's when the big idea came to me; to keep *The Fairy Angel's Gift* alive, all I had to do was tell the story over again, just like I did with *Charlotte's Web*. I usually tell some sort of story whenever I'm doing boring dinner dishes with my little brother, Danny, who's in first grade and is supposed to help me, which means he dries the silverware.

"Danny, I have an offer to make."

"What's an offer?"

"It's something special I'll give you in return for something else. Usually it means money."

"I only get ten cents a week."

"I know—it's not money I'm talking about."

"What?"

"Well, Mrs. Zinc has been reading the most amazing story I've ever heard. It has a fairy in it."

"Fairies aren't real."

"So. This one might be. Do you want to know my offer?"

"Okay."

"I'll tell you the story while we do the dishes *if* you not only dry the silverware, you also dry the plates."

"That's easy."

"Yep. And since you can't reach, I'll put them away, so all you have to do is dry and stack them."

"It's a deal!"

CHAPTER 6

1 9 6 7

MADDIE, I'm ready to hear the story," Danny calls from the kitchen.

"Not yet. There's more dishes to bring in." I grab the glasses from the dinner table and leave the silverware for him.

"There." He tosses a handful of forks and spoons into the plastic tub of soapy water, causing a splash. He turns his pudgy face to me. "So, what happened?"

"Well, a lot of things happened since yesterday. First of all, remember Yram is different from the other fairies. She never did like playing tricks on people and spending the evenings singing and dancing. She wanted to do something important, and because she could fly so high, she thought she had angel wings. She really wanted to be an angel, and Brogan helped her."

"I forget—who's Brogan?"

"He's the wise leprechaun who once knew an angel. He's the one who told Yram what she needed to do. He said, 'In order for you to get a halo, you need to help humans instead of just playing pranks on them.'"

"Do you believe in leprechauns?"

"I'm not so sure. I know Grandma O'Leary used to say that the people from her country believed in leprechauns, but I don't remember her ever saying she saw one. She did see a fairy, though, and I've also seen fairies." I shoot a look at Mom, who's busy cleaning the gunk off the stove.

"I don't believe you saw a fairy, and neither does Dad."

"I don't care, Grandma would have. And you don't have to listen to any more of the story."

"But I want to . . . what happens next?" Danny whines.

I rinse off a couple more plates before I continue. "Because Yram was so different, the other fairies started to not like her. They were jealous because she could fly so high. Her two cousins, Zerko and Zilla, did something really mean to her."

"What?"

"As soon as you finish drying all the silverware, I'll tell you." This always works to get Danny moving.

"Well, Zerko and Zilla snuck into the cave where Yram slept, and they smeared slug slime on her beautiful lavender wings."

"Ew."

"She didn't notice until she tried to fly and could only move in low spirals because more slime was on one wing than the other. Zerko and Zilla started fluttering all around her and then soaring real high and laughing at her. That's how she knew it was them. They kept saying, 'Oh, Dotty'—they never called her Yram—'it's just a joke, hee-hee.'"

"How'd she get it off?"

"Very carefully. Her wings are delicate. She decided to ask Ethan for help. He got her some soap and warm water, and then together they cleaned them off."

"But aren't fairies magic?"

"Yes, of course. They can fly and use their magic to help others fly, like Ethan. But they can't just do any old thing."

"What else happened?"

"Ethan heard that his father planned on going duck hunting, and he wanted to go with him because he knew he was getting stronger."

"It's just about time for homework," Mom announces.

"Maddie has more of the story to tell, can't she please finish it first?"

"I'll be quick."

"Five more minutes," Mom says.

"So, Ethan finally got up enough courage to ask his dad if he could come. His father was surprised that he even asked because Ethan mostly just spent time alone in his room with his books. So his father told him no. He was afraid Ethan would tire out. Here is what Ethan said: 'Yram believes I'm strong enough. Why don't you?'"

"Oh no," Danny says. "I bet that made his dad mad."

I give Danny a quick smile since we both know we'd never get away with talking like that to our father. All we need to do is start to talk back and he'd give us a serious look. If we mumble one more word, his deep voice brings us to a stop.

"Yes, it did. And here's what his dad said: '*Yram?* You're reading too many fairy tales. It's confusing you. The real world is not a fairy tale. Yram only lives in your imagination.'"

Danny's eyes grow wide.

"So of course this made Ethan angry, because he wasn't reading fairy tales. Here's what Ethan said back to his father . . ." I toss the dish towel to the counter, glance over, and see that Mom is sitting within earshot at the kitchen table. I clear my throat and continue in the voice of Ethan.

"'Fine. You can keep your real world, and I'll keep my imagination. At least with Yram I can run and walk.' Then he left his father and went back to his room."

"Uh-oh," Danny says.

"Yep. That's what he said. Ethan was really mad. And he didn't talk with his dad for the rest of the week."

Danny stands still as if hanging in midair like the Road Runner does on cartoons. Before I can stop myself, I start telling the part that had upset me.

"Ethan snuck into the kitchen that evening and overheard his dad say something terrible." Seeing Danny's eyes widen, I remember I really don't want to go back over this.

"What?" he asks.

"Well, it was . . . nothing all that important. You see, his father was confused, and Ethan thought he heard him say something like, 'Why does he believe in fairies?'"

"Oh, I get it. Just like Dad doesn't believe you." Danny relaxes his stance.

"Yeah . . . ," I mumble.

But what I hear inside my head is Ethan's father with our father's voice, saying over and over, "Something must be wrong with him."

CHAPTER 7

2 0 0 5

"HEY, ARE YOU OKAY?" I startle and take a moment before recognizing the six-foot-two frame filling my doorway. The cool air entering from the hall begins to clear my head. Matt Henderson gives me a concerned look and steps inside. "Did I catch you at a bad time?" I nod and grab another tissue. He's exactly who I need to see.

"Please shut the door." I dab at my eyes.

"What's going on?" He settles into a child-sized chair, knees almost reaching his chin. He should have just sat on the little square table in the center. *Oh God, I'm afraid to tell him.*

"I'm not sure." I stand up and point to the stack of files on my desk. "I guess I'm a bit overwhelmed."

He doesn't move. I fall back into my chair. He'll find out soon enough.

"I totally lost it with the third-grade team." I sigh heavily; he remains motionless, focused on me. "I knew they were going to recommend retaining Kaylee, and I could have calmly stated all the reasons why it's not a good idea." My voice breaks at this point. I can't tell if it's anger with myself for losing it or if it's their lack of getting it. Matt patiently waits. "Instead, I blew up." He raises an eyebrow, and I add, "Maybe worse than last week—"

He tilts his head. *How could he not remember?*

"—when Karla Clifford said something was wrong with Josiah's brain."

He flinches, looks away.

Seeing Matt's furrowed brow sends a shot of panic through me. *I'm about to lose my work buddy.* Guilt pokes an ugly finger in the middle of my gut. *I'm losing his trust and everyone else's.*

"I'm so sorry."

He shifts in the small chair. I'm sure he's about to walk out on me. "I must admit," he says slowly, and my heart races. "I miss the steady, calm, wise psychologist." He gives a half smile.

I mumble, "So do I," and glance back at the stack of folders. Waiting.

"Hey," he says, and I turn toward him. "You've been under a lot of stress this past winter. Don't be too hard on yourself." *He's so damn forgiving.*

"It's no excuse." I sigh and can't bring myself to look at him. "It's as though another part of me was taking over, acting out. I'm really sorry." *Oh God, that lump in my throat is about to turn to tears again.* "It's embarrassing," I whisper, swallowing hard, doing my best to stay composed. I straighten up and meet Matt's eyes; they're compassionate. Still, I avoid his face, terrified of what I'll see.

"I know someone who might be able to help."

I squirm and blush, certain of what he has in mind. I'm such a basket case, Matt's about to recommend a damn therapist. *No way.*

Two days pass, and somehow I manage to stay calm and steady. Matt's referral is tucked away in one of the credit card pockets of my billfold. The morning bell rang twenty minutes ago, plenty of time for teachers to take attendance and lunch inventory, and shift into the first lesson. I head off to fetch eight-year-old Jayden, whose parents signed a consent for testing more than four weeks ago. Prior to my mother's passing,

I never delayed longer than a week before meeting with a child.

We spend the morning together in a semi-structured format. He wiggles around on one of two small plastic chairs that snug the square table in the middle of my office, playfully falling off several times, his mop of curly black hair flopping over his dimpled smile. I collect assessment data while he is entertained with questions and answers.

"How are a cow and a cat the same?" I ask.

"That's easy. They both say *mmm* when they start to talk."

I raise my brows in question.

"Listen. A cow says *mmmooo*, and a cat says *mmmeow*."

I smile and nod and then ask, "Anything else that's the same about a cow and a cat?"

"Milk," he exclaims. "Moo, meow; cows make milk, and cats drink milk." He stands up and spins around before settling back into the chair. "And there's something else. Cow and cat both start with . . ." He makes a *cuh* sound and rolls his eyes up as if trying to recall the letter. "I think it's the letter *k*." He grins at me, flashing his big brown eyes.

I love his answer, but I can't give him a drop of credit; the two-point response is that they're both animals or mammals. One point if he had said they both have legs, hair, nurse their babies, and so forth. I'd like to figure out my own scoring system for creativity and enthusiasm.

Next, I tell him I want to see how well he can listen. He dutifully cups his large ears and leans forward while I sit less than two feet in front of him and read a simple sentence for him to repeat back. His auditory comprehension is stellar, and he must have known it. He beams while I pronounce, "No listening problems for you."

He freely volunteers, "Sometimes I don't pay attention, and then I don't hear well."

Sensing he was a smart, creative thinker, I'd started with the fun stuff: puzzles, questions, and mazes. Now it's time to check out the area of concern that prompted the referral in the first place. I begin by displaying a list of words, starting with *if*. When the shiny, laminated page of typed words comes to rest on the tabletop, the game atmosphere vanishes, as though some cruel deity has swooped in and popped a bubble that has kept us both safe.

"Jayden, here are some words. Some of them are easy, and some are hard. I'd like you to try your very best to read as many as you can for me." He stares at me, his eyes frightened saucers. I too begin to panic. *How can I turn this into a game?*

"Look," I say, pointing to *if*. "Can you read this?" He puts his finger under the letter *i* and begins to say a short letter *a* sound and then switches to a short letter *e* sound, long and drawn out, ending with the correct sound for the letter *f*. He gives a quick smile.

"The word is *eff*, just like the letter *f*."

"Nice job. How about this word?" I point to *was*. He stiffens his back and shoulders and bears down, with his finger slowly moving from letter to letter.

"*Wuu aaa ssss.*"

And my heart plunges deeper. He's going at it just as I had suspected he would, letter sound by letter sound, with no concept of blending, believing that somehow the sounds would come together and make a word. After five consecutive misses, in a moment of desperation, I do my best to put on a warm smile.

"Jayden, these are such silly words—not all of them are real. You showed me that you're a master at sounding out letters. Let's get back together tomorrow, okay?"

———————

I return to my pile of folders, each containing an incomplete summary of a child's abilities—a set of numerical facts attempting to pinpoint a disability. Jayden's folder has now joined the stack, abysmally flat, with numbers that fail to capture the creativity of his answers or his intrepid determination to figure things out. Average intelligence. He's anything but average. He's as exceptional as they come. Compared with the classification of "deficient," where his reading skills fall, average sounds pretty good.

Like the others, he'll surely qualify for special education. "Learning disabled" will be on the report, but I know it's dyslexia—a term not used to qualify children for services in public schools. I'll write recommendations, he'll receive an individualized education program, aka, an IEP. Hopefully he'll learn to read and overcome the hurdle of being special.

A heavy curtain descends upon me, making it impossible to move forward. I stare at the pile of reports that are yet to be written and sink deeper. I can't open a single file much less digest the information to qualify a child for special ed. I force myself up and out of my office. I walk the halls and slip into a classroom here and there. I return to my computer and read e-mails that I would typically delete. The entire day passes, and I've managed to aimlessly shuffle among folders, avoiding all the while scoring or interpreting a single test. By four o'clock, I decide it's time to give Matt's referral a call.

CHAPTER 8

1967

MY FATHER is the tallest man I know. Even Mr. Dreadsly, our principal, is not as tall as my father, nor is his voice as loud. If I knew someone as tall as my father, I would want to find out if their voice could fill a room like a loudspeaker just like Father's. When Mom becomes upset by us kids arguing too much or not doing our chores or just fooling around, her voice never stops us cold the way Father's does. She's a lot shorter than he is, and because I am now the tallest person in my class, I think I'm also going to have a loud, strong voice when I grow up.

When we don't listen to Mom, she threatens to tell Father, and all he has to do is say with his thundering voice, "Your mother shouldn't have to ask you three times to clean up your room." He looks directly in our eyes, and this alone can make me feel bad, like he's right. I tighten up to keep my tears from spilling out.

Mrs. Zinc's voice isn't loud like my father's, but when I think about her size, taller than my mother, but really sort of normal, her voice is powerful. What I mostly notice is that she doesn't need to use her loudness, and when she does, we all know she means business. Miss Stanley's as tall as Mrs. Zinc, but like her long flowing hair and scarf, her voice sings out as if it were a song, though only a few of us hear its music. She'd have a terrible time with kids like Bobby Wallace, and for sure Paulette would try to show her how to take charge. Maybe this is why I'm her favorite student: I listen, and we both like learning about saints.

I know Miss Stanley's real name—it's Stacy. *Stacy Stanley* sounds like a movie star. I discovered her name when my mom read the letter sent home the first week of second-grade catechism.

"Stacy Stanley; I remember her. She was a candy striper at the hospital two years ago, a sweet girl."

I couldn't think of Miss Stanley as a girl. I knew she was young, but a girl only two years ago? "What's a candy striper?" Even though I couldn't see the girl version, I sure could imagine her delivering different kinds of candy to sick people.

"Candy stripers are girls who volunteer at the hospital."

"Volunteer passing out candy?"

Mom thought this was funny, but I learned that it had nothing to do with candy except the red-and-white dresses they had to wear made someone think of candy canes. Miss Stanley looks much better in bell-bottoms and scarves the colors of rainbows.

When I first met Miss Stanley, I imagined she might also join the convent like me. After all, with her knowledge of saints and her patient smile, she would surely make a good nun. Maybe we'd end up in the same convent. Now I know she has a boyfriend. I found out about him at the beginning of the school year when Grandma was still alive.

One day after Mom came home, Grandma took me to town to pick up a few groceries at Jordan's Market. We were in the aisle with all kinds of cans, looking for tuna fish.

"Maddie, sweetheart, help me find the tuna fish. You know, that silly picture of the mermaid? Look for that." Grandma understood I do better with pictures.

"Grandma, here it is!"

"Marvelous." She grabbed four cans off the shelf and handed them to me. "Put these in the cart while I get some Spam."

I tossed the cans in and heard the voice that always sounds like singing—Miss Stanley. I looked up, and there she was with a tall man who had long blond hair. Father says long hair on boys makes them look like girls, but I had no trouble figuring out that he was a man. If I had only spied, rather than heard, Miss Stanley next to cans of Jolly Green Giant green beans, I might not have recognized her. She looked different outside the church, but I'd never mistake her voice. I wanted to run to her but suddenly felt shy, and so I pretended not to see her and began to push the cart down the aisle toward Grandma, but Miss Stanley had seen me.

"Madelyn," she called. As soon as our eyes met, I broke into a smile. The man smiled too even though he had never met me. If they had been walking outside, I'm sure they'd have been holding hands. That's when I knew that Miss Stanley probably wouldn't be joining the convent.

"Are you here with your grandmother?" I had parked the cart close to Grandma, who was bent over looking at cans of food. Miss Stanley knew about Grandma coming to stay with us because I had told her. All I could do was nod.

"I'd love to meet her."

Grandma must have heard this even though Miss Stanley's voice is never loud. I was so excited for them to meet, I didn't say a thing. When Grandma stood up and turned toward Miss Stanley, I noticed Miss Stanley take a small step back. She smiled but looked away from Grandma's face. Then I realized it was her nose. It's different.

Before this, I hadn't noticed that her nose was different; I was used to it. The next week, some of the kids in my class had also seen me in town with Grandma. Kids that knew I was a Sparrow for a second year.

"Madelyn, why does your grandma's face look weird. What happened to her nose?"

"It's just the way she is."

"It's ugly. I bet she's like you and can't read," said Bobby.

"Shut up! She can read better than any of you!"

Later, Mom told me the story of how Grandma's nose got that way. She was pumping water in the old country and the handle slipped, breaking her nose. They didn't have enough money to fix it. After Bobby's mean words, I started to notice people staring at her, and then at me, and it made me sad to not want to go to town with her anymore.

"Sweet potato, we need more tea biscuits and other necessities."

Mom wasn't home yet, and my little brothers had just got settled in front of the TV. My favorite time with Grandma was right after school. Alone in the kitchen, we'd share a cup of Lipton tea with sugar and have special tea biscuits that only Grandma and I liked. I'd tell her whatever story my teacher was reading, always making it better.

"I'm busy, Grandma."

"Too busy to come shopping with your grandma?" She knew I didn't have another thing planned.

"Bobby thinks just because your nose looks different it means you're like me."

Grandma left the shopping list on the table, took my hand, and led me to the couch. She pulled me close to her on the center cushion. If she were Paulette or Mrs. Zinc, it would have been "the look," but her eyes made me want to tell her things I'd never told anyone.

"He said you look weird, that you and I both can't read. I said he's wrong. You read really good."

She clasped her hands around both of mine. I felt her strong warmth.

I looked right at her. "Grandma, I don't think your nose looks weird."

"My sweet potato. Promise me," she said, squeezing my hands

together, "you won't ever let anyone decide for you what you're capable of. Remember how fast you spotted the tuna? You're marvelous at reading pictures. Reading words is taking a little longer, but you're as smart as all of them." Her eyes chased mine until I finally gave up looking away. She then held my gaze tight, and even though I didn't understand what she had said, I nodded as if I believed her.

"Promise," I mumbled.

"Bobby's right." She ran her fingers over the small lump of her nose and smiled. "My nose is rather odd. But nobody's perfect on the outside—it's what's inside that counts. Besides, my nose isn't something I ever need to think about."

"Me either," I said. But that was a lie. She kissed me on my cheek and told me to be ready to share a story when she got back. Never again did I go to town with her. Even so, she always brought back the special tea biscuits, the ones only the two of us liked.

CHAPTER 9

I 9 6 7

IT IS 2:20. Mrs. Zinc is planted in front of the class with *The Fairy Angel's Gift* between her hands, each arm forming a downward arrow. The only sound is Bobby crumpling paper as he digs around in his messy desk, but Mrs. Zinc continues to stand as still as a fence post.

I've been waiting, checking the clock every minute since five after two, and now I sit like a statue. But I'm no longer in the classroom; I've joined Ethan and Yram in my favorite scene. Yram tricks Ethan into running really fast. He thought it was fairy magic, but later Yram explained it's the kind of magic we all have: the magic in believing. The next day, the magic left Ethan, and he was afraid to walk much further than his bedroom.

"Yram, you know my parents don't believe in you. They think I'm imagining these conversations."

"What do you believe?" Yram asks.

"I don't know. How can I know you're real?"

"I'm not real to them because they don't believe in fairies. You'll have to make up your own mind whether I'm real."

"I think you are, and I know I really did walk and then run last night. It's just that my parents always told me it wasn't possible, that I need to stop dreaming that I can be like everyone else."

"Ethan, you're more powerful and capable than you've ever realized."

———

"There's something wrong with Ethan?" The sound of Mrs. Zinc's crisp voice brings me back to the classroom, but I missed the question. I raise my hand anyway because I always have the right answers.

"Yes, Madelyn, what do you think?"

"Could you please ask again? I didn't hear the first part."

"In other words, you only looked like you were paying attention but weren't. Paulette, will you repeat the question?"

"Why would Ethan's father think there's something wrong with Ethan?"

"What do you think, Paulette?"

"Well, Ethan was able to read, so that must mean he was smart. I think his father didn't know that Ethan was reading lots of books." Paulette is right. Smart kids read lots of books.

"That's an interesting idea, Paulette. But remember, his father said Ethan was reading too many fairy tales. Does anyone else have an idea?"

I wave my hand, but Mrs. Zinc calls on Bobby.

"Yes, Bobby."

"His father's right. There's something wrong with him. All he had to do was read the newspaper to his dad, and then his father would have known he was smart. But he didn't, so I also think he's stupid."

Everyone giggles, but Bobby's wrong. Mrs. Zinc holds her finger to her lips and says nothing. I whip my hand from left to right and make a small moaning noise. Mrs. Zinc turns her eyes to me.

"You know I don't call on students who are not *quietly* raising their hands."

I shove my hand back into my coat pocket. What Bobby said isn't funny. In my mind, I see the creases above my father's eyes when he came into our kitchen just as Mom was becoming upset because I had done the math worksheet wrong. I had guessed at the directions. He didn't say a single word aloud, but his eyes said it all—something is wrong.

Both my hands are deep in my coat pocket, but Mrs. Zinc calls on me anyway.

"Yes, Madelyn."

"Oh. Well, it's that fathers don't always understand. His father thought Ethan wasn't smart because he kept talking about Yram and . . ."

"Yes?"

"To his father, she's not real, so he thinks Ethan has a problem with his thinking. But he doesn't."

"That's a very good answer. Remember, Ethan's father knew Ethan read, but he thought he read fairy tales. Did Ethan read fairy tales?"

"No," the chorus responds.

"Madelyn's right. His father's upset that Ethan would believe in a magical being that he doesn't believe in himself."

Mrs. Zinc then begins to read, and her voice disappears along with the desks, workbooks, and chalkboard. I listen to Ethan's pleading voice as he shares his problems with Yram, who speaks of ways he can have fun. I see the fairy's long silky hair and purple tunic. I hear her voice speak of possibility. I hang on to every single word, and with each pause, I hold my breath hoping there's more to hear. The chapter ends much, much too soon.

CHAPTER 10

1 9 6 7

GRANDMA would have loved *The Fairy Angel's Gift*. I don't understand why most people think fairies aren't real when smart people, like my grandmother, say they have seen them. Fairies only exist in fiction books. But the Bible isn't fiction, and I think some of those stories, like building a boat so big that two of every animal in the entire world could fit in, well, they're just as hard to believe. I think it's easier to believe that animals can talk to each other, that a pig might not want to be slaughtered, a smart spider can write words in her web, and a fairy might want to try to be an angel.

I miss Grandma the most after school, waiting for Mom to come home. I stay away from the kitchen so I don't remember Lipton tea. Usually, I play on the rope swing or look for frogs by the lake. By the time we reach chapter four of *The Fairy Angel's Gift*, I decide it has been too long since I saw Yram's picture on the front cover of the book, and it's time to draw my own picture of her.

When Yram changed her name, she made herself new clothes so that humans could see her. Most fairies wear green to blend in. Yram chose a purple tunic spun from a silkworm, so I use a sharp colored pencil to draw lots of skinny lines to make it look like woven threads. Her wings are lavender and her hair long and golden. Under my picture, I write the capital letter *B*, and then I study the leaves that are starting to grow on the oak tree I see through my bedroom window and draw one right next to the letter *B*.

"Maddie," calls Danny outside my bedroom door. "It's dinnertime."

"I'm coming," I yell back while looking at my sketch pad.

"What do you have there?" Father asks as I tape it to my bedroom door.

"It's a picture of Yram, the fairy."

"It's quite colorful. Hmm. I see the letter *b*, and then, is that a picture of a leaf?"

"No, it's a *leave*, like the leaves on a tree, and if you put it together it says *believe*."

"Oh, I see. Except what you have is a *b* and a leaf. *Leaves* means more than one, so you would need to put several leafs together for it to be *leaves*. Or," he says, and he gives the quick smile that tightens my stomach, "you could simply spell the word *believe*. Jack or Rob can help with your spelling after dinner."

I settle into my chair across the dinner table from Rob and next to Jack. Father's deep voice leads us in prayer.

"In the name of the Father, Son, and Holy Spirit. Bless us, O Lord, and these Thy gifts, which we are about to receive from Thy bounty, through Christ our Lord. Amen." Our hands make quick motions forming a sloppy sign of the cross, while Father's move straight up, down, and across.

"So, what did everyone learn in school today?" Father always asks this question. On days that we have science and Mrs. Zinc reads from the science book or the *Weekly Reader*, I have lots to report.

Between mouthfuls of mashed potatoes, Jack blurts out, "I started—"

"Jack, don't talk with your mouth full," Father says. Jack gulps big and then wipes his mouth on his shirtsleeve. Father winces.

"My reading group started a chapter book today." Since he's only in second grade, I figure it was a flat chapter book like *Spot the Dog*.

But I'm wrong; it's a real chapter book called *My Father's Dragon*, which my parents and Rob know about. I only look at Jack once and see his chipmunk smile and know that I need to keep my eyes on the mashed potatoes and pork chops.

"We also started reading a new book today," said Rob. "It's really good. It's called *The Hobbit,* and it has three hundred and twenty pages. I'm already on page one hundred and fifteen. I can't wait to get back to it." I practically choke on my mashed potatoes. I knew he read a lot, but is it even possible to read that many pages in one day?

"What's a hobbit?" Jack asks.

"It's a make-believe kind of person. They're like dwarfs, but they have hairy feet. Bilbo Baggins is a hobbit who just wants to stay home and be comfortable, but his friends talk him into taking a big adventure, and now he's on one."

"Sounds like a fantasy story," Mom says.

"It's make-believe," Rob says. "But it seems real when you're reading it."

"When you read a good book, that's what happens—you feel as though it's really happening and you're in it," Father says.

"Even if you don't read but just listen, that can happen," I say.

"Yep, when Maddie tells me the story, it does seem real, but I know fairies are not real," Danny chimes in.

Father clears his voice, and we all look up at him. "Last night, Uncle Joe called. He's in between jobs, and down the road, where that new resort is coming in, they need carpenters. So, Uncle Joe is going to be staying with us for about a month while he works there."

I remember the phone ringing last night and Father looking all serious after he hung up. I knew something was happening; probably he wanted to talk with Mom first before telling us. But now that he has, it feels like Christmas. Everyone except Father is excited.

"When's he going to come?" Jack asks.

"I met with him today. He plans on moving a few things in tomorrow so he can start work Friday with Lakeside Development. He should be here sometime after you get home."

Danny spontaneously claps, and Jack joins in. I thought back to the last time Uncle Joe stayed with us, when he came to help build the garage. He'd listen to the stories I made up, and he had a special name for me—Sister Bard. He always had a funny joke or two, and he's so smart, he knew how to fix the rock tumbler that had broken. Father had said it should be thrown out, but Uncle Joe knew what to do.

"I can't wait for Uncle Joe to come," Danny whines.

Rob looks up from his empty plate of food and asks, "What happened to his other job?"

"Actually, I'm not sure," Father says. "I think Uncle Joe wants to take a little break to think about what his next job might be, but in the meantime, he needs to make money to pay his bills. Rob, were you able to get the information on junior golf?"

Rob looks first at Mom and then Father, and back down at his plate, before answering.

"No."

Father places his fork on his plate so he can give a good hard look at Rob while Mom continues to keep her eyes on the couple bites of potatoes sitting alone on her plate.

In a trembling voice, Rob continues. "I told you, I'm not interested in golf. I want to try out for track."

We all stay quiet, and the silence is so heavy I think it might choke me. Then Danny breaks it.

"What's track?"

"You know, that round racing track behind the kickball field, where the big kids have to run," Jack says, but I can tell Father is still upset, and Mom is staying quiet.

I don't like the quiet, so I say, "I wish I could go out for track." No one responds, so I add, "I'm the fastest one in my class."

"Maybe when you're older," Mom says in her choppy voice.

"It's not all running. It could be jumping or throwing the discus or shot put," Rob says.

"You're right, Rob, it's not all running, but we have already had this discussion. It's much too risky for you even if all you did was participate in the field events. What if you were sixty miles away and had an asthma attack in the middle of a meet? End of discussion."

Rob stands up. His plate is empty, but not all of us have empty plates, and he doesn't even ask to be excused. He turns and leaves. I think of Ethan, how upset he was when his father didn't believe he could handle duck hunting.

"Maddie, I'm ready for the story," Danny says while setting a stack of plates on the counter next to the sink. "I remember what happened."

"What?"

"Ethan stopped talking to his father for a whole week because he was mad. I don't see how that can really happen. And Yram had her wings wiped with slug slime. Did the mean cousins do it again?"

"No, they left her alone. But they started a rumor. Do you know what a rumor is?"

"A room or something like it?"

"No. It's when you say something about someone to someone else and it's not true. Just like at the start of the school year, and I was cold so I kept my coat on, and Bobby started telling everyone that the reason I always wear my coat is because I have to wear ugly clothes. That's a rumor."

"Oh, so it's telling lies. Why did he say you were wearing ugly clothes?"

"I don't know. I think he was mad because I beat him at tetherball in front of everyone. The lie that Zerko and Zilla started telling is that Yram was a cruel fairy who was making children get in trouble with their parents on purpose."

"That's mean."

"Yeah, and it upset Yram because it was sort of true. Ethan was having a hard time getting along with his dad, and he wasn't at all happy. He started feeling more sorry for himself. Yram wanted to help, so she decided to show up at dinnertime."

"You mean she just flew right in the door or something?"

"No, that's not how Yram does things. She made a point of flickering real bright outside the windows. Ethan knew it was her and yelled out, 'Look, Dad and Mom, that's my fairy friend.' Yram waved, and Ethan could even make out a smile. She was hard to see, but he knew it was her. Well, when his parents looked out the window, they started to laugh."

"Why?"

"Because what they saw was not a fairy—what they saw was a firefly. Their laughing made Ethan really mad and hurt his feelings."

"Is that why you get mad when we don't believe you?"

I stop rinsing the plates and turn to face Danny. He stops twirling the damp towel and waits for my response.

"Yes. Because you really don't know what I see." I look over at Mom, who has begun to sweep the crumbs from the floor; I can tell she's listening.

"But this is just a story, and Dad says—"

"I *know*," I snap back. "Danny, you need to help. I've done everything so far. Here, dry this." I hand him a plate and dish towel.

"What else happens?" I ignore him and wait until he at least finishes drying off the plate, and then I continue.

"Ethan wanted to run off. When he got up to leave, he saw the way his parents looked at him. He saw the worry in his mother's eyes and disbelief in his father's eyes."

"Why didn't Ethan's parents see Yram?"

"I'll tell you when I get to that part. But first, here's what happened to Ethan. He took a couple of steps, got all shaky, and his heart started beating real fast, so he fell to the floor. His mother helped him walk back to his room. Once he was alone, he began to wonder if his parents were right, that maybe it wasn't Yram he'd seen. It could have been he was seeing things. This upset him more. Later, when Yram came back, he was mad at her too."

"Why? She did try to show herself."

"Ethan asked, 'Where were you?' and Yram said, 'You saw me waving at you.' Ethan said, 'Why didn't you come in the house the way you always come in my bedroom?' He was still feeling upset about his parents' laughing, which I can understand." I pause and look over at Mom, who is now wiping the counters. "Here is what Yram had to say: 'Ethan, no matter what, they wouldn't have seen me because they don't believe. If you think something is impossible, then no matter what happens, you'll miss it.'"

"I don't get it."

"Yram is saying that if someone has their mind made up that there are no such things as fairies, then no matter what they see, they'll not believe in fairies. Last night, I saw a fairy outside my window, and when Mom looked, she said it was the moon and stars flickering through the leaves."

"Who's right?" Danny asks, darting his eyes from me to Mom and back to me. Mom stops her cleaning and turns toward us.

"We both are," Mom says. "Madelyn saw a fairy, and I saw the stars twinkling. Madelyn has a fantastic imagination. She's able to see things that we don't see."

"But was there *really* a fairy?" Danny asks.

"Yes," I say at the same time Mom is saying, "No."

Danny looks first at me and then at Mom. His face scrunches up as if he's trying to solve a puzzle.

CHAPTER 11

1 9 6 7

THE FIRST THING I do each night before going to bed is make sure my window curtain is cracked open enough to let in a sliver of outside just in case a fairy happens to fly by. I saw one the day after Mrs. Zinc started reading *The Fairy Angel's Gift*. At first, I thought I had seen a giant firefly, but then I realized it was much too big to be a firefly and it was the wrong time of the year because the leaves on the tree were only beginning to push out. When Mom came to tuck me in, I had her take a look, but all she could see were stars.

"Mom, this time I know I saw a fairy. I was lying in bed looking at a star, and it flew right up to my window."

"Honey, it was probably a firefly. Some of them can get pretty big."

"But I thought fireflies were only around during the summer, and it's not summer yet." I gave her my pleading face, and she squatted down next to me, separated the curtains, and tilted her head to peer out the window and shut them much too soon to have seen anything.

"I even saw its wings," I added, because the more I thought about it, the more certain I was.

"What I saw were lots of stars flickering." She smiled the way she always does when I tell her a joke and she knows it's supposed to be funny—but this was not meant to be funny. She motioned me back to bed in her no-nonsense way, like I imagine her at work in the hospital, poking a thermometer under a patient's tongue and reminding him to lie still with his mouth closed.

"I can tell you don't believe me."

"Sweetheart, you have a good imagination, and sometimes you get a little carried away."

"But maybe fairies are real. Lots of people believe in them—I'm not the only one. You know Grandma O'Leary saw a fairy."

"Honey, I think your grandmother was pulling your leg."

"No, she wasn't. She even said that in her country most people believe in fairies and leprechauns."

"Well, the Irish people love to tell stories, and sometimes the stories are so lifelike that people imagine things. Your grandmother was a good Catholic, and Catholics don't believe in fairies."

"I do." I pulled the blankets over my head and tucked my stuffed donkey, Eeyore, under my arm.

I've shared with Saint Rita that I believe in fairies, and I think I heard her answer that she does too.

Each night after tucking me in, my Mom reminds me, "Don't forget to say your prayers." She's always reminding us kids to say our prayers. If we lose something, she suggests we pray to Saint Anthony, the patron saint for lost objects. Mom prays to Saint Anthony whenever she loses her keys, and he always comes to the rescue. They usually show up under a pile of papers on the kitchen counter or in her purse. He helped me a few times, but he also let me down, like when I lost my loose tooth during recess. Mom says prayers don't always turn out the way we want them to.

That's why I plan to be a nun when I grow up. If I'm good at it, I'll learn to do miracles and then go on to be a saint. If I were a saint, I'd work extra hard to listen to prayers and make sure all of them were answered.

I found out about Saint Rita last year when I asked Miss Stanley what a patron saint for lost causes meant, like Saint Jude, who my Mom prays to when she's upset.

"I don't see why anyone would be a saint for lost causes. If I lose something, I pray to Saint Anthony. Does this mean praying to figure out the cause of losing something?"

The other kids in class had giggled just like when I had asked the week before, "If a saint sins, do they still have to go to purgatory?" They never understand the importance of my questions, but Miss Stanley always understands.

"Being a patron saint of lost causes is quite special," Miss Stanley answered in her gentle voice. "A lost cause is not like a lost toy—it's when you want something, and you lose your willpower to get it and you give up. Or when you are in a desperate or what appears to be an impossible or hopeless situation." It had made me sad to think that my mom sometimes feels this way, but at least she has Saint Jude.

"Saint Jude is not the only patron saint for lost causes. There is also Saint Rita, whom I pray to on occasion. Sometimes, I'm in a situation that feels a little hopeless."

I could hardly believe what I had heard: Miss Stanley feeling hopeless? She knows so much about saints and the Bible.

"Like learning a new and difficult song on the organ well enough to play it on Sunday. When I've lost hope, I pray to Saint Rita. She has never failed me."

Miss Stanley plays the organ so beautifully on Sundays, I knew she was right. It must be Saint Rita helping her.

"I didn't know two different saints could be in charge of helping with the same kinds of problems."

Miss Stanley laughed. "There are probably more than two. I just relate better to Saint Rita."

"So do I."

Before class was over, Miss Stanley reached into her desk and handed me a holy card with Saint Rita's picture, and when I imagined a colorful scarf instead of the white habit, I was amazed at how much she looked like Miss Stanley.

Now that I'm in third grade and still a Sparrow, I'm thinking reading's a cause that's so lost even Saint Rita can't help. I still pray to her. I know she's a powerful saint because I listen to Miss Stanley play the organ music on Sundays, and everyone bows their heads to listen, and if clapping were allowed, that's what would happen because her music is perfect.

Mom doesn't need to remind me to say my prayers, and since I had told her I planned on being a nun, I think she knows this. Praying is how I settle down to fall asleep at night. I do more than say a couple of Hail Marys and Our Fathers. I organize the problems from my day and put them in imaginary rooms so I can shut each door and take care of one room at a time. I call it cleaning my rooms. One by one, I open doors and make myself lie still and feel the upset, and then I discuss it with Saint Rita.

Usually, it's teasing or getting scolded for not following along in class. Sometimes it's my father raising his voice. Tonight the messiest room is what happened during PE. That's all I knew when I made a room for it. My thoughts drift back to PE, and my stomach tightens with the image of Bobby and kickball. When I open the door and listen, I know it's not about kickball. I had my best kick all week; I ran with my head held high. I didn't even need to slide into home, but I did anyway because it's fun. Maybe I shouldn't have showed off so much. I know I was smiling when I brushed the dirt from my clothes. Bobby stood waiting for the ball that was still way out in left field.

I play this over in my mind, and my stomach tells me that's not what's making me upset; it has nothing to do with my perfect kick. My stomach stays tight, and that's how I know it's what Bobby said to me that has me tied up inside. The closer I get to it, the more my stomach aches, and, like a loose tooth, the only way to make it better is to pull it out, real fast. I let his voice say what he said.

"Just because you can kick a ball doesn't mean you're smart."

I feel my stomach go into a knot, but right away I tell Saint Rita, "It's just because he was mad. I had caught his pop-up and it was an out. That's why he told me that on the way back to class."

I chant one Hail Mary after another as the twisting, aching feeling is smoothed out, and the room is clean enough to let me sleep.

CHAPTER 12

2 0 0 5

IRENE INGERSOLL, like Matt, is a social worker; not a clinical psychologist. Which I find comforting. I keep a referral list of twenty or more psychologists for parents and teachers. Yet therapy is not something I've ever considered for myself, even when I was getting divorced. I've always worked my problems out using my journal.

My first journal, now a broken-spined, five-by-seven-inch sketchpad stowed under my bed, was a birthday present from my brother Jack. As a child, I liked to draw, but it was writing that ultimately captivated me. Sometime toward the end of seventh grade, when I could read most of my inventive spelling, my sketchpad shifted from pictures to words, which only I could decipher. That first journal introduced me to the pleasures of crafting my thoughts into a meaningful code. I wrote solely for myself, and rules of spelling, grammar, and punctuation were tossed aside. At times, my writing taught me something I neither knew nor thought I might want to know—a painless birth delivering untold satisfaction. I'd create stories about children conquering all kinds of evil forces, and in the course of a leisurely afternoon, regardless of frightful misspellings, I fancied myself a writer.

I arrive a good ten minutes early for my first appointment with Irene. Arriving early is an ingrained behavior acquired from my father. We'd be the kids stiff as icicles standing in subzero temperatures a good five minutes ahead of schedule, waiting at the end of our driveway for the yellow school bus to pick us up. I'm pleased that Irene's office is located on the second floor of a charming Craftsman in my own district of Powderhorn rather than some high-rise in upper Edina.

At the top of the creaky wooden stairs leading to her office, there's a chair and table with magazines and the aroma of herbal tea. I do my best to look as if sitting in a therapy waiting room is nothing new to me. I loop my right leg over my left and refrain from bouncing it. I casually pick up a magazine and place it on my lap. Before opening it, I glance down, and its evenly spaced, bold black letters parading across the cover scream at me: *b-i-t-c-h*. I flip that hot-potato magazine off my lap as if it were on fire, shoving it deep under the pile. I uncross my legs and take a breath. *God, I'm an uptight person. It's just a feminist magazine.* Determined to not look stressed, I riffle through a copy of *Scientific American*.

The door opens, and a current of tension courses through my body. For some odd reason, I can't shake the thought that Mrs. Downing, who had just last week insisted with curled lips and a puffy red face that I retest her child, would be the previous client slipping by me. Relief pours over when no one other than Irene steps out. She appears to be at least my age, possibly older. Not that age ensures wisdom. These days it's the young teachers, those just starting out, who impress me the most. Even so, the prospect of peering into the eyes of a bright-faced twenty-year-old while I attempt to share the crumbling of my professional life has generated a universe of anxiety.

"You must be Mary Madelyn." Irene resembles my mother, which means she's about her weight and at least five inches shorter than I am, but these are the only physical similarities they share. It's her thick dark hair cropped daringly short and a smile that practically spills off her face that grab my attention.

"You can call me Mary." I step in, and I know right away where I'm expected to sit: the overstuffed couch near the coffee table with the box of tissues and squeeze ball. The scent of chamomile and peppermint tea wafts from an end table next to a rocking chair, where a colorful shawl that looks as if it has come from Central America drapes across the back.

"Would you like some tea?" Irene asks.

That's when it hits me that I've made a terrible mistake. It's not at all like me to meet someone, anyone, even someone with a genuine smile, and simply begin to share feelings. I'm the one who listens, or, if need be, writes in my journal. Parading my emotions is not what I do.

I open my mouth to say no, but instead I say, "Sure." My eyes sweep the room, willing a settled calm to ease its way into my veins. I realize what I want, more than anything, is a long leisurely stretch of time to seek out, on my own, the mercurial monster who has taken up residence in the heart of my soul.

I glance over at Irene, rocking steadily, peacefully, as though there is ample time to explore, illuminate, and unearth the unruly residents dwelling in dark corners of my interior rooms. I train my gaze out the narrow window to my right, where snatches of sky peek through leaves, a collage of blue and green shifting gently with the wind. I stare into it, allowing my focus to soften. For a moment or two, I know I belong on this couch in the small room with Irene searching for an opening. I too am searching. But awkward doesn't even come close to describing the discomfort saturating my every attempt to utter something worthwhile.

Long segments of time pass before I'm able to formulate even a beginning of what there is to say. I clear my throat, but nothing comes out. Words can be so inadequate. I long to be alone with my journal, where thoughts release themselves and I don't have to worry about the presentation. My eyes mist over. *What am I doing here?*

"Irene, Matt shared with me how skilled you are, and I'm sure he's right, it's just . . ." My voice grows thin, reedy, unrecognizable. "It's just, I'm not sure therapy is the right thing for me at this time." I catch my breath and then mumble, "I'm sorry," and gaze back out the window. I hear Irene's voice, soft and reassuring; my breathing returns to its normal rhythm. I continue to peer out at the sway of leaves against the blue sky, lost with how to take the next step.

Finally, I turn and look directly at her. "I have no idea how to do this. I don't know where to begin." I feel her intense dark eyes peer beyond the crazy awkwardness of me sitting pathetically on the couch. Her gaze speaks of promise. Suddenly, I'm aware that more than anything, I want her to know I'm intelligent and I'm good at what I do.

"You have begun. There is no right or wrong way—you're doing it perfectly." Her voice is serenely steady, inviting.

It's true—I have begun. *Maybe Matt's right; this is where I belong.* I know I need to fill her in. But where do I start? That I miss my mother and that we were close? Somehow, this alone can't possibly account for my falling apart at work. I move inside myself, taking inventory. I used to call it "cleaning rooms." I realize I may know something of the truth, but I can't quite bring myself to pull it up and take a look.

"Everything changed after my mother died."

"Your mother's been in your life for forty-seven years. This is a big change and a huge loss."

I begin to tell her about my last visit to her house.

"At the end of the afternoon, when I had taken care of everything, I decided to take a look in the hope chest. I knew I'd find her wedding dress, and I was curious what else she had packed away. I had gotten through the entire day without an emotional breakdown."

I take a sip of tea and continue.

"I was very close to my mother. I love and miss her more than I had ever imagined." I feel Mom's hand squeeze mine as she recites, "A daughter is a daughter for life . . ." A surge of emotion wells up. I take a moment to breathe and swallow the lump. "What confuses me is that I really believe I've worked through the stages of grief. I'll always miss her, but I'm well into the stage of acceptance. I know this was a big loss, but it feels like I lost much more than my mother." I look at her pleadingly as if she held the key to my understanding.

"Your life hasn't been the same since her death."

I nod. "Well, anyway. I did find her wedding dress and a pile of saved baby clothes. But then, at the very bottom . . ." My voice cracks as the image of the coat rushes toward me. I swallow and breathe. "I found something of mine that didn't belong in the chest." Irene leans forward. "It was my coat from third grade. I was shocked to have even remembered it. I have no idea why my mother chose to keep it." I give a little fake laugh. I shrug my shoulders.

"Your mother chose to keep your third-grade coat," Irene calmly repeats.

"Yeah. It was like . . . as if she wanted to send me a message. Suddenly, my past jumps in, and what I most remember about the coat is my mother's frowns each day I trudged off to school wearing it. You see . . . I wore that coat all year long. The other kids teased me because it was kind of weird."

I can tell by the slight rise of her brow this has captured her attention, but I'm ready to leave. I glance at my watch and decide to say only one last thing.

"So, when I held it up, I began to cry—a lot. I'm sure it was all about my final good-bye and being alone with her things, and I'm surprised with how much I carried on, but I think I'm done now." Even though I know my sixty minutes of therapy are not up, I make a show of squinting over to the little clock situated on the bookshelf parallel to her rocking chair. "I'm ready to move on and get back to the way things were before." I stretch one leg out at a time, resisting the urge to simply spring up and go.

Reflexively, I reach into my pocket and roll the smooth shell of the acorn between my fingers. There really isn't time to share what I found in my coat pocket. Even if this were not the case, how could I begin to explain what I can hardly grasp myself?

"I see you're feeling restless, and you're impatient with your process. Congratulations for giving yourself this time to explore." Her use of the word *congratulations*, polite and formal, seems out of context. There's nothing to congratulate me for at this point. I'm only trying to get back what I once had. She leans forward on the rocker, and it's clear she isn't going to release me yet. "I have only one more question before we end our session." My stomach tightens, but I see a face that is caring and kind. "It's not at all unusual when a parent dies for childhood memories to surface, to be reactivated. Do you, to your knowledge, have a history of trauma in your early childhood?"

I give her a blank stare.

"I just thought that if there was any kind of abuse or trauma in your past, it would help me, that is, to know the best way to proceed."

"Oh. I see. Actually, I was blessed with two wonderful parents and a pretty typical childhood. I grew up in rural Minnesota and always wished I lived in the city—but I do now." I stand up, adjust my jacket, and give her an awkward smile. As I turn toward the door, a cavernous ache rises from my heart to my throat. An ache that feels as old as the black-hooded coat I had abandoned. The coat had left me feeling raw, but there isn't another thing I could say about it. Yet there is more to be said, something that doesn't come anywhere close to fitting the protocol of abuse, and for sure, there are no perfect childhoods. I turn back toward Irene.

"There's only one thing. That is, from my past."

She leans forward.

"But it's little." I take a deep breath and with a steady voice say, "It took me a really long time to learn to read."

CHAPTER 13

1 9 6 7

AS USUAL, I'm the first one out the door when the recess bell rings. Once out, I hold back to see where Bobby Wallace goes before deciding where I'll spend my fifteen minutes. We both like the same things: tetherball, jungle gym, and racing around on upper field. Because there are only two teachers on duty, he's able to get away with saying mean things, like calling me knuckle-brain or dingbat, so I try to stay away from him. I see him take off for upper field, so I decide on tetherball. Just as I'm about to break out into a run, I hear Paulette calling.

"Madelyn."

I stop but almost keep going.

"What do you want to do?" she asks, and I point straight in front of me to the tetherball.

"You know I can't play that. I wear glasses."

She's right. I know what Paulette likes, all the boring games like hopscotch and jump rope, and most of the time she just walks around talking to other smart girls in the class. I'm not sure why she even likes being my friend.

"How about the bars?" I say, hoping she might have changed.

"I hate the bars. Besides, I don't have shorts on under my dress."

I can't imagine putting on a dress without wearing shorts underneath. Paulette glances around, and I see the group of girls from class that she usually walks with. They must be mad at her about something, probably for being too bossy. She turns her back to them, shoves her brown plastic glasses further up her nose, and gives me her serious teacher look.

"Did you know there's a spelling test after recess?"

"Oh no! I forgot about it."

"Well, you don't have to worry about that. Come play jump rope with me, and I'll make sure you get a good grade." She skips over to the area marked out for jumping rope. I tag behind.

"Madelyn," Paulette says, using her bossy tone of voice, "you turn the rope with Lisa. She wants to jump rope with us." Lisa runs to fetch a long rope out of the tubs where ropes and balls are kept. "I'll start off jumping because I'm the best. Then, when I miss three times, it'll be Lisa's turn because I know you're not too good at jump rope."

"Okay," I say.

As soon as Paulette misses the third time and Lisa begins jumping, Paulette yells across the rope.

"Why do you keep wearing that awful coat all the time?"

"Paulette. Stop it. You said you wouldn't keep asking me."

"But the other kids all think it's really weird. That's why you don't have friends."

"I do too. Besides, I feel cold when I don't wear it. You know that."

"But you didn't wear it all the time last year," Paulette says, while Lisa's head bobs up and down and her blond hair sways from side to side as she jumps in rhythm. Paulette's right; I'm not good at this, and I don't like it. My hand begins to move faster than Paulette's.

"So what," I yell back, and the rope twists. I continue to twirl it faster and faster until Lisa finally trips. Soon, Lisa has tripped three times, and I'm free to leave.

"Madelyn," yells Paulette, "that's not fair to Lisa." Instead of yelling back "So what" again, I race for the tetherball, hoping to get a few good slugs in before the bell rings.

I had hoped Paulette was wrong about the spelling test. I did try to memorize the words when they were passed out last week, but within moments, they flew from my mind, and I was left with a bunch of letters thrown together. Had they been words like *spy, detective, kickball*, or *fairy*, I might have remembered, but these were a bunch of ordinary words. I still made an effort to memorize the order of letters to whatever ordinary word I was looking at so that I might have a chance of coming close.

Mom tries hard to help me pass my spelling tests. She thinks it's easier to spell a word if you can first read the word, but for me, this just makes it twice as hard, and then she gets upset.

"Madelyn, the word is *because*. Reading it will help you spell it." I know she believes this. I did get the *be* part right. I just couldn't remember how the rest of the letters came together. Mom works so hard at helping me pass my spelling tests that it feels like a sin each time I bring home a flunking grade.

Mrs. Zinc stands in front of the class looking like a telephone pole in the middle of a cornfield. Her way of standing is like Father's voice: loud and catching attention. She uses her face, not her voice, to tell us, "I'm waiting for you to quiet down." A smile with tight lips turned up, and it always works. Even Bobby notices. He hates me for being better at kickball and tetherball, but I know he passes all his spelling tests, and I don't think he even tries.

Paulette sits down next to me and gives me a look like I'm some alien from outer space, and then says, "Humph," before turning away. Yellow and cream-colored strands of hair swish this way and that before settling straight down her back, and I know I'm not going to get the help she promised. She's still mad at me for running off from jumping rope. I don't care.

Last week, I was on her good side, and when we had our spelling test, she made no effort to cover her perfectly printed words six inches from my desk, making it impossible to not notice. I did notice that I had started each word out with the right letter. I've gotten good at that. Each time Mrs. Zinc wandered by, Paulette had slid a notebook over the words, glancing sideways at me with a twinkle in her eye. It felt like best friends sharing a secret. My spelling test that week came home with a grade as good as Jack's.

Today, I know she'll keep her words covered up, but I had already made a promise to Saint Rita to not cheat anymore. Nuns don't cheat. Besides, I don't want to have to confess this again on Sunday to Father Stevens.

"The first word is *awake*. If you are awake, you're not asleep. *Awake*."

At least I know what letter it starts out with: letter *u*. Every day in reading circle, we chant, "*U, umbrella, uhhh*." The tricky part is the last letter. If I had been in charge of making the alphabet, I would have said no to making three different ways to spell the same sound: *c*, *k*, or *ck*. I take my best guess and choose *ck*. Then I remember. Since the *a* sound I heard in the middle is the long *a* because it says its name, I need to add a letter *e* at the end because that's how to make the vowel say its name. I write *uwacke*.

Mrs. Zinc continues. "Number two is *surprise*. A surprise party is a party you do not expect. *Surprise*."

I say the word to myself over and over before writing down *srprize*, which sounds right each time I sound out the letters. I can't tell if it looks right because it's not a word that shows up in *Spot the Dog*. I try to take a quick peek at Paulette's paper, but she already has it covered up. She catches me looking and smirks.

Mrs. Zinc finally reaches the last word, *failure*, which I spell *fellyour* because I remember how to spell the word *your*. Mom and I had practiced that one a lot. Paulette's paper is still covered up, and I tell myself it doesn't matter if I flunk again. These are just a bunch of ordinary words that I'll never use in my own writing. At least I won't have to worry about confessing a sin. It's just my parents. My father always says all you need to do is your best, but I can tell what he hopes for is to see good grades, because he always gets so excited when Rob and Jack bring home papers with a letter A on them.

CHAPTER 14

1 9 6 7

On THE WAY HOME from school, I sit three seats behind our bus driver, Mr. Lakowski, lean into a window smeared with sticky nose and fingerprints, and replay the story. Ethan would do most anything for Yram, and so would I. When she whispered, "I need your help," he forgot about his fears; he kept his thoughts pinned on pleasing her.

Yram pulled out a strand of sticky spiderweb and asked Ethan to remember what it felt like to speed through the thicket. That's when he noticed he had run so fast he could still feel his heart thumping up and down in his chest, like a pump. He remembered moving as fast as a deer, and this memory made him shiver with excitement. All at once, Yram lit up, flashing bright like a firefly. She dangled the thread between two tiny fingers, and the thread began to glow, then burst into dazzling golden colors.

The school bus slows to a stop. Rob, Danny, and Jack tumble out while I blink my eyes and whisper good-bye to Ethan and Yram. Jack, three strides ahead, yells out, "I'll race you!" He doesn't wait for an answer, and I don't give him one. Our driveway is long, I have plenty of time to catch up and pass him. Rob stays behind. He could beat us all if he wanted, but he never tries because of the wheezing.

I dash through the kitchen. I never stay too long in the kitchen before Mom comes home because otherwise I'll remember Lipton tea and become very sad. I rush out the back door toward the lake. Midway down the hill, I grab on to the thick rope with a knotted end dangling down from a fat branch. I sprint across the dirt-packed ridge, fling myself over the hill, and fly. Over and over I swing, imagining myself flying with Yram the way Ethan did.

I gulp down a glass of water and meet Mom just as her green station wagon pulls into the driveway. I squeeze my arms around her waist and decide next to look for frogs. I hear the phone ring. I go inside and fill up my glass with more water and pause in the doorway to see who's calling.

"Mrs. Zinc?" Mom answers. I freeze. *Why is my teacher calling?* I stand halfway in the kitchen and halfway out, pretending to slowly drink the entire glass, but I can't swallow another drop. She must have a lot to say, because Mom has stretched the phone cord so she can sit on a kitchen chair to listen. She holds the phone pressed against her face. *Should I run down to the lake or keep sipping my water?* I choose water while I remember all the things I do wrong at school.

At last, Mom says something: "I see."

Looking at her, I can't tell if she's angry or sad. Her lips are pressed together; she squeezes the phone so hard her knuckles turn white. Then she speaks in a voice I imagine her using at work, not at home with us. "Yes, we do need to talk more about this." It must be the spelling test. Or all those times I didn't pay attention. *Should I run down to the lake or stay?* In that moment, I'm not able to do either. I stand stuck at the sink with my full glass of water.

"I understand. We're also concerned."

Oh no.

"I'll get back to you after I have a chance to talk with my husband."

My body takes over and pulls me right to my room. I don't want to hear anymore. Except maybe I do, because I don't slam my door shut;

I leave it open and hear the last sentence.

"Sure, that would be fine. Whatever might help."

Help? What is Mrs. Zinc telling her?

Saint Rita, please don't let this be bad news. I promise to say an extra Hail Mary tonight. I need to know just how serious this is. I wander back to the kitchen to peek at Mom's face. She's sitting at the kitchen table the way Mrs. Zinc likes us to sit, still as a statue, gazing at something so far away no one else can see it. When she sees me, her eyes droop. I give a weak smile.

"Maddie, honey, come here."

Oh no. I scuff jelly-legged to the table.

Her arms are open; I snuggle right in, bracing myself for the bad news.

"That was your teacher who called."

"Why?"

"Well, she has an idea that she wants your father and me to think about for next year, and she wanted to know if we would let you see a special teacher who knows some ways to teach reading to kids who . . ." Her voice goes weak, like she doesn't know what to say.

"What do you mean?"

". . . kids who need a little more help."

"Like kids who have something wrong with them?"

"That's not what I mean." She kisses my forehead. "Mary Madelyn, there's nothing wrong with you. You are as smart as all the others; but you know that reading's been hard. You wouldn't mind getting extra help from someone other than Mrs. Zinc, would you?"

"No . . ." What I really want to know is the idea that needs to be discussed. I can tell from the look on Mom's face that she's not going to share that, and I'm not so sure I want to know after all.

CHAPTER 15

1 9 6 7

I AM THE FIRST to hear Uncle Joe's truck, right after Rob asked if he could be excused. I was still picking through my pile of peas and corn. We don't get many visitors, especially during dinnertime. "It's Uncle Joe!" I shouted, even before I saw his rusted brown Chevy truck that used to be red rumbling down our driveway. Father said Uncle Joe knew how to keep an automobile running no matter how bad off the body was. Uncle Joe is smart.

We all got up at once and ran outside, waiting for the Chevy to pull to a stop.

Uncle Joe doesn't look anything like my father. His face is used to smiling; I see smile lines even when he's not smiling. My father's lines are only serious. It's hard to believe they're brothers. Uncle Joe isn't short, but my father still towers over him. They have the same short haircut, but Uncle Joe's hair is the color of Jack's, not as blond as Paulette's but not brown either. My father wears shirts that are crisp and tucked in; he never wears jeans or boots. I've only seen Uncle Joe in blue jeans, which I think are cool, and tee shirts with a front pocket where he keeps his cigarettes. Another big difference between Uncle Joe and my father is that Uncle Joe has a tattoo.

When I discovered this difference, I didn't know the word *tattoo*. Uncle Joe probably had the tattoo a long time, but it wasn't until last year when he was doing his Popeye the Sailor Man trick that I noticed it. He put his thumb in his mouth and pretended to blow through it, and his arm muscle popped up like a balloon. Jack and Danny were fooled, but I knew that he could make his arm muscle big anytime he wanted. I had spotted something red at the edge of his shirtsleeve. I asked to see. When he pulled up his sleeve, I could hardly believe my eyes—it was a beautiful picture of a red rose.

"Uncle Joe, I didn't know you're an artist. That's a beautiful picture."

"Why, thank you." He looked at it as if for the first time. "I wish I could take credit for that drawing, but I actually paid an artist to draw it for me."

"It's a rose," Jack said.

"That's right. It's a rose for Rosemary Harmon. She's the woman I almost married."

"What happened?" When I saw his face, I knew it was the wrong question. He looked away, and the corners of his mouth no longer curved up. Jack, Danny, and I stood still, saying nothing.

"Sometimes, things just don't work out the way we wish. God had another plan in mind for Rosemary. He wanted her to be with him."

Jack and Danny didn't say a thing. They simply slipped off together. I stood still, feeling sad even though I know Heaven is the best ever place to be. All at once, I hugged Uncle Joe without asking another question about Rosemary.

I kept thinking about how smart it was of Uncle Joe to have an artist draw a picture of Rosemary's name. He could have spelled her name, but he understood that a picture is much nicer to look at than letters.

Weeks later, I don't even remember when or where, I heard a word that sounded funny, and I began to repeat it over and over: *tattoo.* I sometimes do that with funny-sounding words, like the word *bingo,* which I know how to spell: "*b-i-n-g-o,* and Bingo was his name-o." I kept hearing it in my head, and Mom and Father were both in the living room when I asked, "What does *tattoo* mean?" I had imagined it had something to do with cartoons, not the beautiful rose picture on Uncle Joe's arm.

"It's like the ink picture Uncle Joe has on his arm," said Mom.

"That's a taboo?"

"Tattoo," Father said. "It's ink that will never come off. In fact, it's a very painful process and downright foolish."

I looked over at Mom.

"Your father's right. Uncle Joe is stuck with it for life." I was curious about how to make an ink picture on skin last forever and about how painful, but I didn't like the way they were talking about Uncle Joe. It made me wonder if they even knew about Rosemary, because I was sure Uncle Joe was very happy to have this picture of her name on his arm for the rest of his life.

Uncle Joe's truck roars to a stop. We gather around, and Uncle Joe hops out dressed the way I always imagine him, tee shirt and jeans. I'm the one he turns to first.

"Sister Bard, how are you?" He rumples my hair and grins. I want him to lift me up and swing me around like he used to, but now I'm too old for that. I throw my arms around him; he has the same sweet, sweaty smell tinged with cigarettes.

"Why do you call her that?" asks Danny.

"You mean, you don't know what a bard is?"

"No," Danny says, looking over at Jack, who I can tell by his smirk is pretending to know.

"Oh, my dear jester." And he winks at me. "Just like a jester is necessary for any royal family, to keep things light and funny"—he squats down and gives a quick tickle to Danny, who erupts in a squeal of laughter—"a bard is indeed a very talented person. Bards are the original storytellers from ancient days. You must agree—your big sister is one heck of a fantastic storyteller."

"Yeah, she's good. She's been telling me the story of *The Fairy Angel's Gift*. What about Jack and Rob?"

"Well, of course they're important members of the royal family too. All royal families need a knight, someone willing to protect those who might be less able, someone strong but also wise and smart."

"Rob!" yells Danny.

"That's right." He turns and winks at Rob, who is smiling.

"And all knights have an indispensable helper known as the squire, someone who models themselves after the knight, willing to run errands and generally be helpful."

"That's me," Jack calls out. "I'm the squire, and Rob's my knight."

"And we, your parents, are the king and queen," says Father with a lightness in his voice. "We're about done with dinner, but there's plenty if you're interested."

"No, thanks. Grabbed me a burger on the way over."

Even with the excitement of Uncle Joe, like an early Christmas, as soon as we step back into the house, our mom reminds us that it's a school night, and there's homework to be done.

"I did all my homework in school except for math," I report.

"Okay, let's take a look at your math papers."

Reaching into the depths of my book bag, my hand lands upon a crumpled paper, and I'm sure it's the math homework, but as I pull it out and take a look, I see that I am wrong.

"What's that?"

"Nothing." *It's something that belongs in the wastebasket.* I start to shove it back in, but I'm too late. In plain view, before I can hide it, is the spelling test I failed, with a big F written on the front. At first,

Mom says nothing. Then she squints and leans forward, snatching it from my hand.

"Mary Madelyn, I don't remember practicing these words with you this past week."

"I'm sorry, Mom. I forgot to bring them home, and then the next thing I knew, we were having a test."

"No one can expect to do well if they don't study."

I look over and notice her hand holding my paper is trembling, her face reddening. I bring home at least one F every week, but this time something's different.

Her voice rises loud and angry as if I had spilled paint all over the carpet. "How can I help you if you don't bring the work home?"

I stare, my mouth hanging open. She shoves her chair back and stands up. This isn't my mother.

She turns, and I catch her eyes thick with tears. I want to tell her that at least I didn't cheat and don't have to confess this, but the words stay stuck in my throat. She leaves the kitchen, heading for the hall bathroom. She's right. I forgot on purpose because I hate spelling.

I pull out the math worksheet that I could have finished in school if someone had read it to me, but now I don't feel like doing math. I just want to go to bed.

I sit in the kitchen alone. I hear Uncle Joe and Rob talking in the living room. It's not fair. The bathroom door opens and closes, but I don't turn toward Mom.

"Get your pencil ready. I'll read, and you work out the problems." Mom begins reading in a voice like Mrs. Zinc's instead of my own mother. I take a quick look; her eyes are red and puffy. When we're halfway through the page, Father walks into the kitchen with Jack trailing behind him, hopping up and down like a kangaroo.

"Jack has good news to share." Father's face looks a little like Uncle

Joe's as he holds up a spelling list of words with a big letter A written on it. I turn away but not soon enough to miss Jack's smiling chipmunk face. When I look up again, his masterpiece is taped to the fridge.

After kissing Jack on the cheek, Mom continues to read the math problems in Mrs. Zinc's teacher voice, making the heaviness inside me turn into an anchor. Down I sink; down to the sadness of remembering that Mrs. Zinc is almost done reading *The Fairy Angel's Gift*. My heavy head drops to the table.

Mom raises her voice, sinking me further. "Madelyn, how do you think you'll pass third grade if you don't even try to finish your homework? I'm doing all I can to help you, but you need to do your part."

I can't move; too heavy. She finally takes my arm and leads me off to bed.

Even with all the heaviness, I can't settle myself down to sleep. My rooms are too messy to visit—all I can do for now is close doors. Still, the messiest one figures out a way to grab and twist my stomach. This is the room with the phone call from Mrs. Zinc. I see Mom's face, over and over, while she holds the telephone with Mrs. Zinc's voice pouring into her ear, telling her how horrible I'm doing in school.

Then I remember. Mom said she'd discuss it with Father. I sit up in bed, look over at my window, where a small strip of light has found its way into my room past the tree. *Do I want to hear?* I tiptoe to my door, crack it open, and listen to voices short and choppy, like Mom grabbing my arm and leading me to bed. Her kiss good night was a quick touch to my cheek, nothing more. Father's voice rumbles like thunder moments before the loud bang. I stand in my doorway as if on the end of the dock making up my mind whether or not to jump into the cold splash of water. I can't hear what they're saying; I only feel their voices, thick like a storm moving in. If I return to my bed, I'll never know what's going on . . . but I'm still not sure I want to.

I need to use the bathroom. As I step lightly down the hall, the voices turn into words. I duck into the bathroom and no longer feel the urge, only the churning of my stomach. I stand in the doorway and listen.

"She's going to turn out like Joe if we don't do something," Father says in his thundering tone. Hearing this, my stomach reels, as if this is something terrible. But I want to be like Uncle Joe; he is smart and funny. I even want a tattoo.

Mom's voice has turned soft again, not the one she used on the phone today or the one that sent me to bed. It's a tone she uses to win us kids over, but it's Father she is talking to. "I know she's as smart as her brothers. Why, just the other day, she played me an elaborate story she had recorded on her tape recorder. She made it up herself along with sound effects. I know she's smart."

"She can barely read," he says. My knees tremble; he knows I'm still a Sparrow.

"Last year, Mrs. Smith said she just needed more time, and that's what Mrs. Zinc said at the beginning of this year. I agree, what's needed is more patience and time."

More time for what?

"That's what you said when she left kindergarten and only knew the letter *m*. Extra time is not working. You've got to face it, there's something wrong with her. Jack can read more than she can, and he's just in second grade—that's where she belongs."

My legs go weak, and I grab on to the bathroom counter.

His voice continues like a clap of thunder. "Dora, Madelyn has a problem. She'll never be successful next year. Never."

My stomach lurches; I crawl to the toilet, gasp for breath, and instead of breathing out, a churned-up smelly sickness gushes from my mouth. My eyes blur up with hot tears.

CHAPTER 16

2 0 0 5

"DR. MEYERS!" Diane Adams calls out to me as I step into Room 11. She's aglow. Her wispy strands of blond hair appear windblown; her forehead shines under the fluorescent lights. Diane holds a child's fragile hand. Clayton, who has a tendency to buckle his legs and flop down while his arms fling spastically in all directions. She turns to the grimacing boy and supports his chest while his upper body moves in jerking motions, his lower collapsing like Jell-O.

"Show Dr. Meyers how you can say your phone number," Diane instructs.

Clayton arches his back and twists his head, gives a high-pitched squeal, and then barks out a set of numbers only Diane seems able to interpret.

I high-five him; he tumbles into ecstatic joy.

This is why I entered through the back door of Milton Elementary, into the far reaches, where Room 11, like too many self-contained special education classrooms, was purposefully placed—hidden from the hub of activity. For me, its location is a convenience, since my office is also located toward the end of the hall—we're practically neighbors. This morning, admittedly, entering through the back had more to do with arriving a good hour late and not wanting to parade past the office staff.

Diane works as an instructional assistant with Kelly, a talented special education teacher. Everyone loves Diane. She's a mom figure for more than her four children. If that were not enough, she's PTA co-chair, and a foster parent for the Humane Society, which means she often brings a four-legged ward to work. The children in Kelly's class love to take turns walking the orphaned pups.

What I treasure most about Room 11 is that it embraces a concept of normal that includes everyone. It's a classroom where grunts and pointing are acceptable modes of expression. I glance to my left and see Kelly, her thick, gorgeous, wavy chocolate hair toppling over her shoulders as she squats down to where Christy is propped comfortably in a beanbag chair so that Sammy, the golden retriever rescue-turned-therapy dog, can nudge her hand. Kelly glides Christy's hand over Sammy's soft head. My father's words regarding the square peg in a round hole come back to me. I've always suspected he considered me a square peg and had serious doubts about my passing through the round hole. Indeed, it was a squeeze.

Although my father died close to a decade ago, lately his presence has occupied my psyche. He had a thing about fitting in. He gave my older brother such grief when Rob insisted on wearing wire rims. Later, when Rob refused my mom's buzz cut so as to have hair that grazed his ears, my father fumed again, accusing Rob of wanting to be a hippie. Had Father casually sauntered through Kelly's class, he would have experienced himself as a square peg. Kelly's class of beautiful misfits, each shaped so unusually that we'd have to go beyond even calling them square, would have been unfathomable to my father. They require their own classroom, and yet, it's a learning space buzzing with excitement, celebrating the simplest of victories.

I tumble to the floor and lean into Christy's beanbag and feel Kelly's eyes upon me. I assure myself that as far as she knows, I've already attended a SIT meeting and am simply popping in to say hi before the final bell. Before I know it, my hand is also rhythmically stroking the soft curves of Sammy's upper dip from nose to head and down past ears. I glance at Christy, who is drooling with delight. In this moment, we are sisters, appreciating the calm presence of our sage four-legged companion. I give a nod to Kelly and say, "This is a great way to start the day."

My struggle to get myself to work on time comes with a thick package of guilt. I want to blame it on the coat, the therapy, and the intense dreams that have interrupted my nighttime tranquility. I can't even remember what it was like before Mom passed.

My eyes fall upon a student who doesn't belong in this classroom but nonetheless struggles to fit in. Grace Adams, Diane's third-grade daughter. At age eight, I'd for sure have been swinging on bars or hitting a tetherball up until the final school bell. Here is Grace, burrowed in a quiet corner, hunched over a pad of paper, brows creased, writing intently.

It was toward the end of Grace's kindergarten year when Diane came to me, convinced something was wrong. I was aware of Diane's older children; they were all high academic achievers. Grace is the youngest of five. I rarely evaluate a child in kindergarten—after all, they're just starting out. Since her teacher hadn't schedule a SIT meeting or expressed her concerns to me, I'd wondered if Diane was caught up in comparing Grace to her accomplished siblings. Maybe Grace was simply average in academics while accelerated in other areas. I took a wait-and-see approach. Diane wanted to believe I was right, that it was simply a matter of time and unfair comparisons.

When winter break came and went, and Grace could not reliably get the sequence of letters correct in her name, I decided more than likely this wasn't an issue of typical development being compared with high achievers. Her teacher held back bringing Grace to SIT because of her strong verbal skills. She shared Grace's illustrated alphabet book—fanciful renditions of letters shaped as animals that bore no other resemblance to writing. Z was not a zebra but rather a python rising up to attack. Grace grasped visual similarity but failed to understand a reading fundamental: letters symbolize sounds that compose words.

When I did an evaluation, Grace's IQ was in the superior range, despite her inability to grasp the relationship between letter shape and sound.

I rise up from the beanbag and take a step toward Grace. Kelly calls out, "So, Ms. Mary, are you signing up to join our field trip to the zoo next week?" She can tell she has caught me off guard, and gives me a wink. I'd go in a heartbeat if it weren't for the stack of reports waiting to be written.

Grace is oblivious to my presence. Her attention is upon a sheet of lined notebook paper. Since meeting her in kindergarten, every encounter stirs an incomprehensible ache, as if she were my own child and I had somehow failed to meet her needs.

"You're looking like a serious scholar this morning. What's up?"

She tries to hide the lined paper, which holds multiple repetitions of single words—the oldest tactic on the planet for learning to spell. I avoid looking too closely, sure I'll see the slip from the correct version of the word to the incorrect, ultimately reinforcing the wrong spelling. It never worked for me, the copying over and over. All at once a peculiar phrase comes to mind. *Believe anything is possible through a special secret.* I have an odd sense that this string of words somehow has something to do with spelling—and yet, how zany.

"You studying for a test?" I ask.

She peers up at me from large, powerful brown eyes. Her round wholesome face is framed by a traditional below-the-ears cut. Her even bangs across the forehead remind me of my third-grade school snapshot.

"Sort of. I just. Well, some words keep messing me up."

"Ah. I get messed up by some words too."

This catches her attention. She tries to interpret the expression on my face and finally says, "You're joking."

I laugh and shake my head left to right. The veneer of professionalism has thickly painted itself upon my very real insecurities. What Grace sees is my art in perfecting an image of competence.

"No, I'm not. I keep a dictionary close by at all times."

"Well, it's different in my class."

I nod because some part of me knew this as well.

"I'm the only one who writes stories that no one else can read," she says.

"No one else?"

"It's the spelling. Only I can read them."

I nod and remember something I was once proud to have written, yet found to be unreadable.

"It's good to work on the spelling—believe it or not, I still do. Some of us are just slow learners of spelling. But your story is yours even if it's not spelled correctly. Don't give up on telling your stories."

I can see this doesn't make sense to her. I'm not sure it does to me either. I almost chuckle as I hear Uncle Joe proclaiming me Sister Bard. I'm no nun, that's for sure. A bard? Maybe in the faraway past.

Grace says nothing, and I find myself desperately searching to say something, anything supportive. I'm practically trembling with the desire to fix this sad situation. I open my mouth, thinking a kernel of wisdom might spill out, and the school bell rings. Grace scrambles to get to class. As she walks out the door, I remember. She won the poetry slam contest—why didn't I congratulate her for that?

CHAPTER 17

1 9 6 7

I HEAR MY ALARM clock go off like a distant siren, but I can't move. It gets louder and louder. Mom comes in dressed in her white nurse's uniform. Usually, she's leaving for work just as I'm getting up.

"Maddie, honey, how are you feeling?" When I moan, she places her hand on my forehead. "You don't have a fever. I think you just got yourself a little too worked up last night, and the pork chops were a little too greasy, especially for someone who worries." She leans down and kisses me on my forehead. "I'm sure you're going to have a fine day at school. You need to get up and have some breakfast. Your stomach is empty."

I arrive at school with my coat zipped up tight, and that's how I plan to keep it. The sky is cloudless, and I squint while trudging toward the square brick building. Usually, I race so I can swing on the bars and climb the jungle gym before the morning bell, but today, even with the sun coming up, my world feels dark. I don't belong in school. More than ever, I want to join Ethan and Yram. I almost cry when I remember the story will soon be over.

A single soft musical ring fills the classroom and quickly fades. Its sound is the opposite of the recess bell. Mrs. Zinc stands holding the silver triangle with the thin striker still raised, waiting for her one light tap to bring about the shuffling of desks and chairs into four groups: Eagles, Bluebirds, Robins, and Sparrows. Ours is the smallest. The others start reading to each other while Mrs. Zinc gets us going.

I drag myself over to our corner. Moments before, I was thinking of asking to see the nurse, but this meant *asking*. I don't want to talk to Mrs. Zinc ever again.

"Today," Mrs. Zinc announces to the four of us sitting in a circle, "we're going to start a new story." She holds up a small flat paper book with big letters. "Who would like to read the title?" Three hands lift up. I have no interest, and Mrs. Zinc stares at me without blinking. I stop myself from blurting, "I know what you told my parents last night."

"Go ahead, Darren."

"*Tom the Cat.*"

"That's right." Mrs. Zinc turns to the blackboard. "First, we need to review our sight words. Let's say these together. Ready?" She bounces her pointer from word to word on the blackboard. "*With, some, found, fight, race, park, climbed.*"

I half listen while Darren reads, "Tom can sit and run"; Cheryl reads, "Tom had a fight with the dog"; and when it's Jason's turn, I'm wondering if dream catchers are as real as fairies. A dream catcher would be a wonderful thing to have, maybe even as powerful as saints. I don't know who to ask. Maybe Miss Stanley knows. Then I hear my name.

"Madelyn, you look like you're not paying attention."

That's because I'm not.

"Jason, could you please show Madelyn where we are?" He touches my book like it has cooties or something, but I pin my eyes down on the spot and then my finger, even though I don't care if I get it right or not. I do know the first word.

"Tom." I look up and see from Mrs. Zinc's face that I'm right. "Had so me—"

"Tom had some," Mrs. Zinc says.

"T . . . rr . . . eee—tttrrees he cllll . . ." I search the blackboard, and there it is, the same letters, *c-l-i-m-b-e-d*. But they don't form a word for me. I can't remember what word those letters make, so I guess. "Clam bed—"

"Climbed," Mrs. Zinc says.

"—in the krap."

Laughter explodes; even Mrs. Zinc tries to hide her giggling. *Did I really say what I think I just said? I must have, that's why they're laughing.* I pull my hood up and bury my face in my hands. *How could I have done this? Father's right; something's wrong with me.* Finally, Mrs. Zinc gets them to be quiet.

"Even though that was a funny mistake, it was just a mistake. We all make mistakes. The word is *park*—Tom had some trees he climbed in the park. Darren, will you continue?"

His voice sounds funny, like he's trying to choke down his snickering while reading. I used to feel sorry for him since he really should be in fourth grade, but now I can't stand him. I try to think of thoughts that will keep me from crying. *It doesn't matter. I don't care because I don't need to be a reader. Besides, this is a stupid story.*

Finally, it's time for recess. I race to the upper field, imagining that I'm a wild stallion galloping across the country, leading my herd to safety. Out of breath, I slow down to chew on some grass; it tastes sweet and juicy. Behind me, I hear my name being called, and I recognize the voice. Bobby comes galloping by, pretending he's a horse with his own herd of followers. I turn and run back down to the tetherball, and he calls out, "Tom climbed trees in the crap." And bursts out laughing. So do the others, and they weren't even in my reading group. I pick up speed, the wind blowing against me. I can still be a beautiful wild black stallion. Down the hill I run.

In the middle of the best kind of math worksheet—one with no words—the kind that I can finish before everyone else, Mrs. Zinc interrupts me. She tries to do it in a private, secret way, but that's not possible, and everyone looks up and watches. A chill shivers through me while my stomach feels as if Bobby has smacked me real hard. I'm thinking she has decided to tell me about flunking, and even though I know that's what she told my parents, I'm not ready to hear it from her. Not in front of everyone else. When I slow down my breathing, I hear her say "someone special" and remember.

Standing in the doorway, I can see a teacher who's the opposite of Mrs. Zinc—short, fat, rosy-red cheeked, and smiling. I look up at Mrs. Zinc, who hardly ever smiles, but now she is too, and I feel like breaking my pencil in half.

Once outside the door, I hear Bobby's voice calling out, "Where's Madelyn going?"

"Madelyn, this is Mrs. Ellen. She's a reading specialist, and she'll be working just with you two days a week starting today."

Both Mrs. Zinc and fat Mrs. Ellen are grinning as if they've won a prize. Again, I stop myself from blurting out, "I know you called my parents last night, and I know what you told them." I used to like Mrs. Zinc but not anymore.

"I'm looking forward to getting to know you, Madelyn. Come with me." And off Mrs. Ellen marches. She's wearing a skirt the color of the dingy brown floor, and I can see every fold of her skin move up and down as she parades toward the gym. I hold back a good four strides and then pretend that I too have some business down the hall.

I have no idea where she is going, and suddenly she opens a closet door. I hadn't noticed a closet next to the gym. I know where Mr. Griffin, the PE teacher, keeps all his field equipment, and I've even seen where he has his own office space, but I've never seen this closet.

It's small and stuffy like a broom closet, but this teacher has turned it into a miniature classroom. There's a wobbly table, a blackboard nailed to the wall, and three wooden chairs. I take a quick peek under the chairs and see hard mounds of old gum stuck in clumps. On a small bookshelf that looks like it was meant for cleaning supplies are a stack of folders and flat books. More books are on the table, except I don't see any real ones. Kids like Paulette and my brother Rob who read chapter books would never need to visit a closet.

Mrs. Ellen is now chatting away in a happy voice, but I'm too busy trying to figure out what I'll say to the others when I get back to my real class to listen to her.

"Madelyn." Her eyes catch me; she must have figured out my pre-tend listening. I look across the small table at her bright cheeks and curly silver hair. "I need to do a little testing to see where you're at with your skills. All you need to do is try your best."

Hmm, that's the same thing Father always says. And it's never good enough.

Mrs. Ellen holds up a list of words, and, of course, I know the first five: *I, the, of, up, for.* I'm not that stupid, but the other words don't look like real words, and who knows, maybe they aren't and she's tricking me.

"Madelyn, surely you know this word." She's pointing to the letter *I.* I give her my blank look; besides, I doubt that she has any idea how to fix whatever is wrong with me. If it wasn't a lost cause, Saint Rita would have done something by now. Instead of prodding me like Mrs. Zinc would, this teacher lights up like a Christmas tree. She pulls her chair back, stands up, and says, "Watch this." She then picks up the stubby piece of chalk and begins to write the alphabet on the chalkboard.

Of course I know my letters; it's just the ones that look alike that are confusing. I turn toward the door. What I really want is to get back to my real class where I can make up my own stories while pretending to do worksheets, but Mrs. Ellen acts all excited and begins to sing the alphabet song in a funny sing-songy voice. If I wasn't looking in the other direction, it would be hard to not smile and maybe even laugh.

Mrs. Ellen stops at the letter *I* and circles it. "This letter is so important, it gets to be a word. Look, Madelyn, here it is, the first word on this list, and it's the alphabet letter." She then lowers her voice and continues.

"Here's a secret." She waves her puffy hand over the list of words. "When you learn all the words on this page, you'll recognize most words on any page because these are the words that show up the most. When you're ready, I can teach you ways to learn them, but first you need to decide if you want to learn."

I wonder, *Why is Mrs. Zinc doing this to me?* Then I hear loud banging coming from the gym.

"Oh my," Mrs. Ellen says, "I bet that's the PE teacher. What's his name?"

"Mr. Griffin."

"That's right, now I remember. He's a nice man; I just met him this morning." She stands up and looks as though she's trying to make up her mind. "Excuse me, I'll be right back." She walks out, leaving me alone in the closet with the alphabet and list of words.

My eyes dart around to the dimly lit corners as I wonder if there are spiderwebs. Whenever I think of spiders, I think of Gwendolyn and Yram. I'm about to get up to take a closer look when Mrs. Ellen returns with Mr. Griffin by her side.

"Madelyn, Mr. Griffin could use your help. Would you mind?"

Of course not. I pop up like a piece of toast ready to do anything he asks.

Mr. Griffin is sometimes crabby, like if we take too long to line up, but today he's smiling at me. "Madelyn, I need to get all these mats down for the next class; we're starting a unit on gymnastics. Mrs. Ellen here says you can help out."

"Sure." Helping Mr. Griffin is perfect.

I come back to class in the middle of Mrs. Zinc's science lesson. As soon as I step in, I know they're all looking at me and wondering. I make myself smile and walk with a bounce so they get the message that I had a good time. When the recess bell rings, Paulette is quick to ask right in front of everyone, and even Bobby holds back to listen; they all want to know where I've been.

"I went to help Mr. Griffin. He knows I'm good at PE, so I helped him get ready for his classes." I then take off running toward the bars.

CHAPTER 18

1 9 6 7

BY THE TIME it is almost dinner, I keep to the front of the house, catching and then letting go of frogs. I'm really waiting to catch some time alone with Uncle Joe. I met Mom when she came home and quickly gave her a hug as usual, but then I ran off to be alone with the rope swing. My stomach still hurts from last night. I don't want to talk with her about the special help from Mrs. Ellen.

Finally, I hear the truck. Uncle Joe gets out and gives a big stretch and then yawns. I can tell he needs a shower and clean clothes.

"Sister Bard, it's a pleasure to meet you in the driveway. What's up?"

"Nothing. How's work going?"

"Well, to be honest, it's work all right and not all that fun, but it pays the bills." He exhales a big breath, and I do too. He leans against his truck and pulls out the pack of cigarettes from his shirt pocket. I lean next to him and stare at the wild grass growing between the oak trees. I feel his eyes on me.

"Your work is school. So, sister, how's school going?"

"Terrible."

"You're so smart, how in the world can it be terrible?"

I look at him to try to read his face. Is this a joke or does he really believe this? "I just get bored, that's all."

"I used to get bored too. In fact, I'm really bored hammering nails all day, but that's what's required to get a paycheck." He shakes out a cigarette from the pack. "Think I have time for a smoke before dinner?"

I nod, hoping he has time for the entire pack. Then, I can't help myself. "Father thinks I'm like you."

"Really. What do you think he means by that?"

I feel my stomach drop. I had thought he'd give an answer. "I don't know." I feel his eyes upon me. I like the smell of cigarette smoke mixed with leaves. I glance over and say, "I just heard him say I might be like you." His face stays serious, so I add, "Like, always figuring out a way to joke about things. And were you good at telling stories when you were young?"

"Not like you. But I guess you can say I had a good imagination, which I think is true for you."

Now I see his smile, and it makes me feel good inside even if I stretched the truth. "That's what my mom says, but I'm not so sure it's a good thing."

"Why is that?"

"It's the way she says, 'It's just your *imagination*.' And Ethan's father didn't like it that he had an imagination."

"Is Ethan a friend of yours?"

"Yeah. And he has a friend who happens to be a fairy."

"Well, that could come in handy. I wouldn't mind a friend like that."

"Me either. Especially if it were Yram."

He takes a final puff of his cigarette and smashes it into the ground. "Hmm. Speaking of imagination, I'm imagining a wonderful dinner at this very moment. How about it, sister?"

"Maddie, I'm ready to hear more of the story," Danny says as he slides on his socks across the white-and-tan linoleum floor.

"Not until you start bringing in some dishes."

He twirls around and returns with a stack of plates. "Okay, I'm ready."

"Well, remember how I told you that every time he was by himself or with his parents, Ethan forgot that he was able to walk and even run with Yram? Yram did do magic and allowed him to fly with her, but Ethan for sure was also running all on his own."

"So why would he keep forgetting?"

"Actually, it's sort of hard to understand. You see . . . he wants to believe it's true that he can do these things, but he grew up believing what his parents told him. He has a weak heart, and he really does get dizzy if he moves too fast. So what Yram noticed is that when he doesn't think about getting dizzy, he usually doesn't."

"But you said he does really get dizzy."

"What I mean is, it's like when you have a bad cold and you have to blow your nose a lot, and the more you think about being miserable, the more you feel that way. But if something exciting is going on, like going to the fair, and you have a cold, it's sort of like magic the way it doesn't bother you as much."

"So, he does get dizzy but sometimes doesn't notice it."

"Yes, that's what I mean. And his parents kept telling him that he needed to use his cane when he walked and that he couldn't be out of bed very long, especially running around. So every time he's not with Yram, he forgets what he was able to do with her and starts believing what his parents say, but it's not quite like that."

"What do you mean?"

"Well, his parents also want him to try and get around more, so it's not like they are saying, 'Ethan, stay in bed, you're too weak to go to school.'"

"What do they say?"

"They keep reminding him of his bad heart and telling him to take it easy, and"—I make a point of pausing and looking right at Mom before saying loudly—"they don't believe in fairies."

"What does that matter? You know that I don't believe—this is just a story."

"Danny, it matters because they . . . well, it's hard to explain. Anyway, Yram saw that Ethan couldn't hold on to what he wanted to believe in and have happen. This upset her because she planned on helping him."

"So what did she do?"

"Remember the leprechaun, Brogan? He's the one who told her what she needed to do to get a halo. Well, he sent her to a thick forest called the Forest of Wisdom to meet a wise spider."

"Ew. I don't like spiders," Danny whines.

"I know. I would have been so scared, and so was Yram at first. She could hardly make herself look at the spider because it was really big. But Yram followed Brogan's instructions and . . ." I look up. Mom's all done with the pots and pans and has chosen to sit and listen. I love it when she does this.

"She met a huge and very old, ancient spider named Gwendolyn. Yram's a small fairy, and the spider was much bigger and had hairy legs."

"Ew, that's creepy."

"But at first what she saw wasn't Gwendolyn—it was her web. The web was made of threads of different colors that sparkled, like gold was mixed in. It was so beautiful that Yram was no longer afraid of Gwendolyn. She knew she was going to learn something very important. So she was able to turn her eyes and look right at the spider and listen."

"What did Gwendolyn say?" Danny stands motionless in the

middle of the kitchen with the dish towel dangling from his hand.

"You need to keep drying all the silverware and put it away, and then I'll tell you."

"But I am. I'm just working slowly to listen carefully to the story."

"Well, this is the hard part to understand. I'm not so sure I even understand everything Gwendolyn was saying. She was passing on some ancient secrets about webs and how they are used by spiders to catch what they need in order to live."

"That's easy to understand."

"Mrs. Zinc said even though Gwendolyn is talking about a web, she is really talking about something bigger. She wasn't talking about humans really using spiderwebs to also catch insects, she was talking about the idea of a web, how it's important to catch and hold on to good dreams and hopes and happy beliefs. That was Ethan's problem. His dream was to be healthy, and he believed it but didn't hold on to the belief—it kept getting away."

"So Yram used a spiderweb?"

"No, Gwendolyn taught her about dream catchers because they work like spiderwebs."

I notice Mom has moved into the other room; it's just Danny and me finishing up. I'll tell this part to her later. Danny's standing still again, wide-eyed. I can tell he likes the story almost as much as I do. I motion to the few plates left in the draining board before continuing.

"A dream catcher is made to catch only the good dreams and to hold on to your hopes and best wishes. The bad dreams don't stick—they fall through it. The dreams that do stick, the good ones, grow and get better. Gwendolyn taught Yram how to make one for Ethan. Before Yram left, Gwendolyn gave her a warning. Let's see if I can remember what she said. It was something like this." I clear my throat and then speak in the halting, crackling voice of an old woman: "'Yram, you must guard against those who place fear above dreams. They will claim to be acting out of care, but they are hope snatchers and dream destroyers in disguise. You must protect the dream catcher from those who don't believe.'"

"Then what happened?" Danny whispers.

"Yram begged Ethan to help her. She said, 'There is something I need to make tonight, something very important that I deeply care about that will not survive if you do not help me.' So, of course, Ethan felt like he was somehow saving Yram. He had no idea that this important thing was the dream catcher she was making for him because it would help him keep believing in what he most wanted."

I stop and take a deep breath so I won't start crying in front of Danny. "Danny," I say, "tomorrow is the last day of hearing this story. We only have about a chapter left." *How can I keep going to school without* The Fairy Angel's Gift *to look forward to?*

"Tell me what Ethan had to do, and did he do it?"

I have to swallow hard and try to take a normal breath before continuing. Danny doesn't understand.

"Yram really did need his help. She needed spider silk to make the dream catcher, and she had several spider friends who had bundles of sticks with lots of sticky, silky web to give her. Except Yram knew that the other fairies, especially her cousins—"

"Zerko and Zilla!" Danny yells out.

"That's right. They don't like her, and it would be horrible if they saw her carrying the silk and found out what she was doing. They'd destroy it."

Danny gasps. I wash the last of the dishes, and then continue. "It had to be a secret. Ethan needed to deliver the thread all by himself."

"Did he?"

In walks Mom, and I know what she's about to say.

"Okay, kids, time to get homework out. Madelyn, get your book bag. We need to see what the homework is."

"Maddie, can you please answer my question?" Danny whines.

"I'll tell you more later, but for now, yes, he brought it to her, and no one followed." I turn to Mom. "You left at the best part."

"You can tell me all about it Saturday when we dust the furniture. Now, what do you have for homework?"

CHAPTER 19

1967

MRS. ZINC STANDS in front of the class holding the paper that only comes out for special occasions. It's bright white, not muddy brown. Even though it's a very sad day, this makes me happy because it means we won't be copying sentences out of the grammar book. Instead, we'll get to make up our own.

"Class, since today I'll be reading the last chapter of *The Fairy Angel's Gift*, we're going to do something special for language arts."

Last week, when the white paper came out, Mrs. Zinc asked us to write what we most liked about *The Fairy Angel's Gift*, and I had so many things to say, all I could do was write single words instead of sentences. Paulette helped me spell them. Mrs. Zinc called it a poem and asked me to read it out loud:

Yram

Flying high

Angel wings

Imagination

Catching dreams

Bobby argued, saying a poem has to rhyme, but Mrs. Zinc said that's not true of all poems. Later, during recess, he said it was a stupid poem and called me knuckle-brain. Mom's voice chanted in my head, *Sticks and stones will break your bones but words will never hurt you.* Mrs. Zinc also believes words don't hurt; I found this out the first week of school when she made it clear she doesn't allow tattletales.

"I'd like each of you to pretend that you were given a special dream catcher like Ethan's." A smile spreads across Mrs. Zinc's face. She holds the stack of crisp paper close to her chest. I'm sitting up tall in my seat, bouncing my right leg. "What are the dreams you would want a dream catcher to catch and hold for you?" I picture myself meeting Yram. My dream would be to fly with her the way Ethan did. "I'd like you to write at least two paragraphs. Remember, a paragraph starts with a topic sentence and then has three or more sentences that provide details."

My heart is racing. I want to fly with Yram more than even having a horse. I look down at the lined white paper waiting on my desk. This isn't a dream I can share; they'd all laugh. I see most everyone else has started.

I write my name in the top corner. I have other dreams. I want to be a nun. Not only a nun, but I also want to work my way up to being a saint. One that does miracles and answers all kinds of prayers. I've only shared this with Mom, Uncle Joe, and Miss Stanley. People who aren't Catholic, like most of my class, don't know about nuns and saints. This is also a private dream.

I look around. Everyone is busy writing, even Bobby. I hardly have to look to see Paulette's paper. It's almost halfway filled with perfect penmanship. Everyone has dreams they want to catch. I look back down at my blank paper. At least it's mine and hasn't landed on my desk full of words needing to be read and blanks that can only be filled with one answer. Thinking about this, I suddenly remember my other dream, the dream that no one will laugh at and Mrs. Zinc will understand. I too begin to write fast, filling up my paper.

Mi drem is to sum ba b a ritr, I wunt to rit storez that r az wondrfl az The Fare Anjls Geft. This wud b mi brem, to rit a duk that evrywon luvs to reed and I can desid hw it ends and wut hapenbs in it.

It's not two paragraphs, but I know Mrs. Zinc is going to be pleased because I wrote sentences, not just words, and it's the most I've written all year. I glance over at Paulette. Her page is all filled up, and her hand doesn't even look tired. She stops, turns to me, and smiles. Then she flips her paper over. I was hoping she was done so she could help me. I sit and wait while she writes another whole paragraph. If I could write as much and as fast as her, I'd be able to write about all three of my dreams. She finally finishes, holds the paper up, looks at both sides, and smiles. I know she's happy with it, and she knows I'm sitting with my mouth dropped open.

"Are you done?" she says, glancing down at my paper, which no longer looks like much.

"Yeah." I hold it up thinking she might be surprised, but when she only sighs, I understand—it's not much.

She takes out the extra piece of nice paper Mrs. Zinc gave her, clears her throat, acting all teacher-like, and then says, "Okay, I'm ready. Tell me what you wrote and I'll write it out for you."

"My dream is to someday be a writer."

"A writer?" She says in a high-pitched voice as if she hadn't even heard of such a thing.

"Yes, that's what I want to be." I decided that I can be both a writer and a nun.

"But you can't be a writer if you can't read. You have to be able to read words to write words."

"That's not true. I just wrote this. I wrote more than I usually do. I *can* be a writer."

"Okay, what else did you try and write here?"

"It says, 'I want to write stories that are as wonderful as *The Fairy Angel's Gift*. This would be my dream, to write a book that everyone loves to read, and I can decide how it ends and what happens in it.'"

Paulette writes neatly and fast. I can hardly believe how beautiful my words look; they fill five whole lines of paper. My body tingles in excitement with each new line. *Maybe I really can be a writer*. I can hardly wait for Mrs. Zinc to see.

"Madelyn," says Paulette in the familiar voice I put up with, "I'm sorry to tell you this, but you really can't be a writer if you're not a reader."

"That's not true!" The words spill from me with such force I hardly recognize myself. "All I need is help spelling the words I wrote." I then say even louder, "*I* wrote this."

"No, you didn't. I did. All you did was tell me what to write." Paulette is so loud, Mrs. Zinc looks up and comes over, and I'm glad she does.

"Thank you, Paulette, for helping Madelyn."

"Madelyn thinks she can be a writer without being a reader. This is not a dream that can work."

Mrs. Zinc bends down and reads the words Paulette wrote that are my words and my dream in Paulette's perfect handwriting, with each word spelled correctly. I wait for Mrs. Zinc to tell Paulette she's wrong.

"Well, Paulette, you're right." She then looks at me while talking to Paulette. "I don't know of anyone who has learned to be a writer who didn't first learn to read well." My face burns red. "Madelyn, I'm happy to see that you're writing complete sentences. And you should thank Paulette for helping you." She then walks away to check someone else's dream, leaving Paulette with a big grin on her know-it-all face. I snatch my paper out of Paulette's hand and shove it deep into my desk. I turn away from her and send my eyes out the smudged window, looking for some place else to be. *I hate school.*

A few minutes later, Mrs. Zinc asks for volunteers to share what they have written. I keep looking out the window, not even pretending to listen. It would be easy to shut Mrs. Zinc's voice out, but I'm finding it impossible to shut out the voice of Paulette sitting right smack next to me.

"Yes, Paulette, go ahead and share."

"My dream is to be a teacher. I'm good at reading, writing, and math, so I know that I will be an excellent teacher someday. I like to help my classmates."

She pauses. I look over to see if she's finally done, but it's a pause on purpose, so she can look me in the eye and everyone will notice. I whip my head back toward the window, but it's too late. Everyone sees and knows what Paulette means: I'm her stupid practice student.

Paulette continues. "I'm good at helping to spell and write words; all my grades are A's . . ."

When she's finally finished, I silently whisper, "You'll make a horrible teacher."

"Yes, Bobby," Mrs. Zinc says.

"My dream is to be a champion kickball player. I'm already very good, so I think I will only get better. I will one day be famous. As a famous athlete, I will travel all over the United States and meet lots of other famous people, like maybe the Beatles. My other dream is to be a champion fisher. My dad and I go fishing every weekend . . ." Bobby and the others are much easier to tune out than Paulette.

CHAPTER 20

2 0 0 5

IT DIDN'T SURPRISE ME to see Wilma Jenkins as the referring teacher for SIT this week. She teaches second grade and is what I think of as a high-frequency flyer. As a former special education teacher, I never referred children to SIT meetings; I was the recipient of the referrals. That is, the children who passed through the evaluation process and were certified as special ed were referred to me. And now here I am, the primary player who does the "certification."

We—the SIT team—only meet once a week. When a teacher takes the time to fill out the required forms to attend this meeting, it's a real commitment to the notion that help is needed. I try to keep that foremost in mind. And yet, Wilma shows up several times each year with variations of the same concern—a kiddo with attention-deficit/ hyperactivity disorder (ADHD). It's made me wonder if she has some personal experience with the disorder—a brother or sister, or perhaps too many classes on ADHD, which can lead to thinking we all have it. Or it might be her "go-to" disorder when one of her students is not as attentive as she expects or doesn't comply with rules as readily as the others.

When she began to paint the picture of Chase as a classic ADHD child, I couldn't help but recall more than a few others in past years, similarly described, who, with a new teacher, settled in quite nicely.

Yet her portrayal this morning was especially grim. As she relentlessly listed all of Chase's inadequacies—his inability to pay attention, lack of organization, unwillingness to try or work hard—it dawned on me that the bulging veins in her temple and neck were truly pulsing from nothing less than genuine concern. She views him as doomed, and this portrait pains her greatly.

I offered to do an observation. Given her dramatic description, I suspected she was hoping I'd suggest moving right to a comprehensive evaluation. If I did this each time she showed up in a SIT meeting, I'd have no time for interventions; I'd be locked in my office testing kids all day. Nonetheless, she was pleased with my offer, surely convinced I would see what she sees—Chase hurtling down a path of failure.

I step into the hushed and obedient second-grade classroom. Twenty-four school desks in rows face forward. A steel-gray teacher desk angles across the left front corner, its tabletop remarkably clear. A whiteboard spreads across the front of the classroom with a neatly printed schedule in the upper-right corner and a morning exercise that even I remember enduring: copy the sentence, correct the punctuation and capitals. The most prominent sound is the scratching of pencils on paper. I hang back, waiting to see if I will spot, without looking at displayed names on desks, the disorganized, hyperactive child Wilma Jenkins described in this morning's meeting.

Ah, a new sound has entered the symphony of pencil scratching: a rummaging of paper; a squirrel foraging among a nest of crumpled worksheets, smuggled-in action figures, and worn-down crayons. Wilma, sitting at her desk, looks over at me with lips held in a tight upward turn, head slightly nodding. I walk toward the redhead, who has now slipped out of his chair to squat eye level with the contents inside his desk. He dives his arm in and pulls out a two-inch pencil with a stubby brown eraser. I see he captured more than a writing device;

he has also snagged a misshapen paper clip. He erases a jumble of letters with enough force that his paper tears. He looks back up at the sentence and then settles in to further twist the thin silver coil.

I stand next to his desk. He pretends not to notice. The clip slips from his fingers to the floor, and he lunges down to retrieve it, shining a freckled face up at me with green eyes that gleam mischievously, a glint I recognize. Uncle Joe; a second-grade version of my uncle Joe.

"Hey," I whisper, having crouched to eye level. "What has your teacher written on the whiteboard?" He startles and then turns his attention to the front of the room. He doesn't squint or seem to be straining his eyes. He just stares ahead. "Well?" I ask.

"I don't know that first word."

"Somewhere," I say.

"Oven."

"Over," I say.

He starts to sound out the next word, and his freckled face erupts in red blotches. I'm just about to say the word for him when he announces, "It's too hard, and it's boring."

"I think you might be right. Instead of twisting up paper clips, why don't you draw a picture?" He dives into his desk again, this time retrieving a handful of broken crayons, and begins to draw. Before I step away, Wilma storms over.

"Chase, this is not art class."

"Excuse me, Ms. Jenkins," I say too loudly, too intensely. Twenty-three pairs of eyes turn toward me. I whisper, "I really need to talk with you," and I cock my head toward the door. She glares at me, then turns to the students.

"You all know the assignment. I expect everyone to be working on it. Now." She turns from Chase, who stops coloring and anxiously scans the classroom.

We step out into the hall, leaving the door cracked open, and Wilma gives me an icy glower. She's got the taut musculature of a wrestler in the lightweight division. I notice my heart pumping. I take a couple of deep breaths and speak slowly.

"He can't read." There's a tremor in my voice as I try to squelch my anger. "What you're asking him to do is like placing you or me in an advanced trig class with the demand that we write out the damned problem and solve it." I breathe deeply, trying to recover my voice without hysterics. *He's not ADHD,* I almost shout.

"I didn't ask you to come and disrupt my class. I asked for an observation. Chase can do the work if he wants to. He's too busy playing and being distracted." Wilma steps away from me and peers into the room. "There he is, playing around in his desk again." She nods in his direction. Anger works its way up my arms, settling expansively in my chest.

"You don't understand. You too would be scratching through your desk if you were made to read Mandarin."

"And you, Dr. Meyers." Her face sharpens at the jawline. "You are out of touch with what goes on in a classroom." The chill of her words smacks painfully against me. "You're so busy minimizing what we teachers deal with on a daily basis, you have no business stepping foot in any classroom." She turns to leave.

"You invited me," I say. "And you're right, it was a waste of time since you won't listen to my recommendations."

Wilma pauses before entering the class. Without facing me, she says in a muffled voice, "Don't worry. You won't be invited back."

Before she disappears through the door, I blurt out, "Every year you bring up kids like Chase, and every year they do better as soon as they're out of your class." Wilma says nothing as she enters the classroom, pulling the door shut behind her.

CHAPTER 21

1 9 6 7

EVEN BEFORE it's two o'clock, my stomach starts to ache, and I almost ask to go to the nurse's office, but if I do, I'll always wonder what happens to Ethan and Yram, and I'll never be able to tell Danny how the story ends. But more than wanting to know what happens is the *not* wanting. Not wanting to have it end.

Mrs. Zinc begins story time the usual way. If I were Mrs. Zinc, I'd do something different so everyone understood that this is the very last time she will ever be reading this story, but she pretends it's like every other day.

"In chapter twenty, Yram met Gwendolyn, the spider. What did she learn from her?"

This is a question with lots of answers because there's so much she learned. I could easily stand up and say at least ten things Gwendolyn taught, enough to fill the entire question-and-answer time, but I keep my hands in my pockets, telling myself it's the last day of hearing the story, and this makes me think of a funeral, the part called the wake where we sit quietly in a small room with the open coffin. And then I remember Grandma's funeral.

I shut my eyes, wishing I didn't have to leave my story friends. Now, more than ever, I want a dream catcher and a fairy. I feel Mrs. Zinc looking at me, but I pretend not to notice and instead answer her questions silently in my head. Yram learned that dreams can float away if they're not caught; dreams need to be protected from fear; and most important, Gwendolyn taught Yram how to make a dream catcher. There's more, but instead I listen to what the others say.

"She learned what a dream catcher was," Paulette says in a chirpy voice. Mrs. Zinc then calls on Cheryl.

"She learned that webs are good to have."

"She learned that webs make things stick," says Jason.

Bobby says, "She learned that even though spiders are really creepy, they can make amazing things."

I turn and look at him. He catches my eye, and before I stop myself, I've halfway smiled.

"You're all right," Mrs. Zinc says in a voice that sounds a little like Miss Stanley's. I can tell she really likes what everyone has said, and maybe she's also sad about reading the very last part. Maybe Mrs. Zinc doesn't want it to end either. But she gets to read the book over again and again. I catch her looking at me because I always have my hand up, and I turn away. A hot flame burns inside my chest, reminding me I no longer like Mrs. Zinc.

"Yram learned a lot from Gwendolyn. Why do you think Ethan keeps getting healthier?"

I answer in my head before anyone is called upon. Ethan was never really all that sick—he was a little sick and believed he was very sick because that's what his parents told him. And the more he thought about how weak he was, the more weak he became. Yram showed him what he could do, helped him change his beliefs. With my answer so clear, I start to raise my hand, but I catch it and remind myself that this is the very last story time with Ethan and Yram.

"Yes, Cheryl, what do you think?"

"I think Ethan was magically changed by the fairy. The fairy did a magical spell on him and made the magic dream catcher."

I notice Bobby waving his hand wildly. Mrs. Zinc notices too.

"Yes, Bobby?"

"It's not that the fairy did a magical spell, and it's not the dream catcher. It's because he finally got out and got some fresh air. Just like we learned in health, you need to get fresh air."

They don't understand. I pull my hood up even though it's not allowed. I no longer care, and Mrs. Zinc pretends to not notice.

Mrs. Zinc opens the book and begins to read. My heart beats fast. I'm afraid of how it might end—I don't want it to end—and I'm trying to keep it all in my mind so I can make the story last forever. Before I know it, the fairy is gone and so is Ethan.

I look up. Mrs. Zinc smiles, the one that says it's done and I'm in charge. I turn toward the window. I hear the book close, and it sounds like a door slamming shut. My eyes spill over with tears, drenching my cheeks. I search for a thought that can cover my sadness. *It's a happy ending; Ethan can now go to school like the other children. And his father knows he's smart. He will no longer be lonely.* None of these happy thoughts make up for the sadness of the story being finished.

From somewhere far away, I hear a bell ring.

"Madelyn, what's wrong? Why are you just sitting there?" Paulette's standing up, organizing her homework. I shake my head and try to remember what I need to bring home. I can't. I grab a few loose papers from inside my desk and shove them into my take-home folder. I glance around. Everyone is rushing on with life, but my heartbeat is slow; I'm still at the funeral. I stand staring straight ahead at Mrs. Zinc's desk. I see the usual piles of papers, folders, and books stacked on both sides. And then, all at once, I can't believe my eyes—tossed carelessly on top, as if it too is a stupid worksheet waiting to be corrected, I see *The Fairy Angel's Gift.*

"What are you staring at?" Paulette asks. I shake my head not knowing what to say. "Aren't you going home on the bus?"

Oh yeah, and now I see the classroom is almost empty. I can't just leave *The Fairy Angel's Gift* where it is. It might get lost or accidently thrown away with all those papers.

"Nothing's wrong. I was just thinking." I grab my homework folder, race to the row of hooks with no coats left hanging, grab my book bag, and see Mrs. Zinc move toward the back of the room. I dash over to her. Too quick; she startles.

"Madelyn."

"Mrs. Zinc. I was wondering . . ." I take a moment to try to breathe normally. "Can I borrow *The Fairy Angel's Gift*?"

Mrs. Zinc's brow wrinkles up, and her lips part as if she silently says, "Huh?"

Before she can answer, I add, "I want to try to read it." Her face changes to a smile, the kind I'd imagine her giving to a lost puppy, the kind of look Paulette gave me earlier when she paused while reading her paper, and I already know her answer.

"Honey, that book is much too hard for you to read."

I begin shifting from one leg to another, wanting to tear out of the room, but I make myself stay while she keeps talking.

"I'm glad you enjoyed the story, and there will be other good stories to listen to, but I'm afraid if you tried to read that book, you'd only be frustrated by all the big words."

I turn to leave before she can even finish her last sentence.

"You need to hurry along to catch your bus."

I make it to the bus just as Mr. Lakowski starts to close the doors. I pull my hood up and lean into the window, swallowing the hard lump in my throat.

CHAPTER 22

1 9 6 7

"I'LL RACE YOU," Jack yells at Danny and me. Danny takes off after him, but I can barely shuffle my feet forward.

"Maddie, why are you walking so slow?" Rob stands waiting for me. He never races.

"I'm feeling heavy."

"Maybe you should take your coat off. I'll carry it. It's not that cold out, and you'll feel lighter." He's wearing a long-sleeve shirt, his tan book bag thrown over his shoulder and the thick paperback, *The Hobbit*, clasped in his hand. He'd never understand what it's like to have a story end forever.

"It's because it's a heavy day . . . my coat feels warm."

"Okay."

I slow down more, letting him walk ahead of me. I imagine him grabbing a snack and going downstairs to read for the rest of the afternoon, and how I now can hardly wait to get to my room and crawl into bed.

"Maddie, I'm doing my part of the bargain. I'm here to dry the plates. Won't you please tell me how it ends?"

"I told you, you don't need to dry the plates, just the silverware, because I'm not ready to tell the rest of the story."

"But why? Did it end really sad?"

"No, it was a happy ending."

"Then why won't you tell me?" He gives me the same pleading look he gives Mom when she tells him it's time for bed and he wants to stay up.

"I just need more time."

Alone in my room, I reach under my bed and pull out the large shoebox that holds my treasures. On top is my collection of holy cards, except for Saint Rita, who I keep next to my bed on the Bible that's not the real Bible. It's a picture Bible, which is okay for now, but someday I hope to have a real one. Under the holy cards are special birthday cards, mostly ones with pictures of animals; horses are my favorite. I also keep a few favorite rocks. The rest of my rock collection is in a box in the garage. In an envelope, I have a feather that I'm sure belonged to an eagle. What takes up the most space in my shoebox is the embroidery kit Grandma got me last year for my birthday. The last present she ever gave me.

Doing embroidery takes patience. There are lots of tiny stitches that need to be done before even a small part of the picture can be seen—it's not like drawing or coloring. My kit is a cross-stitch of two calico kittens playing with yarn. Except I only did a few stitches. Grandma kept trying to keep me going.

"Maddie, honey, you're doing a marvelous job." But every time I sat down to work on it, I'd think of all kinds of other things I'd rather be doing, like swinging on the rope swing. I didn't tell Grandma it was boring, but I could tell she was disappointed with how little I worked on it. Now I have a different plan for Grandma's present.

I pull out the silky thread—purple, orange, yellow—one color at time, stretch it across the hoop, wrapping and tying it. The threads make a colorful web, and I leave plenty of space in the center for bad dreams to slip through. Next, I borrow the honey bear from the kitchen cupboard and smear my dream catcher with the honey so that my good dreams will stick. I hang it with a tack above my bed.

"Madelyn, what's that?" Mom says while tucking me in.

"It's a dream catcher."

"What in the world is a dream catcher? That looks like the embroidery kit your grandmother got you for your birthday."

"I turned it into a dream catcher. Yram made hers of spider silk, but it still might work the way I did it. A dream catcher is a special web made to catch only the good dreams so that bad dreams don't come into your day."

"Where did you hear about this?"

"Don't you remember? It's in *The Fairy Angel's Gift*." Now I know she doesn't listen all that closely while I tell the story to Danny. "It's how Ethan began to believe he could do more. Yram made him a dream catcher."

"Honey, if you're worried about having bad dreams, all you need to do is pray and remember that God loves you and will protect you." Mom reaches down to kiss me good night and, without meaning to, I turn my head. She stops and stands back up.

"Madelyn, is there something we need to talk about?" I can tell she's mad.

"No. Sorry." Besides, I don't like the sound of her voice; it reminds me of Mrs. Zinc.

"Are you upset with something?"

"No." I bite my lower lip. She turns and starts to walk out. "Mom?" She pauses in the doorway, and I turn my back toward her. A moment later, she is sitting on my bed. When I roll over, I notice my night-light has made her face look soft again. "Please don't make me do third grade all over."

"Sweetheart, we're going to leave that up to your teacher. She's the one who knows what's best for you. It's not fair to send you to fourth grade if you're not ready."

"But I am ready. I'll be as ready as everyone else in my class."

"Fourth grade requires a lot of reading."

"But I might get better." My stomach aches. Father's right—I can't read.

"That's what we're hoping for. Now that you have a special teacher, it may make a difference."

I see fat Mrs. Ellen sitting in the closet. *How will she help me get to fourth grade?*

"Maddie, honey, your father and I want to do what's best for you. We love you, and we want you to be successful. If your teacher thinks you need another year before fourth grade, then we'll need to seriously consider this."

I think of Darren, how other kids tease him, and then about how I will be in the same grade as Jack. Will he still be my younger brother? I sit up and almost shout, *No! That's not what I need.*

"Well, we're not going to decide for a while." Mom stands, and I stare up at her. How can she let this happen? "Besides, even if you do third grade again, it's not the end of the world. You'll make new friends and have your old friends, and you'll probably be the best one in math and science and a few other areas."

"But I don't want to be the best in math or science after flunking a grade." I turn over, burying my head in my pillow. Mom doesn't understand. She's just like Mrs. Zinc. My stomach feels sick, and I want to be alone. I feel her hand patting my back, and it only makes it worse.

Her soft voice returns as she says, "Maddie, sweetie, just remember, we love you."

CHAPTER 23

2 0 0 5

I HOLD MYSELF BACK from slamming my office door. If only I could lock it. *Damn.* How did a simple observation turn into a train wreck?

The morning had been filled with promise. I'd imagined myself proclaiming to Irene that I was back to normal—the steady, well-grounded school psychologist had returned. Now I can't believe what I said to Wilma. I slump into my desk chair and stare at the darkened computer screen.

All at once, I recall the session with Irene that became so uncomfortable I had to leave early.

"It's interesting how your childhood coat reappears, and shortly thereafter, you experience the mercurial monster," Irene had said.

"I doubt there's a connection," I said. "But maybe. For sure I'm ashamed at how nasty I've been with some of the teachers. It really isn't me."

"Something about the way these teachers describe students with learning challenges seems to trigger an unrecognized part of yourself."

"Hmm. I guess you could say that."

"I wonder if that unruly part of you is the child who wore the black coat."

I rolled my eyes.

She rocked contentedly in her chair. I shifted anxiously on the couch.

"That little girl who was so misunderstood would identify with these children. Yes?" she added.

I looked up. "I suppose so. But who knows? It was so long ago."

She smiled. The smile was almost flirtatious, like she knew I wasn't being honest on purpose, but I thought I was. And yet, "so long ago" fails to describe Maddie's place in history. Time somehow collapsed with the reappearance of my coat. And these days, I'm vigilant each time I step into a classroom, never knowing if what I have dubbed the mercurial monster will show up and take command. This is nothing I can articulate to Irene.

"Unlike you," Irene said, "she doesn't have a PhD or the professional communication skills to express herself."

I nodded vigorously because I was glad Irene remembers that I have a PhD, even though I know I come across as . . . as who I used to be. "This is crazy talk," I said. "She *was* me, and I'm done with that part of my life. I've gotten over it and have moved on." I almost got up at that moment. But that very week, I had recalled a dream where I was in third grade.

"It's clear to me you've moved on." She gave me a reassuring smile, and I was startled to realize I was angry with her. I like Irene, but this nonsense about nine-year-old Maddie inserting herself into my life now was a little much.

"And yet," Irene continued, "in the process of moving forward, you've abandoned a part of yourself."

I shook my head ever so slightly.

"With the reappearance of her coat, Maddie has found an opening to make her presence known."

That's when I looked at my watch and said I had to leave early.

———————

Now what? Writing reports seems impossible. I need a break. With my briefcase slung over my shoulder, I march down the hall toward the main school office as if I'm late to an important meeting.

"Hi, Dr. Meyers!" a child's shrill voice calls out. Kaylee, at the end of the line as her class moves the opposite direction from me toward PE, is waving enthusiastically. Several classmates turn to see who she's calling out to. Jan stops and faces the line with her finger on her lips as a reminder. Jan's svelte form, and her hair pulled back tight, reminds me of a teacher from my past, and reflexively I imagine clasping my hands obediently on my desk and sitting up tall and straight. I wave back at Kaylee.

"When you have a minute . . . ," Matt calls out as I pass the office, three steps from the school entrance. I stop and turn toward him. "I thought we could touch base on a couple of cases," he says.

"Oh, sure," I say. "How about between two fifteen and two forty? Your office."

He steps closer to me and adds, "Are you feeling okay?"

"I will be. I'm slipping out for a short walk."

"Impressive. Dr. Mary taking a break. Don't make it too short." He flashes me a grin and heads back into the office.

I toss my briefcase into the trunk of my Mazda and begin to walk south on Jackson toward Java Love Espresso. Within a block, the high-pitched yells of children chasing, being tagged, and blissfully swinging upside down on bars fade. My gait gains an extra bounce. Two more blocks, and I'm surrounded by the belching of city buses and thumping bass tones from passing cars with windows rolled half down, and it occurs to me that, quite possibly, the sound of a school bell would be drowned out. Despite the increased density of buildings, cars, and people, I experience a welcome thinning of the air.

Four lanky-legged unisex teens who should be in school pass by me. They look to be fifteen or sixteen, puffing on cigarettes, boisterously exchanging verbal rap. Tenth grade was the year I discovered my vocation. I had been hanging out with a group of kids who were into skipping class and smoking cigarettes, and I thought I belonged. And then, in tenth grade, my psychology class took a field trip to an institution for children who supposedly were mentally retarded. My fifteen-year-old hand had slipped into that of a chubby nine-year-old who walked funny with uneven legs and spoke like a four-year-old. She was my tour guide. I had wondered if she would eventually learn to read.

I flash on the early part of last week's therapy session—not Irene's crazy notion about my nine-year-old self, but when we talked about how I knew I wanted to be a special education teacher after that tenth-grade field trip. I had observed teachers—called special education teachers—talking to children in a way that made it clear the children were incapable of learning anything meaningful. I knew each child desperately wanted to learn. With a conflicted memory of shame and anticipation, I vaguely recalled being ushered out of my third-grade classroom and into a closet. I too had been viewed as retarded.

In tenth grade I had proudly labored through *Les Miserables*, which continues to be my favorite piece of literature. On the way home from the field trip, I told my classmates that now I knew what I wanted to do with my life—I had a name for it. I wanted to be a special education teacher. I knew I would be a different kind of special education teacher, a teacher who could help all children learn to read.

Java Love has pricy, guilt-free coffee. It's fair-trade, organically shade-grown, and served in a quintessential laid-back atmosphere. A large framed photo of Jerry Garcia looms behind the espresso machine. The young man working the counter has straggly dishwater-blond hair pulled into a ponytail that falls below his shoulders. Growing up in rural Minnesota, I missed out on the hippie revolution, and places like Java Love help make up for the loss. I order a cappuccino and surprise myself by taking a seat instead of stiffly striding back to Milton Elementary.

There was more I'd wanted to share with Irene, but I hadn't found the words. It had to do with feeling like an outsider from a very young age. And even now. I had touched my pocket, felt the acorn, and experienced an ache in the upper part of my chest, a blend of dull pain and longing. I'd wanted to say that I'd known my vocation before that field trip. The trip only sharpened an already steeled determination to mend the wings of small birds unable to fly.

I had felt the same urgency when I shifted over from special education to school psychology. And yet, I'm still wrapped in an incompleteness, a strange yearning to be or do . . . something different.

The wide-mouthed ceramic cup nestled between my palms delivers a dose of comfort. I lift the mug to my lips, breathing in a tang of hot milky espresso before sipping a swath of foam. The image of Chase scrabbling through his desk to find a pencil so as to copy a sentence he could not read hurls itself toward me, and I feel myself descend into a state of remorse.

If he had landed across the hall with Marcia, a teacher who understands that kids unfold with different timelines, that one size doesn't fit all, would he be having an entirely different second-grade experience?

If I hadn't blown up, could I possibly have altered Wilma's perspective? Maybe. My chest presses against a heaviness. The laid-back atmosphere and empty chatter that drew me into the café has now become an irritation. I squirm, not ready to leave but no longer relaxed.

Wilma's mind was made up long before I set foot in her class. There was little that Chase could do to escape the brutality of her expectations. I want to rewind events, take back my obnoxious response to her, swoop in, and deliver Chase to a teacher who could see beyond his struggle to read. A teacher who would share a story that would inspire him to tackle letters and turn them into words. I stare at my half-full cup of tepid coffee and hear the distant call of a recess bell.

CHAPTER 24

1967

"MADELYN," Paulette whispers in her "I have a secret to share" voice. She aims her nose toward my paper. "Why did you write," she says, and she cups her hands together and leans into my ear, "*peed?*"

"What?"

She points to the letters I have just copied off the board. "Don't you know *p-e-e-d* spells," she says, her voice dropping to barely a whisper, "*peed?*" She then says, much too loudly, "The word on the board starts with a *d* and ends with a *p*." I erase so hard I tear a hole in the page. Once again, she's right.

"So, guess what?"

"What?"

"I know the next book Mrs. Zinc's going to read because I almost checked it out myself. Remember when she read *Little House on the Prairie* at the beginning of the year?" I nod; it was boring compared to *The Fairy Angel's Gift*. "Well, I walked by her desk before the bell rang and saw *On the Banks of Plum Creek*. That's the next book in the series."

"Oh."

"I think you'll like it because it has pictures." I nod and squirm in my seat, wondering if *The Fairy Angel's Gift* is still somewhere in a heap next to Mrs. Zinc's desk.

"I can hardly wait," I mumble.

She leans into me. "I know something else that might interest you." She gives her knowing smile and continues whispering, "I also happened to see on Mrs. Zinc's desk that Bobby got an F on the math test. Since he gives you such a hard time, I thought you might like to know."

"Thanks." I don't believe her. It was an easy test, and Bobby's smart. I scoot way over toward the windows, pretending to look in my desk so Paulette doesn't get suspicious, and sure enough, sandwiched between piles of papers stacked on the floor next to Mrs. Zinc's desk is *The Fairy Angel's Gift*.

I now wonder if Mrs. Zinc even knows it's there. If it were my book, I'd give it a special place, a shelf of its own so that it could be propped up with the front cover showing. *I bet Mrs. Zinc wouldn't even notice if it disappeared.* And once this thought slithers into my mind, my body stiffens, my heart pounds, and I feel as if I am about to race across the prairie on a wild stallion.

"Madelyn, why aren't you eating?" Paulette is squished next to me on the lunch bench where I sit squeezed in with the girls from our class. My plan had been for Mrs. Zinc to leave the classroom during morning recess so I could slip back in and rescue *The Fairy Angel's Gift*. Mrs. Zinc also had plans; she stayed in the classroom busily writing words on the chalkboard. When noon came and we all marched out together to the lunch line, I needed to figure out another plan. I look down at the mound of white plopped on my lunch tray—an ice-cream scoop covered in a thick brown topping. Eating is the last thing on my mind.

"I'm not hungry. Besides, it's Gravy Train." That's what we call the mashed potatoes with brown gravy because it tastes as bad as what we imagine dog food to taste like.

"Can I have your chocolate pudding?" Paulette asks.

"Sure."

With only one recess left, I need a backup plan—maybe pulling the fire alarm, forcing everyone out, and while they're running for the door, I can grab the book. This is risky. Moments before the last recess of the day, Mrs. Zinc makes an announcement.

"Everyone needs to go out for recess this afternoon. I have playground duty." There's no waiting around. Mrs. Zinc shoos us all out the door.

I race out in front, like usual, pretending I'm a stallion.

"Madelyn!"

It's Paulette. She'll ruin my plans if I turn toward her. I pretend to not hear and run out of earshot to upper field. Recess is only fifteen minutes, so I hurry back down, circling around to the school and keeping an eye out for Paulette.

I spy her walking past the jungle gym alongside Mrs. Zinc, who has her recess whistle to her lips. As soon as they move toward the jump rope area, I race down and scoot inside the building. I keep myself from running down the hall, and then turn a corner, and there in front of me are Lynn and Carol with Cheryl, who's whimpering and limping. Lynn turns and sees me.

"Madelyn, Cheryl fell and scraped her knee. Can you let Mrs. Zinc know we're taking her to the nurse's office?"

"Sure, I just need to do something first, real quick, and then I'll go let her know." Cheryl whines a little louder, pulling Lynn and Carol's attention away from me. *Whew, that's not a lie.* I duck into the girls' restroom, peek back out, and see that the three of them are inside the office and moving toward the nurse's room.

I pad down the hall, trying not to think about what I'll say if I run into anyone else. I only think of Yram and Ethan and holding the book. The classroom door is cracked open, which is weird. Mrs. Zinc usually shuts the door when we leave. This causes my heart to speed up. I slip inside, and freeze. Someone else is in the room; someone else must have also seen the book tossed aside. As I peek around the coat closet, my heart goes crazy in my chest. It's Bobby Wallace!

In my most quiet Indian moccasin steps, I tippy-toe behind the coats and peek again. He's looking in Mrs. Zinc's desk. If he discovers me, he'll call me a spy and figure out what I'm after. I hold my breath. A moment later, Bobby walks right past, missing me snugged up against the hooks of the closet, and shuts the door behind him. I scurry to the messy stack of papers and see the red cover gleaming at me. I slip *The Fairy Angel's Gift* inside my coat, shifting it over so that my lower left arm crossing my stomach can make a shelf, holding the book snug against my chest. I reach for the door, but it opens before I turn the knob. Bobby stares at me, his face white like a ghost.

"What are you doing here?" he asks. He also has a coat on, his right hand in his pocket.

"I . . . I had to get something." *This isn't a lie. I had to save Yram from getting lost in the pile of worksheets.* Bobby stands still, and then he shifts his weight from one side to the other, looking at me, and then into the classroom and back. I don't move a muscle, especially my left arm.

"Me too," he finally says. He turns, and I follow him down the hall and out the door. My legs are shaky; maybe he had spied on me just like I had on him. Once outside, he keeps walking and doesn't turn to see where I go.

The recess bell rings, and I remember to tell Mrs. Zinc where Cheryl, Lynn, and Carol are. She doesn't notice my left arm pinned across my stomach.

Back at my desk with *The Fairy Angel's Gift* cradled in my lap, I no longer care that Mrs. Zinc will be reading a new story. Repeating third grade no longer seems real. With Yram tucked under my coat, I imagine my dream catcher catching the dream I want most.

CHAPTER 25

1 9 6 7

I BARELY MAKE IT off the bus without falling flat on my face. My legs are weak and wobbly, as if I really have been riding a wild stallion. My left arm is snug up against Yram, and my right holds my book bag. I did manage to make it down three giant bus steps. *Mother, may I take three giant steps down? Yes, you may.*

"Why won't you race?" Jack demands.

"My stomach hurts." Which is true. He looks at me, with my left arm stretched across my coat, and I can tell he believes me.

"Come on, Danny. I'll give you a head start." Off they run.

I walk alongside Rob.

"Maddie, what are you carrying under your coat?"

"What do you mean?"

"You're holding something under your coat with your arm." Rob always notices things.

"Oh, that. Well, it makes my stomach feel better." Which is not a lie, but Rob keeps looking at me, waiting to hear more. "It's a book I borrowed from my teacher."

"Cool. I didn't know you even liked books."

"I do. I mostly like listening to stories, but I'm going to get better at reading."

"That's good. I love reading." As soon as he says this, I notice he walks faster. I do too.

And I call out, "I will too once I start reading something I really like."

———

Finally. Safe in my bedroom, my dream catcher glistening in the late-afternoon sun, sticky honey-coated threads dangling over my bed. I slide on my knees to the floor between bed and window for oak tree and fairy sighting. Then I invite *The Fairy Angel's Gift* to slip out from my coat into my room. Yram's picture on the cover is more beautiful than I had remembered. *Marvelous.* I study each of the gold title letters, left to right. I grab my writing pad and, letter by letter, with only one quick look, write each of the four words with perfect spelling. *The,* which I already know how to spell, *F-a-i-r-y A-n-g-e-l-'s G-i-f-t.*

"Maddie?" It's Danny. I feel my heart jump. I prepare to toss the book under my bed. "Are you in there?"

"Yes. I'm busy. I'll be out in a minute." It's dusty and dirty under my bed, no better than where Mrs. Zinc left the book. I need a safe place that's worthy. I stand up and look around. *Of course. Under my pillow.* This makes me smile. I no longer believe in the tooth fairy, but still this seems the perfect safe place for a fairy to rest.

"*The Three Stooges* is a rerun that I've seen lots, so I was wondering if you want to help me catch a really big frog to show Uncle Joe?"

"No. I don't feel very good."

Once I'm sure he won't come barging in, I pull the book out from under my pillow and begin to look at all the words, page after page. Mrs. Zinc was right; there are no pictures, but maybe she's wrong about it being too hard for me to read.

"Guess what happened today?" Danny says after swallowing a mouthful of macaroni and cheese, one of my favorite dinners. I can tell from his twisted smile that he's about to tattle on someone.

"What?" Jack asks.

"Billy got in big trouble. He got caught stealing from the teacher."

"So what?" Jack says, and then asks, "What'd he do?" Everyone at the dinner table is too busy eating to say anything. Usually, Father cuts the tattletaling off.

"He stole Mrs. Andersen's special stickers. He must have snuck in during lunch recess, because after we got back and Mrs. Andersen went to get her stickers, there were none left. Sally sits next to Billy and yelled out that he had a bunch of stickers in his desk."

"So what happened?" asks Jack.

"Billy was scolded, and he had to stay after school. I bet Mrs. Andersen called his parents. He's probably going to miss recess tomorrow too."

My ears perk up to a squeal that isn't a bird or cat, and then I hear a roar like a lawn mower. Moments later, the kitchen door swings open and in walks Uncle Joe.

"Hi, y'all."

"Hi, Joe. We just sat down. There's plenty of food here," Mother says.

"It smells delicious. I'll be there as soon as I do a quick wash-up."

"Yay. He can sit next to me," Danny says.

"No, next to me," Jack whines.

"I'll tell ya what. I'll sit between the two of you bozos."

"Well," Jack says, once Uncle Joe has settled in next to him with a huge plate of food, "last week Debbie was caught stealing. She took my teacher's favorite book." I almost choke on the macaroni. I'm sure Jack is just trying to outdo Danny. I look up, expecting Father to change the subject, but he seems to not be paying attention.

"How do you know it was her favorite book?" I ask.

"Because that's what she said when it was missing."

"Maybe she was just borrowing it or forgot to ask," I say.

"No, she stole it. She also snuck in during recess. It showed up when we all had to clean out our desks before we could go to the library."

"But you don't know. Maybe she meant to borrow it so she could try and read it."

"She should have asked," Jack says.

"What's her punishment?" Danny asks with as much excitement as when he told on Billy.

"She has to stay in for recess a whole week."

"Well." Father's deep voice makes me shiver. "I'm glad we've raised you kids to know the difference between right and wrong. Stealing is a sin, and staying in from recess does not necessarily set things straight with our Lord."

My stomach somersaults. The macaroni and cheese doesn't taste as good as I had remembered. I start to take another bite, but I'm afraid I might throw up if I do. I look over at Mom.

"Maddie, are you feeling okay? You've hardly touched your dinner," Mom says.

"I'm not hungry. My stomach hurts."

"Well, you need to eat to stay healthy," Father says. I pick up my fork and stab at a piece of macaroni.

"I hate to say it, but I sure got into plenty of trouble myself during my school career," Uncle Joe says, shooting a glance at Father before continuing. "But never once did I steal anything." He then starts to chuckle.

"What's so funny?" Rob asks.

"I was just remembering the look on Mrs. Groutchem's face the day I glued the reading book shut. I used to call her Mrs. Grouch behind her back because she had one heck of a temper. She didn't keep

kids in for recess; she used her ruler on their knuckles and sent kids to
Mr. . . . George, what was his name, the PE teacher?"

"Clark."

"That's right, and he'd have you do push-ups or sit-ups or something. Those were the good old bad days. Of course, your father never
had to see Mr. Clark other than at PE time." Uncle Joe shoots a smile
at Father, who doesn't smile back. "The teachers were always com-
plaining that I wasn't like the other Meyers boy." Uncle Joe gives a
little laugh.

I wonder what this means.

"Why'd you glue the book shut?" Rob asks.

"I reckoned I'd had enough of it. Every day, we'd gather in a big circle and take turns reading the most boring stories. I hated it. Usually,
I got into a little trouble just before reading time and was sent to the
corner, where I made up my own story, which was always much more
interesting. For some foolish reason, on that particular day, I took it a
little too far."

If I didn't have a stomachache, I would have shared that I too make
up better stories than the ones read during reading group.

"What'd you do?" Jack asks. Uncle Joe looks over at Father, before
answering. I do too. Father just continues to eat dinner and ignore us.

"While the reading circle was being formed, and Mrs. Grouchy—"

Jack and Danny burst out laughing. Uncle Joe pauses, eats several
heaping forkfuls of macaroni, and then continues.

"—was all busy running the show, I slipped over to her desk and
grabbed the Elmer's Glue and started gluing pages together. Everyone
was so busy moving their chairs around, no one saw me. No one except
Ethel McMillan." Uncle Joe looks over at Father who doesn't say a
thing. "Do you remember her, George? I heard that she ended up the
homecoming queen. She was a prissy queen all right."

Father nods but stays his serious self.

Rob, Jack, and Danny are all giggling, and even Mom has a smile on her face. It's funny, and I start to giggle, but my stomach keeps me from laughing.

"I slipped on over to the circle and took my place. Usually, I was causing some sort of commotion about then and being sent to the corner. That day, I just sat with a smile on my face." He again has to stop. Danny and Jack are laughing so loud that food bits spurt from their mouths.

"Mrs. Grouchy-face put the reading book on her lap and waited for everyone to be nice and quiet before boring us to death with that idiotic story. Once satisfied—and it was hard to not laugh and give myself away—she tried to open the book to the right chapter. The harder she tried, the pages started to tear, and then everyone was laughing. I don't remember what she said—it's her face I can still see to this day. She looked as though a herd of squirrels had taken over her class."

Suddenly, I too am laughing with Danny, Jack, and Rob. I see Mrs. Zinc's tight face as she tries to open *Spot the Dog* that I have secretly glued together. It starts to tear apart.

"Hey, you guys, do you want to hear what happened next?" Uncle Joe waits for the laughing to stop. Father still doesn't find any of this funny, and, if Uncle Joe wasn't here, I'm sure he'd be telling us to settle down and eat our dinner.

"Please tell us, Uncle Joe," Danny whines. Uncle Joe is quiet for a long moment—and then he continues.

"When the book started to tear, Mrs. Grouchy became so mad, her grouchy face turned into the face of an ogre ready to attack! That's when I couldn't stop myself from bursting out laughing. I wasn't alone. Everyone was laughing until Miss Prissy Ethel spilled the beans."

"Oh no, what happened, Uncle Joe?" Jack asks, wide-eyed.

Uncle Joe's eyes shift over to Father, but he doesn't look back. He keeps on eating small bites of food. I continue to giggle at the thought of gluing *Spot the Dog* together and what Mrs. Zinc's face might look like. Except I know I couldn't get away with it the way Uncle Joe could. He's much smarter and funnier. I try to imagine what he'd looked like at my age: light-colored hair and freckles. Like Bobby, he'd be the one getting away with things.

"I don't remember," Uncle Joe says. "I'm sure I saw Mr. Clark more than I wanted to. I also imagine there was a phone call home. Your grandparents were used to phone calls from school."

"Didn't make it any easier," Father says in a voice that startles us all. It's as if he'd been somewhere else and now is talking to someone other than Uncle Joe. "I hope I never receive a call about any of you kids."

It's no longer funny. I look at the pile of macaroni and cheese on my plate. I can't eat another bite, even if it is my favorite meal. My brothers also stop laughing, but I can see their hidden smiles. Uncle Joe doesn't say another thing.

CHAPTER 26

2 0 0 5

MATT'S OFFICE DOOR is cracked open; he sits at his desk flipping through a spiral notepad. I slip in, and he swivels around on his computer chair to face me. My stomach knots with the possibility that Wilma has already shared her version of our conflict.

"How was the break?" he asks, motioning me to the wooden chair next to his briefcase.

"Too short."

"It's a good start for someone who never takes lunch, and leaves after the custodian."

"True. The problem is the lack of productivity. I still have a stack of files two feet high sitting next to my computer." I sigh and glance around his office. If I were twenty years younger, the blue velvety-covered beanbag in the corner would have been my seat of choice. "So what's up?" I snag a squeeze ball from the basket propping up a feelings chart, displaying cartoon faces that range from bliss to ballistic.

"For starters," he says, "Karla is doing better with Josiah." Matt breaks out in a grin, and I'm pulled along.

"How's that possible?"

"I met with her, and it turns out she too was bored in school." I stare in disbelief. Matt doesn't flinch. "What you said to her was painful; even so, she was willing to consider it."

"Really?"

He nods.

"I was so rude and out of line."

"For sure not the Dr. Mary I know."

My upper stomach stings, and I train my eyes to his bookshelf: *Mr. Worry . . . When I Feel Angry . . . Unique Monique.*

"But, as it turns out, she's extremely rigid."

"Tell me about it," I say mockingly, but my lightheartedness has left me.

"I suspect what she was really asking for in that meeting was permission to let this kid be different."

"She sure went about it in an odd way."

Matt waves his index finger. "Now, now." His voice lowers as he continues. "We talked for about an hour after school. She finally understood that it's okay to let him have a different track. In fact, she realized it was what *she* would have wanted for herself."

The broken look on her face as I marched out of the SIT meeting flashes before me. It seems a lifetime ago, but it was just last week. A sadness presses in. I can't tell if it's for her or for myself and the part of me that has slipped away.

"Matt, you're amazing to have forged that kind of trust." I glance out his office window and across the narrow hall. I take a couple breaths before turning back to him.

"I also want to tell you the latest with Kaylee."

My stomach tightens.

"Here's the deal. You know how Reese is."

I nod. Walter Reese, our principal, understands best practices: no holding kids back a grade unless parents are one hundred percent on board.

"Well, the third-grade teachers have a pretty strong conviction."

Based on a strong bias and lack of imagination, I think.

"Your response was, uh, rather upsetting." The way Matt's blue eyes settle into me reminds me of my father. It's hard to hold his gaze.

"So what's their plan?" I ask.

"They want to meet with you again."

Hell no!

But Matt has his eyes fixed on me, Dr. Mary, the psychologist.

"Interesting," I say. "I mean . . . they already know what I think."

Matt raises his eyebrows. He's right. They know how I feel—I wasn't able to articulate how I think. "They'd like me to be there too," he says.

"But you don't agree with them. Do you?"

"Hey, we've always been on the same page about this. Nothing has changed. Including our commitment to listening and being open-minded."

"Sure." I pull my shoulders back. "So, when?"

"The SIT schedule is too full. It'll need to be after school. Next Wednesday works for us." He gives me a questioning look.

Great. I'll tell the third-grade team I can't come because I have a therapy appointment. Which . . . would not surprise them.

"Won't work," I say, kneading the squeeze ball a good three seconds before tossing it back into its home.

"We need to take care of this. You can let me lead."

"No," I say. He shrinks back. "I mean, just, that afternoon won't work. I can be free Thursday or Friday after school." I take a tight breath. "Is that all? I really need to get back to my office."

I'm halfway down the hall before I realize that my teeth are grinding. I turn the corner toward the cafeteria and see the short, stocky body of Grace Adams almost skipping past the classroom doors. Seeing her lightens my mood immediately. God, I used to work so hard at walking instead of racing. This is such a girl after my own heart.

She must be on her way to Penny's class. She's wearing worn-out jeans, which would have been my style if it had been allowed, a loose tee shirt, and tennis shoes. It's hard to believe she's ending third grade—still dyslexic but in the highly capable program.

I call out to her, "Congratulations!"

She startles, turns to me, and a grin spreads across her face.

"I heard from Ms. Stanton that you won the poetry slam contest."

She beams and nods her head.

"I used to write poetry when I was your age, but I never won a contest. That's really special."

"Thank you. I didn't write it. I just memorized what I made up in my head and said it out loud. I didn't even need to read it."

"Wow. I'm impressed."

"Why don't I get to visit you in your office anymore?"

"Well, I need to see lots and lots of kids, and sometimes I get so busy I don't have time to visit."

"Oh," she says, in a tone or two lower. My heart sinks. She gives me a half smile that fails to hide her disappointment, turns, and continues frolicking forward. A part of me wants to dash alongside her and suggest a game of tetherball. I wish I had the time to simply visit. Especially with Grace. But how can I set the work aside to merely visit when I can barely do the job I'm paid for?

It's eleven o'clock, and as usual, I struggle with letting go of this evening's therapy session. I've had a glass of pinot grigio, followed by warm milk, and still the air in my bedroom is alert, bright, edgy.

Accepting defeat, I make my way down the hall to my study. It's a space too small to hold a bed but perfect for bookcases and my beloved computer, dubbed Vespers, the keeper of my journal. Document "writing.9" is first on the queue. Pushing Control-plus End brings me to page 560. Next month, I'll start "writing.10." I try not to let my journal files get too long, but for now, I allow an uncensored release of memories pried loose from this evening's session.

Chase. My blowup with Wilma. And Uncle Joe.

Irene had asked me to describe Uncle Joe, and I'd said, "If I had to pin a face card to Uncle Joe and his big brother, my father, then Joe would be the joker, and Father would be none other than the king— the king of clubs."

The conversation about outsiderness circled back to the alienation I feel as a school psychologist. Maybe becoming a school psych was a mistake. In the beginning, all I wanted was the answer to a relatively simple question: Why is it so extraordinarily hard for some children to learn to read? This query led me through a multitude of research journals, conferences, and seminars that captured five years of my life. And still, for me, there was no satisfactory answer.

In the presence of Irene, I couldn't bring myself to say why it took nine years to get up the courage to apply to graduate school. That I may have a PhD behind my name, but it feels like a hoax. That I pulled it off even though I can't spell or write worth a damn. I just manage to hide it well—thank God for computers.

Nor did I share how unsatisfying I found the answers to my research questions. That I was offered a position as an academic but knew it would have been a life sentence as an imposter. And yet, five days a week, I stride down the halls of Milton Elementary with shoulders thrown back in an air of self-confidence, acting as though I know the answer to why some children struggle so desperately to learn.

I did share what I know for sure to be true: my passport as a school psychologist has given me an opportunity to shape expectations. I have credibility. Teachers and parents listen. Now my credibility is gushing down a drainpipe I didn't even know existed.

I pause at my keyboard. The softening light from the hall pulls me away, and I'm aware of a serene sadness rising up from the base of my throat. A leftover lump, ignored and controlled during therapy, finding its purchase in the soft recesses of my heart. It's Grandma O'Leary. Grandma, who descended from a rich heritage of folktales, alive with leprechauns and trolls and, of course, fairies. Some of her stories were almost real, others wondrously imaginative. I believed every single one of them.

How long did she live with us, Irene had asked. Not long enough. Even though she never smoked a cigarette in her life, she died of lung cancer shortly after I entered third grade. Sitting on Irene's sofa, my mind drifted back to the times before that. All the times I raced down the driveway, twenty feet from the bus, another couple hundred to go, to make out Grandma's plump body filling the doorway, anticipating our arrival, Monday through Friday. This vision set a stream of memories in motion, bubbling up as unexpectedly as eddies in a river, and without warning, I heard my voice calling out, *"The Fairy Angel's Gift."*

Irene was as surprised as I was. I could tell by her momentary break in composure, the way she shifted in her chair. I began babbling, trying to make sense of my spontaneous outburst. It had been thirty-eight years since I had uttered the title of the story that, in third grade, I had imagined would somehow change my life. My memory of the tale has faded, but not the longing I had to share it with Grandma. This was a story about a fairy who I believed at the time would be my salvation.

I stand up, stretch, and move to the window opposite my computer. I pull back the limp curtain to reveal too many city lights to be able to see stars or fireflies. It was easy to say that I believed in fairies. It's a common childhood fantasy. But therapy with Irene spins in directions I can't anticipate. Like last week, with Irene's sci-fi notion of my own nine-year-old self living a parallel life and demanding acceptance.

Much of the time, Irene's silence, stealth-like, pulls up unexpected bits and pieces from my past. My own unwillingness to sit in the absence of words skewers rogue images that could easily have lain hidden and unspoken for a lifetime.

As quiet welled unbearably, I gave in. "Not only did I believe in fairies, I also believed in saints. Can you imagine, I actually wanted to be a nun? Me, a nun. It's hilarious, don't you think?"

To this I received no visible response, so I exploded into a frenzied laugh. With no fan to flame my fire, I once again found myself squirming in the austerity of silence.

Irene finally intoned, "You held your beliefs close to your heart, each one cradled in absolute sincerity."

I nodded and said, "I used to pray all the time to Saint Rita." Announcing her name brought about a shiver, similar to when I'd said *The Fairy Angel's Gift.* Names from a place so distant I'm left with only a whisper of recognition. "I was told she's the saint of lost causes." I spontaneously giggled.

Once I had quieted, Irene said, "You believed in this saint's power to solve a problem that seemed insurmountable." I nodded and quickly became aware there was nothing the least bit funny about my belief in Saint Rita.

I pace back and forth between my curtained window and computer. I hear last week's unflinching declaration from Irene—*Finding the coat provided Maddie a way to reenter your life*—and I question, if there were any truth to this, why wouldn't Maddie be satisfied with what I've accomplished?

My thoughts go to my mother, the day I graduated with a PhD. She bestowed upon me pearl earrings and kisses. Over and over she stated, "I always believed in you." My PhD graduation ceremony seemed to mean more to her than to me or to my father. I suspect my father and I were on the same page—equally surprised and skeptical of this accomplishment. Yet my mother, ebullient, felt vindicated.

Regardless of my doubts, the fact is, I've achieved the pinnacle of education. I've flown higher than any Sparrow would have dreamed. Shouldn't Maddie be satisfied? Is it really necessary, after all these years, to reach back and find acceptance?

CHAPTER 27

1967

MOM SWITCHES ON my night-light before bending down to kiss me while my head lies flat on my pillow with *The Fairy Angel's Gift* beneath. Alone and all tucked in, I slip the book out, and my night-light becomes my reading light. I think of Rob. This is how he spends every night before falling asleep. He said so. My head and pillow are propped against the back of my bed, my knees and legs form an upside down letter V, and this is where I rest the book—on my stomach, leaning into my legs.

I open the cover, and even though I can't wait to read the first chapter, I want to look at every page. Inside the cover, before the story even starts, I see small print and regular-sized print, but what jumps out at me is the blue writing that's not print. It's grown-up writing, and I can tell it's cursive because Mrs. Zinc is teaching cursive to everyone but the Sparrows. This is sloppy cursive, not like the letters Mrs. Zinc writes on the board. I wonder what it says.

Now, to find Yram. Yram first shows up in chapter two, which looks a lot like chapter one: row after row of words. If her name had stayed Dottyrambleon, finding it would be easy since it's so long. I can't even remember what letter Yram starts with. It sounds like an *e* but it isn't, because I had asked Mrs. Zinc and it was a letter that had nothing to do with the letter *e*. *Yram, Ee-r-a-m, am.* I may not know how it starts, but I know how it ends: *a-m.*

My pointer finger runs across one line at a time for two entire pages while my eyes look for words that ended in *a-m*. After the second page, my eyes are so tired I need to give them a rest. *Saint Rita, can you please help me? I just want to find Yram, and maybe I can then read a few other words.*

I turn to the next page, this time looking without using my finger. My eyes move across the page like reckless hands finger painting, brushing this way and that, when suddenly they come to a screeching halt. They land upon a group of letters that are so familiar, I gasp—*marY*. I jerk, and the book falls forward on my stomach. I stare up at the ceiling. *Saint Rita, why is my name in this book?* A shiver runs through me. Not only *my* name, but the Blessed Virgin's name. My stomach twists. If I have committed a mortal sin for stealing, this might be the Blessed Virgin's way of letting on that she knows. My heart pounds so loudly, I can hardly think straight. *Saint Rita, you know I am only borrowing it. I promise to give it back.* My heart continues to race, and Saint Rita helps me to remember what Mom taught me to do when I become upset. I breathe in deeply and slowly—*one Mississippi, two Mississippi, three Mississippi.*

Breathing slowly, I prop the book back up, moving my finger from left to right, this time on the lookout for my own name. My heart starts to speed up as I get closer to where I had seen my name. All at once, there it is! My name! I blink and it flips to Yram. I move my finger from letter to letter and see for sure that I have found Yram right where my own name had been. *Oh my goodness! Yram is Mary spelled backward!*

The book drops from my hands. The bedroom spins around me. I shake my head, peer out the slice of window, and see stars between the branches of the oak. *Mary is Yram spelled backward.*

I jump out of bed to tell Mom about this amazing discovery. But how can I answer her when she asks how the book ended up in my room? She wouldn't understand. *One Mississippi, two Mississippi, three Mississippi.* Two more deep breaths and I'm back in bed breathing like usual with *The Fairy Angel's Gift* on my lap. *Saint Rita, this isn't an ordinary mistake; it is a mistake meant to happen.* I know, because I'm the only one in my class who mistakes *was* for *saw* and *god* for *dog.* I close my eyes tight. *Saint Rita, I think Yram chose her name because . . . my name, and reading both ways . . . she knew I would discover this.*

I place Yram under my pillow and say one Hail Mary after another. I want to make sure the Blessed Virgin knows I did not steal the book; I only borrowed it. The prayer words flow one after another, freeing my thoughts to wander. *What would Grandma O'Leary say? Did Yram know our names are the same?* The prayer words mix together, thoughts turn to pictures, shapes of all colors. The smell of fresh-cut grass fills the air.

I'm standing on the greenest carpet of grass I've ever seen. I touch it and giggle. It's like running my hand over Jack or Danny's newly cut hair, soft and bristly, tickling my fingers.

"I wish I could power kick a ball or run even half as fast as you." I swirl around and meet the sky-blue eyes of a boy with long wavy hair. He grins, and I know him.

"Ethan."

"Yes, and you're Mary Madelyn."

"How'd you know my name?"

"Yram told me. She said you want to be a nun, just like she wants to be an angel. I've been waiting for you."

My mouth drops open. I step closer to him. He's about as tall as Rob and has the same eyes that know so much.

"Can you bring me to her?"

He reaches out, takes my hand. I look up in the sky, so happy to discover this place. My body shivers. I'm so excited, holding hands with Ethan.

"Not yet, Maddie. She needs your help."

"My help?"

"Yes, you know the secret of her name."

"It's my name spelled backward!" *I smile wide, and we both start giggling. It's a secret he knows too, but I discovered it all on my own. I feel myself swelling up like a balloon. I'm ready to float off.*

Ethan's face changes to serious, and so does mine.

"An evil spell has been cast over the land of Forever After. That's where I live."

"Oh no. Like in The Wizard of Oz? Is there a wicked witch?" *I can be brave like Dorothy; I can toss a bucket of water on the wicked witch.*

"Scarier. Do you remember Gwendolyn's warning?"

"Hmm." *I hear Mrs. Zinc's voice reading that part.* "Oh, yeah— 'Guard against those who place fear above dreams.'"

"That's right, and she also said they will act like they care, but really they snatch hope away."

"I remember," *I whisper.* "But who are they?"

"That's the hard part. If they wore black and had brooms, it would be easy. These are shadows that creep around," *he says. I shiver and dart my eyes around the playfield. It's too bright and green for shadows.* "They don't really snatch your hope, they cover it up," *Ethan says.*

"With what?"

"Fear."

"How do they do that?"

"Madelyn, have you ever noticed that as soon as you hope for something really good to happen, you get sort of scared that it might not happen and you'll be disappointed?"

"Oh. Yeah."

"That's fear of disappointment, and it can grow and get big. And it will cover up the hope."

"That's sad."

"Yes, because without hope, dreams fade. The hope snatchers have figured out a way to grow the fear so big it suffocates the hope." Ethan's face looks so sad, I think he might cry. "My family wanted to believe I really did get healthy and went back to school."

"Just like in the book."

"That's right. But Maddie, I think you know the story hasn't really ended."

I look into his blue eyes and nod. I do know this.

"The hope snatchers cast a spell that made it hard for my family to see the ways I had changed. Hey, watch this." Ethan smiles a crazy grin, which makes him look as young as Danny.

He takes off toward home base, bouncing his knees high like a horse prancing. It's not a sprint, it's a lope. He'll never win a race running like that. He returns, and I hear the faint hiss of wheezing.

"I always believed," I say. His smile makes me feel so light I'm thinking of yelling it out again, even louder. I always believed.

"Not my family. They wanted to believe, but they were afraid to."

"But why?"

"Because they didn't want to be disappointed. So they held back from believing. They clung to their fear, and the hope snatchers took over."

"Ethan, how did they do that?"

"First of all, they blamed Yram for spreading false hope and started a rumor that she was a cruel fairy. That's why she can't be here and needs your help."

I shudder and look around at the empty kickball field. Zerko and

Zilla are to blame—they started this rumor.

"What can we do?" I ask. He turns his full attention to me. I feel his eyes looking into mine, but at the same time, I feel a worm in my stomach twist, and I want to take the question back.

"It's up to you to break the spell." He then answers my question before I even ask it. "No one in Forever After can see me or Yram, and besides, it's much too dangerous for Yram."

"What must I do?"

"Help my younger sister."

"You have a sister? This's different from the book."

He smiles and nods. "You know the story has hidden chapters. You're now discovering them, just like your name."

I nod.

"My sister's name is Alice."

"Like Alice in Wonderland!"

"No, she is my sister, and she lives in Forever-After land. More than anything, she wants to learn to read and not repeat third grade."

My knees collapse, and I fall to the ground. I make my legs move into crisscross sitting. I reach down and feel the grass again, look over at home base, and wish in that moment I was up to kick.

"Don't leave me yet." Ethan lowers himself next to me. I know what he means; in this world, I can be playing kickball if I give it enough thought. I turn back to him and study his beautiful face and his long boy hair. For sure, Father would call him a hippie.

With slowness so I can listen, he says, "The hope snatchers steal a person's hope. They magnify the fear and pain of disappointment, making that more real than the possibility." Now he's talking like Rob in ways that are hard to know what he means.

"But what can I do?"

"Teach Alice to read. She's given up hope."

"But, but . . ." I look at Ethan, and the terrible sadness that had covered his face disappears. He draws a deep breath.

"Maddie, you're more powerful and capable than you've ever realized."

I can't help but grin . . . these are the words Yram had said to Ethan in my favorite scene. Now I know for sure it's really him.

"I'm the strongest and fastest in my class." Saying this out loud makes my cheeks get hot, and I can tell they're turning red. It's something I don't think about too often, but maybe I will be a track star someday. "I want to see Yram. Can you tell me where she is?"

"She's hiding, working on her final creation, her magnum opus."

I love those two words! Charlotte used them to describe her masterpiece to Wilbur the pig. Magnum opus. Magnum opus. It's more fun than saying tattoo, or bingo.

Ethan's voice pulls me back. "If the spell is broken and she completes her masterpiece, she'll get her halo. But she needs your help to finish."

All I can think of is Yram's magnum opus, and I shout, "Ethan, you can count on me. Let Yram know that I'm going to break the spell."

CHAPTER 28

2 0 0 5

I ENTER THE conference room and sit across from three third-grade teachers poised to get their way. The air has a thick, anxious scent of a battle. To my right is a sweet special education teacher. *God, I'm glad I insisted that Penny be here.* Soon, at the head of table, will be Matt. Waiting, we all sit listening to the silence while mentally rehearsing our arguments.

Even with the intensity of the room, I squelch down a yawn. I blink hard and draw a deep breath, trying to ward off a bout of afternoon fatigue. Ever since therapy, I've struggled to sleep at night, and when I do sleep, my dreams wake me up. I wonder if Irene is into dream interpretation. I swear last night's is one I've had before, a long time ago. I woke experiencing a familiar haunting echo. I was being challenged to do something extraordinarily difficult. It was necessary, and only I could do it. Then I lay awake for hours trying to recall the details, to fit the pieces together.

Last week, I made a point of dropping into the resource room during Kaylee's literacy time. I needed to see for myself what her reading progress looked like. I stepped into a class of six students and Penny all doubled over in ear-splitting laughter. Within three seconds, I too began to laugh—without reason other than being captured by their hysterics. Eventually, I pulled myself out of this frenzied state and realized that Penny had read the same article I had about the newest craze in the city: people gathering for the sole purpose of laughing together to experience the therapeutic effects. Penny must have decided to create her own laughter yoga club.

In due time, Penny's arms began swinging wide to capture the students' attention. She sidestepped over to the lights and flicked them on and off a few times. "Okay, now that we're all feeling happy and good inside, let's have fun with words!"

In a flash, manila folders appeared. I circulated from student to student, smiling and high-fiving as I passed. They all have some memory of me: the one who pulled them from their classrooms to answer questions, solve puzzles, and test their academic skills. Inside the folders were lists of words. The phrase *"Read It lists"* jumped from the depths of my memory.

As I approached Kaylee, she called out, "Ms. Meyers! Can I come with you?"

That's my role. I typically pop in and snatch up one of the students to do the routine three-year reevaluation that's required. Sometimes, it's just to check in and see if the special education program is making a difference. Lately, I haven't had enough time to check in and simply visit.

Penny used a voice I never hear in SIT meetings—strong and determined—and brought her students to attention. They began to read words that I remember struggling with. The laughing exercise paid off. I saw smiles and confidence. Penny pointed to a chart with long words broken into syllables, and together she and the students read *un-der-stand-ing, in-for-ma-tion, un-pre-dict-able.* She leaned into me and whispered, "It's important they get to read words other third graders can read." She followed up with a wink.

"Ms. Meyers!" Kaylee called out. "Did you know that *tee-eye-oh-en* can't be sounded out?" She was clearly bragging to the others, and it was completely charming.

"Yes, I did happen to learn that." I smiled at her, and then turned my gaze to Penny, who grinned. "So, what sound does it have?"

Kaylee's voice was drowned out by the others all vying to be right. "It says *shun*, ending like *sun* but starting with *shine*."

Penny beamed. I was never the teacher she is, and I even had the luxury of seeing only two or three kids at a time.

Matt enters the conference room charged with things unsaid. "I'm sorry. I was ambushed by a parent." We collectively give a sigh of understanding. Something about five women waiting for the guy to get us started is a little off-putting, but I'm relieved he's here.

He settles in and makes the rounds greeting each of us, keeping a serious face but spreading a welcoming smile.

"We're here to discuss an issue with strong feelings on both sides." He pauses, glancing first to his left at Penny and me, and then to his right at the three third-grade teachers. "I think it would be helpful to begin by listing the advantages and disadvantages of having Kaylee repeat third grade." I hear a collective inhale of breath; they're all ready to do battle, but I'm on a different track.

"I disagree," I say. "I think the best way to start is to share what we hope the future holds for Kaylee." I scan the three faces, left to right, ending at the head of the table, looking at Matt. I can't tell if he's giving me the "I'm glad you're back, Dr. Mary" look, because it's been too long since I've seen it.

No one says anything, so I continue. "I know she's bright. She scored in the high average range on the IQ test I gave her. She has ambition. She wants to be an environmental scientist. She loves learning. Reading is hard, so she finds other ways to gather information—such as the Discovery Channel. My hope is that she makes it to college and beyond, and becomes a biologist or wherever her passion leads her. Most of all, that she doesn't give up."

The room is silent, and in that moment, I feel a shift. No longer does it smell like a battlefield, but rather a mixture of rain and sun, like spring—intense heat and then a shower, and all so unexpected.

"I agree," says Jan. My heart races. "Kaylee is very enthusiastic about learning. It breaks my heart watching her try so hard and still hardly able to read or write down her ideas." Jan appears the most sincere I've ever seen her. She looks directly at me and adds, "I also want her to achieve her goals and not give up."

I nod and feel a quiet urge to reach across the table and shake her hand.

"I want to see her confident and *reading*," says Donna in a clipped, sharp voice.

"I think she's happy about herself right now," says Shelby, and I notice she is more bold and perceptive than I have given her credit for. "I'd hate to see that change."

I nod and glance at Matt. The expression in his eyes gives me the go-ahead.

"Seems like we're all on the same page as far as wanting to support Kaylee in achieving her goals," I say, and they nod, but there is tension. It's all about reading.

I turn to Penny. "Do you have fourth- and fifth-grade students who read several grades below level and still participate in their classes and are not overly frustrated or wishing they had been held back?" I don't even finish, and her head is bobbing up and down loud enough for all to anticipate her response.

"Well, there's Fernando, Silas, Sandra, Terrance, and Emily. They're in fourth and fifth grade, and we work on second- and third-grade reading skills. They all have achieved so much growth, and they are such smart kids. Kaylee is making the same kind of progress."

"I see frustration with Kaylee," says Jan. "When she goes to write, she can't figure out how to spell almost any single word. I help her, but then she can't even read what I have helped her write."

"That does sound frustrating," I say. "But maybe once she gets your help and her ideas are expressed in a way others can read, she may feel so good about this that the initial frustration fades from her memory."

"I've seen many kids give up when the work is too hard," says Donna, her face still tight. "Fourth grade will be much too difficult for Kaylee." She leans back with arms crossed. I notice Shelby squirming, her cheeks red. I turn toward her, and my focus brings everyone's attention to her.

"I need to say something personal. I was retained in first grade. My birthday is at the end of July, and I just wasn't ready for second grade." I hold my breath, waiting for a testimonial about how good the decision had been. "I think my parents and teachers did what was best for me, but it took a long time for me to get over it." Her face flushes, and I hear the shakiness in her voice. "I still remember my friends all going to the next grade, but not me. It was a big issue for a very long time."

And it still is.

"Kaylee's in third grade. She'll never forget how it feels."

Matt and I exchange glances, and I know the meeting is over. Kaylee will move on to fourth grade. I stand up and hold the back of my chair to steady myself as relief courses through my body.

CHAPTER 29

1 9 6 7

"MADDIE, *Scooby-Doo*'s on." Danny knows it's the cartoon I get up for on Saturday mornings. But not today. I have *The Fairy Angel's Gift* on my lap.

"I'm sleeping in." *Oops, that's a venial sin I'll need to confess.*

"Are you sick?"

"No, I just want to rest." I hear him pad off down the hall, and then the rise and fall of TV laughter. Too bad he can't keep a secret. Having this time alone with Ethan and Yram is better than watching *Scooby-Doo*. I study the picture on the cover. Looking at her golden hair and lavender-colored wings, my favorite color, pieces of last night's dream come back to me: holding Ethan's hand, being asked to help break an evil spell, the kickball field with grass so green it didn't even look real.

I open to the first full page. It's so different from the books I check out at the library; they all have pictures and that's what I look at. I've never spent time studying a page with only words. What I notice is that all the letters start and end at the same place on each side of the page. It's as if someone first drew a square around the paper's edge and then poured letters in to fit inside, except for the paragraphs, which I know about from paying attention to Mrs. Zinc's writing lessons. My eyes float across all the small letters grouped together. There must be over a hundred different words on a single page. How in the world does Paulette, or Rob, or anyone learn to read so many words?

Then I remember what Ethan told me—hidden chapters. If a

chapter is hidden, it wouldn't start like a real chapter announcing itself. I close the book and my eyes. *Saint Rita, I know you know where the hidden chapters are. Please help me to find them.* I open the book somewhere in the middle and land my pointer finger in the center of the page.

I see a group of letters that don't make sense, the kind I usually give up on right away. But now I look carefully at each letter. Saint Rita must be helping, because I know the word *for*, and that's the first part of the word my finger is pointing to. I sound out each of the next three letters: *e-s-t*. Faster and faster I say the sounds, and all at once, I know the word: *forest*. That's a word that would never show up in one of those flat books Mrs. Zinc gives us Sparrows to read.

I begin to look for other words starting with *f-o-r*. Three pages later, I find the word *form*. I remember the word *forest* from the story because Gwendolyn lives in the Forest of Wisdom, but I don't remember Mrs. Zinc reading the word *form*. Lucky me, right next to form is the word Mom made me memorize for my spelling test last week: *change*. I read the two words together, *change form*, over and over. I set the book down and go to my window and gaze at the oak tree. *Change form* is part of a hidden chapter. Yram must be telling me that fairies like to live in the forest, and sometimes they change form.

It's almost lunchtime before I finish rubbing a rag over the furniture, doing my Saturday girl chores while my brothers get to work outside. Even as I stir up the dust from end tables and chairs, I remember Grandma O'Leary telling me that fairies are hard to see during the day because they like to stay hidden in thick woods and dense bushes, and I'm remembering such a place. It used to be my favorite hide-and-seek hideout, and it looks like a forest.

"Maddie," Danny yells just as I head toward the thick tangle of bushes Mom calls the hawthorn hedge. It's so dense with sticks and weeds, even Danny can't crawl in deep enough to hide, but it's perfect for a fairy. If I were a fairy, I'd think of it as a forest.

"What?" I say, trying to ignore him.

"Where're ya going?"

"Nowhere. Just exploring." I hear him shuffling behind me.

"Can I come?" I turn toward him. His pudgy face holds a serious look. I glance down and see he's wearing his cowboy boots on the wrong feet. "Jack and Rob are working on the go-cart. They won't let me help."

"I'm not doing anything you'd be interested in doing."

"Like what?"

"I'm checking something out." I start moving toward the hideout.

"Can I help?"

"Well, you don't believe, and I plan on seeing if the fairy I saw the other night lives in our old hiding place. And since you don't believe in fairies, you'll only make things worse."

"I didn't say that. Dad said they're not real, and so did Rob. But I might believe."

"It'll be boring because all I'm going to do is sit and watch. And you'll have to be quiet the whole time."

"I can do that."

I knew the hedge was overgrown with grasses and pokey sticks, but I'm not ready to meet the spiderwebs crisscrossing this way and that. I shudder, and Danny steps forward with a stick whacking the webs away. Frogs and lizards are fun to play with, and I don't even mind pulling a leach off my legs after swimming in the lake, but spiders always give me the creeps. I wonder as I watch them scatter if one or more of those spiders might be as wise as Gwendolyn.

I crawl in first, and Danny squishes in beside me. Both of us wrap our arms around our legs and touch our chins to our knees. I have a view of Big Pine Lake and make myself not think of the many spiders inches from my back, crawling around in the thicket.

Danny surprises me by being as quiet as I am. I feel his elbow next to my thigh and hear him breathing. Soon the buzzing of mosquitoes presses against my ears. I feel my right leg start to go numb with pin-pricks. I shift my weight off my leg, and all at once, a dragonfly the size of a hummingbird flies toward us and lands six inches smack in front of my face on a stick. Its wings are lavender and its body a deep purple. I'm breathless. After what seems like longer than I can hold my breath, I glance at Danny, and he too has fixed his eyes on the incredibly large dragonfly.

"Danny," I whisper, "that's a fairy in disguise. They do that. They can change form. It's in a hidden chapter." *I read it.*

The dragonfly leaves the stick and begins to fly in large careless circles around the hedge. Danny stays frozen, just the way Mrs. Zinc likes us to sit. I creep up, move toward the oak tree in front of my bedroom window, and wait. Sure enough, the dragonfly notices me, and flies over, landing within reach. I hold out my hand, certain it will come to me, and it almost does before flying away.

I turn to Danny, who has also crawled out from the thicket and is facing me, his lower jaw dropping open.

"Now do you believe me?"

"Maddie, how do you know that wasn't just an extra-special dragonfly?"

"Number one, dragonflies hardly ever leave the lake to come up here. Two, they're never this big or that color—purple and laven-der, the colors Yram chose to wear, you know that. And three, it fol-lowed me to the oak tree. It knows I believe in fairies. I've seen fairies flying outside that window," I say, motioning to my bedroom window, "almost every night." I sigh, look him in the eye. "That was a fairy in disguise."

"Wow," he says, and I can tell he's finally beginning to believe.

"Danny, I think we need to keep this our secret."

"Why?"

"Because when other people don't believe in fairies, and we listen to them tell us they don't believe, then it's harder to see the fairies ourselves."

"Oh."

We pause at hearing the sound of Uncle Joe's Chevy. It roars down our dirt driveway leaving a cloud of dust behind it.

"Uncle Joe's home," Danny says before racing over to greet him.

I hang back, looking at the tree in front of my window and the bramble bush within six or seven big steps. In my head, I repeat the words, *change form*, words I'm sure were never read by Mrs. Zinc. This had to be part of a hidden chapter.

I look over and see Uncle Joe give Danny a tickle. He must have said something about the corny boots, because Danny plops down to the ground and begins pulling them off and switching them over.

"Hey, Sister Bard," Uncle Joe calls out, waving his hand at me and taking a few steps in my direction, "whatcha up to?" Before I can answer, Danny blabs.

"Guess what. Maddie and I saw a huge dragonfly that we think might really be a fairy. She read that some fairies . . . what'd you say, Maddie?"

I try to give him the look Mom gives when he's talking too much, but it doesn't work. Danny's eyes are on Uncle Joe, who now turns to me.

"I said they change form."

"The huge purple dragonfly followed her over to the oak tree," says Danny.

"Is that so?" Uncle Joe asks.

"Yeah," Danny continues. "I'm not sure if I believe in fairies, but Maddie does."

I turn and look toward the lake, thinking how nice it would be to break out running for the rope swing.

"I believe in fairies," says Uncle Joe. I turn back around to see if he's teasing me. If he is, I can't tell.

"Really?" Danny asks.

"Well, sure. Just because they're good at hiding doesn't mean they don't exist."

"Grandma O'Leary said she saw one," I say.

"There you go."

Danny looks up, tilting his head at Uncle Joe, who smiles brightly. "Dad and Rob don't believe in fairies. I'm not so sure." Danny pauses and then turns toward the garage where Rob and Jack are walking out and heading toward the house. Without another word, he trots off toward them, leaving me alone with Uncle Joe. I notice Uncle Joe's shirt has big wet patches.

"Uncle Joe, you're all sweaty."

"What do you think? I've been swinging a hammer on a rooftop for the last couple of hours." He smiles at me, and I notice how the sun shines off his damp forehead. "You sure don't want to end up like your Uncle Joe, getting all sweaty for a living."

"I don't know. It'd be a lot more fun up on a roof hammering than having to dust furniture like I do every Saturday morning. I like working outside."

"Well, Sister Bard, believe me, it could be worse. I feel bad for the boss's son." His smile drifts off his face; he's now looking out toward the lake. I do too, and notice how blue and beautiful it is. I'm sure a lavender-winged dragonfly would never come up here unless it were a fairy. "He's about your age, dark hair, crew cut. I think his name is Bobby. Do you know him?"

"Bobby Wallace? He lives where you work?"

"Why, his dad is the boss. Tough son of a bi—gun. I feel bad for the kid. He was on site by seven thirty in the morning with a pail in his hand, picking up nails. His father was boasting how he makes Bobby spend Saturdays finding and straightening out the bent nails so they can be used again—the cheapskate."

"That's not the Bobby I know. He's always bragging about going fishing with his dad every weekend."

"Well, the only fishing he does is for nails. Poor kid. He gets yelled at plenty too. Just before break, he missed and hammered his finger, and he let out a big holler. His father turns to him, takes one look, and says, 'That was a stupid thing to do.' Then he turns to me and says, in front of the kid, 'He ain't that smart.' I tell ya, I almost had a few words for the bast—uh, boss. Wouldn't have hesitated if it weren't for the fact that I need a paycheck."

It couldn't be Bobby Wallace. Bobby's not stupid; he's an Eagle. It must be a different kid.

"Let's go see if we can find us some lunch," Uncle Joe says as he walks toward the house.

CHAPTER 30

1 9 6 7

I'M SITTING with my back to the thicket of weeds where Danny and I had squeezed in earlier, and I'm looking out at the lake. I'm hoping that fairy in disguise will come back. I glance over at the oak tree in front of my bedroom window and notice the leaves have grown. Even though Mom says it can still snow in the first part of May, today feels like it won't be long before school is over and summer will be here. My stomach twists at this thought. Will I be going to fourth grade?

I jump up and race down toward the lake and the rope swing. I hear steps behind me and see Danny chasing after me. I ignore him, grab the rope, stampede across the dirt ridge, plunge myself over the hill, and imagine myself flying high with Yram.

Out of breath, I flop down on the hillside. Danny sits next to me.

"Danny, I've discovered there are other chapters in *The Fairy Angel's Gift* that Mrs. Zinc didn't know about."

"But what about the ending?"

"I told you it was happy, but the story's not over."

"What do you mean?"

"Well, in my dream last night, Ethan spoke to me."

"But dreams aren't real."

"How do you know? Maybe they are and we just forget about them. But I remember mine. And I met with Ethan." I want to tell Danny about why I was chosen to break the spell, but I can't trust him to keep a secret.

"Maddie, this is weird, and it's making me scared because when I have a nightmare, Mom always says dreams aren't real."

"You don't have to believe dreams are real. But I do know that the story has hidden chapters, and I can tell you about them. This is how I knew today that fairies change form. But it might just be too scary for you." I pull up a dandelion and pluck the yellow petals off, tossing them in the light breeze.

"You know I'm not afraid. Tell me." He grabs a small stone and flings it down the hill.

"Ethan did get better, and when his family began to believe, something terrible happened. While they slept one night, it got thick and foggy outside, but it wasn't just the weather, it was the attack of hope snatchers."

Danny's eyes grow wide, and I know I have him.

"What do hope snatchers look like?"

"They can't be seen, otherwise it would be easy to get rid of them. They're like the sandman—invisible. But instead of sprinkling sand in your eyes to make you sleepy, they sprinkle fear and worry in people's eyes. This makes them stop believing in what they think might be possible."

"Maddie, you don't believe in the sandman do you?"

This makes me giggle. "Of course not! But I might believe in hope snatchers. They took over the entire land of Forever After, where Ethan lives. He lives there with his parents and a sister named Alice, but not Alice in Wonderland."

"I didn't know he had a sister."

"That's because it's in the hidden chapters."

"Where's Yram?"

"Well, remember Zerko and Zilla, the mean cousins?"

"Yeah, they started the rumor."

"The hope snatchers kept the rumor going, and soon it was impossible for Yram to help anyone in Forever After because they didn't believe she was a good fairy. So she needed to find someone to help who didn't belong to that town and didn't get sick from the poison smog."

Danny looks up at me, waiting. I'm not sure what to say next. He doesn't think dreams are real, and my dream is as real as this very moment.

"Yram asked Ethan to find someone to help, someone who believes in fairies and believes he really did get better."

"Who?"

I look at him and wish he were two years older and my sister. I've always wanted a sister. I need to think fast.

"They chose a girl named Mary."

"That's your real name."

"Right. It's a name lots of girls have. That's why I go by Madelyn." This isn't a lie. It's the truth. I smile because now I know I can keep telling my dream.

"Maddie, tell me more about the hope snatchers."

"Like I said, they're invisible, and remember, Gwendolyn told Yram they act like they care, but they really snatch hope away."

"Why would they do that?"

"Ethan said it's because sometimes when you care about someone, you don't want them to get disappointed. The hope snatchers figured out that if people no longer hoped for good things to happen, they wouldn't ever get disappointed. They also make everyone worry too much."

"Like Dad worrying about Rob going out for track?" Danny's right. I hadn't even thought of this.

"Yeah, because Father is worried, it's not possible for Rob to do well, that he might have breathing problems, and that's what happened to Ethan. His parents didn't believe he really could do the things Yram showed him."

We both sit quietly for a few moments listening to a flock of starlings overhead. It's a lot to think about.

"The hope snatchers live in the land of Forever After." I pause, waiting for Danny to look at me, and then add, "Not here. They cast a spell on the land, making it hard for everyone to see what's possible. Ethan is the only one who didn't get fear put in his eyes. Yram protected him. But because of the spell, no one can see him. And Alice, his sister, has lost hope."

"About what?"

"She no longer believes she can do well in school."

"Why not?"

"I told you. The hope snatchers."

"But what do you mean 'do well'?"

"She's smart like Ethan, but for some reason, she's taking a long time learning to read."

"Oh." Danny looks at me without saying anything, and I'm so glad he doesn't understand about Sparrows.

"You see . . . Alice has a father who's under the spell of the hope snatchers. His hope is that she does as well in school as her classmates and that she learns to read. If she doesn't, she might flunk."

"That's awful. I'd hate to flunk."

"But now her father is so afraid she'll never learn to read, he has given up hope and never even listens to her try. He's always correcting her spelling and giving her the look that something is wrong."

"What's going to happen?"

"Remember I told you that Ethan and Yram chose a girl named Mary who believes in fairies to help break the spell?"

"Oh yeah, but you didn't tell me why she was chosen."

"It's because Yram knew she liked to read words backward."

"Why would anyone want to do that?"

"Because it's fun. Did you know that the word *dog* read backward becomes the word *god*?"

Danny rolls his eyes upward, and I can tell by the movement of his lips that he is seeing and reading those two words in his mind. "You're right! That's really neat."

"Well, this girl happened to notice something special about her name and Yram's name." I grab a stick and motion him over to the packed dirt ridge. I write my name and copy it backward. I then point to Yram's name. "This happens to be how Yram spells her name."

"Neato!" he yells.

"It's neat all right, and Yram thought so too. That's why Mary was asked to help."

Danny looks up at me with a serious face. "So, how in the world will Mary break the spell?"

"You'll have to wait until next time when I tell more."

I like going to bed early these days, now that I have Yram to look forward to. Once Mom kisses me good night, I squirm around and peer up at the wall behind my bed. With only the night-light on, the dream catcher is hard to see; I have to squint to tell where it ends and the wallpaper begins. I know Grandma O'Leary would have called my dream catcher marvelous.

I pull *The Fairy Angel's Gift* out, study Yram's picture on the front, and open the book up somewhere in the middle. I close my eyes and pick a spot with my finger. Carefully, I look at all the words around my finger and right away I see one I know: *help*. It has a period next to it, so I back my finger up to the beginning of the sentence and read, "I need your help." That's what Yram had told Ethan.

I close my eyes and see Ethan, and he has the same message for me: "Yram needs your help. You know the secret of her name."

CHAPTER 31

I 9 6 7

THE RECESS BELL rings, and I can't wait to slug the tetherball. I hate when math is spoiled by words that make it impossible for me to do it without Paulette's help.

"Madelyn, you know this word. All you have to do is sound it out."

"*Wu-at.*"

"No! It's *what.*"

"Paulette," I whispered, "you don't need to shout it."

"Why can't you remember?" she asked, still using a loud voice. I shrugged my shoulders.

I'm first to reach the tetherball line. I grab the ball, ready to take on whoever steps up. It's Bobby. I forgot to watch where he went. If I had seen him before grabbing the ball, I would have changed my mind; he's such a sore loser, but here I am facing him. He rolls his eyes and turns slightly away. I can tell he also would have planned differently if he knew I was who he had to play against, because I can easily whip him.

I eye the ball resting in my left hand, make a fist, and prepare to slug it my hardest. I glance over at Bobby. He's ready to hit back, and I notice a fat Band-Aid with gauze wrapped around his finger. I missed seeing it this morning when I passed by his desk, but now it stares back at me, big and ugly.

I smack the ball hard and it wraps three times around the pole before I remember where I am. Uncle Joe really must have been talking about Bobby.

The ball begins its tight, fast circling. I blink hard, step in closer, and begin clobbering it with all my might, making it arc out of reach each time. Bobby is jumping and swinging, and he looks funny, like a puppet. The ball is wrapping tightly around in my direction; he doesn't move in fast enough to stop it. One more blow will surely finish him off, but for some reason I don't step in and give that final blow. The ball slows down, and Bobby catches it in time to turn it around. I step back and watch him bring it to a tight wrap in his direction. I see his face change from a cartoon-screaming look to his usual slight smile. He wins but doesn't brag. I walk away.

How could his father think he's stupid?

I bend down, pretending to get papers out of my desk, and peek at Mrs. Zinc's messy stack on the floor next to her desk. It looks the same minus *The Fairy Angel's Gift*. Now I can settle into work.

"Madelyn," Paulette whispers, loud enough for Ricky and Tommy sitting behind us to hear. "It's time for you to get your extra reading help."

I'm busy copying words from my grammar book onto lined paper. I don't want to bring it home for homework or Mom will try to make me read the words. I ignore Paulette.

"Madelyn." I look up and see fat Mrs. Ellen taking up the entire doorway. Paulette made me tell her where I really went last week, and now I wish I had lied. I'm the only Sparrow who has to leave class and go into a closet for an extra reading lesson. I slam shut my grammar book a little too loud; Mrs. Zinc puts her finger to her lips. She'd have made a good librarian, always hush-hushing everyone. I don't want to go, so I'm slow to get up.

"Madelyn." Mrs. Zinc's quiet voice booms through the classroom. Everyone turns to face me like I'm in trouble or something. I've waited too long to get out the door, and now they all know it wasn't just to go help Mr. Griffin. I shove my unfinished work into my desk and shuffle toward the hall. I pass Bobby and notice he is all done with his grammar assignment and is now trying to finish the math page from this morning. This makes me feel good. Maybe I am better at math than he is. But he's watching carefully, and I know he'll find out why I'm leaving class.

I keep my head down while walking out, pretending I don't know Mrs. Ellen. But as soon as the classroom door shuts, she's acting all excited to see me, as if she missed me or something. Once I brought *The Fairy Angel's Gift* home, I completely forgot about her.

I follow four steps behind until we reach the closet next to the PE storage room. Maybe Mr. Griffin will need to take more things out and make lots of noise. This hope makes it easier to slide into the chair Mrs. Ellen pulls out for me. I watch Mrs. Ellen squeeze around the table and into her own chair and then grin wildly.

Why am I here?

"We're in for a treat. We're going to play word bingo." She places a plastic grid filled with words and a stack of word cards in front of me. I don't like bingo. It's boring, and I always lose.

"Here, Madelyn. All you need to do is place a card in each space. Don't worry about reading words, just listen carefully while I read them."

I hear a little noise next door. *It's Mr. Griffin!* Maybe it's loud enough for her to hear.

"Mrs. Ellen, I think I hear Mr. Griffin."

"Hmm, maybe. He's not being too loud today."

"But maybe he still needs my help."

"Madelyn, I think Mr. Griffin can manage today without your help. Do you want to learn to read?"

I hate this question. I want to get out of the closet. I turn away. I don't know her rules about pulling up my hood, but I decide to pull it up anyway. I'm not sure what to do next. It's quiet. If I run out, that'll only make Mrs. Zinc mad, but I'm certain I can outrun Mrs. Ellen.

"I think if you give it a try, you'll like this game. And it'll help you with reading. You're a smart girl, and I bet more than anything you do want to get good at reading." This reminds me of what Ethan said about his younger sister, Alice, how she forgot because of the spell, forgot that reading is what she wanted to learn more than anything, but I make myself stop thinking about this. It's too sad. I turn back toward Mrs. Ellen and keep my hood up; she doesn't seem to mind.

"I can read some words." *I'd like to read more.* I'm so glad she doesn't say anything—she just smiles—and her smile is different from Mrs. Zinc's. I like her smile.

Mrs. Ellen begins to say one of the words on the grid, but I don't know which one it is. She says it slowly, the way I sometimes sound out words. I've never heard a teacher do that before. Usually they say the word so fast that I don't hear letter sounds. I begin to wonder if Mrs. Ellen is different.

"*Lli-i-ft.*"

I know it starts with the letter *l*, but that next sound . . . I can't remember if that sound is for the letter *e* or *i*. To me, both these letters mostly sound the same. Mrs. Ellen seems to read my mind and says the key word for letter *i*: "*Igloo, ih.*"

The game is easy and sort of fun. All I have to do is figure out what word it is that Mrs. Ellen says and then put a marker on it. If I'm wrong, she gets to put her marker down. This is a very different way to play bingo. And a very different way for teachers to say words—slowly, making it possible for me to figure them out. I just don't like being the only kid in my class who has to see Mrs. Ellen.

I try to slip back to my desk without anyone noticing, but it's impossible. Everyone is working on a writing assignment, and Mrs. Zinc makes sure the class is quiet. I peek in the door, and because Bobby sits next to the door, he looks right up at me. I know he's wondering why I'm not at my desk working.

"Madelyn, we're supposed to rewrite each of these sentences so that they make sense and have the right punctuation," Paulette says.

I look at the blue ditto worksheet full of words I can't read. I'd rather be doing math, but Mrs. Zinc doesn't allow it. Then I think, all I need to do is copy a few and that'll satisfy Mrs. Zinc. It's how I always handle these dittos. I look over at Bobby. He's writing fast. I start to copy down the letters and then stop. Things are different now. I'm reading words from *The Fairy Angel's Gift*. I learned new words with Mrs. Ellen. And if I don't try harder, I'll flunk third grade, something Paulette and Bobby have no idea about.

CHAPTER 32

1 9 6 7

THE FIRST THING I do after getting home from school is shut my bedroom door and bring out *The Fairy Angel's Gift*. I've been waiting all day for this. Every time I close and open the book, landing my finger somewhere in the middle of the page, I find something important to read. The word my finger lands on now is big, seven letters, and it looks impossible to figure out. I start by saying the sounds of the first two letters: *dee. Deeliiive*. I've never heard of *delive*. I notice a period after it, so I move my finger to the beginning of the sentence. *Saint Rita! I know these words*. I don't even have to sound them out: "Come with me, all you have to do is," and now I know the last word, "believe." It's from my favorite scene! Of all the sentences in this entire book, my finger has brought me here.

I spring up and grab the picture pinned to my bedroom door, with the letter *b* and the leaf, because now I can write the word the way Father wants me to. I find a black crayon and write out *d-e-l-e-i-v-e* under her picture. I pin it back up, and I'm ready to look for fairies.

I slip out of my room, happy that Danny doesn't notice, and head for the hiding place where I had seen the fairy in disguise. Parting the bramble with a stick, I clear a spot to squeeze in and crouch down on my knees. Soon I hear Father's car pull into the driveway. I listen to his heavy steps move toward the house. He doesn't even see me, and this makes me think that I can be a spy. At school, everyone notices me even though I try to not to be noticed. I keep a lookout for something small flying through the air. My legs begin to ache, and soon I hear the roar of Uncle Joe's truck. I've spent enough time watching for a fairy.

Uncle Joe lifts one leg out at a time. He stands and stretches next to the truck. When he sees me, he grins and reaches his arms out in front. I rush up and give him a hug.

"Hi, Uncle Joe."

"Hi, Sister Bard, whatcha up to?"

"Nothing much."

"Hey, maybe you can help me out with this." He reaches into his shirt pocket, the same one with his cigarettes, and pulls out a piece of newspaper. "A buddy of mine at the work site gave this to me. It's a job announcement for something a little more up my alley. The print is so small I can't make it out. I need a pair of reading glasses."

"You have glasses?"

"Like I said, I need a pair. But your eyes are young. I'm sure you'd have no problem at all reading this one here." He points to a paragraph with a circle around it. I glance up at him and he nods.

I think of all the words I've been reading and decide for sure I will be able to figure out a few. Maybe enough to make sense. Uncle Joe's right; it is little print. The first line of words has so many letters thrown together—I have no idea how to begin to sound them out.

"Oh, I see what you mean, it's written small. I think I might also need glasses." I pull the newspaper clipping close to my face, then move it out away and look closely at the letters. Several groups come together. "This word here is big enough to see. I think I know it, it says—"

"Madelyn."

I startle and look up. Father is striding toward us. "What's wrong?"

"Your mother needs your help inside."

I look back down at the paper. I'm able to make out three words.

I start to say them, but Father reaches for the paper before I can say anything. "Dad, I'm just going to read it for Uncle Joe."

"Uncle Joe doesn't need your help." He looks angrily at Uncle Joe. "But your mother does. Now go on in."

I stand still, looking at him, trying to figure out what I did wrong. He holds the paper like it has something bad written on it. I feel my tears about to burst out. It's his loud voice. I turn and race toward the house.

Mom is stirring something over the stove that smells good. "Mom." I catch my breath. "Father says you need my help." I'm able to keep the tears in, but my voice is all shaky.

"What's wrong, sweetie?"

"He yelled at me for no reason," I say. Mom turns away from her cooking and looks at me. "Uncle Joe asked me to read something for him because he needs glasses."

"Hmm, is that so?" A slight smile forms on her face.

"I'm getting better at reading, Mom. I've been practicing, and I was just about to read some of the words, and then Father yelled at me that you needed my help."

"Maddie, honey, I think your father was worried that you might feel awkward or upset trying to read something for Uncle Joe if it was too hard."

"He didn't have to yell at me. Besides, I knew some of the words. I saw *car-sales-man*."

"Honey, it's just that he loves you so much he didn't want you to be embarrassed about not reading *all* of the words. And I can always use some help setting the table."

"But he could have let me read some of it. I am getting better." I count out seven plates and arrange them around the table with silverware. I peek out of the kitchen window and see Uncle Joe and Father still talking, but it looks like arguing.

"How much longer?"

"About ten more minutes. The boys are playing down at the lake. Why don't you let them know?"

"Okay."

I go out the back door but find myself drawn toward the voices at the front of the house. I inch closer and hear Uncle Joe, but it doesn't sound at all like him—it sounds harsh and angry.

"What do you mean she can't read? She's in third grade."

I fall back against the house. I know it's Uncle Joe, but he has Father's angry voice. I want to tell him it's not true, I can read, but my body doesn't move. It melts into the wood siding.

"Joe, you don't understand. Something's wrong."

No! I scream the word inside my head. I'm ready to run off, but my legs are collapsing. I feel dizzy and wonder if this is a dream.

"Then you've got to do something about it."

Is this Uncle Joe or Father?

"Don't they have special classes or something these days for kids who can't read?"

Does he mean me?

"I mean—she's no dumbass like me. You don't want her to drop out."

Finally, my body snaps into action. I take off running down the hill toward the lake where Jack and Danny are throwing stones. I'm breathing too hard to call out to them for dinner. I crumple on the hillside next to the rope swing. I cover my ears and shut my eyes. If only I had read the words faster and showed them both that I can read.

"Maddie." Rob stands on the stairs leading down to the lake. "Are you hurt?"

"No. I mean yes, but I'll be okay."

"It's time for dinner, did you tell Jack and Danny?"

"No," I mumble. He takes several steps down the hill and yells out to them. He comes over and holds out his hand. At first, I don't know what he's doing, and then I understand, and the warmth of his hand helps me get up.

CHAPTER 33

2 0 0 5

IT'S EIGHT THIRTY when I pull into Milton's gated parking lot, and I navigate around tight corners, knowing I'll be lucky to find a spot. I'm used to arriving at seven forty-five, in time for an eight o'clock meeting, avoiding the bulk of teachers and staff. I squeeze my Mazda in between a couple of Subarus, feeling so relieved to have time to myself before stepping into consultation mode or facilitating a meeting. It's a godsend no SIT meeting is scheduled this morning.

I decide to walk around to the back of the building, avoiding the main office swarming with teachers and parents, and enter through the door by the playground. I notice a few kids hanging on bars and punching the tetherball, waiting for the morning bell to ring. Recess was a favorite time for me. It thrills me that more than three decades later, schools still have tetherballs and bars. I'm not so happy that teachers continue to insist upon students copying words from what's now a whiteboard.

I unlock the double-paned door and look down a long stretch of hall with lemon-yellow and gray tiles glistening in the bath of fluorescent light. I pause in the doorway of Room 11, and spy Kelly's lush dark curls spilling over her shoulders as she peers into her computer screen. I proceed down the hall to my small windowless box of an office.

Up ahead, someone is waiting for me. I slow down, considering an about-face out of the building, hoping whoever wants to talk will come back later, giving me the quiet morning I've anticipated. I amble forward and recognize the short, small-featured frame. It's Diane Adams, Grace's mom.

She spots me and waves with a smile. Her light-blondish hair is tucked behind her ears, and a small shiny patch on her forehead catches the light in an interesting, welcoming way. I've wanted to ask her how Grace is doing in the gifted program. Even though Diane works within earshot down the hall, we're both so busy racing from kid to kid to meetings, we rarely have a chance to catch up.

"Hi, Diane," I call out. "Hey, I've been meaning to ask you for months how Grace is doing."

I love that, despite everything, this child's overall brilliance is recognized. Late last spring, Geraldine Bronson, supervisor for the highly capable program, invited me to join the final round with the selection committee. Evidently, the director of special services made it clear they needed a psychologist on board. Among the candidates being considered for the district's gifted program was Grace. Her verbal, visual-spatial, and creativity aptitudes soared above all the other candidates. Their concern: weak reading and writing scores. I reminded them that she has a disability, and as a federally funded program, there can be no discrimination. Grace is an example of double exceptionality: she is gifted and dyslexic. They'd need to make accommodations.

Standing in front of Diane, it occurs to me she most likely has not placed herself on my office stoop anticipating my desire for an update about Grace.

"Actually, Grace is why I was hoping to see you this morning." She doesn't have the usual sparkle in her eyes. "Dr. Meyers."

"Diane, really, just call me Mary."

She rolls her eyes. It's an ongoing feud. I open the door and motion for her to enter my office.

"Dr. Meyers," she starts in again, earnestly, and settles down into an elementary-sized school chair. She looks more serious than I'm used to seeing her. Diane is one of the most upbeat people I know. "Do you have a few minutes?"

"Sure do." I take a seat across from her, also in a child-sized chair. "So, what's up?"

"Grace is struggling in the gifted program. It's breaking my heart, her taking it all so seriously and . . . it's not working."

"Not working?" My voice is thin and frail. I feel something inside me start to crumble.

Diane nods. "She thinks she doesn't fit in, and I don't blame her."

Please, no, I plead to a long-forgotten saint. I tighten my stomach, not wanting to hear what Diane is about to say.

"She's frustrated trying to get her ideas down on paper. Her spelling's so atrocious, she can barely read what she writes."

"But . . ." I try to protest. *They know she has dyslexia.*

"The books they assign are all beyond her reading level, and she's spending every second of free time trying to show that she's as good as the others." Diane sighs. "It's so painful to watch. She rarely lets me help her."

I see Grace's determined face boring into a page of words, trying desperately to unlock the meaning. She's much smarter than I ever was. She has every right to be in a gifted program.

"Does . . . does she want to continue in the program? I mean, she wants to, doesn't she?"

"You know Grace, she never gives up."

"Right. She's very determined."

"But it's tearing her apart. I'm not sure what to do. I think she'd be better off back in the regular program." Diane gives me a pleading look. *Oh God, Grace needs to know what she's capable of, that someone does understand.*

"Dr. Meyers," Diane says. I look up, and blink away the wetness that has filled my eyes. "It's not that bad. Really, it's just, I'm wanting to make a plan for next year—are you okay?"

I stand up and grab a tissue. "It's allergies. Spring. Have you talked with—"

"Geraldine, yes. Her only response was this is how we do things. Grace does well with the class discussions. She's good at answering questions."

Dammit all. I'll go talk to her myself. "Do you mind if I talk with her teachers?"

"I don't think it'll do any good. Grace hates to be isolated. In fact, she doesn't want to go to the resource room anymore."

My heart speeds up. "Would you like me to talk with her?" I whisper.

"I know how busy you are, but yes. I'm her mother. She no longer listens when I tell her how smart she is. All she knows is that she doesn't fit in with the other gifted kids."

I can tell her otherwise. I can share that it's possible to move beyond this. For a blessed moment, I'm at complete peace with the prospect of sharing the truth about myself with Grace. More than at peace, the bright aura of rebirth flirts with me. Grace would understand.

I breathe in deeply, and in my mind I see an image of a nine-year-old with bangs and hair chopped just below the ears. She's smiling. I shake my head and gaze back at Diane, who now has the sparkle back in her eye.

"I know you'll say the right things to her." The possibilities of what I might share with this child practically bring me to tears, and I nod in agreement.

Diane glances at her watch. "Oh my gosh. I told Kelly I'd show up early to set up a new workstation."

She rises out of her child-sized chair, and reality slaps me silly.

Of course, anything I say to Grace about myself will be shared with her mother. And from there with Kelly. And after that, it might as well be the entire school district. Never again will I be able to walk down the halls without wondering who knows the truth: I'm a Sparrow in disguise.

"Diane," I call out. My heart is now beating like a flock of captured geese. I'm standing up, and I'm wondering if I moved too fast as I need to sit down before I faint.

"Dr. Meyers?" She looks concerned.

I swivel my adult-sized office chair around and collapse into it. "I may have spoken too soon. I'll try and see Grace, but . . ." I motion behind me to the stack of file folders next to the computer monitor on my desk. "Spring is always the busiest time for me." *What in God's name was I thinking?*

"Thank you so much," Diane says, as if she did not heard my last two sentences. "I understand how busy you are. I really appreciate this." I do my best to form a smile, and my stomach begins to twist.

"Diane, you're an incredible parent. Grace is lucky to have you."

"And sometimes it takes a village."

I make an effort to smile back, ignoring the ache in my heart. I can't give Grace what she needs.

CHAPTER 34

1 9 6 7

"I KNOW YRAM," *Alice says as she turns away from me toward the sink to start the dish water. I step closer; she looks familiar. She faces back to me. "We all know about her. She's known as the cruel fairy."*

"That's not true!" I shout back.

"Yes, it is. She does things that make children get in trouble with their parents."

I stare at her. I don't like her. "You're wrong. That's a rumor. Yram only does good." I run out of the kitchen to the dining room and look for Ethan. The air is thick and damp, puffing dread into my lungs. I see a shadow and think of the hope snatchers. Maybe they aren't invisible. I start to race across the room, but I can hardly move. The shadow lifts from the floor and shapes into a human body. I can't help but look, and when I do, he sprinkles dust in my eyes, and I know for sure: I'm just like Alice. I can't read, I'm not smart, and I too will flunk.

"Madelyn, what's wrong? Why aren't you getting started?" Paulette asks. She's halfway done writing the stupid sentences from the chalkboard. I wish I could have stayed in bed all day like Ethan. Last night's dream fills my mind. I can't read the book, and I can't read any of these words. I look over at Paulette. *Can she see that I'm going to flunk?* "You need to try first and then I'll help," she says.

"I am. I'm just tired, that's all." I stare down at the empty paper.

All I need to do is to get at least one sentence written down.

I sit up and begin copying the letters: *uncledob cameto visitus lastnight*. This is an easy one to fix. I cross out the first letter and write *U* and then put a period at the end. Paulette leans over and looks at my paper.

"Madelyn, that's supposed to be a *b* not a *d*. It's *Uncle Bob*, so you need to make the *b* capital too."

Hmm. If I had known that word was uncle, *I could have figured that out on my own.* I write the next line, letter by letter. It doesn't matter to me what the letters say; it's something stupid. I move my body to block Paulette from seeing my work and telling me how to do it right, because I really don't care.

I'm so happy to be resting my head against the bus window with nothing to do except wait to be dropped off at home, where I will see if I can find another hidden chapter with a few words I can read. Today was long and boring. I would have liked to see Mrs. Ellen. She's so different from Mrs. Zinc. My head vibrates against the window, and the bus noise of voices and clanking blends together. Suddenly, I'm hearing Uncle Joe telling my father something about having special teachers for kids who can't read. I yank my head off the window and sit up straight. *That must be why I'm sent to Mrs. Ellen. I'm someone who can't read.*

I'm slow getting off the bus. Jack and Rob are walking together, talking about the go-cart Uncle Joe is helping them with.

Danny hangs back with me. "I can tell you don't want to race."

"That's right. I don't feel like it."

"Can you tell me more from the hidden chapters, how Mary breaks the spell?"

I fall into step with him, and before I even think about it, I respond.

"First of all, remember, Mary's good at reading."

"Of course. Anyone who can read backwards must be good."

"That's right. So she thought it would be pretty easy to break the spell. All she needs to do is teach Alice—who is not in Wonderland—to read. Besides, Mary likes to teach other kids. She's even thinking she might be a teacher someday. Not a bossy one, like her friend Paulette, or my teacher Mrs. Zinc, who is sometimes crabby, but a fun one who teaches kids who need help with reading. So anyway, to her, this seems easy." I take a deep breath. Danny looks wide-eyed, believing all of this. "But she had no idea how tricky and creepy the hope snatchers were. This part is scary. Are you sure you want to hear it?" I slow down my walking, letting Jack and Rob get further ahead.

"Of course. I don't ever get scared."

"Okay." I want to say that it's a nightmare, but Danny will just argue about dreams not being real. "Mary tells Alice—"

"Who's not in Wonderland." Danny grins.

"Danny, don't interrupt. Are you sure you want to hear?" I ask. He nods, so I continue. "Mary says to Alice that she knows all about Ethan, that he's invisible because of the spell, and she knows how to break it. She's sure Alice will trust her. But instead, Alice argues and says, 'Ethan's invisible because Yram made him that way.' She then repeats the rumor—do you remember the rumor?"

"Yeah, it's what Zerko and Zilla said, that she's a cruel fairy."

"Well, Alice believes this because of the spell. She also believes she can never get better with reading because she thinks she's not smart. And this is what makes the hope snatchers feel like they're in charge. When Mary tries to tell her none of this is true, that Yram is a good fairy, Alice won't believe her, and Mary gets upset and loses her temper. She decides to leave and go talk to Ethan about this. And that's when it gets all scary." I pause and get my thoughts together. I shiver, remembering how scary it was in my dream.

"Okay, I'm ready to hear about it."

I stop walking, take a deep breath, and allow the nightmare to come back. "She's mad, so she starts to run out, and all of a sudden, she feels cold air and pinpricks on her skin. She grabs her coat."

"She wears a coat like you?"

"Yep. Lots of kids do. So she stops and pulls her hood up. It gets all dark, but the darkness is really a huge shadow that has fallen over her, and even though she wants to run out, she can't move. She stands and looks at the shadow, and it turns into the shape of a man. She stares at him, and his eyes are emerald green. She looks inside them, and it's really a hope snatcher. He sprinkles dust into her eyes, and all at once, she forgets how smart she is. All she remembers is when she was little and made lots of reading mistakes."

"Oh no. Now she can't save Alice."

"That's right. She isn't sure she can even pass third grade. She thinks there might be something wrong with her." I sigh and feel my body grow heavy. Danny is looking at me. I look back and say, "That's all for now."

"Can't you tell me a little more?"

"No. Remember, this is coming from the hidden chapters, and it may not have a happy ending."

CHAPTER 35

1 9 6 7

"SO, WHAT DID everyone learn in school today?" Father asks as he piles sloppy joe meat on an open hamburger bun, making it all soggy. I wish we'd just have regular hamburgers.

As usual, Jack shows off. "I got another A on my spelling test today. It was easy. I even got the bonus word—it was *Minnesota*."

"I bet I can spell *Minnesota*," says Danny. "*M-i-n-a-s-o-t-a*."

"Wrong," says Jack.

"But that was really close," Mother says. "How do you spell it, Jack?"

"*M-i-n-n-e-s-o-t-a*."

I wonder why there would be an *a* at the end when it sounds like the letter *u*, and how in the world does Danny know that it ends with an *a*?

"We're learning all about our state. Danny, do you know the name of the capital of Minnesota?" asks Jack.

"What do you mean by *capital*? Do you mean to make the letter *m* a capital?"

"No, the city that's called the capital of the state. It's St. Paul. We also had to spell that for bonus points." Jack turns to me. "Maddie knows so much about saints, I bet she can spell the word *saint*."

I'm thinking he's right, but I can see the look in Father's eyes and I know what he's thinking.

"Jack, eat your dinner, this is not a spelling contest," Father says.

But as soon as Jack said the word *saint*, I began to picture the holy cards in my Bible that I can't read, but I know the red lettering spells *saint*, and I'm able to see it.

"Jack's right, I can spell *saint*, and it's never even been on my spelling list."

"Well, like your father said, this is not a spelling contest," Mom says.

Looking first at Mom and then at Father, I can see it clearly: neither believes me. They think I'll mess up and Danny and Jack will laugh. I bring up the picture of the holy card in my mind with the letters neatly printed at the top, repeat the letters in order, and then call out, "S-*a-i-n-t*." I know by the look on Mom and Father's faces that I got it right. I'm glad Uncle Joe is at the table too. After wiping the drippy meat from the corners of his mouth, he gives me the smile I recognize.

"No, that's not how St. Paul, Minnesota, is spelled. It's spelled, *s-t* period. I know that for sure," says Jack.

"Jack, you're wrong," Rob says. "Maddie did spell *saint* the right way; *s-t* is an abbreviation."

"Well, I got it right on the test. Besides," Jack says, turning toward me, "I'm sure you couldn't spell *Paul*. I was the only one in class who got it."

"Jack, that's enough," Father says in a voice that sends a chill throughout the dining room.

I go to work clearing the table as fast as I can so I'll have plenty of time with my book. Just as I bring the last of the silverware in, Uncle Joe comes into the kitchen.

"Sister Bard, impressive spelling. I never did well with spelling, still can't spell worth a da—darn. Got to watch my language around a future nun." This makes me giggle, and when I look up, he winks.

"I was lucky to get that one," I say before slipping past him to where I gather up the empty glasses. "I'm not very good at it either."

"I guess that means you take after your uncle here."

"Maybe. I also think the stories we read during reading time are boring, and I make up much better ones myself."

"I'm sure you do, but hopefully you don't make the bad choices I made: screwing off and getting into trouble so as to escape it."

I set the glasses next to the plates. "No, I hardly ever get in trouble." As soon as the words leave my mouth, my stomach somersaults. I scurry past Uncle Joe to grab the rest of the dishes.

"That's right, it is *Sister* Bard." He again winks at me when I turn to look at him, causing me to break into a smile. I scoop up the used napkins and return to the sink.

"My teacher read us the most wonderful story ever, even better than any I could make up."

"If that's the case, it's got to be pretty good, because I sure have heard some amazing stories from you."

"Oh, it's much better than any of my stories." I bend down to get the dishpan out, continuing the conversation in my head. *Just yesterday, I read the word* believe *all on my own. I'm reading the book myself.* I set the dishpan in the sink with hands trembling. "Uncle Joe, I'm getting better at reading."

He says nothing.

"The small writing you wanted me to read said *car-sales-man.*"

He gives a quick smile but then starts looking around the kitchen.

"Dad didn't need to get so mad when I was about to read the small writing for you."

"Madelyn, he wasn't mad." He says this so fast it makes me wonder if *he's* mad at me, and I stiffen. "It was just bad timing. He had a hard day, and like he said, your mother needed your help."

When I look at Uncle Joe, he looks away. I know what he said isn't the truth. I turn the hot water on full blast. He moves back and forth across the kitchen, like Danny does while waiting for dishes to dry. I keep the water blasting, and just as it starts to overflow, he leaves.

CHAPTER 36

1 9 6 7

"MISS STANLEY, have you ever heard of a dream catcher?" It's Saturday, and I follow Miss Stanley into catechism class while the others are running around outside waiting to be called in.

"Why, sure. I read that Indians made dream catchers to keep bad dreams away. Where did you hear about dream catchers?"

"It's in *The Fairy Angel's Gift.* A wise spider named Gwendolyn shows Yram the fairy how to make one to keep dreams alive."

Miss Stanley sets her purse down on the large wood desk and pulls a Bible out from the drawer. She turns to me. "That's an interesting title. I've never heard of it—sounds really good."

"It is! I'm reading it." Because I don't want to leave Yram alone all day, I slip the book out from my coat and hold it up for her to see.

"Oh, what a beautiful fairy on the cover."

"That's Yram." I almost tell her about Yram's name and my name, but instead I hand the book over to her and watch as Miss Stanley opens to the first inside page.

"This book was written a long time ago—nineteen forty-five. Well, this is interesting. Is Frieda Zinc the name of your teacher?"

"Her name is Mrs. Zinc. How'd you know?" I lean over and see she's looking at the blue cursive writing. "Can you read that to me? I'm not good at reading cursive."

"It says, 'Congratulations on achieving your dream. Soon the day will come when you're reading this charming tale to your own class of students. Mom.' And then there are *x*'s and *o*'s, which is a way to say hugs and kisses in writing." She looks right at me, but I'm just staring straight through her. "Your teacher's name is written above this. She must really trust and like you to share this special book of hers." I see her smiling at me, but I don't feel it.

I try to smile back, but all I can do is say, "Uh-huh," and move toward the back of the class.

I hear Miss Stanley's voice, concerned, ask, "Madelyn, are you okay?"

"I don't feel so well."

"You look pale. Here, honey." She takes my arm. "You have a seat here, and I'm going to call the class in. Thanks for bringing the book in to share. Someday, I'll have to read it."

Frieda Zinc? Hugs and kisses, Mom? Mrs. Zinc's mom gave her the book? Why didn't she tell us? Why would she toss it in a pile of papers? Now I know for sure she'll notice it missing.

I don't raise my hand and join the discussion today. It's about Jesus being tempted by the Devil in the desert, which I know all about. I sit with *The Fairy Angel's Gift* resting against my chest under my coat and wonder: *What was Mrs. Zinc's dream?* I can tell she's been a teacher her whole life. I think of her being like Paulette when she was young. She probably was good at reading the first day she entered kindergarten. My thoughts continue on, keeping me from hearing anything Miss Stanley says, until suddenly I see Miss Stanley standing in front not saying anything, and then, just like with Mrs. Zinc, it becomes real quiet, so loudly quiet, I notice. Usually, it's hard for Miss Stanley to make the class quiet.

I look up at the clock. It's almost time to leave. I gaze back at Miss Stanley and notice how different she looks today. She's wearing clothes that are big and puffy, tent-like, instead of bell-bottoms and a sweater. Her face looks more round. I had been too busy wanting to share my book to notice.

"I have some sad news to share."

My stomach lurches, and I can tell that she looks sad. Maybe she's sick and dying. I'm ready to cry before she even starts to tell us.

"I've decided I need to take a long vacation to take care of some personal matters. I'd love to keep being your teacher, but . . . I'm not sure I'll be back in the fall."

It's so quiet I hear everyone breathing. I open my mouth to shout, *No, that's not fair,* but nothing comes out.

"So, next time we have class will be my last day with you, and then you'll have a new teacher, someone I'm sure you'll like."

No, no, I won't like the new teacher.

She lifts her hands up as if to say, "Time to go," and more quietly than usual, everyone but me turns toward the door and leaves. I can't get myself to move. Suddenly, my head feels hot and heavy. I drop it to my arms crossed upon my desk and begin to sob.

"Sweetheart, is there something bothering you?" Mom's tucking me in. I felt sick all afternoon and didn't eat much dinner. I can't tell if it's a real sickness or sadness. They feel the same to me. She puts her hand on my forehead.

"Miss Stanley's going away. She's my favorite teacher. I've known her since second grade." I work hard at not crying.

"I'm so sorry to hear this." She means it. I can tell. "Actually, I got a letter from Father Stevens. I didn't realize you were being told this week or I would have prepared you. I know you'll miss her."

A letter? "But Mom, why does she have to leave?"

Mom's quiet. She starts to answer, but then she doesn't.

"What did she tell your class?"

"Something about needing a vacation—but I thought vacations only happened in the summer. She didn't look like her usual self. I'm worried that she's sick and might be dying."

"Sweetheart, that's not the case at all. Miss Stanley's in fine health, and she's made the best decision for herself that she can. We need to accept that."

"But you'll also miss her, Mom. Everyone will, because she plays the best organ music."

"You're right. We'll all miss her." Mom brushes my bangs back and kisses me on my forehead. "It's time to say your prayers and get some sleep. You'll feel better tomorrow."

When Mom leaves my room, I'm too tired to pull *The Fairy Angel's Gift* out from under my pillow, but I can tell Mom knows something more about Miss Stanley. I'm ready to turn over and say my prayers, but I also want to understand. I wait long enough for her to settle into the living room, and then I sneak to the bathroom. The TV makes it hard to hear their conversation. Mom says something that's completely drowned out by the sound of a commercial; but I hear Father, his thunderous words, loud and clear.

"It's really a shame she didn't act more responsibly." My body tightens; I know he's talking about Miss Stanley the same way he does to us when we do something wrong. Before he says another thing, I race back to Yram and my dream catcher and prepare to visit my rooms so I can settle down to sleep.

CHAPTER 37

1 9 6 7

AFTER NEATLY folding up the Sunday newspaper, Father changes into his work clothes. I always slip out of my dress and into my jeans as soon as we get home from church. Miss Stanley played the organ for the last time, and it was beautiful. I kept thinking about her praying to Saint Rita and how I'm now reading words in *The Fairy Angel's Gift* because I too pray to Saint Rita. I tried not to think about her leaving.

Father heads outdoors. For some reason, I begin to think about how it took Ethan's father a long time to notice Ethan was getting healthier, how he didn't believe it at first. I know what chore Father has in mind. He's always busy on the weekends, and usually I stay away, but today I decide to help him rake the leftover leaves from fall that have been covered by snow. Father shares how it's special to be raking leaves in the spring when most people only do it in the fall. It's because the snow comes so fast that we never have time.

He's surprised to see me show up with a rake and wearing my only pair of boy jeans. Sometimes, I wonder if it would be different for us if I were a boy too. Usually, I do girl jobs inside the house, but I really want to learn how to work outdoors. Maybe it would be different if, like Jack or Rob, I too brought home As. Danny's too young, but I know he'll also bring home good grades.

I'm happy to have a rake in my hand. Father doesn't understand that this is better than a dust cloth. The leaves are damp and thick. They take a lot of muscles to move, not like the light, crispy ones we'd pile up like a small haystack in early fall and then, unable to hold back, leap into the pile, tossing leaves into the air, and then start over again. It's much more fun to rake in the fall. Now it's spring. Spring and then summer. Usually, I'm excited to think of spring turning into summer, but this year, Mrs. Zinc has taken the excitement away. I might be flunking.

Father's wearing his brown brimmed hat, making him look even taller. Even though it's May, it's chilly outside. I notice how his strong sweep with the fanned-out metal rake scars the dirt as if a mini-plow has passed through, while my rake only skims the top, catching a small handful, causing me to do a second and third sweep. We work for a long time in silence while Jack and Danny run around pretending to be stacking up loose sticks, but I can tell they're playing their own version of tag. I think about joining them but don't.

"Dad, I'm getting better at reading." I keep sweeping my rake over the small area that's finally coming clean. After the third pass, I look up, not sure if he has heard me.

"Madelyn." Now his rake has stopped. "Mrs. Zinc has shared with your mother and me her concerns about how you'll manage in fourth grade."

"Oh." I want to tell him about the book and the words I'm learning. Instead, I begin raking so hard that I too make the dirt look like a plow has passed through. Then I remember. "Dad, I got an A on my science test."

"Mrs. Zinc told us. But she said you couldn't have gotten that grade if she didn't have the volunteer read the test to you." I had forgotten that part. "Fourth grade is a lot harder than third, and it requires a lot more reading."

"I know . . . but I'm getting better." Now I also have a sizeable pile of leaves. My rake is all gummed up with soggy leaves. I use my rubber boot to kick them loose and see an acorn lodged between the spokes. I pull it out and am about to hurl it across the yard when I feel Father next to me.

"Look at that," he says.

"It's an acorn," I mumble.

"Sure is. I'm surprised the squirrels missed this one." Now he holds it up, having slipped it from my hand. He takes out his white handkerchief, rubs over it, and examines it as if he had never seen an acorn. "Take a close look, Maddie. This small seed may someday grow as large as the oak in front of your bedroom window." He hands it back to me. I look closer than I've ever looked at an acorn and see for the first time tiny ridges not so different from the rake's marks, even and straight. The shell shines and feels smooth. The cap sits on top as if someone grand designed the perfect hat. "An acorn is God's way of reminding us something small and ordinary can grow mighty and extraordinary, just like that beautiful oak tree."

Even though a moment before I was ready to fling it far, and thought how good it would feel to hit the tetherball really hard, taking a close look at this acorn somehow calms me down, just like listening to Miss Stanley's organ music. I think about burying it so it can grow up and be a big tree, but instead, I decide to keep it to myself, safe in my pocket, so I'll remember.

It's almost dinnertime when I wander into the garage, where I find Rob, alone. Rob and Jack spend lots of time here, often with Father. When I step into the part that's not for the car, it's like stepping into someone else's house, someone who lives far away and whom I don't know very well. I see tools I can't name, jars filled with different size screws, and wooden boxes divided into sections of nails of all sizes. No matter what time of the year, the garage always has a cool, greasy smell to it. Rob is sorting out screws or nuts or bolts. I can't tell the difference—maybe they're washers.

"What are you doing?" I ask.

He startles. "Dad wants me to put all the nuts and bolts back into their right spots. You know, cleaning up."

I glance over at the wood-and-metal frame. "The go-cart looks cool. When will it be done?"

"Depends on when Uncle Joe has time to help us with the engine."

"Well, I think it looks pretty neat."

"Thanks."

"Do you want some help?"

He turns his gaze to me for a moment and then returns to his sorting. "No, thanks." This isn't a surprise. He thinks just because I'm a girl I can't sort screws and bolts.

I'm about to leave, but instead I ask, "Did you hear about Miss Stanley not coming back?"

He continues to put small metal pieces in various drawers and, without looking at me, says, "Yeah."

"Oh. Who told you?"

"I just heard. Some kids."

Why does everyone know about my teacher? "She's the best teacher I have. I don't want her to leave."

He stops and eyes me. "Maddie, you wouldn't understand."

"What do you mean?"

"She did something that's a big sin."

"No, you're wrong. Miss Stanley prays to Saint Rita, and Saint Rita answers her prayers."

"Well, it's true. She sinned."

I want to argue, but instead I keep standing there watching him go back to sorting little metal pieces and putting them in their special drawers. Rob is smart.

"So, Father Stevens is *making* her leave?"

"Probably, but she also has to."

"Can you *please* tell me? I really want to know. She's my favorite teacher."

"Haven't you noticed she's sort of fat these days?"

Oh, that's what's different. I nod. She's nowhere near as fat as Mrs. Ellen, but she does look different.

"That's because she's pregnant and is going to have a baby."

"That's impossible; she's not married."

Rob rolls his eyes. I wonder if it happened the way the Blessed Virgin became pregnant with Jesus, but that wouldn't be a sin.

"You don't understand." He turns away from me and continues to sort through the nuts and bolts.

CHAPTER 38

2 0 0 5

MATT, THE GENTLE GIANT, is shuffling down the hall with a wiggly second grader at his side. *David and Goliath.* The curly-haired boy breaks into an exuberant gallop. I hear Matt's patient, firm voice calling out, reminding him of the no-running rule. Curly-haired David is back at Matt's side now, giggling and hopping like a bunny. I wave at Matt when he turns back toward his office, controlling my own impulse to gallop ahead.

"Matt, do you have a few minutes?" I follow him into his warm, spacious office.

"Yeah, about ten before the friendship group starts. By the way, you did a fabulous job facilitating the meeting with Kaylee's teachers."

"Thanks. Shelby sure was impressive," I say. Matt simply nods. "Obviously, she's still dealing with it," I offer, but he doesn't say a thing. "To share with all of us that she had to repeat first grade, that took courage."

"True. But like she said, she had a late birth date and just wasn't ready."

"But Matt, still this is a big admission. It still haunts her."

"She seems to me to be at peace with it."

I stare at him. He doesn't understand. In fact, like my own brother, he skipped a grade, so how could he understand?

"Well, I'm just glad she made it clear how hard it would have been on Kaylee. Teachers rarely get this."

"Hmm. So, what's up?"

I glance at my watch. Five minutes before the friendship group. "I met with Diane Adams this morning. She's worried about Grace. Evidently, even though the highly capable folks know she's in special education and needs accommodations, they're basically treating her like all the other kids, and it's not working."

"Are you going to talk with them?"

"You know it. She's working her heart out trying to keep up. It's taking a toll on her self-esteem. Matt, she's brilliant but doesn't think so." My voice chokes as I weep inwardly at this thought. "So, yes. I'll definitely have a word or two with Geraldine."

"Maybe you should try to make time to talk with Grace," Matt says.

"Of course. And that's what I planned on until I realized just how many new referrals I've received. I've been totally slammed. You know how it is during spring." My heart picks up speed. "Actually, I was wondering if you might have time to see her. She could use some counseling."

"Dr. Mary." A tentative smile plays along the edges of his lips. "You already have a relationship with her."

"Matt, I wouldn't be asking if I thought I could fit her in. Besides, you're the counselor."

He flinches, says nothing, and I feel like shit. *What the hell is wrong with me?*

"I'll see what I can do," I say, and quickly add, "I just don't have a lot of time." I move toward the door.

"Wait."

I pause and look at him, hoping he's changed his mind.

"So how are things going with Irene?"

"Fine. I guess." I open the door to leave.

"Hey, wait a minute. Are you sure things are okay?"

I sigh and turn toward him. All I see is sincerity; he's one damn good counselor. And he's the only one who knows I'm even in therapy. I step back in.

"It's going better than I thought it would." I pull out a chair from the small round table and sit down.

"Yeah?"

"In all honesty, I'm sure therapy had a lot to do with how that meeting went with Kaylee's teachers."

"Dr. Mary, you're back in the game."

I think of Grace and wish he were right. I force myself to smile anyway.

"The thing is, I often feel as though I'm living parallel lives—my past and present. The past keeps popping up in unexpected ways, and I never know what will trigger a gush of tears. But on the way to work today, I decided I'll go to the new sculpture exhibit at the Minneapolis Art Institute this weekend instead of doing the usual." Which would have been too embarrassing to say: sleeping until noon, spending hours with Vespers writing random thoughts.

"Great! Sounds like progress to me. Therapy can start out feeling like uncharted territory. When Beth and I got together, I began acting way too much like my father, who was one mean son of a bitch. He gifted me with a terrible role model for being in a relationship, and I cared too much to let my relationship with Beth suffer due to my own issues."

"You're so brave." I think of my failed marriage. Therapy simply didn't occur to either of us.

"I've seen a few counselors over the years. Irene is good. She helped me sort out a lot of old garbage. I think it helps to know what to expect."

I thought I knew.

"How'd the homework go this week?" Irene asks.

I put on an air of confidence. Something about sitting on this sofa in a scheduled time frame fully activates my competent, intelligent persona. Or perhaps this persona emerges in reaction to the humility I feel at having been given homework in the first place.

"Ah, yes. No time to write it down, but I definitely paid close attention to the situations that angered or upset me."

"And?"

With ease, I share my outrage at the highly capable program, at Geraldine, the incompetent coordinator, at their failure to acknowledge Grace as both having dyslexia and being gifted, the need for the program to be under different leadership. I share a few other instances of my noticing and pulling back from reacting, of calming myself down. A bubble of silence follows. I'm comfortable with it, sure that I've received passing grades on my homework.

"And what are your thoughts regarding your resistance to seeing Grace?"

I catch my breath, my face reddens, and anger ignites. "Like I said, I'm extremely busy. I have six new evaluations due within two weeks."

Her serene expression makes it clear she's not buying this. Not only that, she isn't even going to argue with me, which, by now, I should expect.

I turn toward the window, welcoming the quiet moment as I scramble to pull myself into a state that resembles competence.

"I can see you care deeply for this child," she says. All I can do is nod. "You feel a tremendous amount of empathy with her struggle to overcome her disability and to assert her pride in herself."

I nod again, the anger melting away. I drop my head so she won't see my eyes filling. A tear slips onto my lap and I hold my eyes wide open, hoping to contain the rest. *Damn, this is hard.*

"Who does she remind you of?"

I squeeze the couch cushions and notice the breeze from the partially open window. It's so inviting I imagine myself floating out into the open sky . . . but here I sit, smack in the middle of the couch with a tissue box in front of me. I breathe deeply, turn toward Irene, and give an honest answer. "Myself."

For a fleeting moment, I see her: Maddie. Hand raised, swinging back and forth. She has the answer to her teacher's questions. I feel the heaviness of the black coat. Its weight sinks my body deep into the couch. No longer can I contain the flow of tears streaming down my face. I'm shamelessly grabbing tissue after tissue. *When will this misery end?*

CHAPTER 39

1 9 6 7

"**STAR, PART,** *small, walrus.*" I've never read so many words, and not one had I worked to memorize. It's like meeting someone new and knowing right off what to say.

"Mrs. Ellen, look how fast I'm reading these!"

"When letter *e* shows up at the end of the word, letter *a* changes its mind about giving up its own sound," says Mrs. Ellen. "Sort of like saying, 'Wait a minute. If you're going to join this party, I want everyone to know my name.' Like with most words ending in letter *e*, it feels a need to say its own name. Except," Mrs. Ellen says, and she cups her ears and leans forward, whispering, "hearing letter *a* say its name is hard. You have to listen carefully." She winks and then continues. "Instead of hearing the clear sound of *a* as in *came*, you'll hear something that sounds like the word *air*, such as the air that you breathe." She sucks in a huge breath of air and holds it long enough to turn her cheeks redder than a radish, making me giggle.

"Listen carefully," she says in a regular teacher voice. "Say the long sound for letter *a*—its name."

This is easy enough.

"Now, say it again and add the *r* sound."

I give it a try, *a*, followed by *errr*—it does sound like *air*. *Mrs. Ellen is smart.*

Mrs. Ellen is now pointing to the first word on the next Read It list. It's *care*, and now I know why it's not read as *car* or *carry*.

———————

Two minutes before the afternoon recess bell, Mrs. Zinc passes out the list of spelling words for the week. I shove it in my take-home folder, clear my desk, and prepare to dash to the front of the line as soon as the bell rings. Paulette is busy putting her things away when her spelling list travels over to my side of the desk. Just as I'm about to swipe it back, my eyes catch hold of the first word on the list.

"I know this word."

Paulette turns and looks at me.

"I know this. The word is *believe*."

Paulette snatches the list up. "You're right," she says, then neatly tucks it into a folder.

This has never happened before, and it makes me curious. Maybe I know the other words. I grab my take-home folder and pull out my spelling list. The words look like they usually do: a bunch of letters thrown together. But I did get the first word, *believe*, an important word, the word Yram pointed me to in the book. For the first time ever, I really want to know the other words.

"Paulette, will you read these to me?"

Paulette is still straightening her desk for recess. "Madelyn, the bell's going to ring any moment."

"I just want to know what the words are."

"I thought your mother helped you with that." Paulette's mad at me for not playing jump rope with her. A moment later, the bell rings, but I stay at my desk. When everyone has left, I grab the spelling list and go to Mrs. Zinc who holds the door open.

"Mrs. Zinc, I know this first word. It's *believe*."

"Very good, Madelyn."

"Can you tell me the other words?"

"Sure. And remember, from now on, you only need to practice the first five for the spelling test."

I had forgotten this new rule. I hadn't looked at Paulette's test for three weeks in a row. Mrs. Zinc must have decided there were too many words for me to learn all on my own.

"Here are the words you need to know." Mrs. Zinc points to the string of letters after *believe*. "The words are *possible, through, special,* and *secret*. Now you better get going or recess will be over."

"Thanks, Mrs. Zinc." I shove the list back in my take-home folder and begin to say them over and over so I won't forget. *Possible, through, special, secret.* I then make up a sentence to help me remember: *Believe anything is possible through a special secret.* I get in line for tetherball, and when it's my turn, I say to myself one word for every hit. *Believe. Anything. Is. Possible. Through. A. Special. Secret.* When the bell rings, ending recess, I know I won't forget the words. Now all I need to do is memorize the letters so I can spell them.

On my way home, three seats behind Mr. Lakowski, snugged up against the window, I pull out the spelling list. The letters to *believe* jump out at me. The others are just letters in a row, but now I have a way of knowing what the words are. I say my sentence and touch the words in order, looking carefully at the letters. *Believe anything is possible through a special secret.* After six times through, the letters finally begin to look as if they belong together.

My three brothers and I tumble off the bus onto our dirt driveway. It's a day to show both Danny and Jack that I'm the fastest one. I look back once as I race ahead. They're trying to keep up and can't. Rob, who has never raced, is also jogging. I pretend to not notice him. I gulp down a glass of water as soon as I reach the house. Jack and Danny hit the pantry for a snack, and then Rob comes in. His breath sounds funny, wheezing. I try not to look at him so he won't be embarrassed. He also gets a glass of water.

"Will Dad let you do track?"

"No. But don't tell him I'm going to try out to be manager. My math teacher told me about this. It's cool. If I get the job, I'll be the one to help keep the score, and I can still practice when I'm not having a breathing problem."

I look away. He's so much stronger than all of us, and it doesn't make sense that he can't breathe the right way when he runs.

He's holding *The Hobbit*. It's three or four or five times thicker than *The Fairy Angel's Gift*. Probably lots more small words too. Even though he's smart, I don't think he'd understand the story hiding under my pillow . . . at least not the hidden chapters.

"Are you almost done?"

"Yeah, I'm going to finish tonight. But my teacher will keep reading it for the next couple of weeks."

"It's sad to end a story. My teacher finished *The Fairy Angel's Gift*. I miss listening to it."

He looks at me in a funny way as if he doesn't understand. And I remember, for him, books never really end; he can read them over and over.

"You know, Maddie, when you're old enough, I think you'll be great at track."

"Thanks."

Off he goes to read, and that's what I do too. Knowing four more words, I'm certain I'll read even more. I begin by taking another look at my spelling list. "*Possible, p-o-s-s-i-b-l-e*." Then I hold the book, gaze out my bedroom window at the oak tree, and open it to wherever. I place my finger in the middle of the page and start scanning, expecting one of my spelling words to jump out at me, and one does—the word *special*. And it sits next to a word I can sound out—*web*. *This must be the part about Gwendolyn and her special web.* The letters surrounding these two words make no sense, but that's okay. I'm ready to find a web like Gwendolyn's, and I know exactly where to go.

Outside my bedroom, I hear Danny and Jack laughing with the TV. I tiptoe past them, go through the kitchen, and then dash out the door to the hiding place. I can hardly believe it—there's a new web stretched across the opening. It sparkles in the late-afternoon sun. I grab a stick to remove it but stop before touching it. It's new and perfect. It too is a special web.

I look more closely. Each square of space between the thin lines of web makes a pattern reminding me of Grandma O'Leary's quilts. I wonder if Grandma knew spiders also made quilts. I still don't like seeing spiders, but I want to touch the web. I put my finger to it, and when I pull it back, the web vibrates as if it has come alive. On the opposite side, I see the small sandpaper-colored spider move out from its hiding spot and place one tiny flawless leg on its marvelous web.

I drop to my belly and inch myself into the hideout without disturbing the masterpiece. I wait. Finally, off in the distance, I spy a flicker of lavender wings. I scoot out to follow, but Mom's green station wagon pulls into the driveway, and Jack and Danny come racing out to meet her. I'll join up with Yram later.

"It's dinnertime," yells Danny. I lift myself up from my bedroom floor where I had sat leaning against the bed, paging through my book. I don't see Uncle Joe's truck out the window. I'm sure I would have heard it anyway. It feels weird to be glad that he's not here for dinner. In the kitchen, I smell sweet tomatoes, rice, and hamburger bubbling together in my favorite casserole—Texas Hash. Mom's pulling the casserole out of the oven, and Jack is looking in the fridge for ketchup.

"Will Uncle Joe be coming?" Jack asks.

"I don't know, honey. If he gets here, I'm sure there will be plenty of leftovers."

A wave of sadness settles into me. I've always been happy to see Uncle Joe, but not tonight. I'm still mad at him for acting like Father. And he didn't tell me the truth.

Once dinner is over, Danny begins to clear the table without anyone asking him. He sees me noticing.

"Maddie, have you discovered any more hidden chapters?"

"I sure have. As soon as we get all these dishes into the kitchen, I'll tell you." I let him do most of the clearing. I pull out the dishpan and start the water before I begin the story. "It's not as easy as Mary thought to break the spell. Remember, she got poisoned and no longer believed she could read. So, of course, she couldn't teach Alice. What she really wanted was to find Yram, because she thought since Yram helped Ethan, she could also help her."

"But you said it was too dangerous for Yram—there's the rumor and hope snatchers."

"That's right. But Mary wanted to believe this wasn't true, that she could still find Yram. She also didn't want Ethan to know that she now didn't think she could read. She remembered how Gwendolyn had helped Yram, so she found her way into the Forest of Wisdom. Just like Yram, she was very afraid. Gwendolyn is wise, but she's still a large spider."

"What'd she look like?"

"Very big and ugly, like all spiders. But her web was more beautiful than anything you can imagine. And she sort of spoke like Grandma O'Leary during the time she was sick. Her voice was growly with lots of clearing her throat."

Mom walks in and looks around. "It's so nice to see you two getting started right away and getting along so well."

Danny and I smile at each other. I wait a few moments for Mom to leave. She might interrupt.

"Gwendolyn reminded her that dream catchers are important. You see—Mary now has to grow back her reading skills. They left her—but not really."

"How can that be?"

"Danny, if you really believe something's not possible, it won't be. Mary *can* read, but the hope snatchers made it so she no longer believed this."

Danny squints his eyes and tilts his head. He's getting ready to argue about this, so I continue.

"But she knew how important Ethan's dream catcher was, so she wanted to learn how to make one. Gwendolyn told her she first had to practice."

"Practice making dream catchers?"

"No. Remember how Yram tricked Ethan into practice running and how it worked?"

"Yeah."

"Well, Gwendolyn told Mary she also has to practice so that she can start believing again. So, Mary finally asks Ethan for help, and he tells her about a special teacher, one who believes in fairies and is fun and very good at teaching reading."

"But you said she was afraid to tell Ethan about her not reading."

"Oh . . . that's true. She didn't want him to think she wasn't smart. But after talking to Gwendolyn, she knew she needed help. But what she really wanted was to find Yram because she hoped that Yram would do some quick magic." I pause to look at Danny, wondering if he remembers that Yram didn't do magic to help Ethan run. I can't tell. "Mary begs Ethan, 'Please, can't you tell me where Yram is?' And Ethan says, 'I don't know. I just know she is hiding, and she's busy making her magnum opus.'"

"What's that?"

"Your teacher hasn't read you *Charlotte's Web*?"

"No."

"Well, Charlotte is the wisest spider around, except for Gwendolyn. *Magnum opus* is the word she uses to mean her masterpiece. This's what Yram told Ethan that she was doing in hiding—making her magnum opus. So anyway, Ethan then tells her about this special teacher who is good friends with Yram. He tells her how to go and see her. What Mary really needs is the teaching. But her hope was that this teacher would tell her where Yram was.

"The teacher's name is . . . uh . . . Teacher Elly. She is shorter than I am and has a big smile, red cheeks, and ears that look like they are elf ears."

"Elf ears? You mean she's really an elf?"

"Let's just say she's not like the teachers at our school. She is really different. And *yeah*, she is an elf."

Danny smiles at this. "Neato. That's why she's short, right?"

"Yep. When Mary shows up, all she wants to do is find Yram. She starts off by saying, 'I was sent here by Ethan, and I'm supposed to meet with Yram. Please let her know I'm here.' Well, this teacher is a good teacher. She's fun, but she's also serious about her lessons, so she says, 'Not until my lesson is over. You may have a seat.' Mary wasn't expecting this."

"I wouldn't either if my teacher looked like an elf."

I giggle and try to imagine elf ears on Mrs. Zinc. "Mary didn't pay attention to the funny elf ears. She was mad because she wanted to meet Yram right away. So she didn't even try to learn."

"But she should have."

"Yep. She should have, but do you ever . . . I'm thinking of how Mom says it. She sometimes says you get stubborn and cut off your nose to spite your face."

"I don't remember her saying that, and I don't know what it means."

"It's when you really want to go to town, but since Jack grabs the front seat before you do, you get stubborn and say you're not going after all."

"But that has nothing to do with my nose."

"I know. It's kind of weird. But even though Mary knows she needs to get back to learning to read, she had her hopes up about seeing Yram right away. So, at first she tried not to pay attention. But this teacher is so fun and exciting, she couldn't help but learn!"

Danny claps and yells out, "That's because her teacher is really an elf!"

I grin at him.

CHAPTER 40

1 9 6 7

I'M WRAPPED in a dark mossy-smelling green thickness. I want to snuggle in deep, bury myself, but where is the edge of the blanket to pull up? I stumble forward, searching. I'm dizzy and stumble upon a log. I tumble to the soft dark ground. Looking up, I see light and color. I reach for the log, move toward it, pulling myself onto it. I gaze at the light and see threads of a gigantic quilt, colorful, and like the moon, shining in the darkness. My chest grows heavy. I'm missing Grandma.

"Grandma. Grandma, I need you!"

"My sweet potato, no need to worry." It's Grandma's voice, but all I see is a huge web of threads.

"Grandma, where are you?" I want to feel the tightness of her arms around me. I want to bury my face in her softness. I wrap my arms around my knees.

"Sweetheart, I'm here. I'm part of this web. And so are you."

"No, I'm not. Yram and Ethan need my help, and I can't help because I can't read." I squeeze myself tighter and press my forehead to my knees.

"My sweet potato, you forget who you are."

I shake my head and then try to bury it between my knees.

"The stories. The stories you tell are beautiful."

I close my eyes, remembering Uncle Joe sharing with Danny why he calls me Sister Bard. He always likes my stories.

"But Grandma, why can't I read?"

"But sweet potato, you can. Remember, believe anything is possible through a special secret."

"I read those words."

"You sure did, and you also read 'change form.' We all change form."

My alarm rings. I slam it off and then lie in bed trying to hold on to my dream. I squirm around and look up at my dream catcher, then out my window at the leaves on the oak tree that are now double in size. I think of the dragonfly. *We all change form.* I miss her. I miss Grandma O'Leary more than anything. I bury my face into my pillow and weep until I hear Father's knock and then voice at my door.

"Madelyn, are you up? It's time to get going."

The bell ending our last recess of the day has just rung. I hang back and look for a stray ball, and I find one. Instead of lining up, I volunteer to take it to Mr. Griffin's ball bin, right next to the closet with Mrs. Ellen. I pass her closet, but the door is closed. I plop the ball into Mr. Griffin's bin and return to Mrs. Ellen's space, but the door is still shut. I really want it to be open. I planned for her to be waiting for me. But now I need to get back to class before Mrs. Zinc notices. I stand, not knowing what to do. And then I decide to knock. I knock, and it opens.

"Madelyn, what a surprise."

"Mrs. Ellen, I was just returning one of Mr. Griffin's balls, and I wanted to tell you something."

"What is it, dear?"

"Mrs. Ellen, can I see you every day? I think it's working."

"Oh, sweetheart, I'd love that, but I see kids from all the different grades, and there just isn't enough time to pull you out any more than twice a week."

"What if I come in during recess time?" I can see that she's alone in the closet, so she does have time for me.

"Now that's an idea. But would you want to miss your recess?"

"I don't mind." *I'd rather miss recess than do third grade all over again.*

Mrs. Zinc usually puts on an excited face just before she begins to read to us—even if it's a boring story about a girl named Laura living on the banks of Plum Creek and what it used to be like living in Minnesota way before my parents were even born. Today, Mrs. Zinc looks like she has swallowed a handful of sour grapes. It means we're in trouble. After everyone settles into sitting as still as statues, she begins, not with the story, but by saying, "Class, I have a concern to share with you. Mrs. Smith in Room Twelve has asked to borrow *The Fairy Angel's Gift*."

My heart flips in my chest and thumps so hard I'm sure Paulette will hear it. Then I remember her messy pile of papers has been cleared away. *But still . . .*

"When I went to get it for her, I discovered it's no longer where I placed it."

I gasp. Paulette whips around and stares at me. I cover my mouth pretending to stop the hiccups.

"I believe someone took it. In fact, I think I might know who took it." She stands quiet and looks at all of us. "But I'll wait to see if this student chooses to do the right thing and return it."

Now I grip the sides of the chair. *Yes, I'm still sitting.* My heart's behaving as if I just galloped faster than ever to upper field.

The class is dead quiet except for my pounding heart and Bobby fiddling with something inside his desk. I shoot him a quick look. *Had he seen me and did he tattle?* I try to breathe normally. *I can't return the book. Not now. Mrs. Zinc had tossed it in a pile of junk. How can she remember where she had put it? Saint Rita, I didn't sin, did I? I was saving the book.*

A finger pokes into my ribs. Mrs. Zinc's now reading the boring story, and usually I'd be making up my own with Ethan and Yram. I turn to Paulette, who motions me with her hand to lean over.

She whispers hotly in my ear, "Don't tell anyone: Bobby took it. I saw him. I'm going to tell on him tomorrow if he doesn't return it on his own."

When I look at her, she gives that I-know-everything smirk, and it sends a shiver down my spine. She must have seen him sneaking back into the classroom.

Please, Saint Rita, don't let Bobby get in trouble. He'll kill me when he finds out.

"In the name of the Father, Son, and Holy Spirit . . ." Father's deep voice leads us in prayer while the smell of Pillsbury biscuits makes our stomachs rumble. As soon as Jack has piled his plate with tuna casserole, he begins to brag about his new reading group. I try to shut him out and think about how exciting it was to read the words *special web* and then discover the most amazing web ever. The thunderous roar of Uncle Joe's truck brings me back to dinner. Now I wish I hadn't asked for a second helping; I no longer feel hungry.

"Hiya, all," Uncle Joe calls in his usual cheerful voice.

Danny and Jack yell out "Hi." I keep my eyes on my plate of food.

"Whatcha got cooking? Whatever it is, it sure smells wonderful."

"Tuna casserole and biscuits," Jack yells.

"It's my favorite," Danny says.

"Uncle Joe, I found some more pieces for the go-cart," Rob says.

"Great. We'll be in good shape for Saturday afternoon."

"Uncle Joe, are you going to be living with us forever?" Danny asks. He holds a forkful of food midway between his plate and mouth.

"Danny, my jester, I'd love to live in this beautiful palace forever. Especially with you entertaining me all the time."

"Will you? Stay forever?" Danny is serious.

"I can't. Consider this an extra-long visit. I have a place of my own that I need to get back to. But I sure enjoy being part of this wonderful kingdom."

Now everyone's focused on dinner, and I begin to take small bites of my second helping. I'm thinking of how Ethan kept getting better and better at walking and how exciting it was for him to fly with Yram.

"Madelyn, how was school for you today?" Mom asks.

"Okay," I say, hoping to not talk about it anymore.

"I've been meaning to ask you. How's it going with your new teacher?"

"You have a new teacher?" Jack asks. Everyone stops eating and looks surprised, as if I've been keeping a big secret.

"No," I say, "not really." Mrs. Ellen isn't a *new* teacher, just a helper, and I'm about to say this when Father fills in the empty space.

"Madelyn's lucky. A special teacher is working with her to help her get caught up with reading."

Before I can stop myself, I talk back. "But I don't really need a special teacher." It comes out so fast and sure, I hardly recognize my own voice. No one else seems to either. For a brief moment, it's dead quiet. What I want to share are all the big words I've figured out by myself and that I'm also reading a chapter book all on my own, but looking up and meeting Father's eyes, I know he won't believe me.

"Madelyn, you do need help, and I don't want to hear another thing about it," Father says. My eyes pretend to look at my food, and still I feel Uncle Joe staring at me. I start to take another small bite, but I'm too full to eat any more.

Uncle Joe stands leaning against the entryway to the kitchen while I go from the table to the sink bringing the dishes in. I know he wants to say something, but I don't feel like talking. I don't even look at him.

"Madelyn," he says. I try to figure out what voice he's using: the fun one or the angry one. Maybe in between. "Hey, if you have some sort of special teacher, I think that's great."

So what. I walk past him, looking straight ahead at the dinner table, stack up the plates, and walk by again without looking.

"Your father's right. You're lucky to have a special teacher. It's a good thing."

I grab the dishpan and start filling it with water. Uncle Joe sounds more like Father than like my favorite uncle. He stands watching me quietly and then walks out of the kitchen. I turn off the water and wish I had at least said Mrs. Ellen is nice.

"Mom told me I need to help you," Danny says, arriving late like usual. "I'll dry the silverware when you get them washed."

"Thanks."

"I know," he proclaims, as if he has come up with an answer to some unspoken question. "You can tell me how the story ends. You never did."

"I need more time to think about it. But I'm remembering some parts Mrs. Zinc read that I never shared. Do you want to hear?"

"Okay," he says.

I put some silverware in the drying rack, and I motion to him to get started. "Remember how I told you that Ethan really did have something wrong with his heart and that's why his parents were always worried?"

"Yeah."

"Well, ever since he met Yram, he started getting out of bed more. Sometimes at night, he'd chase after her and go on adventures. Those were the times he wasn't so sure it was real. But during the day, he was also getting up more often to see if he could. He kept trying to do more."

"I know. You told me that. So, what happens?"

"Well, I was remembering something I didn't tell you, and it's important. When he went to his doctor for a checkup, they said he still had a bad heart, but it had gotten stronger. It's like . . . he kept growing it or something. He made it get better little by little."

"Then what?"

"That's what I was remembering. That he kept working on getting stronger, and he did. Yram helped, but Ethan was also helping himself."

CHAPTER 41

2 0 0 5

THE DOOR CREAKS, and Wilma looks up from her desk with a pair of readers perched precariously upon the end of her nose, and a pile of second-grade papers stacked in front of her.

"Good morning," I say, glancing at the plate-sized clock on the opposite wall. It's ten after eight; we have another five minutes before Chase's parents arrive.

"I was just trying to find his unit math test. He got one of the best scores." She resumes her search, punctuating each passing page with an audible click of her tongue. I snag a couple more chairs from surrounding desks and move them over to the table in the back of the room.

"You're quite right about Chase's artistic abilities," Wilma says. "Look." She points to a colorful poster illustrating planet Earth surrounded by a ring of animals drawn in detail. The words DON'T LITTER IT'S BAD FOR THE EARTH are printed across the top—all in capitals. He's clever. Write in caps and you don't have to deal with the confusion between *d*'s and *b*'s. "Other than help with spelling the words, this was his idea and design."

I walk over and take a closer look.

It has been three weeks since I apologized to Wilma for insulting her during my observation of Chase. His freckled face, erupting into red blotches as he tried to read the words, continued to haunt me. A talk with last year's teacher convinced me to take what I saw in

Wilma's room seriously. Upon suggesting I evaluate Chase, everything changed between Wilma and me.

Wilma's phone rings. I head for the office to meet Mr. and Mrs. Babcock. I recognize Mr. Babcock at once: Chase's red hair, green eyes. I imagine freckles on a younger face. Dressed in cargo pants and a plaid shirt, he hangs back under a cloud of discomfort. Mrs. Babcock immediately reaches to shake my hand. She's wearing a tight skirt and jacket, costume jewelry, and a frosted lipstick smile that seems out of place.

We walk down the gleaming yellow-and gray-tiled hall toward Wilma's class. Mrs. Babcock's heels click half a step behind me. Mr. Babcock's soles don't make a sound. My gut tells me it's best to start with the conclusion and gloss over the gloomy details surrounding the severe discrepancy. I can't help but feel strongly sentimental toward Burt Babcock—a visage of Uncle Joe. I wonder if I should start this meeting by sharing that I used to teach students who struggled with reading and then move on to some success stories. I glance out the window at the playground and notice a girl hanging upside down on the bars, a zipped-up black jacket bunched around her upper body. My stomach knots as the image of Maddie doing what she loved the most in third grade wells up inside me.

Wilma is standing at the door waiting to greet us. She reaches out, lightly touches Mrs. Babcock's upper arm, and motions them both to Chase's poster. I see the first glimmer of a smile form on both Mr. and Mrs. Babcock's faces. Who wants to attend a meeting to hear that their child has a disability? I feel grateful for Wilma in this moment. I want her to keep showing all the ways Chase is part of this class, that he's as typical as all his classmates. Before I know it, she is ushering them toward the round table with four chairs.

Wilma sits with a class planner and yellow notepad in front of her. She holds a pen in hand. Mr. and Mrs. Babcock have shifted their chairs slightly closer to one another, maintaining a certain distance from the table. They did not come prepared to take notes. I have a manila folder labeled with Chase's name tucked under my arm. All eyes are upon me as I lay it on the table and pull out my evaluation report.

I dart my eyes from face to face, looking for contact while holding in mind everything about Chase I have grown to appreciate, hoping his parents glean this from the expression upon my face. Wilma responds in kind; she too has discovered a treasure of strengths. The Babcocks avoid looking at me as if I'm some smooth used-car salesman.

I begin the way I always start these meetings: highlighting the strengths. I sense the Babcocks see my sharing as a gimmick to win them over, but I am being genuine. Chase is brilliant in many ways.

"His art stands out in part because he has exceptional visual-spatial skills. On a test that measures this, he scored better than ninety percent of children his age. Within this skill area, he's gifted, and you see it in his artwork." I pause and feel a heaviness that may be impossible to cut through in the next twenty minutes.

"Chase qualifies for special education under the category of specific learning disability," I say.

Burt flinches. Mrs. Babcock is wide-eyed.

I speak swiftly to reassure them. "Overall, he's a very smart boy. It's just that he has a few specific areas of weakness that require special help for him to improve."

Mr. Babcock becomes fidgety, bouncing his right leg while his left hand taps on the stationary leg. His wife speaks up. "We've always been told the problem is that he's not paying attention, not that he has a problem with learning." She glares at Wilma, who avoids eye contact.

"When a child struggles with reading or writing," I say, pausing to take in a slow, one Mississippi, deep breath, "it's only natural for them to avoid these difficult tasks, and this avoidance looks as if they're not paying attention."

Mr. Babcock clears his throat. His left hand now grips his thigh, squeezing. I'm helpless in stopping this surge of uneasiness. His voice is halting as he speaks. "You're right about one thing—he's smart. And I won't allow the school to be putting him in no special-ed class. They did that to me. Put me in with a bunch of hoodlums and hicks. There's no way I'm going to allow any of you to do that to my son."

He stands up. Mrs. Babcock springs to her feet and lightly touches his arm.

"Burt, let's give the psychologist a chance to share her findings. We don't have to agree . . ." She looks over at me, and I notice Burt studying me and I'm worried there's not a thing I can say to change his mind.

"You're right. You don't have to agree," I say in a voice contrived to be pleasant in an effort to cover a desperate plea. "And no one wants to take Chase out of Ms. Jenkins's class. He qualifies for some extra help in the resource room, but let's come back to that."

Mr. Babcock mumbles something under his breath and sits back down.

"Mr. Babcock, I would never recommend that Chase be placed in a special education classroom. I just want him to receive specialized help. He needs this. So he can learn to read." He maintains eye contact, so I continue. "You're right, special ed has had some problems in the past." I pause; "some problems" is definitely putting it mildly. "But it's changing. Things are better these days."

"You need to understand." He breathes heavily and breaks eye contact, focusing somewhere beyond the rows of desks and the gleaming whiteboard. "I won't have my boy go through what I did." He pushes his chair back but stays sitting down with arms crossing his chest.

"Things *are* different."

"Well, I sure as hell hope they are. All special ed did for me was give me a label—reading retarded. They never did teach me to read. I finally had enough of their bullshit and dropped out when I turned fifteen."

I cringe. He continues to cast his gaze forward beyond the room.

"I'm so sorry." I try to catch his eyes, but he looks away. His fair complexion, the way he moves his mouth . . . images of Uncle Joe bubble up. He has no idea how sincere I am. "Teachers these days are more skilled," I say. "Children who struggle with reading do learn to read. In fact, I know an adult who struggled with reading as much as Chase does. She was able to get help and went on to get a PhD in education." I wait, but no one seems to have heard what I just said. I glance at the clock; soon the morning bell will ring.

Mrs. Babcock gives a quick sigh, glances at her watch, and then, directing her focus to Wilma, says, "Well, I'm not so sure this isn't an issue of Chase choosing to play around instead of paying attention." She flashes her eyes at me and says, "Besides, like you said, he's a very smart boy."

I'm now certain Wilma, during the fall and winter conferences, went on and on about his not paying attention, just like she had during the SIT meeting. My irritation toward her returns, especially since she's remained quiet this entire meeting.

I look directly at Mrs. Babcock, who has no problem maintaining eye contact, and say, "That's exactly why it's so important we give him the help he needs to learn to read. He is smart, and because he has a hard time making sense of the printed word, he finds ways to be distracted."

Burt Babcock's eyes remain focused elsewhere, and his leg is once again bouncing. I've lost an opportunity to reach him. I turn toward him anyway.

"He doesn't need to be placed in a special-ed class. He just needs special help with reading."

Burt behaves as though he hasn't heard. He stands up, this time with unmistakable intent; his wife follows him to the door. Wilma and I remain sitting, caught off guard. He turns and says one more thing.

"We're not going to be signing no special-ed papers. I don't want him going through school with some idiotic label. He deserves better."

In stunned silence, I blink hard and try to look unconcerned, but as silence lingers, guilt finds a noose in Burt's bitter words, pulling into a knot. I can't stop myself: *Would it have been different if he'd known I was once a Sparrow?*

CHAPTER 42

1 9 6 7

PAULETTE never gets to school early; she doesn't have to since she lives in town and walks to school. I'm always a good fifteen or twenty minutes early, and usually I play on the bars before going in. I'm about to grab a big ring and swing across like a monkey when I can't believe my eyes. I blink and see Paulette standing over by the jungle gym talking to Bobby. She's shoving her glasses up her nose and nodding her head as she chats away.

"Go!" shouts Jason in my ear. I fling myself forward and grab the next ring but keep my head turned toward the jungle gym. *Why is she here talking to Bobby?* By the time I reach the end, I know. Blabbermouth Paulette couldn't wait. She had to tell him that she knew.

The bell rings. I race toward class, acting as if I saw nothing. Paulette slides in next to me and takes out her plastic pencil case. I turn toward her, wondering if she noticed I had seen her talking with Bobby.

"Bobby's not fessing up," she mumbles. I ignore her and she continues. "I decided to warn him that I knew; that way, he wouldn't get in as much trouble with Mrs. Zinc by telling himself instead of me tattling."

"But maybe he really didn't take it," I say. Now she gives me "the look." I drop my gaze to the empty paper on my desk.

"I saw him sneak in. I was walking with Mrs. Zinc helping her with duty when I noticed him going back into the school."

My heart speeds up. I need to say what I need to say. It's worse than jumping off the dock into the ice-cold lake upon a dare. I squeeze my eyes shut. *I have to do this.*

"Paulette, I know who took the book, and it wasn't Bobby." She stares at me with eyes that slice like a knife. Her face looks confused; I can tell she has no idea that it's me I'm talking about. I start copying the letters from the board onto my lined paper. My hand is shaky. I have no idea what words I'm writing.

"What do you mean?"

I wish it were recess. I'd run away. I look up with nothing to say.

"Whoever it is, you had better tell Mrs. Zinc soon, or I'll let her know that you know and won't tell."

"Paulette, please. Please wait. The person who took it plans on giving it back. I know it."

"Why won't you tell me who?"

"I will, but not today. If you keep it a secret, I promise to tell you."

The morning recess bell sends me galloping off for upper field, as far from Paulette and the others as I can get. I gallop like a horse, and when I'm out of breath, I walk the fence that divides our school playfield with the neighbor's cornfield. Soon I hear breathing behind me and the clicking of a stick running along the chain-link fence. I flip around and see only Bobby. He drops his stick. We quietly eye each other the same way we do across the tetherball pole.

"Madelyn?" He says my name as if he isn't sure whether he can ask a question, nervous-like. Usually, he runs in a pack. I know he's figured it out.

"What?"

"I saw you leaving Mrs. Zinc's classroom during recess time a few weeks ago."

"I know. I had to get something." And then, without planning to, I say more. "You had to get something too, because before you saw me, I saw you leaving after getting something from Mrs. Zinc's desk."

"You were hiding?"

I nod. "But I wasn't spying or anything. I just needed to get something."

"Mrs. Zinc's book?"

"Maybe. But you also needed something." We fall into a silence, and I notice he still has the Band-Aid on. "Bobby, my uncle Joe works for your dad. He told me about . . . your finger. Is it getting better?"

He wiggles it and gives a slight smile. "Yeah. Does your uncle tell funny jokes and have short hair that's sort of blond?"

"Yep, that's him, Uncle Joe. And he has a tattoo on his arm. He's really strong."

"Yeah, I know him. He's nice." This makes me grin. Bobby's the only one at school who knows my uncle Joe.

"Bobby, I took the book."

"I figured."

"I'm only borrowing it." I notice he's not scowling or making a face at me. "I'm practicing my reading with it."

"Cool."

"I told Paulette I know who took it, and I told her it wasn't you." I see his face relax. "I said to her if she kept her mouth shut for a few more days, I would then tell her who took it. Because I know I need to give it back, but I'm not quite ready." I pause, wondering if it's safe to tell him about my discovery of hidden chapters and that's why I need to wait. "So, you don't have to worry about getting in trouble."

He shifts uneasily from one foot to another. And then I remember that he was sneaking around in Mrs. Zinc's class too. I look right at him.

"So, what were you doing in Mrs. Zinc's class?"

"I took something. I was borrowing too."

"I know." But I don't know what. So I give him a look the way Paulette does to me, to see if he'll just fess up.

"Flash cards. I like to study flash cards."

"Bobby, I can make you flash cards."

"But I like flash cards that have answers on the back."

"If you slip Mrs. Zinc's flash cards back into her desk, I promise to make you some. I'm good at numbers." *Not so good at letters.*

"Cool." He gives me a smile and turns toward the school. He looks back at me and calls out, "I promise I won't tell."

"Me either," I yell, and we race each other from upper field down to the school. I could have won, but I let him.

"Let's start with our Read It book," Mrs. Ellen says, holding it up. "Today, we're going to discover the different sounds that letter *o* makes when it's right next to another *o*. Remember *loose caboose*?" A vague memory of a silly poem she had recited brushes through my mind.

"Say with me, 'It's loose, the wild caboose, and clever goose.'" After repeating three times, Mrs. Ellen pauses and then asks, "What sound does two *o*'s have together?"

As if I just saw something really cool, I call out, saying, "*Ooh.*"

Next, there's a list of words in the Read It book that look to be more difficult than what Mrs. Zinc has us Sparrows read. But knowing about *loose caboose*, I read word after word, letting the sounds slip effortlessly from my mouth: *smooth, spoon, pool, harpoon, raccoon.*

"Look at this group of words. They also have two *o*'s in the center, except they don't belong to *loose caboose*." Mrs. Ellen reads the first word, *book*, which I sort of recognize, and knowing the sound in the middle makes the rest of the words easy to read: *cook, crook, look, shook, wood, stood*.

"Now, it's detective time. What do you notice about these words besides that same sound?"

"They end in *k* or *d*."

"Good observation, Sherlock. So, if there are two *o*'s ending with a *k* or *d*, this is what you say to remember the sound: 'I am a good cook.'" Mrs. Ellen giggles. "The truth is, I'm not a good cook." She winks. "When you see the double letter *o*, what will you do to remember the sounds?"

"*Loose caboose* or *good cook*."

"Perfect."

"Mrs. Ellen, can you teach me to read some really big words?"

"At the rate you're learning, it won't be long until we start working with two- and three-syllable words."

"Wow," I whisper, even though I have no idea what a "silly bull" is.

"Are there some words you have in mind?"

I think of the really long word inside the cover of *The Fairy Angel's Gift* that Miss Stanley read. "*Congratulations*."

"That indeed is a very long word." She smiles and then repeats it slowly, clapping to each part. "Five syllables. Notice I clapped five times?" She does it again and makes me clap with her and count. She then writes the word on a fresh notebook page of my Read It book and underlines the last group of letters. "If you learn the special sound of letters *t-i-o-n*, you'll be able to read lots of long words. How about we work on this next time?"

Before I can stop myself, I clap.

I sit with *The Fairy Angel's Gift* on my lap, leaning against my bed and looking out the window. I'm wearing the same jeans I wore when Father talked about the acorn. I reach in and pull it out of my pocket. He's right. It seems impossible this seed can turn into the tree I'm now looking at. How does that happen? I study the acorn more closely than ever. I don't see the secret. I reach around and place the acorn under my pillow and return to looking at words. Together, the entire book, page after page, seems like the grown-up oak tree, so huge compared to the few words I'm learning. This makes me sad. I have to give the book back, and I'll never get to read all the words. I turn to the first page inside the cover and look at the blue cursive writing. Mrs. Zinc's mother gave it to her. My parents would never give me a book like this because they know I could never read it.

I dive under my bed and grab my notebook where I try to write stories that are later hard to read. I'm going to start my own Read It book. I'll need to work hard since I don't have much time. I start by writing the words I know: *fairy, angel, gift, once, upon, time, Ethan, change, form, believe*. I pause, and the sadness lifts. I know more words than I thought.

I'm half running toward the rope swing, and I can hear Danny's light feet following behind me.

"Maddie," he calls out, breathless. "Is Mary learning enough to break the spell yet?"

I pause, turn toward him, and say, "It's harder than she thought." I sprint ahead and grab the thick rope. Letting my hands slip down to the knot, I fling myself off the sloping hill. Two rounds and Danny is now sitting on the ridge waiting. I let the rope dangle, and join him, feeling calm inside with each deep breath.

"What did Dad mean when he said you have a special teacher?"

"Danny, it's not what you think."

He looks pleadingly at me. I jump up, grab the rope, and swing around a couple more times. He doesn't budge.

"It's really nothing. It's just something I do to make Mrs. Zinc happy." He doesn't say anything. "There's this new teacher who wants to practice teaching, and Mrs. Zinc asked me to help out. *Okay?*"

"Okay."

"So, you want to hear more about hidden chapters, right?"

"Right."

I take a deep breath and get back to feeling calm. "Even with Teacher Elly, Mary keeps doubting, because the hope snatchers put lots of sand in her eyes. So when her teacher started teaching about big words—"

"What do you mean?"

"I mean like reading the word *congratulations*. Guess how many syllables that has?"

"I don't know. What's a syllable?"

"All big words have them, and this word has five, which means it's really long and hard. Mary could, of course, read this word and other big words, but she didn't believe it."

"Oh."

"So, what happens is, she feels so scared about flunking, I mean failing, that she runs out on her lesson. And this makes her feel like a failure even more. It's just what the hope snatchers knew would happen. So she wanders around, not sure what to do, and she ends up back in the Forest of Wisdom."

"That place is sort of scary, right?"

"Yeah. It creeps her out because there are lots of spiders in the forest. She gets there and is suddenly confused. It's dark and so creepy.

Can you imagine being alone in the forest at night with big spiders?"

"Noooo!"

"Well, she has to run to get out of there fast."

"Maddie, is all of this in hidden chapters?"

"Yes! How else would I know? She's running and falls over a stump that is all thick and grassy from moss. This slows her down, so she looks around her. The forest is quiet, and then all of a sudden"—I swallow big and breathe. If Danny wasn't sitting next to me, I know I'd cry. I do my best to keep a steady voice, but it quivers—"she hears a voice that she has missed every day of her life. It's Grandma's voice calling out to her."

"Do you mean Grandma O'Leary?"

I nod.

"So she *also* has a Grandma O'Leary?"

"Danny, even though this is about a different Mary than me, this part seems like it might really have happened. I heard Grandma O'Leary speaking to me in my dreams."

"Dreams aren't real."

"That's what you think, but I heard her talking to me, and this is what she said. She said, 'We all change form.' Just like Yram and the dragonfly. She said that's why I couldn't see her; she has changed form. But she's still alive."

"Oh."

"Mary was upset. When her grandmother spoke to her, she listened. Her grandmother reminded her that she really was smart, that she was especially good at telling stories."

"Like you."

"Thank you, Danny. That's called a *com-plane-ment*. Then Grandma's voice was replaced by Gwendolyn's, and all at once, Mary was staring at the beautiful web of Gwendolyn's and saw Gwendolyn crouched in the corner. Gwendolyn sort of scolded her, saying, 'Mary, you have all you need to break the spell. You need to believe in yourself and turn away from the fear that the hope snatchers have created.' Mary understood this but still said, 'Please, let me see Yram, and then I know I can break the spell.' Gwendolyn then told her where she would find the fairy. 'Yram likes to hang out at the bramble bushes where the elf children sometimes play hide-and-seek.'"

"Elf children?"

"Yes, that's who Teacher Elly usually teaches—elves."

"So, kind of like where we saw the large dragonfly?"

"That's right. And that's why I figured it was a fairy in disguise. They like bramble bushes like that.

"So Mary goes there, secretly hoping that Yram will use fairy magic and wipe out the dust from her eyes and make it possible to read again. She waits around, and then crawls into a little space pretending to be playing hide-and-seek. All of a sudden, she looks up in the sky and sees something small and colorful that's moving fast and drawing a picture in the sky. An elf from Teacher Elly's class comes running over and points to it. She reads it because Mary never was good at reading cursive, and this is in cursive. It says 'Help.' Mary is shocked. She's the one who wants help, and even though Ethan had told her Yram needs her help, she didn't really believe it."

"Oh, I know. It's like when she asked Ethan to help her get the sticky web. It was so he'd get practice running."

"Danny, you're smart. It is sort of the same thing." He grins, and I reach over and pat his back. "Then Yram drops something from the air that at first looks like a small parachute. As it comes closer to the ground, Mary can tell it's a huge leaf. An oak tree leaf. It comes toward her, but one of the elf kids grabs it before she can and an acorn falls off it. Mary quickly puts the acorn in her pocket, thinking it must be special since it came from Yram. The little elf girl is nice. She looks at Mary and says, 'I think you should keep this leaf. Yram meant for you to have it. Look at the pretty picture she drew on it.' When Mary takes a close look, she doesn't see a picture, she sees letters!"

"Cool! Could she read it?"

"No, because it was a word with lots of letters and syllables."

"Like *congratulations*."

"Right. And maybe it was *congratulations,* because Mary wouldn't have known. But she did get the idea that Yram meant for her to go back to school and, even if it seems much too hard, to keep working on her reading skills. It was easier to do this knowing that she was helping Yram. And she wanted to read the special word on the leaf."

I pause, and then add, "Mary loves Yram."

CHAPTER 43

1 9 6 7

MISS STANLEY'S last words come like an unwelcome pat on the back. I had been watching the clock and knew there was only going to be enough time for a quick good-bye; but when the time came, it came much too fast. Everyone gets up and leaves as if it's an ordinary good-bye instead of a forever good-bye. I stay in my chair waiting.

"Madelyn," she says softly. Most of all, I'll miss her voice—it's so much nicer than Mrs. Zinc's. "I know someday you'll make a wonderful nun if that's what you choose to be. In fact, I can even imagine you as a saint. Your heart is pure."

I gasp. I don't know what a pure heart means, but I never dreamed Miss Stanley would think that I could someday be a saint. I have to take a deep breath before I answer.

"It's the real reason I want to be a nun. If I can be a saint, I'll make sure everyone's prayers are answered."

"I'm sure you would."

"Including yours, Miss Stanley. You look sad about leaving, and I don't believe it's a vacation." My heart beats fast. I hope she doesn't think I'm being fresh.

"A vacation is a break. I need to take a break from my job here at the church. But you're right, it's sad for me to leave."

"But why? I know you're going to have a baby, but lots of people do, and they don't go away." I thought she'd be surprised that I know this, but she isn't.

"Madelyn, the church teaches that it's a sin to have a baby before you get married. I made a mistake, so some people think it's best that I take a break to think about it."

A mistake . . . that's not as bad as a sin, but I know it's really a sin, just like Rob said. I can't think of her as someone who sins.

"Saint Rita still answers your prayers."

"Of course she does. And yours too."

"Miss Stanley, I wish you could just go to confession and then keep being our teacher."

She smiles at me in a way that I wish I could keep forever, and then she opens her arms and I fall into them. I've never hugged a teacher, but she's special, and will no longer be my teacher. I try not to notice her big, solid stomach.

I'm finding all kinds of new words in my book. I write them down: *garden, upset, sudden, understand.* Now that I know about syllables, I'm good at reading big words. I start to write another big one that I figured out, when I hear Uncle Joe's truck. I look up. I usually greet him on Saturdays, but I'm still mad at him.

Then I remember. I have something to say to him that's not about me. I place *The Fairy Angel's Gift* under my pillow, dash through the kitchen, and out the front door, where I see his truck roll to a stop. I change my mind and pretend I came out to the bramble pile where I saw a fairy. I hear his door open, sticks and gravel breaking under his thick boots as he makes his way toward the kitchen door. I want to hug him even though I'm mad at him for lying to me. I'm surprised my brothers haven't grabbed him by now. This thought makes me run toward him. And stop.

"Sister Bard!" he calls. I feel sad right away. He says my name like it's a treat to see me, but I've been holding back. I don't say a single thing. "How are you? Have you had a good day?"

I can't begin to answer. *I read big words. I hugged Miss Stanley, who thinks I'll make a good saint.* I stand staring at him and then remember what I want to say.

"Uncle Joe, you're right about Bobby Wallace."

"The boss's son. He's your classmate?"

"Yes. And he said you're cool. I told him that you're really strong. He's my friend now."

"That's good to hear. He seems like a nice enough kid. I'm glad you're getting along. How's school going?" I know what he really wants to know.

"It's going good. I can read big words like *congratulations*."

"Well, Sister Bard, what I have to say about that is, congratulations!" He laughs and walks away toward the house. I don't see what's so funny about this. I wish he hadn't laughed.

I wander into the garage and know right away it's not a place I belong, but I'm always curious. All three of my brothers are standing around talking excitedly about the metal frame with a lawn mower engine stuck in the back and a couple of pedals. I take a closer look and notice a steering wheel, but I don't see what the big deal is. But then, I don't understand why Jack and Danny watch *The Three Stooges* every day when we get home. I understand why Rob reads. I turn away to go look for a special web or maybe just hang out by the rope swing or catch a few frogs. When I leave, Danny follows.

"Have you found more hidden chapters?"

I have, but I'm not sure what. I keep walking. He's like a shadow, and I end up at the rope swing. I turn toward him.

"Yes, I have."

"Tell me."

I smile slightly and plop down with a view of the lake in front.

"After seeing Yram and getting the leaf, Mary took her reading lessons much more seriously. She also thought about the acorn in her pocket and remembered something her father had said about acorns, about how they're little seeds that can grow into really big trees. Did you know that Danny?"

"I think so. You mean if you bury an acorn like Mom plants cucumber seeds, it'll grow into a tree?"

"That's right. Mary's father had told her that acorns are special because it means something small can change and grow really big." I'm looking at all kinds of big things: the lake, trees, and the sky stretching across the lake. I wonder if they all started out small. I turn to Danny, and he's poking around with things that are small: a pill bug in the dirt, a small twig he places in front of it to see what it does. But I know he's listening.

"She wasn't sure why Yram had dropped the acorn, and maybe it just happened to be attached to the leaf. But for sure the leaf was on purpose because it had a word on it with letters that only she could see. Mary decides to skip her recess to get even more help with reading because she really wants to help Ethan and break the spell. But she also wants to get her reading skills back. Teacher Elly taught her that reading big words is like reading small words. Here, let me show you."

I get up, grab a sturdy stick, and with the palm of my hand, I smooth out the dirt and write the word Mrs. Ellen taught me the other day. *Fan-tas-tic*. Except I write the syllables in a column so that they look like a list of different words.

"Danny, can you read this?" I point to *fan*.

"Of course, it's a baby word that I learned a long time ago." He's just like all my brothers—good at reading.

"Now read each of the words that aren't really words but syllables, and then do it fast."

"*Fantastic!*" he yells out.

"That's right. And it is a big word with three syllables."

"Teacher Elly is a smart teacher."

"Yes, she is. But still, for someone who has forgotten how to sound out letters, it's hard. Because Mary is especially interested in reading long words, Teacher Elly teaches her a secret sound that you can never figure out on your own, but it shows up in lots of big words."

"What's that?"

"Listen to the last part of congratula*tions*." I pause and then scratch out in the dirt *t-e-u-n*. It looks funny; maybe it's because of writing in dirt. I know the sound but can't quite remember the letters, but Danny won't know. "These letters together make the *shun* sound. You can't sound it out, you just need to know that. And lots of big words have it. Listen: *creation, invitation, nation.*"

"*Vacation!*" he yells. "So now I can read those words too."

"Probably."

"What happens next in the story?"

I pause and wait until I'm sure Danny is listening closely. "The word on the leaf is much longer than she has ever remembered reading. While her teacher shows example big words on the board, she notices small words in the word on her leaf and starts sounding them out the way she was taught. First she sounds out *trans,* and then she notices a small word she knew, *form,* then letter *a,* and the last group Teacher Elly had been teaching, the letters that say, *shun.* Like in *congratulations.*"

"So, what's the word?"

"*Trans-for-ma-tion.* It has four syllables."

"What in the world does that mean? Is it a real word?"

"Mrs. Ellen says—"

"Who's Mrs. Ellen?"

"I meant Teacher Elly. She said it means to change form or change the nature of things. This is a word that's usually said by people who go to college. So this makes Mary feel like a very good reader, and now she knows she can break the spell, because she too was under a spell, thinking she couldn't read anymore, and now she knows she can. She jumps up in joy when she figures out the word. And she runs to the bramble bush area thinking Yram will meet her, and she will yell out, 'Yram, I've figured out the word on your leaf! I did it!'"

"But that doesn't happen?"

"No. Instead, she meets Ethan, and he has advice for her."

"What's his advice? I bet he's happy for her."

"Oh yes, he is. He says, 'Congratulations!' Then she says, 'Where is Yram?' and he says, 'She's still waiting for you to break the spell.' And then she remembers. She broke her own spell, the one the hope snatchers cast on her, but not the one that has Alice and the Forever-After land where Ethan lives. But because she just read the longest word ever, a college-level word, she is full of hope, and that's the opposite of what the hope snatchers want." I pause, look at Danny, and he claps. I smile at him and then continue. "Here's Ethan's advice, he reminds her of—"

"What?"

"Danny, I just remembered. I haven't told you how the story ends when Mrs. Zinc read it to us. You need to know this to understand how the hidden chapters end."

"But when will you?"

I stand up and stretch. We both hear Mom's voice calling down to us from the back of the house; it's dinnertime. I turn to Danny and say,

"Maybe later." And we race up to the house.

After figuring out a difficult word all on my own—*situation: the situation between Ethan and his parents*—I close my eyes and notice my stomach twisting. If I don't return *The Fairy Angel's Gift* tomorrow, Paulette will tell Mrs. Zinc that I know where the book is. I slide Yram under my pillow and prepare to visit my rooms. I'm feeling a sickness build up inside me, more than the usual twisting that happens when I need to settle something inside a messy room. I can't tell if the sickness is real or not, but I think it is. I go to my bedroom door and call out, "Mom."

"What is it, Madelyn?"

"Can you come?" I scurry back into bed.

"I just tucked you in. What is it?"

"I think I have a fever. I feel really sick."

Mom's hand presses against my forehead. "You don't have a fever. Where does it hurt?"

"All over. Especially my stomach."

"What you need is a good night's rest. Is there something bothering you?"

"I don't think so." I keep my fingers crossed, hoping this makes it not a sin.

"Say some prayers to Saint John. He'll help you feel better."

"Who's Saint John?"

"He's the patron saint of sickness. When I feel a cold coming on, I'll say a few extra prayers to Saint John, and usually, I'm feeling better by morning."

"Mom, do you ever pray to Saint Rita?"

"Saint Rita . . . there're so many wonderful saints. I can't say I have."

"She's the saint that Miss Stanley prays to all the time to help her with the organ music." I reach over to my nightstand where my Bible sits and pull out my favorite holy card. A pang of sadness rises up—Miss Stanley had given this to me. "Look." I hold up a card with a shiny face framed by a white habit, the face that looks like Miss Stanley's. I can tell that Saint Rita also has peanut butter–colored hair under her habit. "I'm going to really miss her."

"She's lovely, Madelyn. It says 'Patron saint of lost causes.' I'm sure she'll hear your prayers."

I'm not so sure anymore. I'm still a Sparrow. I don't want Mom to think less of Saint Rita because, after all, she answers Miss Stanley's prayers. I decide not to pester Saint John because I know he can't help me feel better about having to return *The Fairy Angel's Gift*.

CHAPTER 44

2 0 0 5

I LEAVE the SIT meeting feeling calm. We came to an easy consensus. Theo, the first grader in question, was not a candidate for repeating first grade and would not need a special education evaluation. Upon listening to his single-parent mother share the stress of trying to feed and house the two of them on a minimum-wage job, a shift in understanding united us all to dig in and come up with ways to further support Theo's schooling: summer school, the Big Brothers program, and homework club in the fall.

Outside the conference room, I notice Wilma Jenkins pass the office; she catches sight of me and gives a look that's all too familiar.

Whenever I dare to venture into the staff lounge, a place I go only in desperation to snag a teacher and solve a scheduling problem, I'm assailed by "the look." I smile back, aware that it's not me they're seeing; they're seeing the child they intend to bring up to me—Jason, Sara, Ava. I've become a physical prompt, reminding them of the students they are troubled by. I see it now in Wilma's eyes.

A mixture of guilt and leftover resentment churns into a nasty concoction as I lay eyes upon Wilma. She had misled Chase's family—it wasn't ADHD that propelled him into all kinds of creative antics to avoid reading. They had come prepared to hear about his deficits with paying attention, not with learning to read and write.

Wilma stands squarely in front of me, daring me to pass without acknowledging her. I breathe deeply and prepare myself to let the conversation run its course.

"I didn't sleep a wink last night. I can't believe parents would keep their own child from getting help. What are we going to do?"

"Like I said, it's their right to refuse services. In the meantime, since we know he has difficulty with reading and writing, it's important to give him the help he needs in the classroom."

"But he needs so much more than I can ever give. I don't—"

"Wilma," I say in the tone of a teacher reprimanding a student, "now that you know he can't read the sentences you write on the board, maybe together we can figure out some alternatives."

"I just don't think it's enough."

"You're right, he needs more. But at least now you know what's going on with him." I pull my gaze away from hers and call to mind Chase's freckled face. "He wants to do his best—we all do. You know he's very creative and skilled in math. Play that up, help him feel good about this, and don't make him read words that are way beyond his level."

I see her mouth open to say something else, but I turn away. There's nothing more I can add in this moment. I walk to my office, intent upon leaving the problem behind me.

I slump in the chair in front of my computer and stare at a stack of files a dozen or so high—each one an incomplete tale of a child's life. It's my job to interpret the tests and determine the presence or lack of a disability. The file labeled "Chase" sits on top. Never before have I had a family get up and leave. *"Reading retarded"—damn. No wonder.*

All at once, I'm back in sixth grade. A new year and a new special education teacher in a new location. I'm told to leave class during science—my favorite—to get special help. The new room is no longer in a closet behind the gym, but a glassed-in conference room off the library, and anyone who happens to be in the library at the time can see me. This room has a label outside the door making it official. I ask my teacher to read it to me: "Minimal Brain Damage." She says it means only a little bit of damage.

I lift the stack of files from my desk and place them behind me on the small square table, then turn back to my computer where I click on my e-mail. I end up deleting most. Finally, I turn and face the mound of yet-to-be-written reports. I shuffle through the one on top and find the parent contact information. Burt works for Miles Brothers Construction Co., and Cindy Babcock is an employee at LensCrafters. I pick up the phone and call her number.

"This is Cindy at LensCrafters. How may I help you?"

"This is Dr. Meyers." Silence. "From Milton Elementary."

"I remember."

"Ms. Babcock, I understand your husband's experience in school was awful and demeaning. But special education has changed."

"Why are you calling me at work?"

"Because Chase needs help, and I can't let this drop."

"Ms. Meyers, I can't discuss this now. I have customers waiting."

"Please." I squeeze the phone; my breath quickens. "I'll make it short." I hear her sigh. "I'm calling to invite you to come and see what I mean when I say special help. Come and watch students Chase's age working in a small group with a teacher who's really good at helping kids learn to read. They all love working with her, and they're making progress." I bite my lower lip instead of adding, *You'll be able to help Burt understand.*

"I don't get time off in the middle of a school day."

"I see."

"Yeah. It was hard enough getting the morning off to come to your meeting the other day. So it isn't going to happen again anytime soon."

"I'm glad you came. I just wish we could have ended differently.

Chase needs more help than what his teacher can give."

"If you can get him the help without a label and a special class, Burt and I might consider it."

"I'd really like the opportunity to talk with you both about this. I can stay late and meet with you after work. And if you can schedule the time, I think you'll understand why I'm hoping Chase can have this opportunity."

I pause, waiting for a response, listening for the sound of her breath. Then I say, "One more thing." My heart speeds up. "Please let him know that with help, Chase can learn to read."

"Ms. Meyers," she says. I'm squeezing the phone again. "Burt has never gotten over the way he was treated, and I don't blame him. Besides, I plan to spend more time with Chase so I can figure out what's going on. Burt's right—Chase doesn't need to be dealing with no label." And then I hear the anticipated click of the phone hanging up.

The next hour moves like molasses as I try to focus on writing evaluation reports that will qualify children for special education. My mind keeps playing over the meeting with Burt Babcock. I'm left with a finished but unsigned report that lies uselessly atop a pile of folders. Again, I wonder, would it have turned out differently if Burt had known that I too had been labeled?

It's been five minutes since the morning bell ushered the children back to class. The halls are once again safe to navigate. I step out of my office toward the copy room and hear a high-pitched shriek coming from Kelly's special education classroom. Diane Adams is leading Clayton down the hall toward the doors that open out to the playfield. Clayton holds a tight fist around Sammy's leash. Clayton lets out another shrill squeal, his limbs spasming in a joyous jerking motion while his face erupts in a grin so wide he looks like a cartoon character that has just swallowed a pie plate. Sammy continues to tug forward, his tail wagging. Negotiating the door looks tricky, and I dash over to help. Besides, I could use a few wet-tongued dog kisses.

"Clayton, stay right there while I get the door," says Diane, and then she sees me. I can't meet her eyes.

"I'll get it," I say.

"Oh, Dr. Meyers, thank you." I feel her gaze upon me, and I turn to Sammy and Clayton.

"Hey, Sammy." The gold-colored mutt spins toward me, eliciting another squeal from Clayton. "Clayton, are you taking Sammy for a walk?" Clayton makes a grunting sound and nods his head up and down.

"You're welcome to come," Diane says. "It's been a while since I've seen you." I want to disappear into the yellow-and-gray flooring. Diane is such a sincere person, and here I am avoiding her every move since offering to visit with Grace two weeks ago.

"Wish I could, but I'm so busy I can hardly see straight." I squat down to Sammy's level, hold his head between my hands, and massage the back of his floppy ears. His big brown eyes stare into mine, and he makes licking motions with his tongue. In that moment, I'd love nothing more than to spend the day cuddling with him.

Instead, I return to my office and begin to sort the remaining files by due dates. Next in the pile is Jayden, a good ten days past the mandatory timeline. I see his bright face and curly mop of hair. I flip through the test protocols and see that his answers to the stale standardized questions were awesome. His evaluation should be easy to write as he clearly meets the definition of specific learning disabilities. Six months ago, I would have cranked this report out in no time. Now, I'm haunted by the specter of the label I have grown accustomed to: specific learning disabilities. Sort of like, 'a little bit of damage.'

Why can't I simply label him 'differently abled'—meaning creative and talented in many areas but unexpectedly needs expert instruction in the area of reading? I slap the file back down on the table. Burt and Cindy are right—no kid deserves to be labeled.

It's one fifteen, and I wonder if Matt might be free. I need to get out of my office. The moment I step into the hallway, I realize the stack of files I've left behind has moved with me in the form of a backpack filled with remorse. I've just placed a dozen square-pegged children in a holding pattern where they'll remain unanchored and misunderstood if I don't get busy assigning them a label to address their needs.

Up ahead, I see a familiar figure—a husky, determined girl dressed not so girly and walking down the hall in a leisurely manner. She's swinging a thick hardback book in her right arm. I pick up my pace and catch up with her.

"Hi there. Where're you headed?"

Grace looks up at me, startled.

"To Mrs. Stanton's class."

"Is she being helpful?"

Grace stares, and then slowly nods her head up and down. I catch the title of the book she's carrying, *Harry Potter and the Order of the Phoenix*. It's the newest and thickest in the series, clearly her passport for fitting in with the highly capable kids.

"Your mom tells me you're working pretty hard this year," I say.

"Sort of. I like the science projects. But we always have to write a long report. This week Mrs. Stanton's helping me."

"Well, that certainly sounds helpful."

Grace pauses and looks up at me. I see the quick pain in her eyes.

"I wish I didn't need so much help." We're within five feet of the resource room when I notice a couple of girls Grace's age walking toward us. Grace stiffens, glances at me, and then strides ahead past

Penny's classroom.

"Hi, Grace," they call out to her.

"Hi."

"Where're you going?"

Grace holds up the Harry Potter tome. "My book's overdue. I need to renew it."

"Oh, we're getting our pictures taken for the read-a-thon. See you."

I pretend to look at hallway art. Once the girls have scooted past me, Grace pivots, and with the same swiftness, heads back toward the resource room. This time her head is down, examining the tiled flooring as she travels. I step toward her, ready to catch her gaze and deliver a smile that says, *It's okay. I understand.* But she passes by with eyes averted. I call out just as she reaches the resource room door, "Grace."

She gives me a mortified look, and then I realize she's not looking at me at all. She's looking past me at her highly capable classmates, who reappeared just in time to witness Grace slipping into Penny's special education classroom. The resource room door clicks shut, enveloping Grace, and leaving me on the other side aching.

Outside Matt's office, I can see through his window that he has his hands full with three rambunctious boys. An hour later, unable to write a single meaningful word about any child's disability, I feel woozy. Finally, I go to the school office to let them know I need to go home; I'm sick. Sandy, the secretary, holds me in her gaze, which then travels across my pained face, confirming that I am pale and sickly. She says that the crud is going around, lots of absent children this week. "Go home," she advises. "At once. And get to bed." I'm washed with the same relief I felt as a child when my mother would pull the thermometer from my mouth and proclaim that, indeed, I had a fever.

Once home, crawling into bed seems a ridiculous idea. There's nothing physically wrong with me. I pace around the house, knowing what needs to happen. *Damn.* It's no different from the way I behave when the flu hits. I sit in misery for hours, nursing the nausea with sips of 7UP, delaying the inevitable, but always in the end succumbing to defeat, kneeling before the toilet and heaving. A smarter person would just see the road ahead and get it over with, but I hate like hell retching that acid up from my gut. It hurts. I always feel as though I might choke and die in the process. I pace around a good hour before finally sitting my butt down with Vespers.

File "writing.9" is now over six hundred pages. My journal has taken a huge leap since weekly meetings with Irene began. I started out thinking therapy would only be a once-a-week encounter, but it always extends deep into the following seven days, right here in my home office.

I place my fingers on the keys and thoughts spill out: *Irene's right. I can't do this anymore. I need to know and accept my nine-year-old self.* I take a deep breath and look around the small room. *My God, Grace is nine years old. Third grade.* I pause, and images of the black coat, Mrs. Zinc, bubble up. *When did I stop being Madelyn and step into being Mary? How did this happen?*

Feverishly, I write one memory after another. They spring up from a seemingly infinite reservoir, and I simply type, letting my thoughts flow. Five pages later, I have recounted so much. And yet . . . I feel incomplete.

I go to my window and look out on the sunny skyline. The buildings, all so far from the lake, the oaks, and the bramble bushes. Again, I pace. Unlike evenings I've spent with Vespers, I'm left with nothing but churning agitation. *Oh God, I know what I need to do.*

As I reach for the phone, my teeth begin to grind. My left hand, holding the creased business card, trembles. I censor my thoughts—the slightest reconsideration surely will send the phone slamming back into its cradle. I dial the number. She answers.

"This is Mary Meyers. I was wondering." I swallow down the lump in my throat. "Um, I'm having a hard time. Do you by chance have any extra space in your schedule?" I notice the thick blue veins surface in my right hand as it grips down on my thigh bouncing to a frenzied beat.

"Sure, that would work. Great. Thanks," I say. I hang up and sob. Deliriously relieved to be seeing Irene within the next hour and mortified beyond belief that I would feel such a need.

CHAPTER 45

1 9 6 7

MY HEAD'S POUNDING so hard I'm afraid it's going to explode. I slide under the covers and wrap my arms around it so it doesn't burst open. Finally, the ringing stops, but my head continues to throb.

"Madelyn, are you awake?" It's Mom. She must have turned my alarm off. She gently shakes my shoulder. "Honey, it's time to get up. I need to go to work, and you need to get yourself going."

"Mom, my head, it hurts bad." I mumble into the sheets. Mom pulls the covers back.

"Let's see." I roll over onto my back; she puts her hand to my forehead. "Oh dear, I think you have a fever. Let me get you an aspirin."

Pound, pound, pound, its rhythm loud and even. What if my head explodes while everyone is getting ready to go to school and work? They'll find me dead in my bed with arms wrapped around *The Fairy Angel's Gift*. I have to bring it back or Paulette will tell on me. It's today I had promised to tell her who took the book. Tears start to fall down my cheeks. No longer having the book to myself, getting into big trouble with Mrs. Zinc—it's impossible to stop the crying.

I'm crying too hard to swallow when Mom returns with the aspirin. "Madelyn, what is it sweetie? Where do you hurt?" I point to my head, but now it's my stomach that's hurting, the kind that happens when I'm in big trouble. "Here, I want to take your temperature. Now settle down—you'll be fine. Did your dream catcher work?"

"I don't remember any bad dreams." I choke out and sniffle.

"I don't remember any of my dreams; it must have worked."

"Well, I guess you knew what you were doing, making that dream catcher. Or maybe it was the prayers I said for you last night."

I too had prayed to Saint Rita before falling asleep. Was it prayers or the dream catcher?

"Here, sweetie, open up your mouth." Mom slides the cool, thin thermometer under my tongue. "I'll be right back. I need to let the hospital know that I'll be a few minutes late."

I try to remember my dreams, but nothing comes. I shut my eyes and see Yram's picture on *The Fairy Angel's Gift.* I reach under my pillow and feel its solidness. Even if I wasn't sick, I couldn't imagine bringing it back, not yet.

"Okay, let's see." Mom leans over in her nurse uniform with the funny starched hat pinned to her head, and there is a faint smell of soap. She holds the thermometer up and, with nurse's eyes, silently reads the numbers. "Well, it looks like you have a fever. The aspirin should bring it down." She puts her hands to work feeling my neck for swollen glands.

"Hmm, they don't seem swollen. What's this?" She touches a sore spot on my neck. "You have a little red spot here—is this a mosquito bite? Have you been scratching this?" I run my hand over the spot. It doesn't tickle or need to be itched like a mosquito bite.

"No, it just sort of hurts."

"It must be a spider bite."

"A spider bite? I don't have spiders in my bed!"

"Honey, sometimes little spiders just pass through, and they're harmless. It's nothing to worry about. Listen, your father will bring you a piece of toast, and then I want you to rest. I'll call you at eleven, but you are to stay in your bed until I call, do you understand?"

"Yes."

"If you're still not feeling well, then I'll schedule an appointment with Dr. Dean. But I think the aspirin will help. I want you to stay in bed and get lots of rest."

"Okay, Mom." My head continues to pound, and my stomach twists and churns. Mom kisses me good-bye, and I feel for the tender spot on my neck, and remember: I was racing out of the Forest of Wisdom last night, swatting lots of small spiders that collected around my head and neck.

"Mom," I call out, but it's too late. She's gone.

Father sticks his head into the room.

"I hear you're under the weather and need to take it easy today. I'll bring you some toast and orange juice in a little bit." He gives a smile and then he's gone too.

The house grows quiet, and I drift back to sleep.

When I wake up, I'm alone with my book, and I think of Ethan. I prop myself up in my bed and decide to find Gwendolyn. I eye the book's thickness, take a guess as to how far into the story she appears, and open to that page.

"*Gwen-do-lyn, Ggg-www-aan.*" It's no use; this is a name impossible to spell. I move my finger across the lines of print, looking for a capital letter *G*. Instead, I notice patterns. I slow down to look more carefully. There are lots of big words, which I skip over, but sprinkled among the big ones are words I memorized last year and this year, easy little ones, like *of, you, the, as.* Then there are other words, which I had *not* memorized.

These words catch my attention because I know how to sound them out: *spark, sharp, small.* When I come across two *o*'s together, I look at those two *o*'s and find myself saying, *loose caboose* or *good cook.* I pull out from under the bed the Read It book I made and begin to write a new list of words. Words I discovered in *The Fairy Angel's Gift.*

It's fun to read the words I've written. Some rhyme like a poem. My eyes move quickly from letter to letter with the sounds coming together instead of sputtering toward nowhere. My stomach no longer hurts. Even though I didn't find Gwendolyn's name, I found lots more words I can read.

"Jack," yells Danny outside my window. At first, I think they came home too early. I check my alarm clock and can hardly believe my eyes; my day at home has come to an end so fast. I tear out the pages of words from my notebook and place them with the other two already folded in half in the back of the book. Now I have a total of four Read It pages.

The screen door to the kitchen opens and slams shut, two times. I get up to meet my brothers. In the kitchen, Jack races toward the pantry while Danny trails behind him. Jack now has a pack of graham crackers in his hand.

"Hi, Maddie. Did you have fun today at home?" Jack asks.

"No, I stayed in bed the whole day."

"I wish I could stay home in bed all day," Jack says.

"Sounds boring to me," says Danny, and he starts to follow Jack out to the TV room.

"Where's Rob?" I ask.

"I don't know," says Jack. "He stayed after for something." Then they both go off to watch TV.

Later, when I dash into the kitchen to ask Mom if I can use her black marker to make flash cards for Bobby, I'm surprised to notice it's almost past dinnertime. Father's home, the hamburger-noodle casse-role is out of the oven cooling off on the stove, and Uncle Joe and Rob are not here. I start to ask about Rob and change my mind—Mom and Father sound like they are arguing.

I turn to leave, and Mom yells out to me, "Maddie, will you please set the table?"

Uh-oh, it's the voice that means business. I grab six plates. But if Uncle Joe comes . . . I put seven out. I move about laying out napkins, silverware, glasses for milk, and all the while, I keep an ear to the living room. It's about Rob. I hear his name, but everything else is spoken too fast and jumbled. Once the table is set, I duck into the TV room and go to Jack and poke his shoulder. He looks up.

"How come Rob wasn't on the bus?"

"He said Uncle Joe was going to pick him up. He's doing something for his math teacher after school." Jack turns back to the TV. I go to my room and moments later hear Uncle Joe's truck. I peer out my window and see Rob hopping out. He looks happy. I bet he tried out for track. I return to the kitchen and take the milk out of the fridge. Rob walks in, followed by Uncle Joe. Before anyone can say anything, Father is standing in the kitchen like a period in the middle of a sentence. Uncle Joe nods and leaves. Rob's smile fades; he looks up at Father, and then his eyes fall to the floor. Nothing is said, but now I wish we didn't all have to sit down to dinner. Mom calls Jack and Danny, and I try to pretend everything is like usual.

After blessing, no one talks. Finally, Danny begins talking about using the trampoline in gym class and how much fun he had. Rob keeps his eyes on his plate of food, and so do I. Uncle Joe and Jack both act like they've not eaten in a week. Father clears his throat and says, "So, Rob, I heard from your mother that you've decided to show up for the track team after all."

"It's not what you think. I'm applying to be a manager, not a participant."

"Are you doing math to be a manager?" Jack asks.

"Yes. My math teacher, Mr. Greely, recommended that I apply. I'm learning statistics."

Rob is so smart. I've never even heard of that word. I wonder if he knows the word *transformation*.

"Except it does mean hanging out on a grass field and running errands. Rob, this is not a wise choice. There are other things you can do after school instead of trying to provoke an asthma attack."

"Dad, you don't understand, that's not what I'm doing. And everything was fine today." He covers his mouth, coughs, and makes a wheezing sound. I try to think of something to say to get Father's eyes off him, but there's nothing about my day that will make sense to anyone.

Danny comes to the rescue. "Mrs. Peterson taught us how to add double-digit numbers. They're so big, you can't use your fingers, but now I know the trick and it's easy." He looks around the table. I can tell he's waiting to hear praise. "I brought them home for homework, but I don't even need any help."

"Danny, that sounds exciting." Mom says, and I hear the shakiness in her voice match what I see on her face: there's a big problem between her and Father. "I'll want to take a look at those math problems after the dishes."

Rob stops wheezing, and after only a couple of bites of dinner, he mumbles that he has lots of homework to do and excuses himself.

"Please tell me the end like you said you would today." Danny stands with a dish towel in his hand and acts as if he won't dry the dishes if I don't tell him.

"I know, but I just need a little more time. I have too much on my mind." *He has no idea what I have to do tomorrow.*

"Why can't you just tell me how the real part ends?"

"Because. I need time," I say in Father's firm harsh voice. Danny lets the dish towel drop and runs out of the kitchen. It doesn't matter. He isn't much help anyway.

I'm about to stack the last dinner plate into the drying rack when Uncle Joe walks in.

"Looks like your drying partner done run off on you."

"He's not much help anyway."

Uncle Joe grabs Danny's towel and starts to dry the dishes. I've never seen a grown man dry dishes before.

"Thanks, Uncle Joe, but I don't mind doing this."

"I don't mind either. Besides, I heard you stayed home today. Are you feeling better now?"

"Yeah."

"So I guess that means you missed out on working with the special teacher today," he says. I dump the water from the dishes and start to walk out of the kitchen.

"Mary Madelyn," he says, and I stop. Uncle Joe has never called me by my full name. I look right at him and he continues. "You have a chance to get help. You're so smart, it's important that you accept it."

"I don't need an extra teacher. I'm learning to read on my own." My stomach jumps when I see his expression. *He looks like Father.* I again start to leave the kitchen.

"Maddie, listen. I haven't been honest with you."

I stop again. *Grown-ups don't talk this way.* I turn toward him. He's twisting the dish towel in his hands. *He doesn't really look like Father, but he doesn't look like my uncle either.*

"I want you to know something." His words come out slowly. He puts the dish towel down. I lean back against the counter. "I never learned to read. I guess I was too busy goofing off when I should have been paying attention."

I search his eyes for the twinkle that shows he's teasing. "I don't believe you. You're lying."

"I'm afraid not. Even your father tried to teach me, but I never got the hang of it. I dropped out of school. It was a big mistake." He takes a deep breath, and I feel my knees go weak. "I wish I'd had a special teacher who could have taught me how to read."

"But you're smart, and it's just because you need glasses. Anyway, Dad's wrong. I can read." The word *read* hardly makes it out before my voice turns shaky and my eyes blur up. I wipe them with my sleeves.

"Sister Bard." His voice calls from somewhere far away. It's the tone he uses when listening to my stories. "Sister Bard, I have a confession to make."

I stare up at him and see my favorite uncle, and I already know I'll forgive him for whatever he has to say.

"I . . . I made it up," he says. "I'm sorry I lied to you. I don't need glasses. The truth is, I never learned how to read."

"But . . . I don't understand. Why didn't they teach you?"

"They tried. It didn't work, and I gave up."

A thousand questions race through my mind. *How can someone as smart as Uncle Joe not learn to read?* Before I can ask, I can tell he has more to say.

"Listen, I had the best job of my life selling cars. Loved it. I was good. Until I was asked, in a very important meeting, to read a report. I . . . flipped out. I mean, I didn't expect it and panicked. The next thing I knew, I was out the door running." He steps away from the counter and looks around as if to make sure we're alone, and even though I'm hardly understanding what he's telling me, I can't help but take a step closer to him. He sighs heavily and then says, "I quit."

"Can't you just go back and tell them you want another chance?"

He slaps his left upper pocket where he keeps his cigarettes. I'm sure he's going to pull one out, but he doesn't.

"I wish it were that simple." When he looks at me, his eyes are thick and watery.

"Uncle Joe, I almost quit too, but now I'm really working at it." I draw in a deep breath before continuing. "I also have a confession to make." He leans back on the counter again, and I glance around to make sure neither Danny nor Mom is about to enter. "Two confessions. I do have a special teacher, and she's helping me . . . and I borrowed a book without asking from my teacher. It's a very special book. She wants it back, and Bobby might get blamed if I don't return it. But I'm like you, I don't steal things—but I guess this is sort of like stealing."

"Well, that's between you and God. Bringing it back is an excellent idea. It must be a mighty special book."

"It is, and I'm learning to read it. It's called *The Fairy Angel's Gift,* and you know I've seen fairies. The fairy in this book has a special name. Her name is Yram, but guess what? I discovered it is really the name Mary spelled backward. Do you remember ever mixing up the letters backward?"

"Sister, it's been so long since I have even tried to make sense of letters, I can't remember, but this certainly sounds special." Uncle Joe's wonderful smile returns. I step closer.

"Hey," he says. His arms spread out, and I fall into them. "Maddie, promise me you won't make the mistake I made. Don't ever give up on school."

"Promise."

CHAPTER 46

1 9 6 7

I READ MY Read It lists one more time. Then I lie awake, still knowing that I have very messy rooms to clean. Within moments, my stomach twists: I see my Father's stern face at dinner, Rob wheezing, and Mom's tight way of talking to Danny. I slam shut the doors to these messy rooms and begin to say Hail Marys. By the third one, my stomach relaxes. But there are other places inside me rising up in a new round of stomach tightness. I let my thoughts sweep through what tomorrow may bring, and they land on Mrs. Zinc wanting *The Fairy Angel's Gift* back.

I can't even let myself think about this. I start saying more Hail Marys. By the time I've said ten, my parents' voices, harsh and choppy, cause me to lose my place. Quick, jerky movements in the hall, and the coat closet door opening and closing bring me out of bed and to the bathroom, where I listen.

"Dora, I told you this would happen."

"George, there's no way to have known. It could be due to something entirely different. We just need to take him in before it gets worse."

My heart races. "Mom, what's happening?"

Mom has her coat on, and Father's putting his on too.

"Honey, Rob is having an asthma attack. We need to take him to the hospital so they can help him breathe. Everything's going to be okay—he just needs more oxygen."

But . . . I can't move or say a thing. I'm seeing Grandma O'Leary in her robe and slippers, her bald head propped up by Mom and Father shuffling through the kitchen. Grandma left at night and never came back. I didn't get to say good-bye; I was crying too hard.

Mom swoops down, holds my face between her hands, and stares into my eyes, knowing what I most fear. My heart is beating so fast I think *I'm* having an asthma attack.

"Madelyn, don't you worry. Say some prayers and everything'll be fine. Now you get back in bed. You'll be asleep by the time we get home." Her lips smack my forehead.

Father is now walking slowly down the hall with Rob, who gasps for air as if the wind has been knocked out of him. Father's face looks like a piece of glass that might fall and break at any moment. I reach out and place my hand on Rob's right shoulder. He turns toward me, his face putty gray, his lips quivering.

"Rob," I murmur.

Even before reaching my bed, I'm begging: *Saint Rita, it's okay that you decided reading for me is a lost cause, but please, please help Rob. Please help him to breathe, don't let him die.* Outside my window, the car lights leave the driveway. In the middle of a Hail Mary I hear a knock on my door, and before I can respond, it creaks open. Danny stands shivering in his flannel pajamas.

"Danny, why aren't you in bed?"

"I saw Mom and Dad leave with Rob. I'm scared." He moves closer. Sniffling, he asks, "Can I lay with you for a while?"

"Danny, don't be afraid. Mom said everything will be all right. They're just bringing him to the hospital so he can breathe easier. It'll be all right."

Danny doesn't move, only continues to sniffle.

"You can get in with me, just don't fall asleep and wet the bed."

"You know I don't do that anymore."

"And you don't have to cry. Everything'll be okay. I just prayed to Saint Rita, and she'll take care of things."

"Does she *always* answer your prayers?" He peers into my eyes.

"Well . . ." I can't lie to him. And then I remember. The Read It list—I *am* learning to read. Saint Rita is finally helping me learn to read. It just took longer than expected. "Yes, she *always* answers my prayers. She'll help Rob too. I know it."

This is the answer Danny's hoping for. His tears stop. He climbs in next to me and squirrels around, looking up.

"Maddie, is that a dream catcher you have over your bed?"

"Yes. I made it. And it works."

"I wish I had one."

"Well, I can share mine with you. That is, after tomorrow. I have the stuff to make one more, and I think I know who needs it the most."

"You never did tell me how the story ended. It's not fair. I really want to know. Will you please tell me the ending?" Danny's big blue eyes are still puffy from crying. I feel the warmth of his soft body against me, and I have no choice.

"Okay, let's see. We left off with Ethan delivering the sticky spider silk to Yram to make his dream catcher. But he had no idea what was in the package Yram so badly wanted him to deliver. He imagined it was something so important and necessary that she'd die without it. He ended up running all the way from the thicket to the cave where she lived. When he got there, he noticed that he was breathing hard, but not feeling at all faint. He was very surprised with himself for running the entire way."

"I remember that. Tell me again what happens next."

"He waited patiently, and soon Yram flew in. Then she flew out quickly and back in again. She seemed worried about something, so he asked her, 'Yram, is everything okay?'

"'Wonderful, my friend. I just wanted to make sure no uninvited guests had come.'"

"Zerko and Zilla, right?" Danny blurts out.

"That's right. Yram explained to Ethan, 'I have a few cousins who love to play jokes. They don't understand why I'm spending so much time with a human.'

"'Because we're friends, right?' Ethan asked.

"'Right,' she answered.

"And then Ethan asked, 'What is this package for?'

"Yram said, 'Ethan, I am in the process of making something very special for you. It's called a dream catcher. It will help you to hang on to your good and believe in it.'"

"What does she mean by that?" Danny asks.

"I sort of made it up. She used a big word, *accompany* or *accomplishing* or something like that. But what she means by good are the things you really want to have happen in your life, and the dream catcher will help you hang on to that so you don't get too disappointed and forget about it . . . or so other people won't talk you out of it. Anyway, Ethan then asked to see it, the silk he had brought.

"Yram carefully unwrapped the silk, just enough to show Ethan. She then said to him, 'I need you to do one more thing before I can use this. I want you to think about what it felt like as you were racing through the thicket and toward my home. Try and remember how your legs and heart and whole body felt and what you felt inside.' Well, Ethan had to think hard, and what he mostly remembered was wanting to get the package to Yram as fast as he could. But then he played the ending part over in his mind and said, 'When I reached your cave, I felt my heart beating real fast, and I knew I wasn't going to faint. It just made me feel stronger. I even wanted to race outside and run around. I kept telling myself that it's true, I can run!'

"Yram lit up really bright, she flew in tight circles, and then told Ethan to say, 'I am strong, I can run fast' again and again while remembering what it felt like. Ethan did this, and when he did, he got all excited because it felt so real to him, and at that moment, Yram lit up again, but this time she grabbed the silk threads, and the threads also started to light up and then turned to the color of gold." I pause and look over at Danny.

"Wow, that's really cool."

"I know. It's one of my favorite parts." I take a few moments to think about it some more before continuing. "And then Yram told Ethan it was time for him to return home and that she would work to finish the dream catcher. Ethan walked and ran and made it safely to his room. He crawled in bed and was filled with a wonderful feeling of success. He lay in bed and saw himself rising in the morning and walking into the kitchen and showing off his smooth walking. Just as he was about to close his eyes to sleep, he caught sight of a small brightness moving about. 'Yram,' he called out. The light flew in tight circles, and something about it did not seem like Yram at all. Then another appeared . . . and another. He sat up, feeling uneasy. Finally, he flipped on his bed light. He saw three tiny beings dressed in green. They skipped and danced around. They were also fairies."

"I know," Danny says, "they're the mean cousins, right?"

"That's right. So Ethan asked, 'Who are you?' and they said, 'We're Yram's cousins. We've known her for a really long time, back when she was Dottyrambleon.'

"'Why are you here?' Ethan asked. And they said, 'We thought you should know about Dotty. She's always making up stories. Her latest one is that she will be an angel.'

"'But maybe she will,' Ethan said.

"'Not by helping you!' they shouted, and then they laughed and danced in the air.

"'What do you mean?' Ethan said.

"'There's a reason you're not going to school or playing kickball or hunting with your father. Dotty can't change that. She just pretends.'"

"That's mean," Danny says.

"Yes, I know, I didn't like this part," I say. "Here's what Ethan said: 'But I can walk and run, and I did it this evening.' And they laughed and said, 'That's just a little fairy magic. It has nothing to do with you. Dotty is good at creating false hope.'"

"That's a lie," Danny exclaims. "Is it a sad ending?"

"No, it's a really happy ending. I didn't think so at first, but it is, so you don't need to worry. Everything works out.

"Well, the mean fairies flew off, and the next morning, Ethan didn't feel like getting up. He thought about what had happened the night before, about delivering the package, and it suddenly seemed like a dream, like it wasn't real after all. In fact, his legs felt tired and sore, and he thought he should stay in bed all day long. He started telling himself that he was stuck with his old problems and that Yram was a silly fairy who couldn't change the way he was. Of course, Yram later visited him and knew right away that he wasn't believing in his ability to do more. She flew in as usual, doing acrobatic loop-the-loops and trying to catch his attention. He pretended at first to not notice her. He was reading *Robinson Crusoe*."

"Who's that?"

"I don't know, but Mrs. Zinc says it's a good book. Ethan can read almost anything."

"Just like Rob."

"Yes, just like Rob."

"So after all her usual ways to cheer Ethan up didn't work, Yram finally said, 'Ethan, you can stay in bed and be miserable because you believe what those other fairies have said, or you take a chance and come with me and see what we have created together.' At first, Ethan whined and said, 'I can't, my legs hurt.' Yram right away left him. He then felt lonely and sad. So when she returned later, he was ready to go with her. But first they had a serious conversation. She told him that he was wrong to be mad at her for not changing him. She said the other fairies were right that she couldn't change him; he had to do the changing himself."

I pause and notice Danny's breathing has slowed down. I wait a little longer. He doesn't say a thing, so I decide this is a good place to end the story. But this isn't the ending, the ending that had made me cry even though it isn't a sad ending.

I say another prayer to Saint Rita with eyes I can barely keep open. Danny's breathing rocks me to sleep, when all at once my eyes are wide open. A bright light flashes outside my window. I sit up wondering if it's Yram coming to visit. But it didn't flicker, and now I hear the engine of a car turning off. I roll out of bed and meet Mom and Father at the door.

"Madelyn, what are you doing up so late?" Mom asks. Her red lipstick is fading and dark streaks run under her eyes.

"Where's Rob? Is he okay?"

"Rob's fine. He needs to spend the night at the hospital to make sure he's breathing okay."

Father walks past without saying a thing, and Mom frowns. "Let's get you back in bed. It's way past your bedtime." She kisses me good night and carries Danny out of my room. I turn over and say one more prayer to Saint Rita before drifting off to the world of Yram, Ethan, and Alice.

CHAPTER 47

2 0 0 5

I STEP INTO the serenely silent room scented with chamomile and peppermint tea, and my eyes are drawn to the colorful shawl draped on the rocking chair. I notice its likeness to the crocheted lap blanket that had graced the top of my mother's cedar hope chest. The overstuffed couch calls to me. I surrender, and at once, my tears flow. There's no need to look out the open window. I'm here to welcome Maddie back into my life. I can't live another day without her.

I pause between sobs, direct my eyes toward Irene, and hear my words freely fall upon the canvas of our shared space. Without inward grasping, censoring, or my usual holding back, memory upon memory tumbles forth, beginning with, "More than anything, I wanted to learn to read."

Quite suddenly, I'm aware that I'm sitting on a couch, in a small room, in this other world where I have opened doors. A world that I have been careful to keep hidden, yet I am weeping without shame while a woman with an incredibly warm gaze rocks in her chair, murmuring encouragement. And I also realize that I have said it all, told her everything: Father, Yram, the dream, hope, weaving threads, and a rebirth that still has not been completed. I am weeping pure, refreshing, soothing tears, and I am also incomprehensibly at peace.

"My God," I say, regaining a moment of composure. "It's as if a dam I built inside finally gave way." I wipe my face and notice a buoyancy. "I had no idea." My head moves left to right and back. "It's bigger than a bursting dam." I place my hand across my upper chest. I look pleadingly at Irene while a small swell of doubt bubbles up: *Am I being ridiculous?*

Reading my expression, she answers, "Mary, you're renewing my faith."

"*Your* faith?" I say, grabbing another tissue.

"Yes, my faith in the ever-present possibility of transformation."

I reach into my pocket, fumble, and feel the smooth shell. I take the acorn out and hold it in the palm of my outstretched hand. I'm ready to heal the haunting ache in my heart.

We sit in a long, comforting silence, and for the first time, I feel no need to be anything other than who I am: Mary Madelyn—once upon a time, a Sparrow.

CHAPTER 48

1967

"MADELYN, look out your window." Ethan is standing in my bedroom; my curtains are pulled to the side, flooding the room with sun. Flying around the oak's trunk, weaving up through the branches, I see Yram's lavender tunic and yellow-gold hair.

I dump my coat in a heap on the floor and race out the front door. She's flying in figure eights.

"Yram! I read the word you sent me on the leaf. I figured it out all on my own."

She circles above me, then lands on a small branch within arm's reach. I step closer and peer into her eyes; heat rushes through my body.

"I knew you'd break the spell." Her voice is as strong as Father's and as soft as Miss Stanley's. She's more beautiful than her picture.

"But . . ." I'm not sure I want to say anything and spoil this moment. Yram flutters before me, and I know I can't keep the truth from her. "I didn't teach Alice how to read." Yram smiles, making me smile. I blurt out, "I love that we share the same name backwards!"

"That's what makes you special!"

"Did I really break the spell?"

"You figured out the word. And now that you believe in yourself, you removed the most powerful spell of all."

"The word . . ." It has so many syllables. I look away and remember it ending in shun. I know I read it, but standing so close to Yram, I'm much too excited to remember.

"It means . . . it's like when I saw you as the most beautiful drag-onfly ever. You changed form, and the word, it means change form but also something else." Mrs. Ellen had said change nature, which would be trees. Like the oak tree whose leaves change from green to brown and then crinkle up and blow away. This makes me sad.

"Yram, here is what the word means: Beware—you might change your form, like die or something. But there's hope because you might, like a leaf, come back new again."

"Yes, you're right! Now, come with me, I have something special to show you."

I reach for her, fall forward, and my body lifts. I'm flying through the air as though on a high trapeze that swings only forward.

Soon, the clouds part, opening up to a giant palace in the sky. Yram lands on a crystal, and it's so large I too am standing on it. This has to be where Yram lives. I follow her gaze and almost fall over. In front of us is a web, as large as Gwendolyn's, with threads the color of a rainbow sprinkled in gold dust.

"It's a dream catcher." The silken threads shimmer. Are they spun of real gold? "It's your magnum opus! This is what you've been up to. Ethan told me."

I dart my eyes from one thread to another. When I lock my eyes on to a purple golden thread, it knows—it shimmers and bursts into lavender, blue, back to purple, then it becomes a series of pictures, a movie. I see myself learning to walk, riding a bike, excited to read in first grade, the year I believed I would learn to read.

I turn toward her. "Yram, I know what this is. It's my dream catcher, so I can see the dreams without the nightmares. Just like you made for Ethan. It's so beautiful." Then I notice a hole in the center that doesn't look right.

"Yram, Ethan said you need my help so you can finish your magnum *opus. Is it done?"*

"It will be once you use your own magic and weave threads of gold."

"Ethan told me about this. I remember." I close my eyes, and I think about reading the big words with Mrs. Ellen. Just like when Yram had Ethan remember what it felt like to run strong and fast. I see Mrs. Ellen's eyes light up as I read, syllable by syllable, the biggest word I've ever seen. My chest feels warm, expanding like a balloon. I now see gold threads floating all around me and whisper quietly to myself, "Weave threads of gold." And then I remember.

"Yram, the word is transformation!"

Yram flies toward the dream catcher and begins whirling around faster and faster, swirling around so fast all I can see of her is a bright streak, a ribbon, from which Yram spins herself into multiple fine threads of colors I can't even name. Her arms, legs, hair, all of her stretches out into spindles of gold-tinted thread that weave across the center of the dream catcher, leaving only a small pebble-sized opening.

I'm lost inside the threads; each one is like a musical note, vibrating inside me with its own sound. Each strand I follow with my eyes brings up a memory I want to keep, times I felt like a winner.

"Yram!" I close my eyes, and strands of shimmering color continue to dance in my mind. I want to run my eyes over the threads again and again, bringing to life each magical moment of hope turning to good.

I open my eyes and call out, "Saint Rita, where is she? What happened?"

I know the answer. Transformation. Leaves change form—they crinkle up and die. "Yram, come back," I plead. "Saint Rita," I sob, "I wanted her to help me. I need her." I no longer want to look; I cover my face with my hands. "Why did she have to die?"

"Uncover your eyes and look." Saint Rita's voice sounds like Miss Stanley's! I lower my hands and peer out.

Again, the brilliant colors bring memories, reminding me what I can do. I look toward the center, but even before seeing the center, the excitement of reading new words rushes through me. Yram made me a dream catcher, just like she did for Ethan. I turn my eyes upward.

"Yram, please come back, I need to thank you." High, beyond the dream catcher, I catch a glimpse of halo and the small body of an angel. Instantly, I hear a bell ring.

The bell rings louder and louder. Again, I call out, "Yram, come back!" The only answer is my alarm clock. I slam it off, bury myself under the blankets, and slow my breathing down as if I'm asleep again. Bit by bit, pieces come back to me: threads of gold woven together with all my favorite colors, a web so large it can even capture my father.

"Maddie, time to rise and shine," Father's voice calls from the other side of my door. I can't, not now. I need to get back to the dream catcher. I keep my eyes closed and imagine myself back in her sky cave.

The creaking sound of my bedroom door wakes me up. Without lifting my head, I pull enough blanket from my face to see light coming in my window.

"Maddie, honey." Mom's voice, the concerned nurse's voice. I close my eyes again, lie still, trying to remember the dream, but it's Mrs. Zinc, waiting to have *The Fairy Angel's Gift* that I remember . . . and Paulette's threat to tell on me if I don't fess up. Suddenly, tears are dripping down my cheek, and Mom is peeling the blankets back one at a time. Her worried look makes it all the harder to hold back my sobs.

"Sweetie, what is it? Did you have a nightmare?"

"No," I mumble, dampening the pillow. "My head's hurting again." It's the easiest thing to say, but it's a sin. Mom places her hand on my forehead.

"Hmm, you feel as cool as a cucumber. Are you sure you didn't have a bad dream?"

I nod yes, thankful this is not a lie—it was the most amazing dream I've ever had.

"Are you worried about something?"

"No," I whimper. It's my second lie this morning. Now for sure my stomach is twisting and churning as if to give me my penance before I even have a chance to confess to Father Stevens.

"Sweetheart, I don't want you staying home alone another day. I'll get you an aspirin, but you don't have a fever." Mom leaves, and I search for the cave where Yram has created her magnum opus.

"Sweetie, sit up. Here's an aspirin. Your father doesn't need to be at work until later, so I want you to rest. If you're not feeling good enough to go to school by noon, then he'll drop you off at the hospital, and I'll have Dr. Dean see you."

"What?" I moan.

"Your father will take you to school later. I want you to get a little more rest. You don't have a fever; I'm sure you'll be fine." Mom bends down, her lips press softly against my forehead. I imagine a lipstick mark. I lightly touch the spot and inspect my finger; I think I see redness.

When everyone except Father has finally left, I scoot up into reading position and gaze upon the picture of Yram on the front cover. I'm going to miss her. I can't really draw her like this picture—even Miss Stanley said she was beautiful. And I know I saw her last night, flew with her. I run my hand over the book's cover with my eyes closed as more pieces of the dream come back: Yram changing form, but not into a dragonfly, into something beautiful just for me.

I open the book, and my folded Read It papers slide out on my lap. I begin to read the words aloud, "*Moon, bedroom, mushroom—*"

There's a knock on my door, and then Father sticks his head in. "Good morning. Your mother tells me you're resting up a bit but should be fine in about an hour or so, and then I'll be taking you to school."

"Dad?"

"Yes?"

"Is Rob okay?"

He steps into my room. "Rob's fine. They wanted to keep him over-night and watch how he does today. I'm sure he'll be coming home with your mother."

"Okay." My stomach tightens, but I ask anyway. "Can I show you something?" He walks over to my bed. *The Fairy Angel's Gift* is in full view. I hold the Read It lists, take one quick look at him, and then begin reading the words on the list.

"*Start, card, star, arm.*" I pause to look up, but it's hard to know what Father's thinking. I read the next group of words, "*Stood, wood, cook.*" I look at him again, and this time I make out the hint of a smile.

"Madelyn, that's the best I've ever heard you read."

"I'm really learning, Dad. I've a lot more words here. I wrote all of these words down myself and have been practicing them."

"Where did these words come from?"

I glance at *The Fairy Angel's Gift*. "I found them in this book that I've been trying to read."

He picks it up and pages though it. "This looks like a tough book to read. I'm proud of you for trying to read this. Did this come from the library?"

"No. I sort of borrowed it from my teacher. Dad, I'll keep practic-ing all summer long. I like working with the special teacher that Mrs. Zinc has for me. Her name is Mrs. Ellen, and she's nice." I look away, out my window, and then add, "I don't want to do third grade again."

"You're doing all the right things to improve. We'll see what Mrs. Zinc has to say at the parent-teacher conference coming up." And then he's gone.

I tuck my Read It lists back inside the book and gaze out the window. The sun is beginning to glisten through the leaves of the oak tree, sending streams of light dancing on my bedroom floor, making cool patterns. I pull myself out of bed, and my hand lands on something hard and smooth. I can't believe it—an acorn. *What is an acorn doing in my bed?* I stand up in my nightgown and study it closer. From somewhere far away, maybe my dream, I hear Grandma O'Leary calling out, "It's a message from Yram."

"About what?"

"You decide. But remember, an acorn is meant to grow into a giant tree."

I pull my curtains all the way open and look up at the huge oak tree and then back down at the acorn in my hand. It's so hard to believe. I lean down to look up at the leaves, the way Father taught me to notice, and the light-green color is changing. I remember telling Yram in my dream that leaves die, but they will return.

Back in bed with one hand wrapped around the acorn, I open the book to the first page, the page before the story even starts, the page with the cursive writing. My eyes are drawn to the largest word in the sentence. I study it and notice how the letters group together, and the last set has the special sound, *shun*. With hardly any effort, I read this word: *dedication*. It makes my body quiver with excitement. It's such a long word, bigger than any I read to Dad. Maybe Mrs. Zinc won't be so angry when she finds out how much this book has helped me with reading.

"Madelyn," Father calls from the other side of my bedroom door, "I'll be ready to leave in fifteen minutes. You're feeling okay, right?"

"I'm feeling great." I slip the acorn into the front pocket of my jumper. I pull my coat on, but it doesn't feel right; it's heavy and uncomfortable. Outside my window, it's sunny, but still it's cold out. Maybe Paulette's right, it is sort of ugly, but she has no idea how warm and safe it keeps me. I slide it off and place it on a hanger in my closet and grab a sweater from my drawer. I check once more to make sure I have everything I need in my book bag, including *The Fairy Angel's Gift*.

Father glances over at me as we turn off the dirt road and onto the paved street leading to town. I give him a nervous smile. He doesn't know that I'm trying to figure out how to tell Mrs. Zinc and Paulette. But first, I'll have to go to the office to get a late slip. Thoughts are racing through my mind when my hand falls upon the acorn in my pocket.

"So, you're feeling better?" Father asks.

"Yeah. I had a headache, but now it's all better." Three more blocks . . . a little worm twists in my stomach.

"I hope you're not worrying too much about next year. You need to do the very best you can every day."

I look at him, now wishing we had not yet reached town.

"Dad."

"Maddie."

"Remember what you told me about acorns, how amazing they are?"

"That they're a reminder of God's many miracles, such a little seed that grows into something as large as a tree?" he asks.

"Yeah. Well, I had this dream last night about reading, and this morning, I found an acorn in my bed."

"Hmm, that sounds promising."

"Look."

He gives a quick look. I then realize he can't really look and still drive.

"It's perfect," I continue, wishing he could see it the way I do. "I'm keeping it to remember."

"To remember?"

"Yeah, to remember that something that starts out small can grow to be really big." I take a deep breath. "I think I can catch up with reading."

He doesn't say a single word as he pulls the car over to the curb in front of the school to drop me off. When the car stops, he keeps looking straight ahead instead of at me. I open the door to leave, he turns to me, and I see sadness in his eyes. He says, in a friendly way, a way that I can tell he really means it, "Have a good day."

CHAPTER 49

1 9 6 7

I PACK AWAY my nervousness and skip toward the school building, holding *The Fairy Angel's Gift* upright in my left arm as my school bag dangles from my shoulder. I want whoever is around to notice that I'm carrying a real chapter book. The halls are full of children lined up for lunch, with teachers standing in the front waiting for quiet. I walk fast to the office to get a late slip and return to see the back of Mrs. Zinc's head as she leads my class toward the lunchroom.

I sigh heavily; I had hoped to have a quiet moment to talk with Mrs. Zinc. Instead, I step into the empty classroom and take one last look at *The Fairy Angel's Gift*. I run my hand over the cover and whisper, "I know the secret. Yram is Mary spelled backward." I walk over and place the book on top of a stack of papers on Mrs. Zinc's desk. I shove my school bag in my cubby and head for lunch.

I'm not at all hungry but take my tray of lunch food to the girls' table anyway, where I always sit. While looking for a clear space to set my tray down, Paulette spots me.

"Madelyn, what happened?"

"I had a headache, so my dad brought me late."

"No, I mean, you're not wearing that ugly coat."

"Oh. Well, it's nice outside."

"But you always wear it. You look *different* without it. We can scoot over for you to sit here." Paulette motions Lisa and Carol to move over. I twist like a pretzel to get my legs into the space without kicking anyone.

As soon as I'm wedged in, Paulette leans over whispering, "Madelyn." She then turns to Lisa and says, "Excuse me, I need to have a private talk with Madelyn." My stomach lurches. "Madelyn, Mrs. Zinc is still waiting to get her book back. You said you would tell me."

I take a bite of mashed potato and decide for sure I'm not hungry. I turn toward Paulette, and in my normal talking voice I say, "I put it on her desk before coming to lunch."

Paulette stares at me. Everyone else is now busy eating and chit-chatting. I crane my neck over to the boys' table to find Bobby. He eats as fast as he does his reading worksheets. I start to shift around.

"But you said you'd tell me *who* took it."

Before I answer, I squeeze out from the table. "Paulette, I'm all done eating. If you want, you can have my cookie."

Paulette swipes it up and continues to give me the look. *She'll make a good teacher all right, but not the kind I ever want to have.*

"Tell me," she says. Now I'm standing with my lunch tray, ready to dump the food and chase after Bobby.

"I took it. I only *borrowed* it so that I could work on my reading skills."

"But Madelyn, that book's way too hard for you, and you know that. Besides, it's stealing. I hope Mrs. Zinc doesn't give you a week of detention or expel you."

I have no idea what *expel* means, but it makes me shiver. I can't think about it.

"I did read it. I can read now." I race out as fast as I can without getting a speeding ticket. Once I hit the playground, I tear toward upper field. I see Bobby galloping with a small group of followers. I make my legs gallop, and I give a whinny so he knows I'm coming to join the herd.

The bell rings, and Bobby and I hold back from the others. He turns toward me.

"I think you're faster without your coat."

"Thanks, Bobby. I probably can hang on the bars better too." I then reach into my jumper pocket, not the one with the acorn, and hand him a stack of homemade flash cards. "These are the cards I promised you, and the answers are on the back."

"Cool. Thanks. Did you give Mrs. Zinc her book?"

"Yep. I put it on her desk. I might have to be expelled."

"What's that?"

"Paulette told me. It's pretty bad. We better get going."

Mrs. Zinc stands holding the door open while we all file in after lunch recess. "Madelyn, welcome back." She gives me a funny look, and I wonder if she can read my mind and knows I need to talk to her. I hand her my late slip. "I see you're not wearing your coat. Did you decide to hang it in the coat closet?"

"No, I left it at home. I didn't feel like wearing it today." I follow her into the room where she stands in front of the class. I scan my classmates. Paulette's within earshot, aiming her eyes at me. Bobby's flipping through the cards I made him.

"Mrs. Zinc, I need to tell you something."

"It'll have to wait; it's time for math right now." Mrs. Zinc turns to the class. "The bell has rung; I expect you all to be in your seats taking out your math book."

I scurry over to my seat next to Paulette, who leans over and whispers, "Aren't you going to tell her?" It's now too late. At her desk, Mrs. Zinc is lifting up *The Fairy Angel's Gift*.

"Well . . . ," Mrs. Zinc says, not in a loud voice; hers doesn't need to be loud to catch our attention. She moves her eyes across each row of desks as if reading a large book. The class is as quiet as a string of periods. "It appears that whoever took *The Fairy Angel's Gift* has made the right decision. I'm glad to have my book back, but I would like to talk with the individual who took it without asking."

I raise my hand, and my stomach begins churning so loud I'm sure Paulette hears it. I just hope I won't throw up.

"Yes, Madelyn?" she says in the same tone of voice as when I ask to see the nurse.

"I . . ." Everyone is staring at me.

"Are you wanting to go to the nurse's office? You look a little pale."

"No." I see Paulette out of the corner of my eye leaning forward. She can't wait to tattle. "I'm wanting to say . . . I'm sorry. I took the book, but I was only borrowing it, and now I can read some of the words."

Mrs. Zinc looks at me as if I were someone new in class, as if she's never seen me before. With everyone's eyes upon me, I feel my face burn red. I look over at the door and imagine myself racing out. But I don't. I stay cemented to my chair.

"Madelyn, I appreciate your honesty. However, what you did was *not* borrowing, even if you did bring it back. You'll need to talk with me after school."

My heart beats hard and fast. After school. *Father will find out.*

"Turn to page eighty-nine in your math books," Mrs. Zinc says, as if she has no idea my world is about to end.

In between the stacks of numbers that need to be added or subtracted, I keep a lookout for my special teacher. After adding up three columns of triple-digit numbers, Mrs. Zinc whispers down at me that Mrs. Ellen is waiting. Seeing Mrs. Ellen standing in the doorway with a brilliant smile, even as it catches the attention of most everyone in class, I can hardly stop myself from skipping out of the classroom.

"Madelyn, I'm so happy you're here today."

"Me too. Mrs. Ellen, I have something to share with you," I say before we even reach the closet.

"Wonderful, what is it?" I plop down to tell her and then remember—it's between the pages of *The Fairy Angel's Gift*. Suddenly, the heaviness of it all crashes down upon me as if someone tied an anchor around my waist and tossed me into the lake. I can't take my eyes off the floor.

"Sweetheart, is something wrong?" *The book, staying after school to talk to Mrs. Zinc, expel, my father.*

"I made my own Read It list," I stammer.

"That's fabulous. Did you want to share it with me?"

I nod. "But I accidently left it in my teacher's book."

"What book is that?"

"*The Fairy Angel's Gift*. It's a very special book. Even to Mrs. Zinc. And I borrowed it without first getting permission, so now I'm in big trouble." My eyes return to the floor. *Will Mrs. Ellen still like me?*

"I'm sorry to hear that."

I can't tell if she's mad or disappointed. I sigh. "It's my most favorite story, and I practiced reading some of it and wrote out four pages of words."

"Oh my. I'd love to see them."

I look up, and the usual twinkle has returned to her eyes, and I feel myself being lifted back to the surface. She scoots out of her chair and writes the word *star* on the blackboard. She then places a piece of paper in front of me. *Is she going to make me write my list again?* "This is the word *star*." She underlines the letters *a-r*. "I want you to think of as many words as you can that have the same vowel sound as *star* and write them down on your paper. You wait here, and I'll be back." I hear her heels clicking down the hall.

Mrs. Ellen has no idea that *star* is already on my word list. I quickly begin to write more words: *far, car, part,* and then the word *smart.* I'm about to read them aloud when Mrs. Ellen bursts through the door with a smile on her face and lays my Read It list in front of me. I begin reading word after word, glancing up now and then to see Mrs. Ellen nodding with a grin on her face.

When the three o'clock bell rings, I say two more prayers to Saint Rita, begging her to keep Mrs. Zinc from calling my parents or making me miss my bus. Paulette's slower than usual in gathering her things and for sure she's hoping to listen in on the scolding. Then I see Bobby dodging students and desks to make his way over to me.

"Don't worry," he mumbles. "We've . . ."

I look at him. He's looking stuck and out of place, but what I heard him say is *weave.* It's Ethan reminding me to not forget that I read the biggest word in the entire *Fairy Angel's Gift* just this morning all on my own. Even though my stomach's flipping over and my heart is beating fast, I feel excitement because I'm remembering what it felt like to read that word, and I want to do it again. I grin at him.

He smiles back and says, "We'll talk tomorrow." He turns to leave.

But I want him and Paulette to hear what I can now read. I move like lightning, and before he can take two steps away, I slide to the front of the room where the book sits on Mrs. Zinc's desk. Yram's calling to me.

"Mrs. Zinc," I say in a voice that even I hardly recognize as my own. Paulette, Bobby, Lynn, Cheryl, and a few others on their way out stop cold. Mrs. Zinc, who is collecting a pile of papers from the back table, also stops and looks up at me in a funny way. I grab the book, pause to look at Yram on the cover, and then open it to the first page.

"I really didn't mean to steal this. I wanted to practice my reading. Let me show you."

"Madelyn, now's not a good time. I'll be with you in a couple of minutes." Mrs. Zinc turns back to the papers.

I look over at Bobby, who's staring straight at me with a smile. He understands what I'm about to do. In a quiet voice, he calls out, "Read it." Maybe he's daring me, or maybe he wants to see what Mrs. Zinc does. Either way, I look around the room and notice everyone is waiting. The silence is so loud that Mrs. Zinc places the stack of papers aside and stands up facing me. I don't wait for her to say a thing. I look down at the first page and read word by word my very best reading.

"In dedication to those who chase after their dreams." I feel my chest expand. *I did it! Every word right.*

Mrs. Zinc is making her way to the front of the classroom. She looks over my shoulder at the open page. "Nice reading, Madelyn. You read a very big word, *dedication*. Do you know what that word means?"

Of course I know. Miss Stanley had used the word about women who chose to be nuns, that they had dedication.

"Yes, I do. It means when you choose to offer your life to something important. This is a book about dedication to catching your dreams." I look up at Mrs. Zinc and see a small smile form on her face. She gazes back at me, and this time I think she really sees *me*.

"You're right, Madelyn."

When I glance at the others who have stayed behind, they too are looking at me in a different way. Maybe it's because I don't have my coat on. I think even Bobby sees me differently. I imagine him yelling out, "Madelyn is so smart."

What I do hear him say loud and clear is, "Cool."

"I'm sure all of you have buses to catch and places to go. Madelyn and I need a few minutes to ourselves." Mrs. Zinc glances at the clock. "And we need to do this quickly so she can catch her bus."

Thank you, Saint Rita.

"I'll let the bus driver know she might be late," says Lynn.

"Thank you, Lynn." Mrs. Zinc motions me to the corner.

"Madelyn, Mrs. Ellen showed me the words you wrote down from the book. I want you to know that I'm very proud of how hard you're working at becoming a reader. If you keep this up, it won't be long until you can read a book like *The Fairy Angel's Gift* yourself. This doesn't, however, excuse you from consequences for not asking to borrow it." Mrs. Zinc forgot that I did ask. I keep my eyes pinned to the floor waiting to hear the word *expel*. And then I notice she's waiting to hear something more from me.

"Mrs. Zinc, I'm very sorry. I didn't know. I thought to you it was just another book. But now I know I was wrong." There's something I want to ask her, but the words aren't coming.

"It's a very special book, the only copy I know of. My mother gave it to me just as I was graduating from college."

"Was teaching your dream?"

Her face softens, and I wish she looked like this more often.

"Yes, teaching was a dream that came true for me." Her face changes back to the serious Mrs. Zinc. "I'll expect you to stay in from morning recess for one week starting Monday. Now, you need to move quickly if you're going to catch your bus."

CHAPTER 50

1967

ROB CLIMBS OUT of Mom's green station wagon and looks the same as he always does. *Thank you, Saint Rita.* Danny, Jack, and I have been waiting all afternoon for him and Mom to come home. Jack and Danny didn't even watch TV. Instead, the three of us played Red Light, Green Light, and then I Spy in the driveway.

Once Rob is in the house, he pulls out a funny-shaped pipe thing he calls an inhaler. He says that if he has trouble breathing, all he has to do is breathe through it. Mom lets him show us once. It makes a funny whizzing noise.

"Does this mean you can go to track meets?" asks Jack.

"We're working on that. We need to see how it goes," Mother answers.

"Mom, you heard what the doctor said—he said it would be fine," Rob says.

"I know, but we need to talk with your father to make sure he's comfortable with it."

Jack and Danny head for the TV; Rob goes toward his bedroom. I dash back to my room for the dream catcher I've made.

Rob's stretched out on his bed, head propped up with a pillow. He's holding a thick book. His space is bathed in the dim light of the lamp on his bed stand.

"Rob, I made you something." I hold out the dream catcher.

"What in the world is this?" He takes the embroidery hoop with colored yarns stretched across and honey dribbled over. He turns it over several times, but he's careful with it, and it doesn't fall apart.

"It's called a dream catcher. It holds on to your dreams and makes strong the dreams you want to have happen."

Rob smiles.

"It also makes sure that you don't have bad dreams during the night and only the good parts are remembered. That's why it's sticky."

He touches the sticky part and looks up at me.

"I have one, and I know it works."

"Hmm, interesting. It doesn't have anything to do with fairies, does it?" When I don't answer, he gives a friendly laugh. "I guess it wouldn't hurt to try it out. Thanks, sis."

"You're welcome. I really hope Dad lets you work with the track team."

"Me too."

Once the dishes are carried into the kitchen, I turn to Danny. "Danny, do you want to hear more of the story?"

"Do you mean from the hidden chapters?"

"Yes, because I think I know how it all ends. But first, I want to share the ending Mrs. Zinc read."

"I thought you did last night."

"You fell asleep and missed how it ended."

"Yes," he says, hopping up and down. "I want to hear more. Tell me the part I missed."

"Okay, but remember, this is the ending that Mrs. Zinc read. I think you fell asleep right when I was telling you that Yram had a serious conversation with Ethan."

"I don't remember, what'd she say?"

"She told him that he had no business getting mad at her for not changing him, that he had to do the changing."

"But she's the fairy who can do magic."

"Yes, but she knew if he didn't believe he could walk and run without her help, then he would never be able to have what he really wanted: to be like the other kids and have friends and go to school and go hunting with his father."

"Then what?"

"Well, this is the part that is sort of sad but not really. That night, she told him to follow her for the last time so she could give him the gift. He knew it was the dream catcher, and he was very excited. Like before, he was able to run and follow her, and she used magic that let him fly with her."

"I wish I could fly. It would be so cool."

"It is. I know because that's the dream I had last night, and it could have been real."

"What do you mean?"

"Maybe it really happened, and I just *think* it was a dream."

"Maddie, you're confusing me. Tell me the story."

"Once they got to Yram's cave, it was all lit up, brighter than just the moonlight shining in. Inside was a beautiful dream catcher made with lots of gold thread."

"Like the round thing hanging over your bed? That's a dream catcher, right?"

"Yeah, except this one was made by Yram. Ethan went to it and reached out to touch it. When he did, it was like he was delivering the silk thread again. He was only touching the thread, but he felt the same feelings of winning. He touched it again and again, and each time he touched it, his belief in what he could do grew.

"And this is the sad part. Yram explained that he had everything he needed to be who he wanted to be, and there wasn't anything more she could do for him. She said, 'Ethan, my gift to you is a place where you can always go to remember what you're capable of. It's up to you to choose to believe in yourself.'

"Ethan said, 'Yram, I want you to be my friend forever. I don't have any other friends.'

"Yram then said, 'I'll always be your friend, and you'll make lots of new friends, but after tonight, you'll never see me again.'"

I pause and look at Danny. His expression doesn't change. This was the part where I had to bury my face in my coat because I couldn't hold back the tears. Even now, it makes me sad.

"Yram then said, 'When I become an angel, I'll be your guardian angel. But first, I need to help someone else—that's how I'll get my halo.'"

"Then what?" Danny asks.

"Yram did fairy magic. She told Ethan to touch the dream catcher with his eyes closed and to allow himself to feel the happy feelings. She said that when he opens his eyes, he'll be back in his bed, and the dream catcher will find a home within him. It will continue to catch the good he wants, and when he closes his eyes and sees it in his imagination, his belief in himself will continue to grow."

"Is that the end?"

"No, there was one more last part. Ethan woke up and had a strong feeling that it would be a new day; that he was different. He remembered what had happened, but he couldn't tell if it was real or a dream." This is the other part that had made me cry. I take a deep breath. "That's just like me, Danny." *Had Yram really spoken to me or had I only dreamed it?*

"What do you mean?"

"My dream last night; it was so real I think it really happened. I was flying with Yram, I remember. She showed me a dream catcher that was mine."

"Tell me the rest of the story," Danny whispers.

"So Ethan closed his eyes and thought about what it would feel like to go to school, and instead of being all scared like he usually was, he started remembering how fun it was to walk far and to run, and that running felt real to him. Feeling like you can do something means you have . . . uh . . . *con-fun-dance*."

"What? I've never heard that word before."

"Me neither, but that's the word, and Mrs. Zinc said it means you feel good about yourself because you know you can do something. I think it's short for saying come have fun and dance. Anyway, Ethan's parents saw his *con-fun-dance* and agreed to start letting him go to school, a few hours each day. Later, when the doctor checked him out, he said that Ethan was completely ready to spend all day at school. His father started taking him on hunting trips. Ethan never forgot about Yram, but he did wonder if his father was right, that maybe she was part of his imagination. And his father agreed that it could be a good thing to have a big imagination. Anyway, everything worked out for Ethan."

"That's such a good story."

"It's my favorite one."

"What's the hidden part of the story?"

"Remember Yram gave a message on a leaf to Mary, and she had to work on her reading skills in order to read it?"

"I remember, and it's a college word."

"Do you remember the word?"

"No. Do you?"

"*Transformation*. Even though she read the word showing she was no longer under the spell, she now had to teach Alice to read so that the land of Forever After would no longer be under a spell and Ethan would be visible again."

"Did she do this?"

I pause, and suddenly this part of the story has faded away. I keep seeing last night's dream and Yram saying I had broken the most important spell of all.

"I think so."

"What do you mean?"

"I'm having a hard time remembering this part. There might be more chapters, and because they are hidden, I can't tell for sure."

CHAPTER 51

2 0 0 5

THE SCHOOL OFFICE is abuzz. Sandy clicks away at her computer while fielding phone calls from parents and reminding teachers to turn in their conference schedules. Multitasking must be the measured aptitude for making it as a school secretary. I'd never pass.

"Good morning," I say, smiling. "Here's to a quiet day in the office." I raise my right hand in a token toast. Sandy grins back at me and is greeted by a frazzled-looking substitute teacher. I scoop up a small pile of papers from my cubby, located in the middle of four alphabetically arranged rows of wooden slots. I step into the brightly lit hall, turn toward the wing leading to the school's back entrance, and notice a corkscrew twisting in the pit of my stomach. I glance at my watch and walk at a fast clip toward my office.

Up ahead, I see the buoyant blond hair and compact body of Diane waiting at my door. She must be crazy with curiosity. I had all but pleaded that we meet.

"Dr. Meyers," she playfully calls out. "So, am I in trouble or what?"

"You could say that. Starting with the commotion you cause each time you let Clayton walk Sammy. That kid has a laugh like a siren." We both giggle while I open my door, shuffle around test kits, and free up a couple adult-sized chairs. She plops down like an obedient child at the square table in the center of the room. Her face has an open glow to it. I leave my plush swivel chair tucked into my desk and sit across from her.

An uneasy silence bubbles between us; the twisting in my gut returns.

"I'm really glad you can give me a few minutes this morning." I try to smooth the tremor from my voice. "There's something I need to tell you." My heart pounds wildly. This was not how I meant to start. Diane is wide-eyed, losing all traces of her bright glow. Without intending to, I stand up.

"What is it? Are you okay?"

For a moment, I'm dumbfounded. I had no idea how hard this was going to be. And now I'm freaking her out. I sit back down, give a quick forced smile, and feel the red heat of a blush work its way up from my chest, to my neck and face.

"Diane, I, well, I said I would meet with Grace . . ."

"But you're too busy, I understand that. It's really okay."

"No . . . it's . . ."

"Dr. Meyers, it's okay. Grace will be fine." Her face turns blotchy red, and it's my fault. I've made her incredibly nervous. *Damn.* I search the corners of my mind for the words I had so carefully rehearsed.

"But it's not okay," I say too firmly. She slides her chair back. I see fear in her eyes. I begin again, but I'm trembling. All at once I'm Maddie, screwing up word after word in front of my classmates.

"Please, I need to tell you this." I shift my attention back to my session with Irene. I make myself see Maddie. "My middle name is Madelyn. Those who knew me best as a child called me Maddie. Back then, I was like Grace, actually worse off, couldn't read a damn thing for a very long time." I say it all so fast, I'm practically panting. "I need to let Grace know. I need to tell her that even though it seems so out of reach—I mean, who would have ever expected that I, well, I was in special ed too." My eyes prickle, and I blink them hard. She has settled solidly back in her chair. I can't read her face, but I can only imagine the surprise. I look away, noticing my heart pounding as if I had slugged the tetherball so hard it flew off its tether.

"You're amazing," she says in a relaxed voice. I shudder, and confusion swirls in my head. I'm not sure what she just said.

"What I'm saying is, I used my busyness as an excuse to avoid seeing her. I've struggled with reading as much as, perhaps more than, Grace. It's taken me close to forty years to accept this."

"But look at you now. It's so hard to believe."

"I've hidden it well . . . but I can't anymore. It's part of who I am."

Diane looks directly at me and nods, but she couldn't possibly understand.

"You're so intelligent, no one would ever guess."

I give a weak smile. I squelch the menacing voice inside that says, *Something must be wrong with her.*

"It took so long for me to learn to read, I thought something was wrong with my brain." I cast my eyes across the room to the bookshelf full of academic textbooks. "I had thought getting a PhD would help me feel smart. I don't want Grace to ever question her intelligence."

Diane's face is warm and open. I'm certain Kelly's special children also seek refuge in Diane's soft cushion of acceptance.

"I tell her all the time she's smart, and I'm never sure it's enough," she says.

"I'm ready to meet with her. I think I can help. I . . ." My voice cracks, and I feel my cheeks burn red. "I needed to tell you first."

"Mary, there's absolutely nothing to be ashamed of. I've always respected you; and now, all the more." She meets my eyes, and I'm flooded with warmth. "I would love for you to share your past with Grace. You're right, she needs to know what's possible." Before I can say another thing, she stands up, grins, and says, "Clayton the siren is waiting to walk Sammy."

I return her smile, and as the door closes, I whisper, "Thank you."

I sit at my desk and ponder. Was she uncomfortable with my intensity? Or was my revelation no more complicated than taking Sammy out to do his business? I suspect the latter: done and on to the next task. And yet for me, the universe opened up and shifted. I am newly stepping into the present, firmly holding the hand of Maddie. Never before have I shared outside the walls of therapy the truth of who I am.

I replay our conversation. I allow the feel of Diane's smile to sink in. Of course she's concerned about Grace. But my past, for Diane, is no big deal. And that's exactly the way it should be.

It's a little after ten. Already I've written an entire evaluation. At this rate, there's hope I will finish all reports before the school year's out. I stand up, stretch, and then make my way down the hall to Kelly's class. I peek my head in; Diane is sitting opposite Clayton at a small rectangular table in a corner of the room, prompting him to sort plastic pieces by shape. Sammy is draped on a beanbag chair resting his head on the lap of the new student, Janie, who is jabbering away to him. I would have loved a dog as a classmate. Diane looks up, a little exasperated with Clayton, and notices me. She gives me a grin, and I know for sure that all is fine.

I glance at my watch, wondering if by chance I can catch Matt before his next appointment. I move down the hall toward his office, feeling a lightness in my step. Up ahead, I see his tall frame leaning in conversation with petite Mrs. Lee. I slow myself down, hoping it's a brief exchange. They nod at each other, and then Matt turns toward his office and catches sight of me.

"Dr. Mary. You look as though you have something exciting to share." *Damn, he's good at reading my body language.*

"Do you have a minute?"

He glances at his watch and smiles at me. "For you, I have about five."

Once in his office, without thought, I collapse into the cushiony blue velvet beanbag. His eyebrows rise with a twinkling smile.

"I see you've undergone a transformation." He's trying to be funny, but the astuteness of his comment almost makes me cry.

"This morning, I came out to Diane."

I can see he's thinking: *What the hell, come out? About what?* Sagely, he waits for me to continue.

"I shared that, like Grace, I was dyslexic, took forever to learn to read."

"Never would have guessed."

"Yep. Kept it well hidden. If it hadn't been for therapy, it would have stayed that way. Therapy's been good for me. I'm finally feeling whole again."

He springs from his chair, spreads his arms out, and proclaims, "I'm so happy for you."

"You were right about Irene. She is good."

He smiles and sits back down, and I feel more connected to him than I've ever felt.

"Once I learned to read, I never looked back. Completely divorced myself from who I was and what I had struggled with. After Mom died, it caught up with me." I shift my gaze away from him and consider the irony. The one item of hers I wanted, the cedar chest, became a vessel returning me to my past . . . and the acorn.

I look up at Matt, open my mouth to share, but there are no words to express what I have discovered. I reach into my pocket. "Look."

Matt is back on his feet, bending over as I hold the acorn up.

"It's so perfect," I say. He gives me a questioning look. "It'll take much more than the minute I have left to tell you the story about this acorn. Let's just say, it's an affirmation from my past, and I am now ready to move forward." I scramble out of the beanbag and return the acorn to my pocket.

Matt stands up in front of me with open arms. "Dr. Mary, this is so awesome."

CHAPTER 52

1 9 6 7

I'M SITTING in the backseat of Father's car, alone with both my parents. Being by myself with them feels like a special occasion, and part of me is excited about this, but the heavy quiet takes away the excitement. It's a good thing I decided to wear my coat. I've never been invited to a parent-teacher conference, and when I asked Paulette if she was going, she stared at me before saying, "Of course not, it's only for parents." But Mrs. Zinc wanted me to come. Even Mrs. Ellen will be there, and I'm glad my parents will meet her, because she's now my favorite teacher.

"Did she say seven or was it seven fifteen?" Father asks Mom.

"I'm sure it's seven. I think she said she had scheduled someone else at seven fifteen, and that's why we need to be sure to get parked and to the classroom a little before seven."

"Okay, we're doing fine. We should be there in another five minutes, giving us a good fifteen minutes to get situated."

I had to change in and out of my school clothes twice today. I didn't want to sit around in the house with them on—I needed to play on the rope swing and visit the bramble bush. I don't like how Mom and Father aren't even talking.

"Bobby and I made up a new game during recess that's really fun."

"Bobby?" Mom asks. "I thought he was the kid who called you names all last year and this year."

"Not anymore. Now we're friends. We both like running around on upper field make-believing we're horses. We let the other kids try out to be part of our herd. They have to follow us and keep up. We pretend to go to all kinds of places."

"I'm glad to hear you're getting along with him," Mom says.

"Madelyn." Father's deep voice fills all the empty spaces in the car. "Your teacher asked us both to come and you because this is an important conference." I know this but don't want to think about it. "She wants to discuss whether or not you're ready for fourth grade."

My stomach tightens. I look out the window—we're almost at school. I wonder if Mrs. Zinc might still be mad at me for taking her book. Ethan would be telling me to weave threads of gold. I replay in my mind her surprise, everyone's, as I read the word *dedication*. I wanted to come home and tell my parents, but I didn't want to tell about taking the book. I'm still not sure if it's a sin, but Father would think it is.

The car rolls to a stop. I see other parents walking toward the school and away from the school, but no kids. I guess Paulette's right. This reminds me of the first time I went to see Mrs. Ellen and I was the only one to go, but it will be fun to see her with my parents; I know she'll share how much I've learned.

Father keeps looking at his watch, just like I do with the clock all day at school. When it's exactly seven o'clock, he steps forward and opens the classroom door. Mrs. Zinc and Mrs. Ellen are standing next to Mrs. Zinc's desk, talking. They both stop and turn toward us with big smiles on their faces, just like the day I was being introduced to Mrs. Ellen.

"Mr. Meyers, Mrs. Meyers, and Madelyn, I'm so glad all three of you could make it." It's a serious meeting, but Mrs. Zinc is smiling like she won a prize. She points us to the back conference table where the Eagles read chapter books. I smell bitter tobacco left floating in the air from the last parents.

"Madelyn, you sit here." Mrs. Zinc pulls over a chair from a regular desk. She has already put three big-person chairs around, but Father's knees still touch the table.

"I'm so glad you can all be here." It's another smile time. I look over at Mrs. Ellen. She too is smiling a lot. If this is such a serious meeting, why is everyone grinning? "Madelyn has made a lot of progress since Mrs. Ellen began working with her." I look over, and Mrs. Ellen is nodding her head. I look at Father and Mom, wondering if they heard because they have serious faces. I wish they hadn't made me take my coat off. I want to wrap it around me and pull up the hood. I scoot my chair back a little. Father shoots his eyes at me, and I look at the chalkboard.

"I've spoken on the phone with each of you, and you're well aware that Madelyn is not anywhere near an ending third-grade level. She's significantly behind." Now her smile has flipped upside down into a frown. She doesn't look at me; she keeps her eyes on Father. I squirm because I don't want to sit and listen. Mom puts her hand firmly on my knee.

"Madelyn did progress from a first-grade level to second . . ." Then I remember the test she gave. It had lots of little words that couldn't be sounded out. I might have read a few backward. I do better with big words. Especially if I'm given enough time to sound out each part. I'm feeling dizzy, like I might faint.

I'm squeezing my hands together waiting for Mrs. Zinc to say I read the word *dedication* and knew its meaning. Even Bobby said cool. I see the grown-ups nodding their heads up and down. It has turned into a very serious meeting, and the dizziness in my head is making it hard to listen.

"She's made a year's worth of progress . . ."

I feel my heart race. I look from Mom to Father and back; their faces, flat like a wall, tell me this makes no difference. Mrs. Zinc keeps talking, but she's talking about someone else. It's about Alice in my dreams, not me. This girl made progress but only went from first grade to second, and no one at the table thinks it's a good idea for her to try to be a fourth grader because that's two years behind.

I broke the spell! I know I can do it. I read the words transformation, dedication. *Mrs. Ellen taught me the secret to reading big words.*

They have stopped talking. They're all looking at me with sad eyes.

"Madelyn," says Mrs. Zinc, "we're all here because we care so much that you get the time you need to learn to read." My head is swimming; I can't look at them. Mrs. Zinc, Mom, Father. I hear their voices saying the word *care*, but I don't feel it.

"Another year in third grade will help her develop confidence." *Confidence.* I said it wrong to Danny. It's not *con-fun-dance*, it's *con-fidence*, and I hate that word. Mrs. Zinc says she wants me to keep it, and she wants to keep me, but I *want* to lose confidence and Mrs. Zinc. I no longer like her. I pull my eyes from the table and look up at Mom, but she can't hear the screaming in my head. I look over at Mrs. Ellen, and she's still trying to look happy.

Please, Saint Rita, I don't want to be a Sparrow the rest of my life.

CHAPTER 53

1 9 6 7

I TUMBLE onto the dirt ridge, letting the thick, knotted rope swing on its own. My hands are red and puffy. I'm breathing as if I had just raced up the hill from the lake, except it wasn't running I was doing. I was flying. I'm feeling light without my coat. I'm looking out over the lake, and behind me, I hear the sound of someone coming.

I see Danny making his way to me; *The Three Stooges* must be over. I pretend to not notice him. He sits down next to me anyway.

"I miss listening to you tell about *The Fairy Angel's Gift.* Do you have another story you can tell?"

"Well, remember, I wasn't sure if I had discovered the last hidden chapter or not?"

"Yeah, I remember. You told me you would let me know if you discovered any more. Have you?"

"I have. I can't tell if it's the last chapter or a new beginning—like a chapter to a new book or something."

"Will you tell me about it?"

"Sure. Because they're hidden, it's a little confusing, but I'll try." I take a deep breath. Danny looks at me, waiting. "Remember Alice?"

"Yeah. You said since Mary read the big word, she was able to help her learn to read, and the spell was broken."

"Actually what I said was that Mary was confused. She did break her spell and read the big word, but she didn't teach Alice how to read."

"Oh. So now what happens?"

"Alice is in trouble again. Mary thought since she figured out the big word—"

"I remember, *transformation!*"

"That's right. But reading this wasn't enough." My eyes prickle and I squeeze them shut for one Mississippi. "Even though the spell was broken, there was one sneaky hope snatcher hiding under her bed."

"Oh no. That's why I make Mom always take a look under my bed before she tucks me in."

"Danny, you don't have to worry. This is in the land of Forever After." I give him a quick smile, and he grabs a small stick and starts to crumble it. "When Alice was about to fall asleep, the sneaky hope snatcher sprinkled poison in her eyes. She thought it was the sand-man." Danny squirms and then sits on his knees. "When she woke up, she remembered that she could read well, but she thought she was remembering a dream, that it wasn't real."

"Oh no."

"She told herself reading well was make-believe, and her real life is a big struggle with words." My voice is coming out shaky; I talk slow so Danny won't notice. "She's not sure she even likes reading anymore." I turn my head so Danny won't see the tear dripping down my cheek.

"That's sad. I thought it was going to be a happy ending."

"Me too." Through my watery eyes, I look out at the lake and see the bright green leaves of an oak tree in front of me. Then I remember: the acorn in my bed. "But it still could be a happy ending."

"But now she really can't read?"

"Only a few words. And her teacher is making her do third grade all over again."

"That's awful."

"It is." I look and notice my hands are no longer red and puffy. Danny would get upset if I sprang up now and started swinging, which is what I feel like doing. "But maybe not."

"What do you mean?"

"Her teacher told her she might get something that will make it worth it. If she works hard, she might win something called con*fidence*."

"What's that?"

"Only grown-ups can see it, and when they do, they think it's really good. So, if a kid has it, this means grown-ups will believe they can do most anything."

"Oh. Sort of like Rob? Is that why he gets to be in charge when Mom and Dad go out? And why he gets to stay up as late as he wants?"

"Yes, Rob has it. You can also tell by the way Dad talks to him— not always but lots of times—as if he were also a grown-up. Alice knows she needs help, so when her teacher told her that she might get confidence by repeating third grade, she decides to give it a try."

"What happens?"

"Mary is very sad. She thought she had broken the spell and helped Alice."

"She did, right? It's just that a hope snatcher was hiding."

"Yes, she did. Mary worries that it will take more than repeating third grade to help Alice. Alice needs someone to help break the new spell so she'll never forget that she really can read."

"But you said she might get what Rob has."

"Even if she wins confidence, Mary knows she has to help. She told Ethan she would. She needs to be with Alice to make sure Alice doesn't give up even if she stays a Sparrow."

"What do you mean?"

"Mary needs to be right with Alice, and maybe Mary will also get confidence, but she doesn't want it, because she would rather be in fourth grade. But since Alice is stuck doing third grade again, Mary decides to stay back and help her."

"Wow. Why would she do that?"

"Mary promised Ethan. And she thinks she might want to be a nun."

"Like you?"

"Yeah." I look at him and then just plain tell him. "Danny, guess what?"

"What?"

"I also know a girl named Alice who needs help to get through third grade." I cross my fingers and know I'll need to pray for forgiveness. He stares wide-eyed. I nod and say, "Yep." He continues to stare. "I've decided to stay back and help her because doing good deeds is good for me. I also want to be a nun and someday a saint—one that answers everyone's prayers." I hold my breath and partially close my eyes, hoping he won't ask a single question.

"Maddie, look!" His arm flings across my face as he points to a large purple dragonfly with lavender wings. I gasp. It's flying toward us. We sit motionless. It lands within my reach. A lump forms in my throat. Slowly, I hold out my hand. The dragonfly circles around four or five times before flying off. Danny remains quiet.

I turn to him and say, "That was a fairy in disguise."

CHAPTER 54

2 0 0 5

IT RAINED all night. When I pull into the Milton parking lot, I'm struck by the signs of spring greeting me. The damp black pavement, no longer a mottled canvas of puddles, glistens blindingly in rays from a sun that now shows up by the time I arrive. How could I have missed this even a week ago? The cherry blossoms have bloomed—pink, outrageous, and otherworldly. I step lightly out of my car, sling a bag of files over my shoulder, and pause. Even with the parking lot filling up, it seems impossibly quiet. For more than ten years, I've parked and entered this building poised for work, yet today seems startlingly new.

I have just enough time to respond to all my time-sensitive e-mails before making my way to the main office. The morning bell rings as I approach, and I pace for a few minutes to make sure enough time has elapsed for teachers to take attendance before I ask Sandy to call Grace down to the office.

"It's our future poet laureate," I say as she enters the door to the front office.

"What's that?"

"A poet laureate is someone chosen to be a poet for the whole country, to inspire others to appreciate poems. Who knows, with your talents, you might be that person someday."

She smiles and shrugs her shoulders.

"I decided it might be nice to visit for a little bit. Does this work for you?"

"Yeah. I'll miss boring language arts, where we hardly ever get to write poems."

Upon entering my office, she calls out, "I remember this place!" She's all eyes, checking out the test kits, the posters, and the computer that sits on my desk. "Are all those yours?" she asks, referring to the briefcases full of assessments.

"Well, actually, they're not. They're the tools the district buys for me so I can do my job. Do you remember," I say as I pull out the cubes from the Wechsler, "when I had you use these to make a design?"

"Oh yeah. I love those kinds of puzzles."

"I know. You're really good at this. Did you know that it measures a special kind of intelligence?"

"My mom's always telling me I'm smart." She eyes me, perhaps waiting for a response. "I'm pretty good at puzzles, but . . ." Her voice trails off; she looks away.

"Reading and writing are hard."

"Yeah."

"Hey, reading and writing were hard for me too. Even so, I still was able to get a PhD from the University of Minnesota." Grace gives me a blank stare. "PhD means lots of extra school after high school. But it's school you want to go to. And like the highly capable program you're in, you need to pass tests that show you're smart enough. But I suspect you're much more intelligent than I am. I don't think I would have made the cut for a gifted program. When I was your age, I barely read at a first-grade level."

Her eyes bore into me, and I sense her mind chewing on this information that's at odds with so much of her school experience.

"I can't read *Harry Potter*. I just pretend."

"Sweetie, that's okay. I can barely read it myself."

She grins, and then we both laugh.

"But look, I know you can read these." I whip out a list from an achievement test. It starts with the word *I*. We share a smile, and then she gets down to business, reading word after word. When she gets to *island*, which she pronounces *is-land*, I say, "Congratulations, you made it to beginning second grade. Now, I know that's disappointing, but Grace, I only made it to mid-first at your age."

"Really?"

"Really. And look." I pull out her file and show her that she knew no more than three words two years ago. "You're flying high, girl."

She glows.

"I know it's tough hanging with kids who can read most anything and write pages upon pages, but you're going to get there. I did. You can. Did your mom share that your overall thinking skills are more advanced than ninety percent of children your age?"

"Not like that."

"Grace, you're very smart. Your reading skills will continue to develop, believe me. You and I are different from most. We need more time and a special approach when it comes to reading. I also had a teacher like Ms. Stanton."

I pause and try to recall her name, but in the moment, I can't find it. What I do remember is something called a Read It book, and . . . the excitement when she taught me to read really big words.

"Huh," I say aloud to myself, and Grace gives me a questioning look. "I was just remembering something really special from when I was your age and getting help with reading. My teacher taught me to read a word that I had never heard before. It made me feel smart at the time."

"Do you remember the word?"

I hadn't until this moment; remembering it felt as eerie as discovering my coat. "Now I do. *Transformation*."

Grace jerks back slightly as if caught off guard. "That's a huge word," she says. "Is it like the movie *Transformers*, and the toys?"

"Yeah. It basically means to change form, and that's what transformers do, right?" I capture Grace's eyes and say, "This special teacher of mine really helped."

Grace slowly nods her head up and down.

"It's nothing to be ashamed of."

"Are you really telling me the truth?" She's only nine, but her large brown eyes drill into me as if she were a prosecuting attorney ferreting out evidence. I blink, and for a brief moment, I come face-to-face with Maddie.

Returning Grace's gaze with the same intensity, I say, "Absolutely. I would never lie about this." And I feel a sharp stab in my chest.

I take in her face. I am in confession with none other than Maddie.

"At first," I say, "I remember feeling embarrassed about leaving class to have to see a special teacher. Who wants to be singled out?" I see her nodding. Of course. Even decades later, Grace must be experiencing the same. We all want to be like each other, but not really.

"What I discovered," I say, "is that she truly helped."

Grace nods her head up and down. I do like Irene and remain quiet.

"Ms. Stanton is a good teacher. She's helped me with reading."

"So did . . ." And it comes to me. "Mrs. Ellen. I felt ridiculous at having to leave class to see her—but then, look at me." I wink. "I can read all the words on the list."

I'd had no idea where this encounter would take us, but now the next step is clear. I go to my briefcase and pull out *The Fairy Angel's Gift*.

"Grace, this is a very special book. My third-grade teacher gave it to me. And it was given to her by her mother. It's about having a dream and not letting go. It took me many years before I could read it, and it's a lot simpler than *Harry Potter*."

I pause and experience a warm swelling in my chest. Grace sits motionless across from me.

"I want you to have it," I say. "But promise me you'll take good care of it. And if there comes a time in your life when you meet someone who is struggling to believe in their dreams, you'll pass it on to that person."

Her lower jaw drops, her eyes widen, she reaches out, and I place the book in her hands. She whispers, "I promise." A smile explodes across her face. "It has a fairy on the cover."

"That fairy's name is Yram. It's short for Dottyrambleon. She wants to be an angel, but first she has to do some good deeds."

Grace holds the hardcover more reverently than I had thought possible. She gently looks inside and then back up to me.

"It's very old, isn't it?"

I nod.

"Is it an antique?"

I nod again.

"Wow. I promise I'll take good care of it. I'm going to start reading it as soon as I get home."

"Wonderful. And remember, don't be too disappointed if you have trouble at first. It took me more than a few years before I could read every word. And in the meantime, I discovered all kinds of hidden chapters."

"Hidden chapters?"

"Yes, of course. The chapters I made up in my imagination. They were the best."

CHAPTER 55

2 0 0 5

A CUP OF TEA nestles between my hands—the most soothing cup of tea in the universe. Its warmth seeps into my fingers and up my arms while I breathe in the smell of peppermint and chamomile. Irene rocks in the chair, diagonally across from the couch. This is possibly my last visit. I gaze over at her and smile, but sadly. Perhaps this is how I felt so many years ago when Mrs. Zinc read the last chapter of my favorite book—sadness even with a happy ending. I'd had no idea these sessions would lead me here.

I can't help but glance out the window. It's a pattern of mine, a mini-refuge when intense feelings arise.

My mind drifts back to recent discoveries. Something Irene had said prompted me to notice the stout twenty-four-inch square box sealed in packing tape in the back corner of my closet, which I used as a raised shelf for another layer of shoes. A fixture so permanent, I had long forgotten that as a box, its primary function was to hold and store.

"Where are you?" Irene's question draws me back to the couch and tea.

I give a shrug. "I was thinking," I say, "about how I had unwittingly buried the most important book of my life in my own closet. And how odd that I would so completely forget that I had the book. That thinking about Grace, and reconnecting with Maddie, I would suddenly remember. It's all so mysteriously amazing."

"You buried not only an important book but an important chapter in your life."

"Truly." I sigh and again look out the window. "It's funny. I worked so hard at erasing the memory of repeating third grade, I ended up erasing the best part of it—Mrs. Zinc giving me the book when I finally moved on." In the recesses of my mind, I hear the voice of Maddie: *If I hadn't stolen it, she wouldn't have made me repeat.* Yet I now recall, when she gave it to me, I knew it was a gift. I turn toward Irene and say, "She must have liked me after all. I was never sure."

"Repeating third grade was a bitterly painful experience."

"And it made little difference with my reading, but I survived. I'm sure it has everything to do with the dream catcher Yram created for me." I smile at her, half-jokingly. My dream of flying with Yram and seeing the dream catcher she made for me is as vivid today as it was thirty-seven years ago. I never forgot that dream.

Irene understands. "You've done an admirable job of keeping your dream catcher alive and working. Ethan would approve. Look at all you've accomplished."

"I had no choice but to be a special education teacher. And now, a school psychologist. Maybe it was a dream caught, inviting me in, but it felt more like a calling, a resolution of sorts." I shoot another look out the window. What I say next won't surprise Irene, but I still struggle to voice the desire so dear and precious to my heart.

"I'm now aware of a dream that's been on hold." I pause, make eye contact with Irene, and can't resist. "It's my dream to be a nun and advance into sainthood." My smile completely gives this away, and we both end up giggling. Then she grows quiet. I love the time she allows for me to express myself. It's almost as good as Vespers.

"The dream that's been waiting for me, that I'm ready to claim, and want more than anything, is to be a writer."

"And you are a writer."

She responds so quickly, I stiffen, not at all used to hearing these words. In the course of therapy, I must have shared well over a hundred typed pages of personal insights.

"Yes, I want to think of myself as a writer."

"Be my guest. Writers are, after all, self-ordained." Her voice, velvety light, like water gently rushing nearby, speaks with the authority to carve out all kinds of new terrain.

"I'm going to write a book," I say, welcoming the determined voice of Maddie. She may have struggled years with learning to read and spell, but she was never afraid to acknowledge her dreams. "It may take a very long time, but that's my dream. I want to write Maddie's story. Complete with a wise and beautiful fairy, a dream catcher, and . . ." I gaze upward, trying to find the right words. *Oh God, am I the material of a writer?* "It'll be a story about the dynamics of hope and disappointment. About the importance of imagination. But most of all, I want others to know about Maddie's experience."

A blush burns across my face, and the skeletal voice of Mrs. Zinc intones, "If you can't read, you can't write." I shudder and turn toward the window, casting my eyes far into the distance. *Dare I consider myself a writer?* I focus upon the farthest horizon, darkly clouded, with an aching awareness of my dream's vulnerability.

There is a parting of clouds and a sliver of blue that expands to a patch of brilliance. As I focus upon the nascent clearing, my mother's ebullient voice comes to me: "I've always believed in you." I choke down a lump in my throat, turn toward Irene, and, even though tears are brimming, manage a smile to let her know these are good tears.

Once again the window calls to me. I squint beyond the parting of clouds, where my tear-drenched eyes see a mottled blending of color. And movement. My heart races, because all at once I swear I glimpse, fleetingly, a flock of sparrows flying high.

ACKNOWLEDGMENTS

The introduction of *Once Upon a Time a Sparrow* into the public world will forever represent a significant transformation for me. I pined to write stories at a time in my life when mastering reading seemed impossible. By the time I finally did learn to read, I had internalized an insidious message: if you can't read, you can't write. In adulthood, an incredibly skilled and sensitive therapist gave me the opportunity to reexamine the limited belief system I had adopted. Thank you, Ruth Hooper, for insisting I make contact with my nine-year-old self. Reaching out to her began a journey I had long ago abandoned.

My dear sweet wife, Janis Avery, endured the brunt of my unbridled nine-year-old self finally engaged in what she wanted to do—write stories. Meanwhile, the schooled PhD psychologist in me stood by mesmerized that she was finally writing fiction (instead of research papers). Thank you, Anne Lamott, for coining "shitty first draft," making it an official rite of passage. I lingered long in this phase, and Janis did her best to put on a good face while I was under the hypnotic influence of my elated nine-year-old self. Janis never gave up on me. And when I finally turned out a draft that won her approval, it meant the world. Thank you, Janis, for holding the standard high while never wavering in your belief in me.

My first "break" came when my still-shitty first draft was accepted into a writer/editor workshop, and Kyra Freestar was assigned to me. What I received thereafter was what I had missed out on in failing English 101. Kyra did more than edit; she taught me how to write, comment by comment. She called out what wasn't working and then gave examples. To this day, I can hear her voice as I take a closer look at each paragraph and sentence. I hit the jackpot when Kyra was assigned to my very messy draft of a story.

Without my faithful writing buddies, Dorothy Van Soest and Roger Rothman, there would have been no meaningful progress with my revisions. They took their job seriously, and despite my difficulty in receiving feedback (the nine-year-old protested), they persisted. And changes were made, improving the storytelling. We have critiqued one another's writing for more than a decade. Dorothy is on to publishing her third book and Roger his second. I am blessed to have landed with two incredibly gifted writers who take the craft of writing seriously.

An additional benefit of meeting Dorothy was the introduction to Max Regan. If you are an aspiring writer, I encourage you to check out his website: www.hollowdeckpress.com. Max has a keen sense of what works and what doesn't. He's a master of all brands of narrative. Thank you, Max, for your exquisite skill in delivering substantive feedback. You provided a path for me to move forward, dramatically altering my manuscript for the better.

Early in the revision process, upon making the needed changes, I asked a few friends to read and respond. Lynn LaRiviere, Jennell Martin, and Pauline Erera, who also happen to be well-respected, highly accomplished professionals in the fields of special education, child welfare, and sociology, generously took time to read. I received from each of them the precious gift of affirmations. Their resounding applause gave me buoyancy to forge ahead and not give up. This is a gift of wings. When doubts have arisen, I have brought myself back to their endorsements.

Finally, I would like to acknowledge and thank two additional editors, Alice Peck and Erin Cusick, for contributing further substantive changes, making it possibly for *Once Upon a Time a Sparrow* to enjoy runner-up status in the international novel competition at A Woman's Write. I have a special place in my heart for each of them as they not only upgraded my writing with their editing skills, but also openly shared praise and enthusiasm for the story itself.

———————

DOROTHY VAN SOEST is a writer, social worker, and political and community activist, as well as professor emerita and former university dean who holds an undergraduate degree in English literature and a Masters and Ph.D. in Social Work. She has a research-based publication record of ten books and over fifty journal articles, essays and book chapters that tackle complex and controversial issues related to violence, oppression, and injustice. Her novels, *Just Mercy* and *At The Center,* were published by Apprentice House

DVS: *You chose to use your own first name for the protagonist, and at least one reviewer questions whether "there is a measure of biography in this touching novel." To what extent is the story in* Once Upon a Time a Sparrow *based upon your own life?*

MAK: I never questioned the use of my first name as the protagonist, even as I veered from specific facts of my life. On some level I knew writing this story was an act of redemption. I drew heavily from memory, which of course we know is imperfect, and then allowed myself to dip into my creative reservoir to express metaphorically a truth about myself that I grew into much later in life.

I was indeed severely dyslexic. And, like Maddie, I considered myself a devout Catholic, and sometime late in elementary school, I aspired to be a nun. I prayed to saints and managed my stress through "cleaning rooms." Unlike my protagonist, though, I fortunately was not held back a year.

Looking back, I notice a difference in how I "showed up" as a school psychologist before and after receiving therapy. I went to therapy for different reasons than Dr. Meyers, who was beset by grief upon losing her mother. Therapy was my attempt to address depression. Like Dr. Meyers, I unexpectedly found myself ruminating over my past reading failure. While still in therapy, I had a series of encounters with a girl similar to Grace. I felt a strong yearning to share my story with her, yet I couldn't. Revealing my past with the girl felt too risky. She would share with her mother and I (irrationally) believed other teachers may find out the secret I had carefully hidden. My sense of shame was too great to risk this. The school year ended, and I had missed my opportunity.

This particular event—my longing to tell a child about myself yet being unable to do so—represents a turning point. Since ending therapy, I have shared my story many times with children and occasionally parents in the same vein as Dr. Meyer would share: in an effort to instill hope.

There are also a couple unanticipated parallels between my own life and the book. When my mother read an early draft of my story, she loved it and claimed that I actually did have a black hooded coat I continuously wore. I have no memory of this. As I moved toward completion, my mother abruptly passed away. She died in her sleep. And, as in the novel, "this is precisely how she had hoped to die."

DVS: *Your work as an educational psychologist in elementary schools involves identifying and diagnosing learning and reading disabilities. How does your past experience as a child with dyslexia compare with the experiences of children today?*

MAK: Children with dyslexia continue to have the same initial experience I had. Confusion over why friends and classmates so easily learn letter names and sounds, launching them into the magical realm of reading words. Today, many parents and teachers are as puzzled as my parents and teachers were as to why their child is progressing slowly. It's not uncommon for them to initially assume the delay is due to immaturity, a lack of paying attention, or not working hard enough. After all, these children are generally recognized as bright.

Sixth grade was the first year I received special education services. The service came in the package of twice-weekly thirty- or forty-minute sessions alone with a teacher, who used the time to help catch me up on assignments—which meant reading the worksheets to me so I could do the assignments. For someone who was as severely reading disabled as I was would receive help much sooner today, which is good news.

Unfortunately, the range in skill level among special education teachers continues to be wide. Teachers graduating with degrees to teach special education are generalists instead of specialists. They are expected to understand the needs of children with autism, behavior disorders, attention deficit disorders, and specific learning disabilities (a larger category that subsumes dyslexia). Compounding the lack of specialty is a lack of resources. All teachers are stretched thin. Special education teachers in particular. Children with dyslexia who live in school districts with fewer resources and families that can't afford private tutoring may very well have educational experiences similar to mine. It has been pointed out to me that I am an exception. That is, an exception in achieving success in a career that relies heavily upon literacy skills.

DVS: *What would you say was most challenging for you when writing* Once Upon a Time a Sparrow?

MAK: My writing résumé consisted of research papers and a master's and doctoral thesis. In other words, I had no formal preparation for writing this novel other than the rekindling of a desire I had long ago abandoned. This is a difficult question. Part of me wants to yell out that what was most challenging was not knowing—that is, no one told me (until late in the game)—that novels we read have been revised and edited and revised many times over. And yet, had I known this early on, it may have killed the kindling desire that was sparked. Sort of like if we, as parents, had any idea how incredibly challenging it is to raise a child, our earthly population would dwindle. So, ignorance can be bliss.

In the end, I suspect what was challenging for me is what is challenging for all writers. Writing is not that different from solving a Rubik's Cube. For me, it starts with a vision of what the end product will feel like, and getting there is like a puzzle, with a lot of trial and error until "it works." Tuning oneself into knowing and sensing when it works is part of the process. From my reading, I gather that all writers have self-doubt. It is not unusual that I would as well. My self-doubt comes in the form of "I never passed English 101." I struggle with a profound sense of inadequacy each time I misspell a word such as despite or come to a halt because my spell checker can't find the right spelling for a word I want to use but have no idea how to spell. These, of course, are simple mechanical errors that can easily be fixed. Nonetheless, I have yet to heal all the baggage that comes with misspelling simple words.

DVS: *What are your hopes for this book?*

MAK: This is an easy question. My life expanded when I took the painful step of acknowledging who I am. By doing so, I've embraced what my younger self wanted all along: to tell stories. I am so grateful for the life events that brought me to this place of sharing that which I'd kept hidden for so long. My hope is that Once Upon a Time a Sparrow will be a source of inspiration and understanding for others. If I, who so miserably failed at writing, could learn to write a novel, then others with histories of writing failure can do so as well. I have heard from parents that reading my novel opened a greater understanding in them of their children with reading challenges. Hearing this brings endless satisfaction.